frank portman

DELACORTE PRESS

Visit us on the Web! www.randomhouse.com/teens
Educators and librarians, for a variety of teaching tools, visit us at
www.randomhouse.com/teachers

Library of Congress Cataloging-in-Publication Data
Portman, Frank.
King Dork / Frank Portman.
p.   cm.
Summary: High school loser Tom Henderson discovers that "The
Catcher in the Rye" may hold the clues to the many mysteries in his life.
ISBN 0-385-73291-0 (trade) – ISBN 0-385-90312-X (glb)
[1. Identity–Fiction. 2. Fathers–Fiction. 3. High schools–Fiction.
4. Schools–Fiction. 5. Mystery and detective stories.] I. Title.
PZ7. P8373Ki 2006
[Fic]–dc22   2005012556

The text of this book is set in 11-point Caslon Book.

Book design by Angela Carlino

Printed in the United States of America

April 2006

10 9 8 7 6 5 4 3 2

BVG

And afterwards, in radiant garments dressed
With sound of flutes and laughing of glad lips,
A pomp of all the passions passed along
All the night through; till the white phantom ships
Of dawn sailed in. Whereat I said this song,
"Of all sweet passions Shame is loveliest."

–Lord Alfred Douglas

intro

It started with a book. If I hadn't discovered it when and how I did, everything would have turned out differently. But because of it the first semester of sophomore year at Hillmont High School ended up way more interesting and eventful and weird than it was ever supposed to be.

It's actually kind of a complicated story, involving at least half a dozen mysteries, plus dead people, naked people, fake people, teen sex, weird sex, drugs, ESP, Satanism, books, blood, Bubblegum, guitars, monks, faith, love, witchcraft, the Bible, girls, a war, a secret code, a head injury, the Crusades, some crimes, mispronunciation skills, a mystery woman, a devil-head, a blow job, and rock and roll. It pretty much destroyed the world as I had known it up to that point. And I'm not even exaggerating all that much. I swear to God.

I found the book by accident, in a sense. It was in one of the many boxes of books in the basement, in storage in case we ever got more shelves, or perhaps to be sold or given away at some point. The reason I say by accident "in a sense" is because the book I found was exactly the book I had been looking for. But I had been looking for just any old copy of it, rather than the specific copy I ended up finding, which I hadn't even known existed. And which was something else, and which ended up opening the craziest can of worms . . .

August

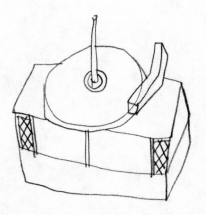

KING DORK

They call me King Dork.

Well, let me put it another way: no one ever actually calls me King Dork. It's how I refer to myself in my head, a silent protest and an acknowledgment of reality at the same time. I don't command a nerd army, or preside over a realm of the socially ill-equipped. I'm small for my age, young for my grade, uncomfortable in most situations, nearsighted, skinny, awkward, and nervous. And no good at sports. So Dork is accurate. The King part is pure sarcasm, though: there's nothing special or ultimate about me. I'm generic. It's more like I'm one of the kings in a pack of crazy, backward playing cards, designed for a game where anyone who gets me automatically loses the hand. I mean, everything beats me, even twos and threes.

I suppose I fit the traditional mold of the brainy, freaky, oddball kid who reads too much, so bright that his genius is sometimes mistaken for just being retarded. I know a lot of trivia, and I often use words that sound made-up but that actually turn out to be in the dictionary, to everyone's surprise–but I can never quite manage to keep my shoes tied or figure out anything to say if someone addresses me directly. I play it up. It's all I've got going for me, and if a guy can manage to leave the impression that his awkwardness arises from some kind of deep or complicated soul, why not go for it? But, I admit, most of the time, I walk around here feeling like a total idiot.

Most people in the world outside my head know me as Moe, even though my real name is Tom. Moe isn't a normal nickname. It's more like an abbreviation, short for Chi-Mo. And even that's an abbreviation for something else.

Often, when people hear "Chi-Mo" they'll smile and say, "Hippie parents?" I never know what to say to that because yes, my folks are more hippie than not, but no, that's not where the name comes from.

Chi-Mo is derogatory, though you wouldn't necessarily know that unless you heard the story behind it. Yet even those who don't know the specific story can sense its dark origins, which is why it has held on for so long. They get a kick out of it without really knowing why. Maybe they notice me wincing when I hear them say it, but I don't know: there are all sorts of reasons I could be wincing. Life is a wince-a-thon.

There's a list of around thirty or forty supposedly insulting things that people have called me that I know about, past and present, and a lot of them are way worse than Moe. Some are classic and logical, like Hender-pig, Hender-fag, or Hender-fuck. Some are based on jokes or convoluted theories of offensiveness that are so retarded no one could ever hope to understand them. Like Sheepie. Figure that one out and you win a prize. As for Chi-Mo, it goes all the way back to the seventh grade, and it wouldn't even be worth mentioning except for the fact that this particular nickname ended up playing an unexpectedly prominent role in the weird stuff that happened toward the end of this school term. So, you know, I thought I'd mention it.

Mr. Teone, the associate principal for the ninth and tenth grades, always refers to Sam Hellerman as Peggy. I guess he's trying to imply that Sam Hellerman looks like a girl. Well, okay, so maybe Sam Hellerman does look a *little* like a girl in a certain way, but that's not the point.

In fact, Mr. Teone happens to have a huge rear end and pretty prominent man boobs, and looks way more like a lady than Sam Hellerman ever could unless he were to gain around two hundred pounds and start a course of hormone therapy. Clearly, he's trying to draw attention away from his own nontraditionally gendered form factor by focusing on the alleged femininity of another. Though why he decided to pick on Sam Hellerman as part of his personal battle against his own body image remains a mystery.

I'm just glad it's not me who gets called Peggy, because who needs it?

There's always a bit of suspense about the particular way in which a given school year will get off to a bad start.

This year, it was an evil omen, like when druids observe an owl against the moon in the first hour of Samhain and conclude that a grim doom awaits the harvest. That kind of thing can set the tone for the rest of the year. What I'm getting at is, the first living creature Sam Hellerman and I encountered when we penetrated the school grounds on the first day of school was none other than Mr. Teone.

The sky seemed suddenly to darken.

We were walking past the faculty parking, and he was seated in his beat-up '93 Geo Prizm, struggling to force his supersized body through the open car door. We hurried past, but he noticed us just as he finally squeezed through. He stood by the car, panting heavily from the effort and trying to tuck his shirt into his pants so that it would stay in for longer than a few seconds.

"Good morning, Peggy," he said to Sam Hellerman. "So you decided to risk another year." He turned to me and bellowed: "Henderson!" Then he did this big theatrical salute and waddled away, laughing to himself.

He always calls me by my last name and he always salutes. Clearly, mocking me and Sam Hellerman is more important than the preservation of his own dignity. He seems to consider it to be part of his job. Which tells you just about

7

everything you need to know about Hillmont High School society.

It could be worse. Mr. Donnelly, PE teacher and sadist supreme, along with his jabbering horde of young sports troglodytes-in-training, never bother with Moe or Peggy, and they don't salute. They prefer to say "pussy" and hit you on the ear with a cupped palm. According to an article called "Physical Interrogation Techniques" in one of my magazines (*Today's Mercenary*), this can cause damage to the eardrum and even death when applied accurately. But Mr. Donnelly and his minions are not in it for the accuracy. They operate on pure, mean-spirited, status-conscious instinct, which usually isn't very well thought out. Lucky for me they're so poorly trained, or I'd be in big trouble.

But there's no point fretting about what people call you. Enough ill will can turn anything into an attack. Even your own actual name.

"I think he's making fun of your army coat," said Sam Hellerman as we headed inside. Maybe that was it. I admit, I did look a little silly in the coat, especially since I hardly ever took it off, even in the hottest weather. I couldn't take it off, for reasons I'll get to in a bit.

I know Sam Hellerman because he was the guy right before me in alphabetical order from the fourth through eighth grades. You spend that much time standing next to somebody, you start to get used to each other.

He's the closest thing I have to a friend, and he's an all-right guy. I don't know if he realizes that I don't bring much to the table, friendship-wise. I let him do most of the talking. I usually don't have a comment.

"There's no possibility of life on other planets in this solar system," he'll say.

Silence.

"Well, let me rephrase that. There's no possibility of *carbon-based* life on other planets in this solar system."

"Really?" I'll say, after a few beats.

"Oh, yeah," he'll say. "No chance."

He always has lots to say. He can manage for both of us. We spend a lot of time over each other's houses watching TV and playing games. There's a running argument about whose house is harder to take. Mine is goofy and resembles an insane asylum; his is silent and grim and forbidding, and bears every indication of having been built on an ancient Indian burial ground. We both have a point, but he usually wins and comes to my house because I've got a TV in my room and he doesn't. TV can really take the edge off. Plus, he has a taste for prescription tranquilizers, and my mom is his main unwitting supplier.

Sam Hellerman and I are in a band. I mean, we have a name and a logo, and the basic design for the first three or four album covers. We change the name a lot, though. A typical band lasts around two weeks, and some don't even last long enough for us to finish designing the logo, let alone the album covers.

When we arrived at school that first day, right at the end of August, the name was Easter Monday. But Easter Monday only lasted from first period through lunch, when Sam Hellerman took out his notebook in the cafeteria and said, "Easter Monday is kind of gay. How about Baby Batter?"

I nodded. I was never that wild about Easter Monday, to tell you the truth. Baby Batter was way better. By the end of lunch, Sam Hellerman had already made a rough sketch of the logo, which was Gothic lettering inside the loops of an infinity symbol. That's the great thing about being in a band: you always have a new logo to work on.

"When I get my bass," Sam Hellerman said, pointing to another sketch he had been working on, "I'm going to spray-paint 'baby' on it. Then you can spray-paint 'batter' on your guitar, and as long as we stay on our sides of the stage, we won't need a banner when we play on TV."

I didn't even bother to point out that by the time we got instruments and were in a position to worry about what to paint on them for TV appearances, the name Baby Batter would be long gone. This was for notebook purposes only. I decided my Baby Batter stage name would be Guitar Guy, which Sam Hellerman carefully wrote down for the first album credits. He said he hadn't decided on a stage name yet, but he wanted to be credited as playing "base and Scientology." That Sam Hellerman. He's kind of brilliant in his way.

"Know any drummers?" he asked as the bell rang, as he always does. Of course, I didn't. I don't know anyone apart from Sam Hellerman.

THE *CATCHER* CULT

So that's how the school year began, with Easter Monday fading into Baby Batter. I like to think of those first few weeks as the Baby Batter Weeks. Nothing much happened–or rather, quite a lot of stuff was happening, as it turns out, but I wouldn't find out about any of it till later. So for me, the Baby Batter Weeks were characterized by a false sense of– well, not security. More like familiarity or monotony. The familiar monotony of standard, generic High School Hell, which somehow manages to be horrifying and tedious at the same time. We attended our inane, pointless classes, in between which we did our best to dodge random attempts on our lives and dignity by our psychopathic social superiors. After school, we worked on our band, played games, and watched TV. Just like the previous year. There was no indication that anything would be any different.

Now, when I say our classes were inane and pointless, I really mean i. and p., and in the fullest sense. Actually, you know what? Before I continue, I should probably explain a few things about Hillmont High School, because your school might be different.

Hillmont is hard socially, but the "education" part is shockingly easy. That goes by the official name of Academics. It is mystifying how they manage to say that with a straight face, because as a school, HHS is more or less a joke. Which can't be entirely accidental. I guess they want to tone down the content so that no one gets too good at any particular thing, so as not to make anyone else look bad.

Assignments typically involve copying a page or two from some book or other. Sometimes you have a "research paper," which means that the book you copy out of is the *Encyclopaedia Britannica*. You're graded on punctuality, being able to sit still, and sucking up. In class you have group discussions about whatever it is you're alleged to be studying, where you try to share with the class your answer to the question: how does it make you feel?

Okay, so that part isn't easy for me. I don't like to talk much. But you do get some credit for being quiet and nondisruptive, and my papers are usually neat enough that the teacher will write something like "Good format!" on them.

It is possible, however, to avoid this sort of class altogether by getting into Advanced Placement classes. (Technically, "Advanced Placement" refers to classes for which it is claimed you can receive "college credit"–which is beyond hilarious–but in practice all the nonbonehead classes end up getting called AP.) AP is like a different world. You don't have to do anything at all, not a single blessed thing but show up, and you always get an A no matter what. Well, you end up making a lot of collages, and dressing in costumes and putting on irritating little skits, but that's about it. Plus, they invented a whole new imaginary grade, which they still call an A, but which counts as more than an A from a regular class. What a racket.

This is the one place in the high school multi-verse where eccentricity can be an asset. The AP teachers survey the class through their *Catcher in the Rye* glasses and . . .

Oh, wait: I should mention that *The Catcher in the Rye* is this book from the fifties. It is every teacher's favorite book. The main guy is a kind of misfit kid superhero named Holden Caulfield. For teachers, he is the ultimate guy, a real dreamboat. They love him to pieces. They all want to have sex with him, and with the book's author, too, and they'd probably even try to do it with the book itself if they could figure out a way to go about it. It changed their lives when they were young. As kids, they carried it with them everywhere they went. They solemnly resolved that, when they grew up, they would dedicate their lives to spreading The Word.

It's kind of like a cult.

They live for making you read it. When you do read it you can feel them all standing behind you in a semicircle wearing black robes with hoods, holding candles. They're chanting "Holden, Holden, Holden . . ." And they're looking over your shoulder with these expectant smiles, wishing they were the ones discovering the earth-shattering joys of *The Catcher in the Rye* for the very first time.

Too late, man. I mean, I've been around the *Catcher in the Rye* block. I've been forced to read it like three hundred times, and don't tell anyone but I think it sucks.

Good luck avoiding it, though. If you can make it to puberty without already having become a *Catcher in the Rye* casualty you're a better man than I, and I'd love to know your secret. It's too late for me, but the Future Children of America will thank you.

So the AP teachers examine the class through their *Catcher* glasses. The most Holden-y kid wins. Dispute the premise of every assignment and try to look troubled and intense, yet with a certain quiet dignity. You'll be a shoo-in.

Everybody wins, though, really, in AP Land.

But watch out. When all the little Holdens leave the building, it's open season again. Those who can't shed or disguise their *Catcher*-approved eccentricities will be noticed by all the psychopathic normal people and hunted down like dogs. The *Catcher* Cult sets 'em up, and the psychotic normal people knock 'em right back down. What a world.

"Did you get in any APs?" Sam Hellerman had asked on the way to school that first day. He hadn't gotten in any APs.

Whether or not you end up in AP is mostly a matter of luck, though the right kind of sucking up can increase your odds a bit. So considering that I put zero effort into it, I didn't do too badly in the AP lottery. I got into AP social studies and French; that left me with regular English and math; and I also had PE and band. "Advanced" French is mainly notable for the fact that no one in the class has the barest prayer of reading, speaking, or understanding the French language, despite having studied it for several years. AP social studies is just like normal social studies, except the assignments are easier and you get to watch movies. Plus they like to call AP social studies "Humanities." Ahem. . . . Pardon me while I spit out this water and laugh uncontrollably for the next twenty minutes or so. This year, "Humanities" began with Foods of the World. The basic idea there is that someone brings in a different type of ethnic food every day. And the class celebrates cultural diversity by eating it. Day one was pineapple and ham, like they have in Hawaii! We were gifted and advanced, all right. And soon we would know how to have a snack in all fifty states.

I suspected regular English was going to be a drag, though, and I wasn't wrong. AP teachers tend to be younger, more enthusiastic, and in premeltdown mode. They are almost always committed members of the *Catcher* Cult, and easy to manipulate. The regular classes, on the other hand, are usually taught by elderly, bitter robots who gave up long ago and who are just biding their time praying for it all to be over. Getting in touch with your inner Holden is totally useless if you wind up in a class taught by one of the bitter robots. You will not compute. Or if you do compute, the bitter robots will only hate you for it.

I didn't get into AP English because my tryout essay last year was too complex for the robots to grasp. So I ended up in regular, nonadvanced English, run by the ultimate bitter robot, Mr. Schtuppe.

"I don't give out As like popcorn," said Mr. Schtuppe on that first day. "Neatness counts.

"Cultivate the virtue of brevity," he continued. "There will be no speaking out of turn. No shenanigans. No chewing gum: *of any kind*.

"Shoes and shirts must be worn. There will be no shorts, bell-bottom trousers, or open-toed ladies' footwear. No tube tops, halter tops, or sports attire. Rule number one, if the teacher is wrong see rule number two. Rule number two, ah . . . if you are tardy, the only excuse that will be accepted is a death in the family, and if that death is your own–mmmm, no, if you die, then that death is, ah, accepted as excusable, mmm . . ."

Mr. Schtuppe's introductory lecture was not only morbid, but had a few glitches, as well.

It is like his bald robot head contained a buggy chunk of code that selected random stuff from some collective pool of things teachers have said since around 1932, strung them together in no particular order in a new temporary text document, and fed this document through the speech simulator unit as is. And sometimes there was some corruption in the file, so you'd get things like "my way or the freeway." And of course, all the girls in the class were in fact wearing halter tops, and practically every guy had on some kind of "sports attire." You can't have a dress code for just one class. It was nonsense. There must have been a time long ago, in the seventies, I'd guess, when he *had* been in a position to impose a dress code, and he kept it as part of the introductory speech because—who knows? Maybe he just liked saying "open-toed ladies' footwear."

Mr. Schtuppe was still droning on about forbidden footwear when the bell rang. He stopped midsentence (he had just said "In case of") and sat down, staring at his desk with what appeared to be unseeing eyes as the kids filed out. I had a feeling that everyone in that room was thinking pretty much the same thing: it was going to be a long year.

HIGH SCHOOL IS THE PENALTY FOR TRANSGRESSIONS YET TO BE SPECIFIED

Despite the ominous beginning, the first day of school had been refreshingly uneventful and easy to take. So, after weighing our options, we decided to go back and do it all over again the following day.

I had been curious about how Mr. Schtuppe would

launch day two of English for the Not Particularly Gifted, and I was pleased to note that he stood up at the beginning of the class period and simply resumed in midsentence where he had left off the day before.

"Fire proceed to the exit in an orderly fashion," he said. "No talking." While part of me was a bit envious of the AP English students, who were at that moment probably watching a movie or eating cookies or something, I was mainly just fascinated to watch my own educational train wreck in progress.

Mr. Schtuppe had a certain charm, if you looked at the situation in the right spirit. He liked to call the girls guttersnipes and the guys "you filthy animals," and he would say it with this weird smile that made him look like, I don't know, the devil or something. A shiny pink devil with a lot of ear hair.

First on the program in Mr. Schtuppe's class, when the introduction had finally ended, was a book called *30 Days to a More Powerful Vocabulary.* "In 30 days, you will learn how to make words your slaves."

This book is a big list of fancy-pants words, and our job as self-improvement vocabularists was to prove we knew what they meant by saying them aloud and using them in sentences.

Mr. Schtuppe's unique twist on this was that he managed to mispronounce around half of them.

"The first word is 'bête noire,' " he said. But he pronounced it "bait noir-ay," with the emphasis on the "ay."

"Bait noir-ay," we said in unison.

"Excellent. Now, class, listen carefully: magnaminious . . ."

(We would have to wait till the end of the alphabet before we witnessed Mr. Schtuppe's finest hour. That would be "wanton," which he pronounced like "won ton." The delicious Chinese dumpling often served in soup at the Pacific Rim's finest eating establishments. That's why Sam Hellerman and I will sometimes refer to a sexy girl as a Won Ton Woman.)

Of course, if I had known how important mispronunciation skills would prove to be in my sex life and in the events that followed, I probably would have paid more attention. But I spent most of the class in my own zone, thinking about the lyrics of Roxy Music's "She Sells" and writing out a track list for Baby Batter's third album, *Odd and Even Number*.

Note to self: one of these days, my next band is definitely going to be Beat Noir-ay. First album: *Talk Won Ton to Me, You Crazy Asian Superstar*. Lots of wok solos.

But getting back to Hillmont:

I used to get beat up and hassled a fair amount in elementary and junior high school, but not so much these days. In part, that's because the normal people of the world, as they mature and become more sophisticated, naturally begin to discover that psychological torture is in the end more satisfying, and easier to get away with, than the application of brute force; and, in part, or so I like to think, it's because of a special technique I developed last year.

What I mean is, actual balls-out physical attacks, where one guy wins and the other gets beaten to a quivering bloody sock monkey, are rare, though they do happen. It's usually more subtle than that. They'll try to trip you as you go by in the hallway; or they'll throw little rolled-up balls of gum at the back of your head in homeroom; or they'll write stuff on your locker, or squirt substances like mustard, milk, or worse through your locker's slats; or they'll superglue your gym locker shut so you can't get to your street clothes. None of these techniques is all that devastating alone; but repeated endlessly and in tandem, they can build up and start to drive you a bit insane. The basic idea is to wear you down with day-to-day social exclusionary exercises, and the repetition of mind-numbingly similar minor pranks and indignities. It's all about ritual abuse, mental and emotional stress, psychological torture, and humiliation. They really are a great bunch of guys.

The best way to handle such situations is to stare straight ahead and act like you don't notice or care. Unless you happen to have some serious equalizing firepower. Which I don't.

My dad always used to say "Fight back," but that's not realistic. Even if you could successfully pretend to be some kind of bad dude there would still be something like eighteen hundred of them and only one of you. On TV, people in that situation claim that they know karate and that their hands are registered as lethal weapons and then they do this yelpy kung fu dance. Someone cues the laugh track and the tension is relieved. Then there's a commercial, and they don't show the part where Matt Lynch rides his skateboard on the guy's face. No thanks.

The only way to get Matt Lynch to leave you alone, if you can't actually take him out, is to introduce an element of uncertainty into his slow-moving, gummed-up "mind." It turns out Matt Lynch has a fear of uncertainty and the irrational. Raising such doubts is not as hard as you might think, though it took me quite a while to figure that one out.

At the beginning of the school year, all the psychotic normal people are mainly concerned with their own affairs, and even the minor irritants and pranks I've described can get off to a slow start. Which is why that first week went by without incident. Well, almost.

September

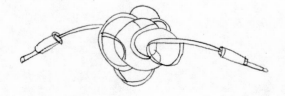

THE WEEKEND STARTS NOW

I say almost because on Friday, at the last possible moment, there was what I guess you'd call an incident. I was in my own world, thinking about Baby Batter, planning my stage banter ("Hey, we're Baby Batter, and this one's called 'Up Your Face.' *Un, deux, trois, quatre...*") on my way out at the end of the day when I bumped into Mr. Teone. Literally, I mean: there's quite a lot of Mr. Teone, and it's pretty easy to crash into him if you're not watching where you're going. It happens all the time. In this instance I must have been going along at a fair clip, because I bounced so hard off his expansive trampoline-y stomach that I almost lost my balance and fell backward. Mr. Teone stood there smirking. No salute this time. Just a weird smile, if that's what it was.

"Henderson," he said, in that mush-mouthed, nasal way he has, stopping me with his hand on my shoulder. He pulled his head back and squinted one eye as he looked at me. Not a pretty sight.

I said nothing, looked up at him warily. What now?

"Say hi to your dad for me."

I gave him one of my "whatever, freak" looks, disengaged, and shuffled off to the northwest exit.

See, that almost sounds like an okay thing to say, if you don't know that my dad is actually dead. But now that you know that, what do you think? I would certainly pardon your French if you were to reply that he's totally fucked up. There's no other way to put it.

This was just a few days before the anniversary of my dad's "accident," which had me in a somber mood, despite all the Baby Batter excitement. At moments like these, it's hard to tell whether you're being too paranoid or just paranoid enough. It sure felt like they were all in it together, all the psychotic normal students along with their buffoonish mascot, Mr. Teone. It's like they sit around all day trying to come up with ways to get to me. Some of the experiments are ill-conceived from the beginning; some are so moronic they wouldn't trouble a retarded monkey; some have promise but go astray. But every now and again there's one that lands. This one had a kind of subtle brilliance.

In fact, I do talk to my dad, in my head, sometimes. Not that I think he hears me, not really. But I kind of pretend that I do think he's listening, and would be dispensing advice and comfort if only there were a way for the human ear to pick up the signal.

Telling him that Mr. Teone said hi just ain't gonna happen, though.

I was feeling kind of weird. When the subject of my dad comes up, particularly when it's unexpected or sudden, I feel funny, kind of disoriented and light-headed. And there's a strange pressure in my chest, like I'm recovering from being punched in the stomach. Mr. Teone's remark had rattled me. Can't they leave you alone for even one week? In fact, I don't think they can. It's in the school district bylaws.

Sam Hellerman was waiting for me by the oak tree across from the baseball backstop, which was our usual afterschool meeting point (unless somebody was already there "smoking out"–then we would meet a little farther down, near the track). We couldn't think of anything to do, so we went over my house.

Friday is my mom's half-day, so she was already home from work, leaning against the kitchen counter with her afternoon highball in her hand, smoking and staring blankly at the wall. She was wearing a shortish, vibrantly colored floral-print dress over white flared slacks, with big clunky boots. And a turban. Yes, a turban.

"Far out, Mom," I said as we walked by, but she was lost in thought and didn't react.

Sam Hellerman followed me into my room. I put on *Highway to Hell.*

"The weekend starts now?" he said. I did the devil hand sign and said "Party."

"Mom says to turn down the teen rebellion," yelled my sister, Amanda, pounding on the door. "She can't hear herself think."

Bon Scott was singing "Walk All Over You." I reached over and turned the volume up.

"What's her problem again?" asked Sam Hellerman.

"Oh, she's at that awkward age." Amanda was twelve and was going through changes. It was like she had a supply of different personalities, a brood of alternate Amandas that she was trying out. You never knew which one you were going to get.

"No," said Sam Hellerman. "I meant your mom."

"She's at an awkward age, too," I said.

I was only half kidding.

Sometimes I accuse my mom of being a hippie, though that's an exaggeration. She just likes to think of herself as more sensitive and virtuous and free-spirited than thou. If that dream leads her down some puzzling or slightly embarrassing avenues in a variety of neighborhoods, it's not the world's biggest tragedy. "I'm a very spiritual person," she likes to say, for instance. Like when she's explaining how she hates religion and all those who practice it. Well, okay, if it makes you feel better, Carol. She's really about as spiritual as my gym shorts, but I love her anyway.

I think she might have unintentionally bumped up her own groovy-ometer just a bit after my dad died. Her eye for fashion certainly went through a strange and magical transformation around that time. I think the technical term is cataracts.

Well, we all went a little bananas. That's to be expected.

My dad was more down-to-earth. He was with her on a lot of the touchy-feely save-society-and-admire-African-art stuff, I'm pretty sure. But he didn't overdo it. Plus, he worked for the police, so he couldn't be frivolous about absolutely everything. He liked war and action movies, which hurt my mom's feelings. And he loved motorcycles, which I think she thought was daring and hot. I think he found her beautiful and quirky and goofy and charming, kind of how I do when I step back. Somehow, you always end up forgiving her for being totally crazy.

Basically, she is a traditional suburban mom with a thin veneer of yesterday's counterculture not too securely fastened to the outside. It's not a good idea to kick the scenery too hard, but if you hold very still and view it all through a squint and from a certain angle, you can just about get a glimpse of how she likes to see herself, and it's actually very sweet. She was quite a bit younger than my dad was when they got married and she had me when she was super young, so she's still quite pretty. By the way.

My dad was married to another lady before he got divorced and married my mom. I know nothing at all about my dad's first wife, except that she lives in Europe somewhere and her name is Melanie. And that my mom hates her guts, even after all these years. She calls her Smellanie, and says she's getting a migraine if anyone ever brings her up. And believe me, you don't want to be around Migraine Mom. I strongly recommend avoiding that subject.

The current man in my mom's life, technically my step-father, is a *full-on* hippie, though. There's just no getting around it. He'd say "former hippie" probably, but that's too fine a distinction in my book.

Our official legal relationship is pretty recent, though he's been around for quite a while. I don't know why they decided to get married all of a sudden. They went away for the week-end to see Neil Young in Big Sur and somehow came back married. They still refer to each other as partners, though, rather than husband-wife. "Have you met my partner, Carol?" Like they're lawyers who work at the same law firm, or cops who share a squad car. Or cowboys in the Wild West. "Howdy, pardner."

Unfortunately, Carol's dogie-wranglin' varmint-lickin' yella-bellied pardner's name happens to be Tom also. Just my luck.

He has tried to establish the system where I call him Big Tom and he calls me Little Dude. So that any observers (like, say, if someone had planted a spy cam in the TV room) could tell us apart. See, you can't have two Toms in the same room. It would be too confusing for the viewer. Well, he can call me what he likes, but I hardly ever say anything at all, so it never comes up from my end. He's the one who calls himself Big Tom. Which is funny because he's very small for a full-grown man. The spy cam doesn't lie: Big Tom is little.

Little Big Tom can be annoying, but I eventually got used to him. Amanda, on the other hand, has never accepted his legitimacy. She spent the whole first year of the "partnership" sobbing. (So did my mom, come to think of it, but that's not the same thing: my mom spends a great deal of time crying regardless of who happens to be married to whom. Odds are she's crying right now. I'll bet you anything.) These days,

Amanda contents herself with methodically running through all the possible ways to give him the cold shoulder, one after another. No amount of bribery or family-counseling gimmickry ever manages to charm her, though he continually tries. It just makes her angrier. She gets pretty excited when my mom and Little Big Tom have an argument, because she's always imagining that this will finally be the one that leads to their getting divorced. It never is, though. It's weird to watch the situation unfold: you never know who to root for.

One time I said "Get a haircut, hippie" to Little Big Tom, because I'd heard him mention that that's what people used to say to him in Vermont where he's from. He thought that was hilarious, and actually seemed quite excited that I'd said anything at all to him, since that doesn't often happen.

He raised his beer and put an awkward arm around my shoulder, and I tried not to stiffen up too noticeably. Then he pushed the mute button on the remote, turned to me, and said, "Kid, you're all right." There was a long silence. Then he took his arm away, de-muted, and sighed heavily. Well, the Giants were down by two.

"Kid, you're all right." How sad is that? What an ass. For a moment, though, I felt a surge of—what? I don't know the word for it. It's like when you feel lonely, but for someone else. I don't know how to say it. Like you feel sorry for yourself, but it's somebody else's situation that makes you feel like that. Not feeling sorry for someone in the usual condescending way, like when you feel bad if you run over an animal or when a midget can't reach a shelf. More like you suddenly find yourself pretending to be the other person without meaning to, and feeling lonely while playing the role of the other person in your head. I guess, well . . . you could do it with an animal, too.

But let's be clear. In no way should this Special Moment undermine our central thesis, which I will always stand squarely behind: Little Big Tom should get a haircut. Seriously. That ponytail has got to go.

When *Highway to Hell* was over, we put on *Desolation Boulevard* and started to roll stats for "War in the Pacific." Sam Hellerman was playing the Japanese. At around "No You Don't," Little Big Tom came in and stood in the doorway. He nodded as though listening to the music; then he said, "How about we go easy on the decibels for a while? Your mom's trying to rest."

I stared at him until he did a little decisive frown-nod and flitted out. Then I reached over and turned the volume up a notch.

Little Big Tom is a pretty nice guy, actually, and it's not fair that I'm so unaccommodating.

He means well. He likes to walk around making little helpful comments.

"Now, don't fill up on milk," he'll say if he thinks someone is drinking too much milk. Or he'll say, "Ladies and gentlemen, welcome to the homework hour!" if he thinks there's not enough homework going on at any given time. "Let's put some light on the subject," he always says whenever he turns on a light.

He also likes to dispense words of encouragement when he's making his rounds. Like, Amanda will be working on this plaster cast of her hand for art class, and he'll come in and say, "nice hand."

Once, Little Big Tom stuck his head in the door while I was trying to play "Brown Sugar" on the guitar.

"Bar chords," he said. "Rock and roll."

Little Big Tom wasn't actually saying that my halting rendition of "Brown Sugar" was rock and roll. No one would have said that.

He likes to say "rock and roll" all the time, but what he usually means by it is "way to go!" or "let's get this show on the road!" or "this is a fantastic vegetarian sausage!" Like, he figures out how to set the clock on the VCR and he'll say "rock and roll!" Or he'll say "rock and roll!" when everyone finally gets in the car after he's been waiting for a while.

Sometimes he'll even say it quietly and sarcastically when something goes wrong. Once he knocked over my mom's art supply shelf. He bent down to pick everything up, whispered "Rock and roll," and sighed deeply.

I'm a bit rough on Little Big Tom, I know, but I'm nothing compared to Amanda. She can hardly bear to be in the same room with him, and she says even less to him than I do. That time he said "nice hand," for example? Her reaction was to pick up the half-finished hand, drop it in the garbage, and walk out of the room without a word. I don't know if it hurt his feelings quite as much as she was hoping it would, but he sure didn't enjoy it, if the strained tone of his whispered "Rock and roll" was any indication.

We had just reached "7 Screaming Diz-busters" on *Tyranny and Mutation* and things had begun to turn around for the Allies in "War in the Pacific" when Little Big Tom stuck his head through the door and said "Chow time!" What he meant was that he had fixed some vegetarian slop with lentils and bean-curd lumps and weird-tasting fake cheese, and that we were welcome to have a crack at choking some of it down. So Sam Hellerman hightailed it out of there. Lucky bastard.

THE BIG MARBLE FILING CABINET

My family goes to the cemetery to visit my dad's grave every year on September 6, which is the anniversary of his death. This year, it happened to fall on Labor Day, so we were off school.

We call it a grave, but it's really this big building on the cemetery grounds with stacks and stacks of dead people in drawers, like a big marble filing cabinet. My dad is in powder form in a little vase inside one of the sealed filing cabinet drawers. It says "Charles Evan Henderson" and "Peace" on the outside of his drawer. There's also the seal of the Santa Carla Police Department, and a little cup you can put flowers in.

As usual, my mom put flowers in the cup, and we all stood there looking at the cup with the flowers on the filing cabinet drawer. It always feels awkward. There's nothing to say. We just stand in a clump, looking up. My mom and Amanda cry, quietly. I feel sad. But for some reason it doesn't make me cry. There may be something wrong with me there. My mom gets mad at me for not crying, like it shows that I don't care or wish to show respect. It's not like that. I got in big trouble once for bringing a book with me on one of these visits. It wasn't even on purpose. I just automatically take whatever book I'm reading with me everywhere I go without thinking. But it really hurt her feelings and she wouldn't speak to me for two weeks after that.

When I get nervous or worried about something, I do this weird thing with my ears. They start to itch way on the inside and I have this urge to move them back and forth on the outside, trying to relieve the itch. My jaw gets involved also. It can make my whole face look funny and kind of warped and disturbing; plus my glasses go a little crooked. Once I start doing it, I can never stop it on purpose. If it stops on its own, because I get distracted or just calm down, and I notice that it has stopped, I'll be relieved for a second, but that will remind me about it and I'll start doing it again. The more I try to control it, the more out of control it gets. It's a real problem.

Standing by my dad's grave with my mom and Amanda is the classic situation for the ear thing. I just get more and more nervous and twitchy. This year, my ears were going like crazy, maybe even more than usual. I was drenched with sweat, too. I tried biting the inside of my cheek really hard to give myself some other irritant to focus on. That sometimes works, but this time I couldn't bite hard enough to have an impact, even though I could taste a lot of blood in my mouth.

As I stood there, not exactly trying to cry but imagining how much of a relief it might be if for some reason I did, I couldn't help thinking of Mr. Teone's mockery. Hi, I thought sarcastically in the general direction of my dad's drawer. The big marble filing cabinet is the one place I never feel like my dad can hear me talking, though. It just feels empty and lonely and stressful. Definitely not my favorite place.

WE ALL DIED IN A PLANE CRASH

I'm regretting how sloppy I've been with my notebooks, now that I'm trying to go back and remember exactly when everything happened. I mean, I write down all our bands, which ends up being a kind of record of events, but I hardly ever put any dates in there, and even though it was only a few months ago, the timeline seems a little fuzzy. My best recollection is that it was around the middle of September, three weeks or so into the school year, when the Baby Batter Weeks officially ended. And when Sam Hellerman came up with a strange and unexpected proposition.

The band broke up in the customary way. That is, one day, when I met Sam Hellerman at the corner of Crestview and Hillmont Avenue on my way to school as usual, he started to whistle the first line of "Sweet Home Alabama." Which told me that he wanted to change the name of the band again. That's because we had our own words to that line: "We all died in a plane crash," which was how all our bands ended. I could see his point. Baby Batter had been a great band, but it was time to move on.

We worked out the details of the new band on the way to school. The Plasma Nukes.

Logo: an intercontinental ballistic missile with a broken-in-half heart dripping blood on the side. "Plasma" superimposed in fancy cursive and "Nukes" underneath in retro computer bubble writing.

Credits:
Guitar: Lithium Dan
Bass and Calligraphy: Little Pink Sambo
Vox: The Worm
Machine-gun Drums: TBA
First Album: *Feelin' Free with the Plasma Nukes.*

Album cover: a woman's high-heel shoe on a chessboard, with blood dripping out of it (front). Band members' heads in jars on shelf (back).

I was Lithium Dan and I played in a cage. Little Pink Sambo was Sam Hellerman. And we just made up the lead vocalist. The drummer was imaginary, too, but for the record, TBA is pronounced like tuba.

* * *

As for Sam Hellerman's bizarre proposition, it went a little like this:

"There's . . . this . . . this . . . sort of party . . . um . . . thing I heard about," he said.

Pause. "Really?"

"Wanna go?"

I gave him a "yeah, right" look. Then I realized he was serious. I stared at him. Sam Hellerman and I weren't the kind of guys who got invited to parties. The last party I had attended had had cake and streamers and a magician-clown. I was five. And I was pretty sure that if I ever did go to a high school party I wouldn't be any more comfortable than I was then. But it was immaterial because there was more chance of gumdrops falling from the sky and all God's crystal unicorns overthrowing the government and dancing on the White House lawn than there was of anyone at Hillmont High letting me or Sam Hellerman into any of their precious parties. It just wasn't gonna happen.

But Sam Hellerman had some old friends who'd gone from McKinley Intermediate to CHS rather than Hillmont. Maybe they hadn't grasped how risky it would be to be seen hanging around with him. Or maybe, for some bizarre reason, they didn't care all that much. They do things differently in Clearview. It's like a whole other culture.

At any rate, Sam Hellerman *was* planning to attend this party, which was being held in a couple of weeks at the house of some CHS kid whose parents were going to be out of town. I could come along, too, if I wanted. In fact, he was kind of insistent. He really wanted me to go. I had a "let's play it by ear" attitude, but he was having none of that: he wanted a solid commitment.

"So," he said, "you're definitely coming, right?"

It's strange to think what a different type of sophomore year I would have ended up having if I had refused, as I almost did, or if, in the event, I had tried to wiggle out of it in some way, which would have been very much in character for me. But for some reason, I said okay. He made me promise to honor that okay, too. I gave him a look but agreed. Maybe he was nervous and needed moral support. No one would know me, so I felt pretty safe saying yes. Plus I'd only experienced this situation in movie and commercial form. I wanted to see what life was like on the other side. Of Broadway Plaza Terrace Camino, that is.

30 Days to a More Powerful Vocabulary didn't take anywhere near thirty whole days in Mr. Schtuppe's English class. So once we reached "weltschmerz," we immediately started over again with "abortive."

Eventually, though, time was up, and the vocabulary section was over. I think we stopped the second go-through at around "dipsomania."

Now it was time to start the reading.

I was bummed, but not terribly surprised, to see Mr. Schtuppe writing *The Catcher in the* . . . on the board. There really is no other book they ever want you to read. I had my own copy. It's standard school equipment.

Everyone is required to carry a copy at all times. Hall monitors stop you on your way to class and won't let you pass unless you show them your valid *Catcher in the Rye*. The Salinger Boys kick your ass and you get expelled if you're caught wandering in the halls without one. Okay, that's an exaggeration. We don't actually have hall monitors at our school. But otherwise, that's pretty much mostly almost exactly how it is.

Anyway, I opened my backpack and pulled out my *Catcher*.

Now, the AP English teachers would have smiled an "aha, one of us" smile and said a silent prayer of thanks to the nonconformist gods. Or they might even have taken me aside to tell me the fond story of how they used to carry around a copy of that book with them everywhere when they were young and how it helped them through troubled times and how their door is always open if I ever need to talk.

But Mr. Schtuppe didn't have that level of interest. He was waiting to die. Why should he care about instilling a sense of tame rebelliousness in the above-average students? I got two extra credit points for having my own book. But then I got three minus credit points for writing "Beat Noir-ay rules ok" on my desk.

Once again Mr. Schtuppe had his own approach to teaching the joys of literature. The first assignment was to copy out chapter one, highlight the words with three or more syllables, define them, and use them in sentences.

I just sat there staring at page one, wondering if it was even possible to mispronounce "autobiography."

THE SPORTING LIFE

PE is probably the most unpleasant fifty minutes of a person's day-to-day life at HHS. For one thing, they force you to wear this brutal outfit consisting of these gay little blue and white George Michael shorts and a reversible T-shirt that says "Boogie Knights." There are many danger zones, but two of the most dangerous are: at the beginning when you take off your street clothes to put on the gay little blue and white shorts and the reversible Boogie Knights T-shirt, and at the end when you take off the g. l. b. & w. shorts and the r. B. K. T. and attempt to put your regular clothes back on.

There are a few seconds there when you are essentially naked, standing among a bunch of big, mean normal guys who hate you just for existing and who are constantly asking each other "who you callin' faggot, homo?" (It's a call-and-response game, the response being: "I ain't no homo. Who you callin' homo, faggot?" This is a self-sustaining loop that can literally go on for hours if uninterrupted.) As a rule, they are so absorbed in this game and assorted homoerotic horse-play amongst themselves that they barely notice you. But if your timing is such that you end up being naked at the same moment that they are partially or fully clothed, and one of them happens to notice you, you can be in big trouble. All the usual high school tortures can come into play here, but being naked while they are happening makes them all much worse. Plus there's something about the PE situation that makes a certain type of socially well-situated psychopath unable to resist issuing threats about how his plans for beating you up include the ambition to stick various things up your butt. Which can be pretty disturbing. Yay, team. What a great bunch of guys.

It's a little foretaste of our fine prison system, I suppose. And it doesn't take much. The lesson is clear: unless you happen to be one of those guys, and if you don't particularly want to be beaten senseless and raped with a foreign object by one of them eventually, stay as far away from sports as you possibly can. I mean, prison.

So around midweek, the Plasma Nukes (that is, Sam Hellerman and I) were walking away from PE class, on our way to "Brunch," which is what they call the seventeen-minute gap between second and third period. We were feeling pretty good about PE. I mean, we had timed everything well and hadn't had any nasty run-ins with any normal psychopaths while we happened to be naked. You get one of those days every now and then. It's like finding a twenty-dollar bill in a library book.

So great was the general feeling of relief that I hardly minded when Mr. Teone, waddling by on his way into Area C, yelled, "Henderson!" and saluted with what seemed like a determined attempt to set a new standard in the field of sarcastic greetings and with the air of a man who believed he was auditioning for Head Idiot and really had a shot at it this time. True, Sam Hellerman winced like he always does when Mr. Teone said "Miss Peggy!" But I could tell even Sam Hellerman was feeling relatively carefree as well. We had made it through PE. We were high on life.

But then something happened.

Sam Hellerman had this funny little hat he got at the St. Vincent de Paul. No one else had a hat like that, which may have been why Sam Hellerman liked it so much. Maybe he liked to imagine people saying to themselves as he walked by, "There goes that fellow with the unusual hat." He loved the hat. He wore it all the time. But I knew that hat was trouble the minute I saw it.

And so it proved to be. We were walking past a group of jabbering half-human/half-beast student replicants when a smaller subgroup of what seemed like angry orangutan people broke away and started running toward us, shrieking in that way they have: *"Oof, oof, oof!"*

As they rushed by, one of them snatched Sam Hellerman's hat and knocked him into the gravel walkway. Holding the hat aloft, they disappeared into the nearest boys' bathroom. Well, it didn't take a genius to figure out what they were planning to do with the hat in the boys' bathroom. But Sam Hellerman had to check. After the orangutan people had burst out and clambered off in search of other victims, he trudged into the bathroom. Then he trudged out again looking hopeless and miserable. The hat was beyond help. He just left it in there.

The look on Sam Hellerman's face was enough to tell me that he was thinking of a Rolling Stones song, either "Mother's Little Helper" or "Sister Morphine." He had already begun counting the minutes till school was out. As I think I've mentioned, Sam Hellerman knows where my mom keeps her Vicodin, which is one reason he always wants to come over my house. In fact, he doesn't really do it all that often, but when he's feeling especially depressed, or in the aftermath of a major tragedy like the unjust loss of a favorite hat, he'll head straight to my mom's night-table drawer and take some of the pills with a tall glass of bourbon that he swipes from her entertaining area. Then he'll fall asleep and wake up after a while with a headache and maybe have to throw up. It can't be too pleasant, but he keeps at it nonetheless. I can relate to wanting to go away for a while, though that method is really not for me.

Sam Hellerman is as low as I am on the high school social totem pole, which is as low as you can get if you can go to the bathroom by yourself and don't need machinery to get from one place to another. But it's worse for him, in a way, because until high school he actually had a sort of social life. I can merely fantasize about what I might be missing. He has experienced it firsthand.

What I mean is, he had quite a few friends in junior high, and he had enough status that he could theoretically walk into a room without everybody laughing or throwing things at him or threatening to kick his ass and so on. Theoretically.

I mean, he could hang out with normal people and be reasonably certain that the whole thing wasn't part of somebody's master plan that would end up with the joke being on him.

And he was just at the level where he could talk to a girl or even ask a girl to "go" with him and the very idea wouldn't automatically have struck everyone as totally outrageous and hilarious.

In fact, he even had a sort of girlfriend for a brief time, Serenah Tillotsen. They used to smoke and make out behind the scout house sometimes, until she suddenly started dressing sexier and realized that dumping Sam Hellerman would be more of a move up in the world than not dumping Sam Hellerman. That sucked, but all in all he still had it pretty good.

In high school, though, everyone suddenly seemed to realize that Sam Hellerman probably wasn't going to grow any taller, and had kind of weird hair and a funny walk, and really didn't have anything to offer that couldn't be acquired much more cheaply and efficiently from someone else. The market, which had once rewarded him slightly for being the same height as the average eighth grader, had now determined that his services were needed elsewhere, and so he ended up at the bottom of the totem pole and at my house every now and then palming Vicodins and swallowing them with some bourbon from Carol's entertaining area.

In teen movies, there is often a guy like Sam Hellerman who is a minor but important member of the "in" group. A glasses-wearing cutup, kind of outrageous, whose sarcastic comments and goofy antics are accepted and appreciated by the others in the group, though they tend to receive his bits of dialogue with a degree of eye-rolling. Sure, he's the second one to get his chest ripped open by the masked psycho with the garden implement (right after the sluttiest girl in the group has her throat slit while starting to take her clothes off). But he had his moment.

That's how it was for Sam Hellerman. His moment was over.

So I met Sam Hellerman at the oak tree, and we walked to my house. He assembled his materials, consumed them, came into my room, and lay down on the floor. I let him slip into the void, and put on *Quadrophenia*. Even though Sam Hellerman was there, after a fashion, I was alone with my thoughts.

After *Quadrophenia,* I put on *The Who by Numbers* and thought rather intently about the lyrics to "Slip Kid." I don't want to take any Vicodin for the same reason that I try never to sit with my back to a door.

MS. RAMBO

PE had started with Track, which basically means you go around the track without stopping for the whole period. You're supposed to run most of the time, though you can take periodic breaks where you walk till you're ready to start running again. Of course, Sam Hellerman and I took full advantage of this loophole and walked most of the time, talking about this and that, like, say, whether the Count Bishops or Slade had had more influence on the sound of the first wave of British punk rock. Every now and then, Mr. Donnelly would notice and would yell something like "Come on, girls! Stop playing with your lip gloss!" By which he meant, though it's not all that easy to explain why he chose those particular words, that we were walking too much and that he wanted to see some "hustle." We would then jog sarcastically for a few minutes till his attention turned elsewhere, and then resume our discussion at a more leisurely pace.

After the Track segment was over, near the end of the Plasma Nukes week, we moved on to Tennis. Tennis is kind of a riot. You're supposed to hit the ball with the racket so that it lands in the space between the white lines on the other side of the net and bounces. Then you hit it back if it somehow manages to get hit back in your direction in such a way that it lands and bounces in the space between the white lines on your side of the net.

No one is very good at this. But I have as much chance of performing this operation as a jar of wet gravel would have of calculating pi to a hundred places.

Sam Hellerman is the same way.

So here's our Tennis technique. We hit the ball as hard as we can so it flies over the fence and lands in the bushes outside the tennis area. Then we spend the rest of the period "looking for the ball."

One day we were goofing off, holding the tennis rackets like guitars and practicing duckwalks and windmills and scissor jumps. I suck at this also, of course, but Sam Hellerman is surprisingly good.

The PE teacher in charge of tennis-related activities is named Ms. Rimbaud, which is pronounced Miz Rambo. She looks a little like a frog. If she were actually a frog, she would be highly prized as a source of arrow poison by the natives of South America because of her rich red color.

She noticed our arena-rock tennis-racket antics and ran over to confront us. I don't think I had ever seen a human face turn quite that vibrant a shade of red.

"How would you like it," she said, "if we all came out here and started playing tennis with guitars?"

New band name: Tennis with Guitars

Logo: name printed phonetically as from a dictionary

Love Love: lead axe

The Prophet Samuel: Bass and rat-catching

Li'l Miss Debbie: vocals, keys, bumping, grinding

First Album: *Amphetamine Low*. Cover is white with the album title in tiny black type on the back. The band name does not appear anywhere on the outside packaging.

Second Album: *Phantasmagoria, Gloria*. Cover photo: a police dog licks a broken doll's face.

Band wears white shorts, shirts, and sweater vests, except for L'il Miss Debbie, the girl singer. She wears a tiny nurse's uniform with big black boots. Instead of guitar solos, I use my guitar to hit tennis balls into the crowd. With a delay on it, this makes a really cool sound when the ball bounces off the strings. Debbie and the Prophet Samuel are married but have an open polyamorous relationship. Band is on semipermanent hiatus because I'm always in Europe getting my blood changed.

Oh, and the drummer is a drum machine called Beat-Beat. Because we kind of had to face the fact that we probably never would end up finding a drummer.

THE ACCIDENT

My mom tends to refer to my dad's death as "the accident." It's true in a way, since that's what you call it when one car crashes into another car, but it's also misleading.

I bought into the idea that he had been killed in an ordinary car crash for several years. But gradually I started to pick up on little hints that it wasn't quite that straightforward. The biggest hint was that my mom and other adults always spoke so carefully about the subject and avoided giving details, even ordinary ones like where it happened and who was in the other car, and if they were drunk, and whether anyone else had been killed. I can see the logic of doing that around a little kid, but as I got older they continued to do it, in pretty much the same way. When details were provided, they were often contradictory. They acted exactly like people do in movies when they're hiding something, and I gradually became convinced that it wasn't an act and that I wasn't imagining it.

The other thing my mom says about my dad's death is that he was killed in the line of duty, protecting people. I can see why she liked to think of it, or for it to be thought of, that way. It kind of contradicted the "accident" theory, though. There may have been a grain of truth in it, even so, but, like the accident story, it wasn't straightforward. My dad was a detective working on narcotics and vice cases for the Santa Carla police, and he certainly did do a lot of protecting people in a sense. But that's not how he died, either.

It wasn't hard to fill in the blanks—some of them, anyway—once I decided I wanted to. I was able to read about it in old newspapers on microfilm at the public library. After I read them, I continued to pretend I didn't know what had happened. My mom pretended it was plausible that I wouldn't have found out. We have a lot of those arrangements in my family.

My dad had been parked on the shoulder of the Sky Vista frontage road late one night. A car had rammed him on the driver side and driven away. He had died from unspecified injuries related to the impact. It was either homicide or manslaughter. That is, he may have been deliberately murdered, or the fact that he died in the crash may have been the inadvertent result of a random accident. They never found the car that hit him, or the driver. The assumption seems to have been that it was a random fatal hit-and-run rather than a deliberate homicide.

But there were unanswered questions hovering over the newspaper articles, much like there were when my mom talked about "the accident." Trying to read between the lines in both situations, you really got the impression that there was a lot of information that was being held back, glossed over, hidden, or buried. I had lived with the uncertainty for six years now, with the strange realization that the more I found out, the more uncertain everything seemed to be. And I admit, even as part of me wanted to know, another part couldn't stand to think about it.

WAGBOG

There's this kid, Bobby Duboyce, who has some kind of skull disease and has to wear this football helmet at all times. The little white chin strap is always fastened because if the helmet comes off and he hits his head it could be very serious. Even though there are ear holes in it, he still has a hard time hearing people, so he's always saying "what?" or "what's that?"

He also has this problem where he is always tired, and he tends to fall asleep at random times. He often spends his time in class asleep, sometimes drooling, sometimes not, with his big helmet resting sideways on the desk. The teachers leave him alone. They don't dare throw an eraser at his big helmet-head because they're afraid his parents will sue their ass.

When he falls asleep in Center Court at lunch, though, it can get ugly. Hillmont High's finest will come up to him and gently write things on his helmet with a permanent marker, like "pussy helmet head" and "I am a fag" and "my mom's a twat." The gentleness is so they don't wake him up before they're done. His parents keep having to buy him new helmets, which they can't be too pleased about. Maybe they have some kind of deal with the helmet people, and a big supply of backup helmets in the garage. He always has a new one the day after, on those occasions when the fine young men and ladies of Hillmont High School's upper crust have decided to indulge in a little lighthearted helmet play.

We (Tennis with Guitars) were on our way to the cafeteria when we saw Bobby Duboyce passed out on the center lawn and realized that our social superiors had developed a new tactic. Some guys from the Honors Society were pouring Coke into one of Bobby Duboyce's helmet's ear holes to see how long it would take him to wake up. Then, when he did wake up, one of them pinned the helmet to the ground and another continued pouring the Coke, presumably to see how long it would take him to start crying. Which was almost immediately. Then they scampered back to their girlfriends, who had been waiting for them by the lockers, and kissed them and grabbed their butts. Ah, young love. Mr. Teone was standing in front of his office door, smiling broadly. Figures.

Sam Hellerman said, "WAGBOG."

Which stands for "what a great bunch of guys."

I mention this because that's when we decided to change the band name to Helmet Boy, with me on guitar, Sambiguity on bass and procrastination. First album: *Helmet Boy II*.

The bell rang. We watched Bobby Duboyce pick himself up and slink off to the boys' bathroom near Area B. Sam Hellerman said, "Wait a sec," and ran after him, either because he had to go to the bathroom himself, or more probably because he wanted to check to see if Bobby Duboyce was all right. Sam Hellerman is like that: he likes to keep tabs on everybody who can't beat him up. After the coast is clear, of course. I was standing by my locker, waiting for Sam Hellerman to return so we could continue on to Band, when I saw Mr. Teone lumbering toward me. Bummer.

Now, Mr. Teone is kind of like the Little Big Tom of Hillmont High School, in that his main job seems to be to walk around making strange comments. With LBT, though, the comments seem more or less good-natured. Mr. Teone's comments always seem to have an undercurrent of malice. And often, they make no sense at all.

He takes some cues from the sociopathic normal students, in fact. For example, my glasses are always slipping down on my nose, and somewhere along the line I developed the habit of pushing them back up with the palm of my hand, so that the palm slides up my nose and kind of hits my forehead between the eyes. And ever since I can remember, kids have mocked me by mimicking this motion whenever they see me coming. It's not a big deal. But there's something weird about seeing an adult do it, especially one who is supposed to be in charge of something. When Mr. Teone isn't doing the Henderson-salute routine, he's doing the nose-forehead slide. And after he has done it, his face will contort into a grotesque parody of a smile, as though to say "ain't I something?" I call that psychopathic-moronic.

By the time Mr. Teone reached me, he was out of breath and sweating like a pig, but that didn't stop him from doing the Chi-Mo nose-forehead slide.

"Naked day of zombies," said Mr. Teone. "Day of suicide-osity."

And then he started giggling like a maniac. I am often at a loss for words, it's true, but at this moment, I felt the loss particularly keenly. What the hell? Maybe I hadn't heard him

45

right—his funny, nasal, syllable-swallowing way of speaking often made it hard to understand him. He wasn't inclined to explain, though.

He made me turn my T-shirt inside out because it had a skull on it, and I guess they had passed some kind of antiskull policy since the last time I'd worn it. I don't look very good without a shirt, so standing there with my army coat between my knees, naked from the waist up while I clumsily reversed the shirt, was pretty embarrassing. Everyone was staring at me. Mr. Teone was staring, too, and laughing and kind of trembling. Pretty creepy.

Sam Hellerman didn't show up at the oak tree after school that day. It was kind of weird. I waited for a while. Then I couldn't think of anything to do, so I just went home.

As soon as I opened the front door, I heard my mom call out from the back patio in the voice she always uses to ask me to fetch her lighter and cigarettes. I didn't really hear how she phrased it but the tone was enough to tell me what she wanted.

And from the sounds coming from the patio, I could tell that I was about to walk in on a meeting of the Annoying Laugh Club.

I braced myself and brought the cigarettes out, lighter on top of cigarette pack in a neat little stack, just like I'd been doing since I was a kid. My mom said the same thing she always says: "Thanks, baby, you're so sweet."

The Annoying Laugh Club has only two members, my mom and Mrs. Teneb, and both of them were smoking and drinking iced tea at the patio table. Mrs. Teneb is one of my mom's friends from way back, maybe even all the way back to high school, and she's also friends with Little Big Tom. My mom has a laugh like a car alarm. Mrs. Teneb has a laugh like a long scream and she says "frickin' " a lot. I stood there for a few minutes watching them smoke and drink iced tea, trying to figure out what they were laughing about, which is pretty much impossible most of the time.

At one point Little Big Tom stuck his head through the door at that funny angle he always sticks his head through the door at. It almost looks like the rest of his body hidden behind the wall next to the door is sideways, too.

"Take the Nestea plunge!" he said, and went back upstairs. He was working on his grant proposal.

Mrs. Teneb and Little Big Tom know each other from the Renaissance Faire and the Community Theater, where they do plays and such. Mrs. Teneb is a woman, but she likes to call herself an actor. Not an actress like you might expect her to say.

" 'Actress' is sexist and diminutive," she'll say, if she thinks you're thinking it's a little weird that she's saying she's an actor.

Carol and Little Big Tom always call her an actor, too, but for some reason Little Big Tom didn't like it so much one time when I referred to him as an actress. He likes to think he has no hangups, but that's kind of gendercentric and unprogressive of him, don't you think?

I'll say one thing, though: whether he's an actor or an actress, he sure is diminutive.

BOOKWORMING

I could still hear the annoying laughter after I entered the house and proceeded down to the basement. I had realized on the way home that I had left my *Catcher in the Rye* in my locker, and I needed it for one of Mr. Schtuppe's brain-dead assignments. ("Define the following words and use them in sentences, noting the page on which they occur: linoleum, hospitality, corridor, canasta, janitor, conscientious, phony, lagoon, incognito, brassiere, burlesque, psychic, brassy, intoxicating, verification, jitterbug . . .") I knew there had to be another copy of that book somewhere in this house. There are copies of that book lying around everywhere.

I soon found one, in one of the many ragged boxes of random books that were stored down there. It was very old, very beaten-up, not a paperback but not exactly a hardcover book, either—it was like a hardback but with a slightly flimsy cover, and it was almost as small as a paperback. The title on the spine had been rubbed off, but was legible on the front cover, which was only hanging on by a few threads. Some of the little bunches of pages were loose. The whole thing was falling apart. It had once been held together by a rubber band, which had now disintegrated, though pieces of dried-up rubber band still stuck to the outside.

I flipped through it idly on my way upstairs. It was really banged up. There was some underlining, some illegible scribbles, and a lot of weird stains. The dedication, *To My Mother*, had been scribbled out and someone had written "tit lib friday" in blue ink on the title page. Heh, I thought, now there's a band name for you. I suddenly realized that, since it wasn't the same edition my class was using, the page numbers wouldn't match up, and I almost tossed it back onto the book pile. But then I saw what was written on the inside front cover, and I stopped dead with my foot on the fourth step of the basement stairs, the assignment forgotten.

It said "CEH 1960." Now, CEH stood for Charles Evan Henderson. So this had been my dad's copy of *The Catcher in the Rye* when he was (doing the math), um, twelve. My God,

I thought: my dad had been one of those people who had carried *Catcher* with him everywhere when he was a kid. He had been a member of the *Catcher* Cult.

I don't know why it came as such a surprise. My dad was from the *Catcher* generation. I guess I just never thought of him as the type. Little Big Tom had given me the "*Catcher* changed my life" speech, of course; I'd have been surprised if he hadn't. But I can't remember my dad ever mentioning any books. I was only eight when he died, though, so maybe he thought I wasn't quite old enough to be initiated into the Holden Caulfield Mysteries.

I didn't much like the idea of his having been a *Catcher* Cult guy, but I guess I found it more fascinating than distressing.

Anyway, I sat down on the steps to examine the book more carefully. I don't know what I was looking for. It suddenly hit me that I didn't know that much about my dad as a person, despite the fact that I would have said, if ever asked, that we had been very close. You can feel you're close to someone you hardly know; people do all the time. But I had never realized that this had been the case with regard to my dad, and I found that it freaked me out a bit. You don't think of your parents as actual people when you're a little kid because you don't need to, I guess, and his half of the father-son relationship had been prematurely frozen at the son-at-eight stage. Mine had continued to develop as a one-sided thing, but we had missed out on quite a bit, and I guess to a degree I still saw him through eight-year-old eyes, though I knew that was a pretty silly thing to do.

For those reasons, there was something spooky about simply holding the book in my hands. I felt dizzy. And I don't know—a little *crazy* somehow. I realized that I was crying. Not just with slightly moistened eyes, like I was used to, and not over-the-top racked-by-sobs bawling à la Amanda either. Just large, silent tears pouring out of my eyes, landing in the open book in my lap, so subtle I hadn't even noticed them till I saw the fuzzy dark circles they made on the page when they started to absorb into the paper. Some stuff dripped out of my nose and landed on the book, too. Revolting. I shook the thoughts out of my head, in that way I have, and forced myself to get a grip and get back to examining the book.

There wasn't a whole lot of information, though. Besides "CEH 1960" and "tit lib friday," there were a few other scribbled words I couldn't make out, a lot of numbers, and what looked like part of a date: 3/something/63. The day was smudged and faded and stained and impossible to make out; the month was also not too clear, but it did seem like it probably was a three. No significance to that date jumped out at me, though by my calculations he would have been about my age in March of 1963. The stains could have been anything: food, coffee, wine, beer, blood. Blood? Uh, yeah. Calm down, now, Columbo. The *first* body hasn't even turned up yet.

There was only one underlined passage, as it turns out. It was the scene where this girl called Jane Gallagher gives Holden Caulfield a back rub at the movies. Why would he have underlined that particular paragraph and no other? It didn't seem quotable or inspiring or meaningful in any way, just more blather in Holden Caulfield's annoying *Leave It to Beaver* lingo. But that was my instinctive anti-*Catcher* bias talking. I made what felt like a physical effort to keep my mind open. I didn't get it now, but maybe there was something to it that I was missing. If the back rub scene had been important enough to my 1960 dad that he had underlined it, there had to be a reason.

Then something else hit me: maybe there were other CEH books down there. I scrambled back to the box area and spent the rest of the day going through them all, book by book, setting aside those marked CEH. It took around three and a half hours. By the end, there was very little light coming through the window on the aboveground downhill side of the basement wall, and I had twelve CEH books, including the *Catcher.* They had been inscribed between 1960 and 1967, when my dad would have been 18 or so. There was also another one that I wasn't sure about, inscribed only "CH" with no date. It looked like the same handwriting, but it was hard to tell.

They sat in a little stack on the basement floor, a crooked, dusty treasure.

Little Big Tom came down and noticed me pawing through the books. He flipped on the light and said, "How about a little light on the subject?"

Then he said, "It's a classic!" And of course I knew without glancing up that he was tilting to one side and looking at *The Catcher in the Rye* when he said it.

LOVE, FOR WANT OF A BETTER WORD

It seems as if I am always horny.

That's bad because the chances that I will ever get to express that horniness in the context of a fulfilling relationship with an actual other person have always seemed pretty slim. It's a thing you have to live with. In fact, before October 1 of this year, I had never even touched a girl in "that way." And even then—but I'll explain all that soon enough.

In youth-oriented movies and books, the guy like me often has a huge crush on a specific blond cheerleader who doesn't know he exists and would never stoop to talking to him. Or maybe she is kind of mean to him even though she's friends with him and asks him for advice on how to get the football guy to make out with her, which drives him crazy, and so forth. Now, don't get me wrong, I'm definitely that guy. But there isn't any one particular girl that fits that formula, and the idea that someone like that would ever be friendly with me in any sense, even as a device to dramatize my own pain and loneliness, is rather preposterous.

But of course I do have this mousy but cute female sidekick who has been right under my nose all along, only I won't realize how great she is till I've learned a few painful lessons about commitment and responsibility and what's important in life.

Just kidding; I don't have one of those, either. Pretty much all the girls in school are cruel and unattainable, and the great majority are also beautiful and sexy and desirable in at least some way. None are at all interested in or available to me, and why would they be? When I dream of how it would be if I were suddenly transformed into the kind of guy that does not repulse the females of our species, I don't necessarily think of any particular girl. Pick any one; it doesn't matter. This whole topic is so in the realm of pure theory that we might as well call her x. Or rather xi, "i" denoting "imaginary." Conceivable in theory, but unrecorded by history and impossible in nature. An imaginary girl.

If it makes it easier to visualize, though, let's say xi is, hmm, how about Kyrsten Blakeney? She's blond and wears really short skirts. I don't know if she's actually a cheerleader, but she looks the part. Real foxy. Looks great poolside, chewing on an eraser, leaning over to buckle her shoe, riding a bike, eating a banana. Looks great paying a late fine at the library, taking out the recycling, buying a newspaper, playing with dogs, whatever. Nice rack. Sagittarius. Birthstone: yellow topaz.

I find myself thinking of how I'd like to express my horniness in the context of Kyrsten Blakeney fairly often. So does practically everybody who has ever seen her—students, teachers, janitorial staff, etc.

In all the movies and books, the guy like me is totally in love with Kyrsten Blakeney and only Kyrsten Blakeney. If you forget the quaint adherence to monogamy in the realm of pure ideas, and depending on how much you want to quibble over fine shades of meaning in the word "love," that's pretty accurate and true to life. And it would be quite true, in the strictest sense, to say she is not aware of my existence. Which is a mercy: I can't see that I would have anything to gain from her knowledge of my existence.

In real life, I admire her from afar and quietly celebrate her beauty, just as I would do if I were playing my character in the finest, most typical teen movie or young-adult novel our civilization has to offer.

In this movie, Kyrsten Blakeney somehow discovers my hidden depths, decides she likes my eyes, smells my pheromones, and goes crazy for my body. She decides to risk everything and shock God and country by becoming the girlfriend of a nameless, sad-sack dork like me. Society is aghast. Parents and teachers wonder where they went wrong. The president declares martial law. Meanwhile, Kyrsten and I make out in the gym at the homecoming dance while everyone stands around in a shocked, silent circle. Then she gets up on the stage and delivers this great speech to the student body, condemning them for their superficiality, insensitivity, and racism (because maybe in the movie I could be black or Filipino or Native American and handicapped, too). And when she's finished, after a panoramic shot of the stunned, silent crowd, one person starts to clap slowly. Soon another starts to clap. Before long, they're all clapping. They raise me up on their shoulders and ride me around the gymnasium shouting, "Chi-Mo! Chi-Mo! Chi-Mo!" just like they used to in junior high, except now they mean it in a positive sense. And my dad comes back from the dead and smiles at me from the bleachers and kisses my mom on the cheek. And as the throng hands me a check for a hundred thousand dollars and carries me out the door to my brand-new car, you hear the voice of my back-from-the-dead father saying, "I'm proud of you, boy. . . ." Kyrsten and I start driving off to Vegas to get married. She gives me a blow job on the highway under the steering wheel and kisses me on the mouth and says, "Chi-Mo, you better get used to this, because from now on you're stuck with me. . . ."

Okay, I got a little carried away there. Take it up to right after the speech to the student body, and change me back into a white, suburban, typically abled, clever, if angry, yet somehow almost loveable mixed-up kind of weird guy. Slightly more believable.

King Dork to wed Homecoming Princess. News at eleven. It's a nice thought, and it turns up all the time in movies and books. The one minor problem is that in reality, it never happens. I don't mean rarely or hardly ever. I mean it has never even come within the ball park of being even slightly close to almost happening in the whole history of high school, since the beginning of time.

Not even once.

It turns up in all those books and movies for the same reason that parents and teachers want you to read *The Catcher in the Rye* all the time. It's the world as they would like it to be. It's the fantasy that the short end of the stick somehow comes with hidden benefits that only people out-side the situation can see. The fantasy that the nonentity in the background is secretly the main guy who has his revenge in the end. It's a nice thought. But it's bogus, man. Total crap.

TOYS IN THE ATTIC

That CHS party was just around the corner, and I was starting to dread it a little. I mean, what good could possibly come of such a thing? Still, I didn't want to let Sam Hellerman down. And anyway, I had more important things on my mind. Because it was starting to dawn on me: the band wasn't going anywhere. We really needed to take it to the next level. Sure, we had great band names and stage names and album titles, and I could play bar chords, though it would sometimes take me a little too long to switch between the E and the A one. Sam Hellerman still didn't have his bass, but I was getting tired of waiting.

Don't get me wrong: Liquid Malice was and is a great, great name. But without songs that are as great, it would never amount to much.

So I decided I would write some songs and we would get together to rehearse them, even if we didn't completely have our shit together.

One thing I learned right away. It's way easier to think up names and album covers than to write the actual songs to plug into them. I wrote this song called "Kyrsten Blakeney's a Total Fox" only to realize that what I'd done was basically rewrite "Christine Sixteen" with new, suckier lyrics. There just aren't any words that rhyme with Blakeney. Kyrsten does rhyme with "thirstin'," and I was sort of proud of that one, but the fact remains that my first song set the band back several stages all on its own.

I was starting to sketch out the lyrics for a new song with

the tentative title "Advanced Placement Is a Scam" when Sam Hellerman finally came over. He had his clarinet and a book of Aerosmith for Reed Instruments.

He had a good point. We could start with Aerosmith and work our way up to our own tunes.

I played the chords on my guitar and Sam Hellerman played the melody line on the clarinet. It didn't sound too bad.

Little Big Tom poked his head in and said, "Dream on!" which I thought was a little mean.

It shouldn't have come as a surprise that I had so much trouble writing songs. They always say, "Write what you know." And that was the problem: I didn't know anything.

The following morning, Sam Hellerman dropped something on my desk in homeroom. It was the "Thinking of Suicide?" pamphlet from the Student Resource Area. (They have a whole wall of poorly written, amusingly illustrated pamphlets to help students sort through their problems. The titles are always in the form of a question, like "Pregnant?" or "Drugs and/or Alcohol Addiction or STD?" "Thinking of Suicide?" is our favorite, though.)

"Oh, Ralphie," I said, because sometimes we call each other Ralphie. "Is it that obvious?"

This was a running joke between Sam Hellerman and me. He would pick up one of the suicide pamphlets and bring it over and I'd say, "how did you know?" And he'd say something like "killing yourself is a cry for help, you know." And I'd say, "but isn't death just a part of life?" "Yeah," he'd say, "it's usually the last part." It passes the time.

But this time around, my mind wasn't on the hilarious banter. Instead, I was looking at the extremely familiar cover of the pamphlet as though seeing it for the first time. "Thinking of Suicide?" has this great drawing of a retro girl in a sweater and a short plaid skirt with her calves apart and her knees together and her stack of schoolbooks falling out of her arms. The expression on her face is supposed to be anguished, but she has her mouth open as though in surprise and to me she has always looked pretty sexy. Her glasses are on the floor near one of her clumsily drawn Mary Janes, which seems kind of sexy, too, for some reason. Glasses have always turned me on. It's one of my favorite pictures, and we had already used it for several album covers (most recently for the Underpants Machine, me on guitar, Sam Sam the Piper's Son on bass and bottle rockets, first album *We Will Bury You.*)

What I was thinking, though, for the first time was, this would make a pretty good song. All I had to do was give the girl a name and feel sorry for myself while pretending to be her. And figure out some lyrics and chords and stuff. It was worth a shot, anyway.

I was distracted for the rest of the day, wishing I had my guitar with me so I could play around with suicide song ideas. It was frustrating. On the other hand, it did give me something interesting to think about while Mr. Schtuppe was trying to teach us how to mispronounce words from *Catcher in the Rye*.

But then my world was plunged into darkness.

We were in PE sitting in the lanai, boys on one side and girls on the other, listening to some lady give a speech on what she called Rape Prevention, but what was really more like a list of dating dos and don'ts. Do be passive and tentative at all times. Don't try to persuade anyone to do anything or not to do anything, nor allow yourself to be persuaded to do anything or not to do anything of any kind at any time under any circumstances. Do recoil from human contact at the first sign of discomfort or awkwardness. Don't go out with anyone anywhere if there's a slight chance that drugs or alcohol will be or have ever been consumed by anyone in the vicinity. Realistic stuff like that. And remember, girls, if a boy does something you don't like, you can always poke him in the eyes with your index and middle fingers, thrusting upward under glasses if necessary.

I noticed some of the girls laughing and pointing my way, plus making these little pained grimaces. I knew that I had to be the person they were pointing and laughing and grimacing at. I just didn't know specifically why.

Later that day in Band, Scott Erdman, who is kind of going out with Molli Miklazewski, one of the girls in that PE period, told me that she had told him that they were laughing because they thought they could see my balls. That's totally believable, because, as I've explained, they force you to wear these extremely small blue and white George Michael shorts in PE, and not only do they make you look completely gay but they're not very effective at fulfilling the minimum requirement for a below-the-waist garment as I see it, which is, if nothing else, to cover the genitals. I guess it works out okay for George Michael, but for me it was far from ideal: if you sit a certain way, like Indian style in the lanai, there's always a chance that something will peek out, and I guess that's what happened.

Not only that, but Scott Erdman said that Molli Miklazewski specifically made a point of saying that it's not seeing just anyone's balls per se that grossed them all out. The girls in her circle, she wanted to emphasize, quite enjoy seeing someone's balls in many situations. Sometimes they see a person's balls and throw a big party in the spirit of reverent and enthusiastic ball admiration. Whether it's gross and makes them want to throw up or not is all dependent on whose balls they are. Now, maybe she was saying this in part just to make sure Scott Erdman knew that she felt okay about *his* balls, but the message was clear. The entire second-period sophomore girls' PE class thought my balls were uniquely and supremely beneath contempt. Great.

Never mind about the date-rape prevention from this end, Ms. Rimbaud. I got you covered. There will be no dating, school district approved or not, going on in the general vicinity of my balls for a long, long time.

But the Lord never closes a door without opening a window, and on the bright side, it could have been much, much worse, as this would have been the perfect opportunity for someone to propose a groundbreakingly embarrassing new nickname. But fortunately, just at the point when the discussion in the band room would have reached the all-important nickname development stage, in walked Pierre Butterfly Cameroon.

Needless to say, Pierre Butterfly Cameroon is cursed with one of the worst names ever misguidedly foisted upon a poor, defenseless kid by adoring, clueless, hippie parents. He's also the shortest kid in school (another wonderful gift from the Whole Earth Mom and Dad: stunted growth owing to a protein-free vegan diet in his formative years). Plus, he had been insane enough back in elementary school to have chosen to play the flute rather than some more gender-appropriate instrument, so when he walked in someone lifted him by the legs of his jeans and shook him upside down till he fell out of his pants and hit his head on a saxophone case and lay there crying in his underwear and everyone started chanting, "Get a belt! Get a belt!" So my balls were forgotten in the excitement. Like I said, doors and windows.

So I guess I ended up having a slight change of attitude about that CHS party. I mean, I was kind of looking forward to it, suddenly. It had disaster written all over it, but really, how much worse could anything get?

TITS, BACK RUBS, AND DRY CLEANING

I had, of course, brought all the CEH books up to my room right after I found them at the beginning of that week. I had cased out the *Catcher* pretty thoroughly, but it wasn't till the Thursday just before the party that I got around to examining the rest of them closely as a set. Sam Hellerman had had to skip band practice to do something with his parents (an obligation I wouldn't wish on a dog–his parents are no picnic). I was on my own. So I put on *Rocket to Russia* and began to go through them.

A couple of the books were familiar from school as *Catcher in the Rye* alternates or runners-up. That is, if *Catcher* is for any reason unable to perform its official duties, they make you read one of the other ones instead. There was *A Separate Peace*, which is about this irritating guy who keeps trying to make this other irritating guy fall and break his leg until he finally does and ends up dying. And there was *Lord of the Flies*, which is kind of like Hillmont High School meets *Gilligan's Island*, except that the goons in charge are prissy English schoolboys instead of normal red-blooded American alpha psychopaths.

There was one pretty cool one, though: *Brighton Rock*. Reading books can be a lot of fun when they're not the same ones that they make you read over and over and over till you want to shoot yourself. *Brighton Rock* seemed pretty interesting. I opened it and read the first couple of pages. But knowing it was my dad's book gave me a weird feeling that kept distracting me from the story, so I didn't get too far.

Really, though, I was less interested in reading the books than I was in examining them for physical evidence. *The Catcher in the Rye*, CEH 1960, was the most beat up and had had the most things written and spilled in it. The others were in better shape, though some had stuff written in them as well, mostly little check marks and lines drawn next to paragraphs at the margin, with an occasional note. Someone had written "Beatles" and the word "wow," as well as the word "HELP," and had drawn what looked like a mushroom cloud on the inside back cover of *The Crying of Lot 49*, CEH 1967. Hilarious. *The Seven Storey Mountain*, CEH 1963, had a business card from a dry cleaner stuck between the pages, and also another little card, which appeared to be from the funeral service of someone named Timothy J. Anderson. What that told me was that my dad used to bring his books with him in inappropriate situations, like the funeral of a family member or friend, just like my mom gets mad at me for doing. And that he may have been into the midperiod Beatles and had a fine sense of irony, as well as things that occasionally needed to be dry-cleaned. Hey, I'm a regular Encyclopedia Brown.

I still couldn't make out a lot of what was scribbled in the *Catcher*. In addition to underlining the Jane Gallagher back rub passage, my dad seemed to have used it as a sort of all-purpose notebook and scribble pad, jotting down this and that inside the covers and on random pages. Which makes sense if it's something you're always carrying around, I guess. I use the white rubber parts of my shoes for the same purpose. A lot of the scribbles looked like they might be dates, and maybe some of them were phone numbers, though I don't know—they didn't look like phone numbers to me. There was never much more than the numbers, either. I could understand if they were phone numbers, which you sometimes just write down when someone tells them to you for temporary purposes. I've got some phone numbers on my shoes that I have no idea what they are. But why would you write down dates with no identifying information, like an appointment or something? A date alone is meaningless.

Some of the pages were missing, but I doubted there was any significance to that. The book was in such bad shape I'm sure pieces of it were scattered to the far reaches of the universe by now. The scribbles that looked like words were mostly illegible and incomprehensible, but, absurdly, of the ones I could kind of make out, the word "tit" seemed to crop up a lot. What the . . . ? All in all, there were four of them, including the "tit lib friday" on the inside front cover. One of the other books, *Slan,* CEH 1965, had some string in it that appeared to have been used as a bookmark and had a scrawled note that said (I think) something "4 tit" something something. Four-Tit Something Something. Great band name. Not much use in any other way.

In the end, the results of this phase of the investigation were pretty negligible. But I did know one thing: whatever my dad had been up to between the ages of twelve and eighteen, it had somehow involved tits, back rubs, and dry cleaning.

October

THE TEEN WITHOUT A FACE

For some reason, I didn't want Little Big Tom and Carol to know I was going to a party, though it would probably have thrilled them to imagine that this could be the start of my finally trying to socialize with other kids. They're worried about me in that respect. While being thrilled, though, they still would have teased me about it. I think the same thing that makes them worry about my lack of socialization would also make them uncomfortable about any attempts at remedial socialization that I might try. My mom would have looked at me dubiously and asked if I was planning to dance with anybody. Little Big Tom would have said something like "the girls better watch out!" or "looking good!" I just couldn't face it.

So I said I was going over to Sam Hellerman's house to play D and D. There hadn't been a late-night D and D session in my world for some time, but they had no way of knowing that. Carol and LBT were watching a pledge drive on PBS anyway and had no idea something out of the ordinary was going on. Amanda knew, but she wouldn't tell because there were things she didn't want me to tell about that she was intending to do. She had teased me almost as relentlessly as I had feared my mom would, but in the end we had worked it all out.

"Call if you need a ride home," said Little Big Tom. "I've got a set of wheels!"

It only took around thirty-five minutes to walk to the party, but once you get to Clearview Heights it feels like a different world. It looks pretty much the same as Hillmont, but somehow you get the feeling that there's an invisible wall between the two towns and that you're on the good side of it all of a sudden. There was a good chance that no one would have any idea who I was over there. I was the teen without a face. There are worse feelings.

We got to the door of the party house and just walked straight in. No one tried to kick us out. Outstanding.

There were a lot of normal people there. But quite a few of the ones other than them seemed to be CHS drama people, which was good.

Normal people freak me out, but I'm not scared of drama people. There are some at Hillmont, of course. They're all right, but they tend to be a bit faux hippie and into "jam bands" and the Grateful Dead and Neil Young, so they remind me of my folks a little too much, and they always seem to be trying too hard to be wacky. The real reason I don't like them, though, is that I know they will never let me into their club. I wouldn't particularly like to be a fourteen-year-old hippie revivalist with embroidered jeans listening to the Dead and playing Man in Auditorium in *Our Town* by Thornton Wilder. But the fact that they wouldn't accept me even if I *did* want to be a f.-y.-o. h. r. with e. j. listening to the D. and playing M. i. A. in O. T. by T. W. rubs me the wrong way.

There is, however, one thing I can guarantee: no drama person has ever beaten anyone up.

The CHS drama people seemed similar to their Hillmont counterparts, but they were faux mod rather than faux hippie, and that's a vast, vast improvement. It seems to me if you are going to express your individuality by adopting the costumes and accessories of a long-vanished youth subculture, you're better off with mod. At least you get some cool-looking boots and short skirts out of the deal, and the music is a whole lot better.

Sam Hellerman stood in line for the keg, then came back and handed me this big red plastic cup of beer.

"What do we do now?" I asked.

"Put cup to mouth at slight angle. Swallow contents. Repeat," he said, demonstrating. But he knew what I meant. He recommended trying to "act normal" (yeah right) and mentioned that there was a TV room downstairs if all else failed.

Then he went off to talk to some of those old friends who, for whatever reason, still felt they could afford to be seen talking to him.

Clearview really was Freedom.

The music on the stereo was all Small Faces and the Who and the Kinks and the Jam. Not too shabby. The mod thing was a bit much, though. There was a guy running around wearing a British flag as a cape, and several people were speaking in unconvincing English accents. They, and their hilarious asymmetrical haircuts, were trying too hard. But that's the thing: trying at all is trying too hard. I granted them an indulgence on account of the fine, fine music and gave them absolution for their lapses in taste. I was in a generous mood.

I slouched around quietly, checking everything out, trying to stay away from situations that might erupt into a sudden ridicule/torture session and blow my cover.

Despite the civilizing influence of the unusually numerous drama people, there were a lot of these situations brewing. I mean: clumps of normal guys horsing around and asking each other "Who you lookin' at, homo?" And gaggles of normal girls, any one of whom might suddenly decide it would be fun to put her arm around you and pretend to be hitting on you to see what you would do, with everyone laughing at you the whole time.

That is one of life's most trying and irritating situations. Sam Hellerman and I have given it a catchy name: the Make-out/Fake-out. I don't know if it has a real name. The object of the game isn't actually to make you think they're sincere and go for it, which no one would be stupid enough to think, but just to watch you squirm and see how you'll try to get out of it. You can't win. You might as well just bite down and break open the cyanide capsule concealed in your false front tooth. If you've got one of those. It was fresh in my mind because there had just recently been a Make-out/Fake-out attempt on my dignity during PE class, and I could still feel the pain of having no cyanide capsule to make it all go away.

The danger zones were easy to avoid, though. Steer clear of the schools of sharks and flesh-eating piranhas. Avoid the sirens. Drift toward the playful mod dolphins, who are so busy being entranced with their own wonderfulness that they don't even notice your ungainly boat paddling in their midst. "It's quite a lagoon you've got here," I said, to no one in particular.

Eventually, I drifted into a little basement room down some stairs at the end of the hall. This was presumably the TV room Sam Hellerman had mentioned. It was quite dark, and almost totally empty. There was a turned-off TV and a sofa, and on the sofa was this girl. She was staring intently at a candle that was burning on top of the TV and holding the smoking stub of a joint in a mall head-shop roach clip. You know, with feathers dangling from it, and I think maybe a pentagram or an ankh.

She didn't have a full-on mod costume, but I could tell she was one of the funky CHS drama people because she had a Maximum R & B T-shirt underneath a crazy-looking denim and—what? Yarn?—yeah, it was a yarn 'n' denim jacket that looked homemade. She had on this black soft cap that looked kind of military. And these little black glasses. I was pretty sure she was older than me, a junior maybe. The Who shirt was tiny and didn't go down all the way and her belly looked really good, what I could see of it. I mean really good.

She waved me over and said, "I'm trying to make the candle go out with the power of my mind."

I walked over, unsure of what to do. She said I should sit down and help her. Concentrate, she said. I sat down next to her and stared at the candle. It didn't go out.

"You call yourself a hypnotizer?" she said after a while.

No. I'm quite certain I had never said I was a hypnotizer. I hadn't said anything. Part of me was off in the corner thinking, Maybe these are my people? Eccentric and funny and weird with good taste in music and off-the-wall hobbies, I mean. Another part of me realized that I was so self-conscious that I wasn't exactly radiating Good Eccentric around here. But the biggest part of me was just staring at her bare stomach, which was, like, the nicest thing I'd ever seen in person, though I was trying to do it kind of sideways, hoping she wouldn't notice. She didn't seem like she was in much of a noticing mood, to be honest.

She asked me if I wanted the roach. Now, the thing I said sounds really stupid and goofy, but I know from having watched people smoke pot all my life that it's the thing you say. I still felt like a big ass saying it, though.

"I'm cool."

Never in the history of the world had there been a less accurate statement.

She shrugged and popped the roach in her mouth—reminding me, weirdly, of my mom—and grabbed my half-filled cup and drank it all in one long swallow.

"Fiona," she said after a lengthy grimace. "I'm in drama. I'm an actor and I also do costume. What's your story?"

Wow, a female actor. Just like Mrs. Teneb. I guess she could tell my jumpy brain was mulling over the concept of the female actor, because she quickly added, in a slightly lecturing tone: "We don't say actress. Everyone is an actor. It's unisex." Then she said, carefully, "Actress is diminutive."

Well, okay. Not that I didn't love how she said "diminutive": with great care and delicacy and solemnity and attention to detail, the way you lean two cards together on a new level of a card house.

But I still had to tell her my "story." What was my story, exactly?

"I'm in a band," I said.

"Yeah? What are you called and where are your gigs?"

"The Stoned Marmadukes," I said, making a mental note to make sure to tell Sam Hellerman the new band name so our stories would be straight. Me on guitar, him on bass and paleontology, first album *Right Lane Must Exit*. Then, out loud and rather lamely, I said, "We're working on some, um, on some . . ." Gigs. As if.

But Fiona had already lost interest in that topic. She was scanning the room to see if there might be anyone else around to liven up the conversation. There was no one, so she started talking, in a distant way, about something or other. But I was getting the feeling that she had started to realize what she was dealing with here and had reached the conclusion that my fitness as a participant in any future spooky telekinesis experiments was in serious question.

I sat there while she spoke, trying not to make it too obvious how intently I was examining her, which I totally just couldn't help doing. She had some really tight jeans on, and black boots. Shiny boots of leather. She mentioned how she was making all the costumes for some play she was in. She always ended up doing the costumes, she said, because she was such a good seamstress.

"You mean seamster," I said.

She paused, and said, as though talking to herself, "Mmm, that's interesting." Then she stared at me. The candlelight made her glasses glisten when she moved her head. At times they looked almost like they were made of liquid. I suddenly noticed that she looked a little sad, or so it seemed to me, but maybe she was just stoned and sleepy. Maybe I was just imagining the sadness for my own purposes–I always think girls are prettier when they're crying.

Now, Hillmont is known as Hellmont, or less commonly as Swillmont. And most of the people at the party went to CHS, so I'd have guessed they probably lived either in Clearview or Clearview Heights. Queerview. So that's why Fiona said, "How are things in Hellmont?" And that's why I said, in response, "Diabolical."

She seemed to spring to life. A bit. I mean, she acted as though she thought that was pretty funny. I was sitting there in silence trying to decide whether she was being sarcastic or not. Well, she was at least a little stoned. But I gotta say, her giggling like that in response to my powerful vocabulary, THC-enhanced and sarcastic or not, was pretty fucking charming.

She was hitting my arm. I guess she had said something while I had been in my own world trying to psychoanalyze her, mesmerized by her belly, which her T-shirt had been de-signed to reveal, but maybe not quite as much as was being revealed now that she was all stretched out on the couch, and which I couldn't stop staring at. I mean, it was almost physi-cally impossible to pry my eyes away from it. I did, though, which made a ripping sound, like Velcro.

I went: "?"

"Getting a good look, hand-jive?"

I drew back, mortified. But she was just kidding around, still laughing and hitting my arm.

"Slut heaven," she said. "Do slut heaven."

Now I was really confused. I think I may have said, "Um . . . ," and half smiled so it would look like I knew what

71

was going on while I tried to figure out what was going on. She grabbed my head on either side, put her face very close to mine, and said, slowly and deliberately, the way you talk to a retarded person or an ESL student:

"How. Are. Things. In. Slut. Heaven?"

It took me a beat, but I realized: she must be from Salthaven, or possibly Salthaven Vista, not Clearview Heights. Duh. I'd never heard that name for Salthaven, but it was a pretty good one, and this time my half-smile was at least semigenuine.

But she was still nudging me.

"Slut heaven, going once, going twice . . ."

"Um, concupiscent?" I said.

See, I was a little slow, but I guess we had established the foundations of a game where she asked how things were in a town, and I responded with the appropriate word from *30 Days to a More Powerful Vocabulary*. She shrieked and clapped her hands theatrically and gave me this admiring sort of smile that I had never, ever seen anyone direct my way before. I swear to God, she did, and it didn't even seem very sarcastic.

The beauty of this moment was slightly tarnished by the fact that in the back of my mind I was thinking of Mr. Schtuppe and how he might mispronounce "concupiscent." In fact, I'm not totally sure I didn't mispronounce it. But I've got to say that I hadn't previously grasped the true benefits of making words your slaves. Fiona was an unusual girl, though, not like any of the Hillmont High girls I'd observed. For one thing, what might cause an ordinary person to recoil, or at best make a mental note never to play Scrabble with you, seemed to make her horny. Well, that and all the beer and marijuana. I hadn't realized I had one, but this was my kind of woman.

So now we come to the weirdest part. I swear to God this is exactly what happened.

Fiona grabbed my wrist and moved my hand over to her belly so that my palm was on her stomach just to the right of her belly button and my fingers draped over her hip. I want to say I almost felt a physical electric-y shock from the feeling of her bare skin. It was so surprising. I knew I was supposed to kiss her, but I wasn't sure how to go about it exactly. She scrunched up to me like she was trying to smell my shoulder and I leaned down and we started to rub our faces on each other in the general mouth area. She made this quiet "mmm" sound and started pushing her tongue all the way in my mouth and sort of swirling it in a circle. Counterclockwise. I started to do that, too, after a fashion, but I knew she could tell I didn't know what I was doing. I was in a clumsy, mentally deficient daze. I started to slide the tips of my fingers downwards just underneath the waistband of her jeans, so it was jeans-fingertips-underwear-skin with one fingertip poking slightly underneath the underwear layer, but she squirmed and said, all mumbly because she had her mouth full: "Uh, no, mmm, baby . . ." Uh-oh, I thought, I blew it, I wasn't supposed to do that yet or at all and the whole make-out scene was officially over, but then she said in a kind of whispery voice, "My tits, my tits." I started to move my hand up the other way and reached her right breast underneath her shirt. I had never touched a breast before. She seemed to shiver a little when I touched it. Somehow, I don't know how, I knew that she wanted me to start pinching her nipple, and then, when I had started squeezing it and rolling it between my thumb and forefinger and she started saying "mmm" again and breathing a little laboriously I knew that she wanted me to squeeze it a whole lot harder. I was really digging into it with my nails, and twisting it back and forth

73

while still keeping up with the tongue rotation thing as best I could. Her breathing sounded more like wheezing than breathing. I don't know about the Frenching, but somehow I knew that I was doing the nipple thing right, how she wanted me to be doing it. Though it must have kind of hurt. Then suddenly her head fell back and she leaned away from me.

"I'm sorry," she said in a whisper. She was still breathing a bit strangely and she didn't look sorry. She looked–how? Conspiratorial? "Look, I can't do anything with you because my boyfriend's friends are all here. In fact, we really shouldn't be sitting here like this."

I didn't know what I should say.

She suddenly leaned in and bit me on the neck right above the shoulder, and hopped off the couch and zoomed out. I didn't know what to do.

Eventually I got up and went upstairs and back into the hallway. I scanned the clumps of drama mods, but I didn't expect her to be there. She had clearly intended to flee the scene of the crime and was already gone. As I walked through the house tunneling through the little clusters of drunk and stoned kids and to the front door and down the walk and into the street and on my way home, I was really glad I had my army coat, which is long enough to cover up the front of my pants.

Otherwise, I might never have made it out of there.

SON, YOU GOT A BAD APTITUDE

Now, I've been avoiding this part, because I find the whole thing a little embarrassing, but I figure I might as well get it over with. I mean the Chi-Mo story.

Back in seventh grade they gave everyone this multiple-

74

choice test to determine what you were supposed to be when you grow up. The way it worked was, certain combinations of multiple-choice answers would point to, say, Medicine, meaning you should try to be a doctor. Or you would get Law, meaning you were going to be a lawyer. There was Business, and The Arts, and both kinds of Technology, Food and Computer. Some kids got Athletics, even though it seems like the wrong type of test to determine something like that, and quite a few got one called Counseling and Social Work. Which sounds like wishful thinking on the part of the counselors and social workers who designed the test, but never mind.

Everyone got two results, so you'd have something to fall back on if the other one didn't work out. No one took it that seriously, but it was supposed to be kind of fun to see what you ended up with. Answer some touchy-feely questions, sit back, and watch the machine reveal your future.

Somehow, I ended up with Medicine (which was normal) and Clergy. Which was not. Clergy was bizarre. I was the only one to get Clergy. What the hell were they doing saying "Clergy" to a seventh grader? My future had never seemed to have much going for it, but this was a dark avenue no one had yet considered. It freaked me out.

There was a Peer Interaction and Response Segment where everyone was comparing answers, and someone saw mine.

"Clergy!"

Most of the kids in the room hadn't even heard the word before. I played dumb, didn't say anything. That can make some situations go away, but not all.

Eventually, though, they figured it out and someone said "Father Tom!" That wouldn't have been too bad, as nicknames go, though it still would have been pretty weird for a seventh grader. But then someone said: "child molester!" Then everyone started saying "child molester." That was shortened to Chi-Mo. And that got shortened to Moe. Or I guess maybe it's technically spelled Mo'.

The process only took around fifteen minutes, ending when Mr. Bianchi threw an eraser at someone and said "settle down" to signal the beginning of the Pause and Reflect Segment. But by the end of that fifteen minutes I was officially Moe, or Chi-Mo, or sometimes Mo-Ped, and that's the way it was ever since.

So there you have it. My nickname is an abbreviation for "child molester," or just "molester," whether the people who use it know it or not. As I was saying before, it's just about the poorest excuse for an insult anyone could imagine. It doesn't even make sense. Still, anyone who calls me Moe, even when they may mean no harm, is a potential enemy. That's just the way it is.

Another thing I've got to explain, and now is as good a time as any, is how I've got this reputation as a Guns and Ammo guy. Otherwise, some of the stuff that happened in the week or so following the party will be kind of hard to understand.

It started as a matter of necessity, more or less a ploy. I ended up getting kind of into it in spite of myself, I admit, but for the most part it's still just a means to an end.

The whole thing goes back to early ninth grade, and it started with this one specific incident at the beginning of the year. Matt Lynch and his friends, who had been hassling me as a sort of hobby ever since I can remember, had stopped me as I was coming out of the boys' bathroom and pushed me back inside.

"Why do you look like a wet rat?" Matt Lynch said, while his friends stood behind him blocking the door.

The question, like all the others of its type, didn't have an answer. But he would keep asking it over and over to watch you squirm and to see what you would do. Then he'd get tired of that and move on to the conclusion: beating you senseless, or as senseless as he had time for or thought he could get away with.

Biff Bang Pow. In the stomach, in the ribs or head after they trip you over. Maybe stomping on the knees or wrist. And finally maybe letting a slow, thin string of spit fall down on your face, if they were in the mood for worrying about presentation. You know, like a garnish.

After I had finished vomiting in the toilet stall and cleaning myself up as best I could, I started to ask myself: how can a person prevent Matt Lynch and his retarded subhuman sidekicks from asking you why you look like a wet rat all the time? I knew the answer had to lie not in trying to apply superior force, which wouldn't have been practical, but rather in figuring out how to mess with his mind.

My idea, which had sounded far-fetched at first, ended up working better than I could have hoped. I started to wear an army coat from the surplus store, and to carry around magazines like *Today's Mercenary, Soldier of Fortune,* and *International Gun.* I'd mention my interest in guns and military hardware and urban warfare techniques at strategic moments when I knew I'd be overheard by people who would mention it to other people who would mention it. And I practiced what I hoped was a wild-eyed, crazy look in the mirror (just the eyes–everything else frozen) till I could do it without thinking. It would have looked better without the glasses, I admit, but unfortunately, I needed them to see. In the beginning, I put on a big pentagram pendant as well, but that was overkill and made me look like a moron, so I ended up ditching the pentagram and just concentrating on the military stuff.

People started to look at me funny. I mean, on the rare occasions that people noticed me at all, they started to look at me in a slightly different funny way than the funny way they used to look at me when I wasn't trying so hard to induce them to look at me funny. I was still a nonentity. But I believe I managed to introduce enough uncertainty about my stability into the equation to give at least some would-be harassers pause when they might otherwise have pushed me back into the boys' bathroom without a second thought.

What I learned was this: people like to pick on people of lower status whom they believe they understand. But if something freaks them out enough, it can plant seeds of self-doubt, and sometimes that can be enough to inhibit action, even when you present no real threat to them. Some people are more easily rattled than others, and everyone has a different threshold. But it sure seemed like Matt Lynch's personal self-doubt threshold was such that his self-confidence started to erode involuntarily when confronted with the guns and ammo trip. I had accidentally stumbled on his number. I lucked out.

There are a lot of factors in the situation, and the gun-freak act may have been only one of them. All I know is that when I started to wear the army coat and carry *Today's Mercenary* under my arm and talk about precision sights and shot group training methods and cordite and so on, Matt Lynch seemed to lose interest in trying to push me into bathrooms and beat me up. Though I'm sure he still participated avidly in the anonymous locker exploits and gum throwing and derogatory Chi-Mo graffiti and so forth. He's only human. In a manner of speaking.

DAZED AND OBSESSED

I couldn't stop thinking about Fiona and her mysterious ways. I could still feel her teeth marks on my neck, from the inside and from the outside. I began to notice this distant, yet somehow intense, constricted feeling in my chest whenever I thought of her, which was—well, a lot.

I don't want to leave the impression that I was obsessed with Fiona, walking around in a Fiona-addled daze. The reason I don't want to leave that impression is because it would be pathetic. But I don't know who I'm trying to fool here: of course I was dazed and obsessed.

The Fiona couch episode had been the most successful interaction with a female in my life, surpassing many of my least plausible dreams. A case could be made that it had been my only genuine interaction with a nonrelated female ever, the previous ones having taken place in my head as pure fantasy or in the real world where I had been an object of amusement rather than a true participant.

How could I not be obsessed? It was the most significant event in my life so far. *By* far.

But there was a lot about it I didn't get. She was a mystery. I'm not going to go into all the different angles from which I tried to examine the Case of the Disappearing Fake-Mod Girl. But the central, most important question was: why had Fiona decided to kiss on me and everything, when no previous girl I'd ever come in contact with would have been caught dead in that situation?

I came up with six points, or topics for discussion, which I present in ascending order of validity (one being the most valid) along with some of my notes.

Six: She was impressed with the band.

True, she hadn't seemed too interested. But when I first mentioned the Stoned Marmadukes she said, "Yeah?" and there was something about that "yeah" that seemed a little more fascinated than other "yeah's" I had experienced in my life. Dubious, yet possible.

Five: She was captivated by my masterful command of the English language.

By my count, I had said no more than twenty-one words to her, and that's only if you count "um." And my first bit of dialogue had been nothing less retarded than "I'm cool." But clearly my ability to make words my slaves had had some comedic effect. And girls dig guys who can make them laugh. At least, they do according to scripts written by TV and film comedy writers. Likely, but not necessarily crucial.

Four: She had no idea who I was, and hadn't figured out that I was an Untouchable.

Lack of accurate information had to have been a factor. And anonymity. I only knew her first name and she didn't know any of my names. But was that enough? The mere fact that my reputation had not preceded me? Could I have come off as some kind of Cool Dude when disassociated from Chi-Mo, the dork, the myth, the legend? Hardly. I still radiated me-ness, I'm sure. Relevant, but insufficient.

Three: Fiona prefers dorks.

I've heard that there are girls with this fetish. It's a complicated matter that I don't completely understand, but I'd guess it mainly applies to girls who for one reason or another can't do any better and who persuade themselves that settling for a degree of dorkiness is better than nothing. Are there any girls as hot-looking as Fiona in this category? No way. But maybe her instinctive alterna-ness (in her capacity as a CHS drama mod) made her more tolerant of dorkiness, less repelled by it, even when it radiated from the anonymous King of the Superdorks.

Two: She knew no one was watching.

This one almost goes without saying.

One: She was totally high.

Well, obviously.

MR. JANISCH'S UNDERGROUND BUNKER

I was mulling over some of these points in Geometry that Monday when I felt an eraser hit me on the forehead.

"Somewhere else you'd rather be, Thomas Charles Henderson?" said Mr. Janisch. He always calls people by their full names as they appear on the roll sheet. Just to be a dick.

"No, of course not, Mr. Janisch. Copying these problems and their proofs from the front and back sections of this book respectively is the realization of a lifelong dream."

Of course, I didn't really say that.

What I did was: I gave him a look that was intended to convey the impression that I had been contemplating the mysteries of the world of Pure Geometry and that I had been on the verge of discovering an Important Truth that would have been a boon to humanity and would also have had considerable commercial value had my concentration not been shattered by his supremely ill-timed, inappropriate, and possibly actionable eraser assault.

But at the same time, I was in no mood for Mr. Janisch's foolishness, so I'm not surprised that my look may also have managed to convey the sentiment "No duh, Einstein."

Six of one, half dozen of the other, really.

The punishment for this sort of low-level insubordination is usually that you are made to copy out something, typically a dictionary page, onto a sheet of notepaper. This is no big deal. There is little difference between this penalty and the other assignments they give you as part of your "academic" work. The only difference is the thing you're copying. A dictionary page is preferable to a chapter from *The Catcher in the Rye*, even, because, well, at least the chances are good that it will be a page you've never copied before and that's special.

Mr. Janisch, for reasons known only to him, likes to make you fill a page of notepaper, front and back, with zeros, in groups of three like this: 000,000,000, etc. The weird part is that he seems genuinely pleased when you hand him the finished page of zeros. It's like he gets caught up in the excitement and forgets that it's supposed to be a disciplinary measure. My theory is that he saves these pages in a series of black binders in a specially designed rebar-and-concrete lead-lined underground bunker. When the bomb drops, or on Judgment Day, or by the time he retires and goes underground to plot his revenge, he'll have thousands of binders filled with millions upon millions of zeros. Then he'll add a one to the beginning and suddenly he'll be in sole possession of the world's largest number in manuscript form. Or I guess it'd be even better to add a nine. Then he can laugh maniacally and die happy.

Whatever gets you through the night, big fella.

Anyway, that was my punishment this time. I enjoy it, actually. It's mindless, routine, repetitive, familiar, and no more pointless than anything else they make you do in school. The hand moves automatically; the pen goes circle-circle-circle-tic, circle-circle-circle-tic, a soothing rhythm; and the mind is free to wander. I started trying to think up some lyrics to "Trying Not to Believe (It's Over)."

THE FLOWERPOT MEN

One thing that was slightly freaking me out was the thought that even though I felt I couldn't be more different than the

CHS people at the party, we did seem to like a lot of the same music. Because I love the Who. But I'm not a fake mod like the dolphins at the party. Not at all. I don't dress up like anything. True, I did let my hair grow a little longer and started to wear flared jeans over the summer when I got more into seventies bands and stuff, as a sort of tribute to their fine work; and I've got the army coat, though that's more of a practical tool than a fashion statement. But I don't "dress punk," or mod or metal or goth or garage or rockabilly or anything. I don't wake up every morning and put on a music-genre-oriented youth-culture Halloween costume—that's what I'm saying.

My tastes do tend to be a bit retro, though. I'm really into the Who, the Kinks, the Merseyside/British Invasion sort of thing. And like I said, I also like a lot of seventies stuff, which I find myself listening to more and more often. 1975 was a great year for rock and roll, and don't believe anyone who tells you different. But I can find something to appreciate about most pop music—it's all part of rock and roll history, which I'm trying to know everything about. I have a pretty big record collection of mostly old stuff, and I'm totally proud of how schizophrenic it is. I even kind of like Wishbone Ash. And I'm not even exaggerating all that much. But for some reason I'm not necessarily too interested in very much of what was recorded after I was born. And, as a matter of principle, I don't dig whatever mindless, soulless crap all the normal people are into at any given time, because what would be the point of that?

My personal ultimate in art rock will probably always be, well, either the Who or the Sweet. Or Foghat. But I'm also really into Bubblegum, and that's probably what confuses people most.

Bubblegum is this music they had in the seventies, created and marketed for little kids, and, apparently, not taken very seriously by anyone involved. But it somehow ended up being brilliant by accident without anyone realizing. I love that. I have a pretty big collection of Bubblegum records. Now, I admit, maybe I got into it at first because it was so clearly the opposite of what everyone else liked. But whatever: it's some of the best rock and roll music there ever was. I think normal people think it sounds corny or wimpy, not realizing that there would have been no Ramones without "Yummy, Yummy, Yummy." But I'm quite confident that when we're all dead, history will clearly conclude that my retro rock revival was years ahead of everybody else's retro rock revival.

Sometimes, when I'm trying to cheer up Little Big Tom by finding some interest we can temporarily pretend to share, I'll ask him about the music of the sixties and seventies, which was his era. Back then, he and all his friends didn't pay attention to most of my favorite music from the time. They thought it was childish, not serious, meaningful music like, say, Led Zeppelin. Now, Led Zeppelin is all right (good drums and guitar, anyway, though that singer should have been silenced or muzzled or something–frankly, I prefer it in Yardbird form to be honest). But Little Big Tom's example of how serious and important and adult it all was? "Stairway to Heaven." I kid you not. Don't get me wrong: I like hobbits and unicorns and wizards and hemp ice cream as much as the next guy. And I suppose it's the antimaterialist message that seemed so sophisticated and meaningful to those guys– no one does antimaterialism better than multigazillionaire rock stars. But my view is that there's something seriously wrong with a subculture that would prefer "Stairway to Heaven" to "Wig Wam Bam." Come on: go listen to "Wig Wam Bam" and tell me I'm wrong.

I was thinking about all this, and kind of counting the

ways in which the Sweet ruled Led Zeppelin's relatively sorry ass, when I returned home from the first post-Fiona school day. On my way in through the patio, I noticed Little Big Tom using a sledgehammer to break big pieces of concrete into little pieces that would fit in his wheelbarrow. (He was trying to turn the backyard into Spaceship Earth by reversing the paving process and planting ferns and vegetables so that one day they might be able to film a margarine commercial there.) I heard him whistling a tune I recognized from my own record collection: "My Baby Loves Lovin' " by White Plains, originally recorded as a demo in their previous incarnation as the arguably superior Flowerpot Men. It is the perfect pop song, more or less. I had just been playing it pretty loudly the previous day. So—here I was, influencing Little Big Tom with an unjustly rejected gem from his own era. Kinda neat.

So I went over and started singing "My Baby Loves Lovin' " and doing this little Greg Brady/Jackson Five dance—well, not a dance, exactly. It's more like genuflecting and using your knees to move your whole body up and down while smiling like an idiot. There is simply no bait that Little Big Tom will leave on the hook. He broke into a big smile as well and faced me and started singing "My Baby Loves Lovin' " and doing the Greg Brady/Jackson Five genuflect dance, too, though I suspect he may not have been aware that it was the G.B./J.F. g. d. So there we were, rising and descending, facing each other, singing "My Baby Loves Lovin'." Amanda came through the back door, stared for a few seconds, and then turned on her heel and walked back in. I really couldn't blame her.

It got old quickly. But Little Big Tom was having such a great time that I hated to pull the plug, so I continued doing it for a while, looking at him with a frozen yet fading smile that gained and lost altitude while I tried to figure out a way to end the baby-loves-love-a-thon gracefully. He couldn't take a hint, though. Finally, I just had to say:

"Hey, you know: I've got some things to do."

Probably not the best way to handle it, but I was desperate. I went into the house, hearing his trademark sigh and eventually his sledgehammer-on-concrete sound.

WOMEN GETTING IN THE WAY

Maybe it was more or less predictable that the whole Fiona situation would eventually start to affect the band. It's well known that that has been the downfall of all the great bands of the world: women getting in the way.

Sam Hellerman had a weird attitude. At first I thought he was mad at me for leaving the party without him, but it turns out he didn't care about that at all. It was Fiona.

When I told him what had happened, at our first post-Fiona band practice—and then told him again, presumably so he could pay attention once he realized I hadn't been making it up—he said: "Fucking bitch."

Now, you have to understand something about Sam Hellerman. He never swears. I don't swear much, either, out loud, but that's mostly because I never say more than a couple of words at a time. I keep it to myself, but in my head, I'm like a late-night cable comedy special. Everyone would be shocked if they had access to a transcript from my head. I don't know about Sam Hellerman's head's transcript, but he talks out loud all the time, and as he's talking you can almost see him struggling to avoid saying swear words. Like, he'll always say have sex instead of fuck, or boobies instead of tits. The first works sometimes, though it can sound awkward; the second is pretty much inexcusable and reflects poorly on

him. Once he said crotch instead of nuts when he was describing where Matt Lynch had been trying to kick him during a recess scuffle. That alone was good for a couple more
beatings. I think his parents are Seventh-Day Adventists or
Mormons or something like that.

That was part of the reason Serenah Tillotsen had to
break up with him. Not the having Mormon parents. The
swearing thing, I mean. To be dateable at the time, you had
to excel in at least two of the following four areas: swearing,
bullying, smoking, sports. And to go out with a girl who
dressed as slutty as Serenah Tillotsen you probably had to
have mastered at least three, and even that might have been
pushing it. Sam Hellerman had the smoking down, but he
was a disaster at all the others.

Sam Hellerman's swearing thing had already affected the
band a bit, but so far only in a good way. He objected to the
song "Normal People Are Fucked Up" in favor of the alternate version "People Who Are Normal People Are the Most
Retarded People in the World," which turned out to be a
much, much better song.

So it was shocking to hear those words come out of his
mouth. He was taking the whole thing pretty seriously. Now
I admit, I may have *slightly* exaggerated when I told him the
story. Just a little, in that I may have managed to imply that
things with Fiona might have gone a little further than they
actually had. But even considering that, it was still just a
stoned teen party grope-a-thon any way you sliced it. He
should have been happy for me. Maybe he was jealous; I
guess I would have been.

In any case, that's so not how I saw the situation: for me,
Fiona was not, literally or in any other sense, a "fucking
bitch." I had nothing but esteem and admiration for her and
her sinful ways. And I had a kind of high-minded reverence

for her memory. Sure, there was much I felt remorseful and embarrassed about, and I had had absolutely no luck trying to figure out a way to understand her confusing behavior. But I blamed all the awkwardness and most of my current predicament on my own deficiencies, and I was quite sure I was right about that. So was I bitter and hate filled at the thought that that had probably been my one opportunity to participate in a make-out session in this lifetime? Sure. But I could hardly blame the one girl who had been sporting enough to give me a shot at it: it just made me hate everyone else even more, which automatically made me love Fiona more by comparison. See? It's all a matter of proper hate calibration. You have to take a balanced view.

I haltingly asked Sam Hellerman if he could ask his CHS friends about her, try to find out, um, I wasn't sure exactly what. But could he ask around, find out what her deal was, in some way?

"Her deal?" said Sam Hellerman. He said "deal" mockingly, and did that thing where you put your hands up on either side in front of you palms out and wiggle your fingers sarcastically. Sometimes it just means "ooh, I'm scared." But sometimes it means, "the word that I am now quoting back at you is so absurd that the human voice alone is insufficient to convey the appropriate level of sarcasm, and therefore I must use my hands as well, as they used to do in the days of the silent cinema and in vaudeville where they had to make sure that everyone way in the back who couldn't hear the dialogue would still get the point that the person being addressed is a total ass."

It was in this sense that Sam Hellerman did the sarcastic hands thing on this particular occasion. I thought it was a bit over the top, frankly.

"Her deal?" he repeated. "You mean, other than the whole cock tease thing?" Again with the swearing.

Yeah, that's what I meant, Hellerman. Thanks for breaking it down. I really didn't get his attitude. So I just stared at him.

But I almost forgot to mention how the Fiona Deal was affecting the band like I said. (See what I mean? Making out with Fiona really seems to have poked permanent holes in my brain that I can feel even now. Plus, well, you don't know about it yet—it happens toward the end of the year and I'll explain it all when it comes up because I'm really trying to describe things in the order that they happened—but I'm still recovering from this massive head injury I got from this attempt on my life. What I'm saying is, for a variety of reasons, the Fiona Deal among them, my thinking tends to be a little fuzzy these days.)

Anyway, it wasn't just that the Fiona Deal made Sam Hellerman act like a total dick. It had to do with the songs.

Sam Hellerman tended to like the topical songs the best. He liked "Mr. Teone and His Lady Butt," and "Matt Lynch Must Be Stopped (from Spawning and Generating Ungodly Offspring)." Political stuff like that. But he would tolerate the personal, sensitive tunes, too, even though I sometimes wondered whether he thought they were too corny. He liked "World War B" and would even tolerate "I'm Only a Page of Zeros but You Are the One," for example.

But somehow he could tell what "Trying Not to Believe (It's Over)" was about, and it was way too Fiona oriented for his taste.

"We're not doing that one," he said.

Well, the difference between the ones we were "doing" and the ones we were not "doing" was not easy to spot, as most of them didn't yet have many or any lyrics, and very few of them had repeatable music yet. Even the ones with words *and* music were—well, I'd play them on the guitar and mumble the words I had and say "mmm-mmm-mmm" for the ones I didn't have and Sam Hellerman would play random notes on his clarinet.

What I'm saying is, I'm not sure the set list matters enough to take personally at this stage in a band's career.

Luckily, I realized what was going on soon enough to refrain from telling him about "My Fiona" or "I'm Still Not Done Loving You, Mama." He would have hit the roof. If it's possible to hit the roof in the spirit of utter contempt and condescension.

I had wanted to keep the Stoned Marmadukes going for a little longer, mostly as a tribute to the band I said I was in during my one conversation with her. And also because of this very unrealistic line of thinking that went: were we to keep the name long enough that we would still have it when we finally got instruments and learned to play them, and were we to have a "gig," and were that *still* to be our name even then, and were she somehow to find out about it, well, then she might remember me and my powerful vocabulary and decide to show up or something. (Rock legend in the making: "Who is this mysterious Fiona that Moe 'Fingers' Henderson puts on the guest list every night?" "No one knows. But she never shows up." "And Moe is alone and silent with his mysterious pain?" "Yeah, that's right.")

Now, even I could see how pathetic that was. But it was also kind of random and off-the-wall. Sam Hellerman was starting to develop a nose for the Fiona-related, though, and he could sniff out the vaguest hints of it. And he sure didn't like how things were smelling lately at 507 Cedarview Circle, Hillmont, CA.

"Here's an idea," he said. "The Fionas. You on guitar and Fiona-phone, plus Sammy 'I Heart Fiona' on bass and Fiona

Reconstruction Therapy, first album *F-I-O-N-A! What's That Spell? I Can't Hear You! Fiona! Fiona! Yay, team!*"

Hmm, I thought . . . but I knew he wasn't being serious. He was kind of funny even when he was being a dick, though, I'll say that for him. I'll admit also that he may have had just a teensy-weensy point. But it still left something to be desired attitudinally from my point of view.

"The. Name. Is. Ray. Bradbury's. Love-Camel," he said firmly, before walking out and slamming the door.

Then he had to come back because he had forgotten to take his clarinet case with him.

He left again silently. But two seconds later he came back again, stuck his head through the door LBT style, and said very quickly: "Ray Bradbury's Love-Camel, you on guitar, Scammy Sammy on bass and calisthenics, first album *Prepare to Die.*"

Which made me feel a bit better.

JANE GALLAGHER AND AMANDA HENDERSON

Meanwhile, I still didn't quite know what to make of the CEH library. I had all but given up trying to interpret the scribbles, the dates, the whole tits/back rubs/dry cleaning puzzle. There was a story there, presumably, or at least an explanation, but there just wasn't enough information available to figure out what it was. It was lost in the past, for good, probably.

Still, I had developed this crazy idea that by reading the books my dad had read at my age, I could get to know him better retroactively. Maybe reading his books would provide some insight into his character, an indication of the kind of person he had been and the sorts of things he had been interested in and had thought about. Now, in one way, this insight was something I desperately wanted. In another way, though, I wasn't sure I wanted it badly enough to go through the ordeal of reading *A Separate Peace* again. I had been forced to read it last year and had found it to be among the most annoying of all of the state-mandated novels about disaffected East Coast prep school juveniles. Was anything worth that? On the other hand, *Brighton Rock* looked promising. I decided to start there and save *A Separate Peace* for last.

Of course, while I was reading *Brighton Rock* on my own and rereading *Catcher in the Fucking Rye* for the zillionth time for Mr. Schtuppe's class, I was also obsessing about Fiona. This turned out to be a pretty weird setup. Mr. Schtuppe would mispronounce something from *Catcher*, and it would spur cascades of competing thoughts of my dad's teenage years and of the mystery girl's breasts at the same time. Particularly when the subject was sex, which turns up quite a lot in *Catcher in the Rye*, though it tends to be expressed rather quaintly. And particularly when the girl being talked about was Jane Gallagher, because of the underlined Jane Gallagher back rub passage in my dad's *Catcher*.

Mr. Schtuppe's tests were always true-false or multiple choice, except for the last question, which was an essay question. An essay question is a multiple-choice question with the multiple choices left off, and three wide-spaced lines where you're supposed to write the answer.

On one of the tests, the essay question was "What was the cause of Holden's fight with Stradlater on page 43?" By some entirely characteristic oversight, the identical question had also appeared above in the multiple-choice part of the same test. The answer to the m-c version was (b) Jane Gallagher. The answer Mr. Schtuppe was looking for in the essay question version was Jane Gallagher without the (b), or possibly something like "the cause of Holden's fight with Stradlater on page 43 was Jane Gallagher."

The real answer is that Holden Caulfield had the hots for this girl, Jane Gallagher, though he was too scared to try anything. And he was worried that his roommate might have hooked up with her before he got the chance to. But in the quaint world of *Catcher in the Rye,* the phrase they use for fucking is "giving her the time." I kid you not. Giving her the time. Another one is "crumby," which is how they spell crummy, but which you can tell from the context really means fucked-up. Seriously. It's like this thing was written by Sam Hellerman or something.

Actually, it's kind of cute.

Just to amuse myself, instead of writing "Jane Gallagher" in the essay-question space like I was supposed to, I wrote:

```
Jane Gallagher had wanted to know
what time it was, but for some reason
Holden Caulfield hadn't wanted Stradlater
to tell her. When Stradlater refused to
tell Holden Caulfield whether or not he
had told Jane Gallagher what time it
was, Holden Caulfield became enraged and
attacked him in a fit of horological
savagery, possibly because he was
mentally ill and hated anyone but him
knowing what time it was.
```

I thought I'd get the question wrong, but when Mr. Schtuppe handed back my test, I got a hundred. The name Jane Gallagher had been circled and the circle had been checked. I guess he only needed to read the first two words.

I was sad for a few minutes that my brilliant humor had gone unappreciated, but then I got over it.

Now, everybody's favorite guy, Holden Caulfield, has a younger sister named Phoebe. I've never found her very believable. She's way too sweet and loving and Holden-o-centric. She's nothing like my sister, Amanda, that's for sure. On the other hand, if Phoebe Caulfield had had a crazy mom, a dead father, a goofball stepfather, and a King Dork brother, and if she had grown up in blank, characterless Hillmont instead of rich, atmosphere-laden, fancy-pants Manhattan, who knows how she might have turned out?

Also, HC makes no secret of the fact that he is a pathological liar, so the real Phoebe may not have been all she was cracked up to be. (Some might say I'm one to talk, but I'm really not a p. l. like HC. I'm more of an exaggerator than a liar, really, and unlike Mr. Wonderful, I don't do it as a sick compulsion or a recreational activity.)

Amanda *is* hard to peg, though. She has many modes, some of which seem to be battling for supremacy over the others. There's her Harriet the Spy mode, where she's kind of a grumpy, introverted oddball, constantly scribbling and drawing weird stuff on these notepads that she won't let anyone see. And then there's the budding bitch-princess mode, where she and her friends seem to be going through training exercises to prepare for when they finally emerge as full-fledged sado-psychopathic normal girls. She's a pretty girl, and all indications are that, when she grows up just a little more, she'll be a knockout. The thing is, she's way too intelligent, and—what? individualistic?—to pull off the normal mode very convincingly for too long. And I'm not kidding about the intelligence: she doesn't always express it perfectly in words, but she's supersmart, and in a sort of deep-thinking philosophical way that is nothing like my clever and glib but shallow preoccupation with sex and trivia. Sometimes she'll say these simple yet unexpectedly true things that make me want to consider giving away all my worldly possessions, taking a vow of celibacy, and devoting my life to studying at her feet. But then she'll spoil it by doing the nose-forehead slide or mimicking my walk. Honestly, I find her clumsy attempts at normalcy more cute than insulting, but you know: it does kill the Yoda mood.

I do wonder if she'll make it as a normal person in the end—though simple hotness can make up for a lot of other deficiencies, it's true. The worry is that she'll have to over-compensate by being even meaner and more psychotic than usual in order to draw attention away from her Harriet the Spy–ness and pass as normal psychotic. If that's what she ends up wanting to do with her life.

Protonormal Amanda doesn't seem to think too highly of me and isn't too fun to be around. I prefer the HtS Amanda, because I can relate to her better. We don't interact much, but generally we get along okay.

There's one more Amanda mode I have to mention, the mode she assumes whenever anything has to do with our dad. In those situations, she suddenly turns into a Phoebe-like little girl. She'll cry, and sniffle, and reach out to hug me. Sometimes she'll put her arms around my neck and squeeze so tightly that it seems as though her little arms could make permanent indentations. She doesn't have anyone else to talk to about him. My mom is crazy and best avoided, and she hates Little Big Tom, so I guess I'm it. In fact, though, we never actually do much talking. We just hold on to each other and cry. Well, she does.

FILLING IN THE SO

My mom has this funny habit of ending practically all of her sentences like this: "[Random sentence]. So . . ."

There's another part that comes after the so, but it's either so obvious that it's not necessary to say it, or she doesn't quite know what it is and gives up trying to figure it out.

"I've got to get to work early tomorrow. So . . ." That means "I've got to get to work early tomorrow. So I'm going to bed early and I don't want anyone making too much noise." Or possibly: " . . . so I'm taking this big glass of bourbon into the bedroom and I do not wish to be disturbed and I'm seriously considering giving you the silent treatment for the next couple of weeks starting now."

More interesting, and sometimes more disturbing, are the mysterious ones where you can't figure out exactly what's supposed to come after the "so."

"Elaine [old lady down the street] said she's sorry she decided to have children after all and wishes she had spent the money on herself instead. So . . ."

"When I was growing up, they didn't expect you to go to college. High school was enough. So . . ."

"Well, they do say if you ignore something, it goes away on its own in ninety percent of all cases. So . . ."

I bring this up because of the following:

Sam Hellerman had somehow talked his parents into giving him an advance on his Christmas present and had mail-ordered a bass from the Guitarville catalog. Now I needed to get my act together and get an electric guitar. I was currently playing my dad's old nylon-string folk guitar, which I cherished because of my respect for him but which really wasn't the right tool for heavy rock. If Silent Nightmare (me on guitar, Samson on bass and gynecology, first album *Feel Me Fall)* was ever going to get off the ground, we needed pro gear.

Somehow, I couldn't see the Christmas present advance concept being comprehensible to Carol Henderson-Tucci, but I figured it was worth a shot.

I brought it up with a great deal of subtlety, mentioning that Sam Hellerman's parents had given him a bass as an early Christmas present and that it had been very easy to order it from the Guitarville catalog. I let my voice trail off.

Her answer amounted to a no, which didn't surprise me. But for the life of me I really, really couldn't fill in the so.

"Baby, don't even talk to me about Christmas right now," she said. "More people commit suicide on Christmas than on any other day of the year. So . . ."

THE ENTIRE CONTENTS OF MY ROOM

"Hey, chief," said Little Big Tom. "We'd like a word with you. If you've got a minute."

It was the Thursday evening of the first post-Fiona week. I followed Little Big Tom into the kitchen, puzzled and a bit apprehensive. He only called me chief when it was serious or when he was nervous about something. He had this grim expression, like he wasn't even trying to look cheerful the way he usually does. I figured they must have found out that I went to the party in Clearview instead of Sam Hellerman's house on Friday night, but boy was I wrong. Well, I mean, I guess they *had* found out about the party, indirectly, but that wasn't the main issue.

My mom had on her Picasso *Guernica*-print shorts, cowboy boots, a red and white checked halter, and a polka-dot scarf worn like a headband, and was leaning against the counter smoking one of her Virginia Slimses. You've come a long way, baby, I thought. It was shocking to think how much she wasn't even kidding.

Little Big Tom started to caress his Little Gray Mustache at the corners of his mouth with his thumb and forefinger, as though he were trying to stretch it out to get that extra droop that used to drive the ladies crazy in Vermont in the seventies.

There was an uncomfortable pause while we all looked at the kitchen table. A whole lot of my stuff was spread out, neatly arranged in little piles. Some books. Some records and CDs. Some random martial arts materials. My Talons of Rage fantasy blades that I got from Ninja Warehouse, which had been used as a D and D prop long ago and were now purely decorative. Some of my old role-playing military strategy games, and some board games, including Risk and Stratego. Some of my dad's stuff: videos of Clint Eastwood movies and war movies. *Tora! Tora! Tora! The Enforcer. Patton.* The bowie knife he gave me for Christmas the year before he died. My army coat. Jane's *Military Small Arms of the 20th Century* and the *Tanks and Combat Vehicles Recognition Guide.* A couple of my notebooks. (Uh-oh.) My "Kill 'em All and Let God Sort 'em Out" T-shirt. And a big stack of my weapons-and-tactics magazines, fanned out like cards on a blackjack table.

"What is this shit?" said Little Big Tom, eventually.

"The entire contents of my room?" I said.

Well, it wasn't quite everything, but that was essentially the correct answer. See, in real life parents raid their children's rooms and confiscate the porno magazines and drugs; in the back-assward world of Partner and Mrs. Progressive at

507 Cedarview Circle, they leave the porn alone and confiscate everything else.

There was another bumpy stretch of awkwardness, during which all you could hear was the rhythm of my mom's sucked-and-blown Virginia Slims 120s. Short, hissing intake. Pause. Long, exasperated release. It sounded like a factory in a cartoon, or in an educational film on how they make steel tools. Ordinarily, it can be very soothing.

"Why," Little Big Tom finally said, "do you feel the need to read this garbage?"

Why, I thought, do you feel the need to try to impersonate Jimmy Buffett and wear shorts and sandals with black socks and eat tofu loaf on Thanksgiving? Some questions have no answers.

"I don't know what to say. Your mother and I hoped to set an example so you would respect and share our values."

Now *that* was funny. I just looked at him. The look that says: "what are you, high?"

Then he said something that totally threw me.

"It's very important to have respect for women."

I stared at him.

Well, now I'm going to skip ahead to the part where I ended up figuring out what the hell Little Big Tom was getting at.

It was hard to piece together because very little of what he was saying made much sense, but here's my best guess as to what had happened. Little Big Tom, making his rounds, had overheard the conversation about the Fiona Deal and had found it disturbing. He hadn't liked the way Sam Hellerman had referred to Fiona (I hadn't, either, though I doubt we had exactly the same reasons). I don't know how much of the rest of the conversation he heard, but if he missed anything, he could have read all about it in my notebook. I'm ashamed to say that one of my notebooks contained, among other embarrassing items, some tortured "letters to Fiona" I had scribbled out during a stretch of maudlin, sleepless nights. And I'm sure he wasn't thrilled about the lyrics to "She Likes It When I Pinch Her Hard." And many of my other songs, I'm sure, like "Gooey Glasses."

He must have read the notebook. Otherwise, how would he have reached the conclusion that my "relationship" with "my girlfriend" was undermining his generation's sacred achievement of the institution of easygoing touchy-feely ouchless deodorant-optional crunchy-granola *Hair*-sound track butterflies-and-unicorns sexuality?

But I'm getting ahead of myself here. After overhearing the conversation, and in the throes of a full-blown paranoid, sex-obsessed, politically correct midlife-crisis meltdown, he had decided to search my room for evidence of more disturbing-ness and had basically freaked out over what he'd found.

He was much, much more bothered by the war stuff, the magazines, the nunchakus, the "Kill 'em All" shirt, and the Stratego than he had been by the cock tease conversation. And there's where he made his mistake. He tried to combine two discussions, the one where you tell your stepson it isn't nice to call girls bitches and the one where you express your inner turmoil over the fact that being into war and weapons betrays the deeply held values of the generation that stopped the Vietnam War. The result was incoherence, confusion, and the least successful attempt at Family Conflict Resolution since the White Album told Charles Manson to give the world a big hug.

For Little Big Tom, these issues were like two sides of the

same coin. He could jump from Stratego to Respect for Women without realizing he had changed topics, but he was the only one who had any idea what he was talking about. Even my mom, smoking in the corner, seemed confused.

I'm just speculating here as to his state of mind, but I think he looked at everything in my room, along with his very mistaken imaginative reconstruction of my "relationship" with "my girlfriend," as a kind of personal attack on him and his fabulous generation. And he saw everything in my world only as it related to his own self-image and personal style, which he held in pretty high regard. He wasn't too interested in hearing where he had things wrong, either. The theory confirmed his suspicions and he liked it that way. My first make-out session was all about him. So were the Talons of Rage fantasy blades. And so was Stratego from Milton Bradley. Plus, I think he was embarrassed, worried that some of his PC friends might see me wearing the wrong shirt or something.

His version of my life was pretty hilarious, at any rate. I wasn't treating "my girlfriend" with enough respect. I didn't understand how sex was spiritual as well as physical. "My friends" and I were in a "space" of negativity and aggression, which wasn't healthy. The music he had confiscated was mostly metal, since those were the album covers and song titles that fed into his theory. But he left the Rolling Stones alone: see, they stopped the Vietnam war, too.

All the references to "my friends" threw me at first. Had he really failed to notice that I had no friends other than Sam Hellerman? Then it hit me that he was assuming that some of the band members in the Sam 'n' Moe bands I'd written about in my notebook were actually real people. (What tipped me off: he mentioned a Debbie, and I was like "who's Debbie," until I realized he was talking about Li'l Miss Debbie, the imaginary nurse-slut vocalist of Tennis with Guitars. It's a good thing he didn't realize that some of "my friends" were really me: it might have turned his mind into a pretzel.)

All this from Stratego and a few fantasy blades? Un. Real.

At one point my mom chimed in: "Baby, all we're saying is you have to try to find harmony between your masculine and your feminine natures." I heard a tremendous guffaw from Amanda in the other room. Thanks for that, Mom. I knew I'd be hearing about my feminine nature from Amanda, and till the end of time.

The one bit of reality in the whole scene did come from my mom, however, though it was the kind of connection to reality that reveals an even deeper disconnection from it.

"Are you having trouble with the kids in school?" she asked.

Bingo. Well spotted. Give the lady a cookie. But on the other hand, how could anyone who knew me or anything about me even have to ask that question? The mind reels.

The whole sorry affair wrapped up like this: we wheeled and dealed for the stuff. Little Big Tom kept the magazines, the "Kill 'em All" shirt, some of the albums, and the throwing stars, nunchakus, and decorative weapons (all except for the bowie knife, which I was allowed to keep for sentimental reasons). I got the books, the coat, most of the videos, the notebooks, some of the albums, and the games. He agreed to respect my privacy and I to respect his values from that point forward. If you're thinking that that sounds like a joke, well, you're right, but one of the unspoken terms of the truce was that we couldn't actually laugh at it till we were out of the room.

My mom said, "Baby, if you ever need to talk, we're always here." I gave her a little "right back at ya, babe" salute.

Little Big Tom, under the impression that he had achieved something by accusing me of being criminally insane and taking half my stuff, rumpled my hair and said, "Growing up is rough for everybody. Even old geezers like me. I'd like to think I'm not above learning a thing or two myself sometimes." That was supposed to be self-deprecating and lighthearted and philosophical and tension relieving. Hey, I'll take it. Anything's better than getting in touch with your feelings in show trial form.

I knew he had fully snapped back to his old self when he turned his head slightly sideways, handed me my notebook, and said, "Some righteous tunes in there! Very creative!" I thought I heard him sighing heavily as I walked out, but of course, that was normal too.

THE HELLERMAN EYE-RAY TREATMENT

There's a scene in movies and situation comedies where the main kid starts to be "interested in girls" and the dad is supposed to take the kid aside and give him a lecture that used to be called "the birds and the bees" but is now usually referred to as "the sex talk." The dad doesn't want to do it and has to be goaded into it by the mom. If there's no dad, the mom finds some dad substitute to do it. The dad or replacement dad module is nervous and dances around the subject and uses funny euphemisms and analogies, and the joke is that the kid is already very knowledgeable, a thirteen-year-old Hugh Hefner or Prince. Sometimes the kid will even be shown in an armchair wearing pajamas and a robe and smoking a pipe while the dad figure is squirming. And the live studio audience laughs and laughs.

It hadn't occurred to me, but when I told Sam Hellerman about Little Big Tom's Stratego Sex Inquisition, he pointed it out: I had just been a participant in the most retarded version of the sitcom sex talk the world had ever seen.

So maybe my *mom* had heard the cock tease discussion and had told LBT he had to talk to me about sex. He was reluctant but couldn't refuse. And in the course of his research he got sidetracked by Stratego and–boom! My sexual awakening was suddenly all about Vietnam.

Meanwhile, Sam Hellerman still seemed bent out of shape about my Fiona obsession. And I still couldn't figure out why. It seemed like more than just being bored by the subject, which I tended to go on about: that I would have understood. Was it related to his Serenah Tillotsen experience, in which he had felt the rejection so keenly that any description of a less than totally available and compliant female would push mysterious buttons and automatically send him into a blind fury at the injustice of love and those who snatch it from the mouths of the needy? And would ignite a fiery desire for revenge on behalf of all unfortunate lonely hearts, or at least on behalf of those lonely hearts he happened to be in bands with? That sounded pretty good. Maybe so. But I had to wonder if he knew something he wasn't telling.

So why didn't I just ask him if he knew something he wasn't telling?

Not a bad idea.

"Do you know something you're not telling?" I asked.

I suspected that this was just the kind of question that would send Sam Hellerman into another furious spasm of over-the-top sarcasm, and I wasn't wrong. He no longer needed to resort to words. He just stared at me with bugged-out eyes that he appeared to be trying to spin in opposite directions. I believe his line of thinking went something like this: maybe if I stare at this creature long enough with these supersarcastic eyes, his head tentacles will eventually retract into his head, his back tentacles will retract into his back, his leg tentacles will shrivel up and drop off, and the external lung in the polyp on the side of his neck will burst, depriving the alien brain pod of needed oxygen and forcing the mother ship to relinquish control of the mind and body, after which the host organism will come out of its coma, rub its eyes, and say, "who's this Fiona everybody's always talking about, anyway?"

Well, it was worth a shot. Maybe Sam Hellerman didn't know more than he was telling after all. All I knew was, I was feeling a little feeble and vulnerable after that intense Hellerman eye-ray treatment. It's a killer.

In fact, however, despite Sam Hellerman's persistent bad attitude about a certain faux-mod seamster who had one breast that had experienced just a little less of this life than the other, he was still my friend by alphabetical-order relationship, and that means something.

So, to my surprise, it turned out that he *had* asked his CHS friends about her for me.

But none of them knew a drama mod named Fiona. In fact, as far as anyone could tell, there was no one named Fiona in the CHS student body at all. There were, of course, many hot brunettes with sexy stomachs, but that wasn't much help. And no one recognized the most unusual feature, the funky homemade denim and yarn jacket.

But what about the little black glasses? That should narrow it down. Hot b. with s. s. and l. b. g.?

"I'm sorry, man," said Sam Hellerman, because we had started to say man recently. "She doesn't exist."

PROTEST SOMETHING

They had managed to make Foods of the World in "Humanities" last several weeks. We were well into October, on the Monday following Little Big Tom's Sex/Stratego campaign, when we finally left the gifted and talented snacking behind and moved on to the Turbulent Sixties. The first assignment was, I kid you not, "protest something." So of course, the entire class just didn't show up the following day. You can get away with stuff like that in AP, as long as you can write a couple of sentences afterward explaining how your class cutting is analogous to marching from Selma to Montgomery. I'm sure the teachers kind of expected it and enjoyed the free period, too.

I was on my own for my "protest." Sam Hellerman hadn't made it into Humanities, so he was stuck in normal social studies, copying God only knows what from some inane textbook, no doubt.

I decided to go off on my own to read *Brighton Rock,* which I was beginning to think was the best book ever written. I was getting to the end and I was excited to find out what was going to happen. So I went out to a deserted part of the school grounds, the slope behind the outfield of the baseball diamond, and lay on the grass to read. It was damp, but a pale sun was out, and I had on my waterproof all-weather army coat, so it didn't faze me.

One thing I did while I was reading was pause every now and then and turn back to the inside front cover to look at the "CEH 1965." Then I would try to imagine what the circumstances were when my dad had read it. Listening to "(I Can't Get No) Satisfaction," "Mr. Tambourine Man," and "Help Me, Rhonda" on the radio? Riding the streetcar wearing neat but rumpled midsixties student-type clothes, with older men in suits with skinny ties and women wearing gloves and little hats? At the dinner table, with my *I Love Lucy* grandma hitting him on the head and telling him to cut it out already? In the few photos I had seen of him from that time, he looked kind of Beach Boys–collegiate, so that was how I pictured him, with a little button-down short-sleeved shirt, floods, and Brian Wilson hair, sitting on the curb waiting for the bus, *Brighton Rock* open on his knees. It was kind of fun to do that. It was all bullshit, too. But in spite of myself, I had this feeling like I was getting to know him in a way I never had. I would get to a good part and I'd think, where was he and what was he doing when he read it? What did he think about the fact that Pinkie said he didn't believe in anything yet was totally convinced he was damned? That kind of thing.

It wasn't only the story but the physical object that did something to me. Just being aware that I was holding it made me feel kind of–what? Spooky? Reverent? If I started to think about it, I'd get kind of dizzy sometimes, and start to have this ringing in my ears, and I felt almost like my mind was spinning, rising backwards toward the sky. Maybe I *am* crazy, I thought. For real, I mean, not as a ploy.

The lunch bell rang, but I was pretty into the story, so I stayed where I was and continued reading.

Before too long I was down to the last few pages, and it was really exciting and suspenseful. I was feeling spacey because of the spooky thing I mentioned before (and maybe even more than usual because there were a lot of priests and so forth in the book and that always adds to the spookiness). And then a shadow suddenly fell on the page. I saw an elongated shadow head and shoulders on the grass in front of me and felt the presence of someone behind me. Then, and this was all in just a second, not how long it's taking me to describe it, I saw some stuff splashing on the page, though first

I think I heard the sound of it hitting the page, which was very, very loud in my ears.

"The fuck?" I said, and turned around. It was Paul Krebs, one of Matt Lynch's pals and as psychotic a normal person as ever there was, pouring Coke out of a can onto my book and giggling like a simian maniac.

Now, this all happened in a split second, like I said. Paul Krebs was up there on the crest of the slope giggling, doing this little taunting dance, like a boxer or something. My ears were ringing so loudly I couldn't hear much else, and I was seeing little multicolored blobs that started small but expanded to obscure my field of vision slightly before they dissipated and new ones would take their place. Little circles of green, yellow, and red. A liquid kaleidoscope. I got up and he kind of danced away from me, still giggling and yammering. I couldn't make out what he was saying. I started to chase him, and somehow, I don't know how, I managed to trip him and pull his legs upward so that he fell down on to the rough gravel path. He must have hit his head pretty hard on one of the bigger rocks that lined the pathway, because there was a tremendous amount of blood seeping from a cut near his hairline. I had fallen in a big patch of mud in the process. I scrambled to get up, sliding around a bit, but he was just lying there blubbering and bloody. I grabbed his hair and smashed his head into the gravel as hard as I could. Then I stepped on his neck and said, "I will kill you." And we both knew I totally meant it.

While I had been chasing him, I had still had *Brighton Rock* in my hand, but I had dropped it when the whole head-smashing thing was happening. It was lying open on the path, with little splotches and splatters of Paul Krebs's blood on it, reflecting the sun, shining on the page. Somewhere in the back of my mind I was thinking, stupidly, maybe this is how *The Catcher in the Rye,* CEH 1960, got bloodstains on it.

My first impulse was to run like hell in some random direction, but for some reason, instead, I sat down very deliberately on a big stone over on the other side of the path and read the last couple of blood-spattered pages of *Brighton Rock*, tuning out the sound of Paul Krebs's gentle moaning. Then I paused and stared off into space. It was a great ending, the best ending of anything, book or movie, I'd ever experienced. Then I closed the book reverently and walked back toward the campus, because I needed to get myself cleaned up and fifth period was about to start and I didn't see any reason to be late.

POD HIPPIES

It was a day or two after I accidentally beat up Paul Krebs that two very, very surprising things happened.

The first was that Pierre Butterfly Cameroon, the diminutive, flute-playing, hippie-parent-stunted, relentlessly picked-on PBC, my brother in dorkdom, started "going with" Renée "Née-Née" Tagliafero. For real. I mean, eating together, having third parties deliver notes to each other, and spending lunch period walking in a circle around the perimeter of Center Court, just like all the normal freshman and sophomore couples did. (I've never really understood why couples do the joined-at-the-hip lunchtime laps. They stop doing it junior year because once you're a junior you can leave during lunch and go to the Burger King instead.)

Now, when I say that Pierre Butterfly Cameroon is my brother in dorkdom, I mean that we are both at roughly the same low level of the social structure. The Untouchable level. I don't mean brotherhood in any other sense. I mean, I don't know him. Hanging out with each other would just make us both look even more pathetic. Sam Hellerman is kind of friendly with him, as he is with everybody who isn't a dangerous normal psychotic. I'm more of a loner. Still, if I'm the king of hearts in the dork deck, PBC is definitely one of the other kings.

But Pierre Butterfly Cameroon was no longer Untouchable, or so it appeared from where I was sitting when I first saw them walk by. Née-Née Tagliafero was touching him quite frequently, in fact. They looked weird as a couple because he was not much more than half her height. But more than that: such things just didn't happen. It was inconceivable.

Née-Née Tagliafero was pretty and popular, with no handicaps or defects except, perhaps, for a very slight mustache, which she was able to bleach into insignificance. And she had pretty big breasts, too, which counted for a lot. I'd never seen her picked on by anyone. She had a kind of punky hair and thrift-store clothes thing going on, but that was fashion rather than true alienation, like it always is. I mean, she was definitely one of "them," that is to say, mostly normal, not actually one of society's unwanted. I would classify her as subnormal/drama. She'd had several normal boyfriends before. What the hell was going on around here? It was mindboggling.

The other thing that happened was hardly less surprising. Sam Hellerman suddenly started hanging out with the Hillmont High fake-hippie drama crowd. I swear to God.

This came without warning. I walked out of fourth period expecting our paths to converge at around locker number 414, as usual, and to continue on to our usual lunch-period routine of eating at the cafeteria and trying to remain unobtrusive and unharassed till the bell rang. But I walked past locker number 414, and he wasn't there. I backtracked, looked around, and finally saw him sitting on the lawn near the drama hippies. No, not near–*with* them. I can't remember ever having been so surprised. He must have known I'd be looking for him, of course. I tried to get his attention, but he deliberately avoided looking up to the exit of building C and locker number 414, where he had to have known I'd be.

God only knows what they were talking about. He didn't seem to be doing much talking, but it was hard to tell. Somehow I couldn't see him actually becoming a faux-hippie drama person himself–that would be too bizarre. But how would I know? Maybe that's how it always begins: you sit with them on the lawn during lunch; then, later that night, a pod grows under your bed with a little fake-hippie version of you inside; then the fake-hippie you hatches, kills the original you, and takes your place. Before you know it you're embroidering your jeans, singing "Casey Jones," smoking pot from a pipe you made out of an apple, and playing Motel the Tailor in the class production of *Fiddler on the Roof.*

Could that really happen to Sam Hellerman? Ordinarily I'd have said no, but after witnessing the courtship rituals of Pierre Butterfly Cameroon and Née-Née Tagliafero, I had to admit that my sense of what did and what did not constitute a believable thread in the fabric of reality suddenly didn't seem very adequate.

I wasn't about to barge in on that groovy Happening, I can tell you that. Instead, I went on alone to the cafeteria, semidazed, with a lot on my mind.

THE BAD DETECTIVE

Channel two was showing two horror movies back to back every Wednesday and Sunday night for the whole month of October. I was in my room brooding over this and that–Fiona, my dad's library, Paul Krebs, and the whole weird Sam

Hellerman pod-hippie situation that had erupted earlier that day. Strangely enough, the first movie on channel two that night was *Invasion of the Body Snatchers,* which has pretty much the same pod-oriented story line. It almost made me feel as though I was on the right track with the pod-hippie theory. I put on *Taking Tiger Mountain (By Strategy)* and turned the TV volume almost all the way down, watching the movie while listening to the music, and thinking things over.

I know it doesn't make much sense, but somehow the puzzle of my dad's teenage library and the mystery about his death had become connected in my mind. I would decipher part of a cryptic notation in *Catcher,* CEH 1960, or be struck by something in *Brighton Rock,* CEH 1965, and it would somehow feel like I'd gotten somewhere on the "accident" issue, too. At weird moments, like that night, I'd also have this crazy sense that the other puzzles in my life, like Fiona and Sam Hellerman's increasingly odd behavior, were somehow connected to my dad and *The Catcher in the Rye* as well. I mean, they all got muddled together sometimes.

I'd always wondered why the police, at least to judge from the newspaper articles, appear to have put so little into the investigation of my dad's death; usually when a cop is killed, they turn the world upside down to see justice done. Maybe it was obvious to them that it hadn't been a murder, and the newspaper had just played up the ambiguity. They hadn't found the car that hit him, which was weird, too. Or possibly they had found it, and it just hadn't been thought newsworthy? I wished there was someone I could ask about it, but I wouldn't have known where to begin. The reporters who wrote the articles? Hmm. I would also have given quite a lot to know what he had been working on when the "accident" happened. I'm sure that played a role in the investigation, but if it had ever been mentioned publicly, I had missed it. I even dared to try to ask my mom once, but all she did was cry. And what was Fiona doing tonight? And what the hell was up with Sam Hellerman anyway?

But what this all had to do with tits, back rubs, and dry cleaning, I hadn't the barest clue.

I'm a bad detective, though, really. I let my emotions and prejudices dictate what I choose to investigate, rather than trying to look at the whole picture with an objective eye. I hadn't looked at *A Separate Peace* and *Lord of the Flies* very carefully because they hadn't been obviously marked up and pummeled like *Catcher,* CEH 1960, but mostly because I had something personal against them. And because of that I had missed something pretty important.

Invasion of the Body Snatchers had ended, and *Rosemary's Baby* had begun. I put on *Sabbath Bloody Sabbath* and turned to look at my dad's books on my desk. I was reaching for *The Journal of Albion Moonlight,* CEH 1966, which I had decided would be next on the agenda of my one-man book club, when I accidentally knocked the stack of books to the floor. *A Separate Peace,* CEH 1962, fell in such a way that it was open under the bed, and when I went to retrieve it, I noticed a slip of paper that had fallen out. It was half a sheet of graph paper that had itself been folded in half. On the inside of the folded paper was this weird clump of letters, neatly written in the graph paper's squares in dark blue ink:

```
q f f q g a r f q q f a s u
 x q d f q j g u q y e u m d
  q y u m V e q x x u m d q z
   g r j g m g f e m H q d h u
    g e m e x u m f q P o q e q
     q z a y m d u m x q v f q d
      u a e d q u t F Y g h u m V
```

And on the other side, in black, and hardly less weird:

```
Mon cher monsieur,
The bastard is dead. Thrown into the
fire. Long live Justice and the
American Way.
Regards,
Tit
```

So Tit was a person? "Tit lib friday"—an appointment at the library with Tit? And someone was dead? And it had something to do with Superman?

The note was dated 6/31, but the six was heavily and awkwardly inked and clearly had originally been a five.

My first thought, influenced no doubt by having been watching *Rosemary's Baby* with a Black Sabbath sound track, was that the little parallelogram of letters might be a magic charm or spell of some sort. And maybe "thrown into the fire" alluded to the burning of witches or something like that? Or perhaps the charm was an element of some kind of death spell, a spell that had apparently worked, if the reference to the "dead bastard" was any indication. You send this magic parallelogram to someone, innocently disguised as an ordinary note, and soon after seeing it, the person dies. Except that that would mean that my dad would have been the one who died. But of course he had died, only not for thirty years or so. Maybe he'd received the note as a kid but hadn't actually looked at the evil parallelogram till six years ago. Or the death spell had a built-in delay, a kind of long fuse.

And now I had seen it, too. I started to calculate, wondering how long I had. . . .

I got a little creeped out. Then I realized that was nuts.

Getting a grip, I looked at it again. Perhaps it was the

kind of puzzle where you search for words and circle them. But all I could find were things like "fux" and "yum," and none of them were even in a straight line like they're supposed to be. There was "mmmmm" running diagonally from the upper left to the lower right. All that stuff reminded me of Fiona somehow. But that was the only intelligible thing about it.

It didn't take me too long, though, to realize that it was probably a code. Then it took about twenty minutes of staring at the note and thinking about the CEH library to develop what I thought was a pretty good theory about what sort of code it was, and how it might work. But several solid hours of scribbling yielded only gibberish. Either I was totally on the wrong track or I was missing something. I even swallowed a bit of my pride and phoned Sam Hellerman to see if he had any ideas. But there was no answer at Hellerman Manor.

I eventually had to admit defeat. I closed my notebook and settled into an uneasy, half-asleep night of fretting about Tit, the dead bastard, zombies, pod-hippies, Halloween, witchcraft, my dad, my mom, murder, Sam Hellerman, Mia Farrow, Little Big Tom, Amanda, Black Sabbath, Paul Krebs, Roman Polanski, Anton and Zena LaVey, Matt Lynch, Nostradamus, Mrs. Teneb, Superman, Dr. Dee, Elvish, Klingon, *Brighton Rock*, Fiona, and Jane Gallagher. It was exhausting. When I finally dropped off, I had a dream that I solved the code and that the revealed message suddenly made it clear how it all fit together perfectly as part of a single story that explained everything. But when I woke up, I couldn't remember what it was.

Ordinarily, I'd have immediately run, not walked, to Sam Hellerman with Tit's mysterious note. He hadn't been too interested in my dad's teen library when I'd told him about it. He only liked science fiction and fantasy. Basically, if a book didn't have a map of somewhere other than earth in it, he couldn't see the use. He had a point, but then, he didn't have a mysteriously deceased dad to investigate. I had tried to tell him how great *Brighton Rock* was, but he had just rolled his eyes.

Tit's note would have been right up his alley, though, and I'm sure he would have been able to help. He's a clever guy. However, things were a bit strained between us because of the Fiona situation, and because of–well, something was going on with Sam Hellerman, something hidden from me. It wasn't just that he was being a dick about Fiona and hanging out with hippies. He was also acting weird toward me in general, kind of distant and secretive.

Calling him had been my first impulse upon finding the note. But of course, he had been out. Later, when I asked him where he had been, he said, "Visiting my grandma," which I didn't believe for a minute.

A thought struck me.

"Hey," I said. "If you ever happened to be somewhere like another party or something and you happened to see Fiona there, you'd–you'd tell me, right?"

He just looked at me like I was the most pathetic creature he had ever seen. Which was well within the realm of possibility, especially since Sam Hellerman didn't get out much.

He was also evasive when I probed for the story behind the new Hellerman/drama hippie nexus.

The first thing he said was "I didn't expect a sort of Spanish Inquisition."

"Nobody," I said blankly, "expects the Spanish Inquisition," supplying the required response but continuing to stare at him as though to say "there is a time for quoting Monty Python and a time for choosing another path."

Then he said: "trust me, you don't want to know." Then, after watching me continue to stare at him for some time, he cleared his throat and claimed that, actually, he was considering going out for drama and trying out for *The Music Man.*

I allowed my expression to change from "your feeble attempt at false jocularity will never succeed in changing this subject" to "who exactly is this moron and why is his Sam Hellerman impression so laughable and unconvincing?" He finally said, lamely: "There is a thing called hanging. It's not a big deal." And he asked me what my problem was, though I don't think he expected me to answer. He added that it "probably won't be for much longer anyway." Which sounded pretty fucking weird to me, but he clammed up after that, and no amount of eye-rolling, sarcasm, or even long, steady, unblinking stares would induce him to say any more.

Look, I never said it was a "big deal." Just that it was unusual. And the more he tried to make it sound usual, the more unusual it seemed. That's all I was saying.

We were more or less civil to each other, and still spent a lot of time together working on the band (the Medieval Ages, me on guitar, Samber Waves of Grain on bass and bodywork, first album *That Stupid Pope.*) And we were still alphabetical-order friends, and that's forever. But there were now some topics that were more or less off-limits, and that made me feel self-conscious about bringing up other matters. Rock and roll was okay, but not too much else. Plus, for the first time since the Order of the Alphabet had brought us together back when we were little kids, I was on my own for lunch.

I have to admit, though, that apart from all that, I kind of wanted to keep Tit's note to myself. Even though it was little more than nonsense, the fact that only I knew about it made it the most intimate thing connecting me and my dad. Similarly, and rather selfishly, I hadn't told Amanda about the CEH library, even though I knew she would have been pretty interested in it. I had no clue what the coded message might be, but I had developed this absurd idea that if I did decode it, it would turn out to be a kind of message to me. I wasn't sure I wanted anyone else to know what that message was. I wasn't even all that sure I wanted to know it myself. While it remained unsolved, it retained boundless promise. Solving it could only disappoint. On the other hand, you can't just leave an unsolved code kicking around in your life.

LOU REED

It was in the midst of all the pod-hippie business that Sam Hellerman's bass finally arrived. I had to admit, it was sweet. It almost looked like a copy of a Fender Jazz Bass, but it was made in Korea and the fine craftsmen in the Korean bass sweatshop had put their own collective individual stamp on it. And by that I mean the name on the oddly rectangular head stock was not "Fender Jazz Bass" but rather "Apex Dominator 2."

He didn't have an amp yet, but we figured out how to plug it in to the back of the Magnavox stereo console in my living room so the sound would come out of the speakers. It sounded kind of distant and rumbly and fuzzy, but sort of cool, too. Famous recording engineers and producers spend millions of dollars experimenting with effects and overloading preamps and poking holes in speakers with pencils and even pouring foreign substances over circuitry to achieve the sort of thing Sam Hellerman could accomplish just by being too cheap to buy an amp. We are geniuses.

He looked cool with it, too. He had it slung so low around his neck that it hung well below his knees, and in order to reach the G string he kind of had to dislocate his right shoulder a little. He appeared to be in considerable pain. Like I said, way cool.

We had just finished working on the band's signature tune, "Losers Like You," which goes:

Catcher in the Rye is for losers
Losers, losers,
Catcher in the Rye is for losers
Losers like you

(The Sadly Mistaken, Moe Vittles on guitar, Sam "Noxious" Fumes on bass and landscaping, band name spelled out in bullet holes on the side of a family station wagon, first album *Kill the Boy Wonder.*)

It sounded a lot better with bass instead of clarinet, I'll tell you that right now.

We were playing the next tune when Little Big Tom popped in.

"Nice!" he said. "Lou Reed, right? 'Sweet Jane.'"

"No," Sam Hellerman said. "'My Baby Who Art in Heaven.' An original."

Little Big Tom tilted his head in that birdlike way he has and said, "Hmm. I thought it might have been Lou Reed."

Then he tilted his whole body from one slight angle to the other by raising first the left foot, then the right, but keeping the rest of his body stiff, and stuck his lower lip out slightly while bringing his chin firmly downward, as though to say "I have just performed this little dance to celebrate the fact that I believe we've accomplished a great deal with this illuminating discussion."

Then he said, "Rock on!" and flitted out.

Sam Hellerman and I looked at each other for a while with the same thought, though he was the one who said it first:

"You know, 'My Baby Who Art in Heaven' does sound an awful lot like 'Sweet Jane.' "

"Fuck," I said.

Sam Hellerman couldn't believe I wasn't more pissed off at Little Big Tom for snooping in my room and confiscating all that stuff. I mean, I was pissed off, but not enough to go crazy about it. I was embarrassed about the notebook and resolved to take steps to protect my data more carefully in the future, but practically, it meant nothing. The magazines had already served their purpose. And as it happened, I had another "Kill 'em All" T-shirt as a backup. I didn't even care too much about the confiscated records: I was at the point in my creative life where listening to other people's music was just a distraction from my own stuff, and what he confiscated was mostly lame crap anyways. And believe it or not, I was finding I could get along just fine without the Talons of Rage fantasy blades. Just knowing the Talons of Rage fantasy blades existed, somewhere out there, was enough for me. I guess I was growing up.

But the real reason I wasn't more pissed off is that I'm a sentimental fool, and I couldn't stop feeling sorry for myself while pretending to be Little Big Tom. I could understand why he and, well, anybody, might be freaked out by me and the Talons of Rage fantasy blades and all the other Guns 'n' Chi-Mo paraphernalia. Though I still think Stratego is pushing it.

When you stare at people, saying nothing for long periods of time while they try to think of ways to fill in the space, and they know they don't get you at all, they can get a little tense, and sometimes how tense they get is proportional to how likely they judge it to be that you might have access to some kind of dangerous weapon. I developed the method to use on Matt Lynch. Little Big Tom just got swept up in the net by accident, a dolphin with the tuna. That had never been my intention.

I think it may have been the image of him as an uncomfortable, flailing, sitcom dad substitute caught in a net suspended from a crane on the port side of a Japanese fishing boat that made me decide to make a peace offering.

I took out a sheet of paper and wrote:

```
Dear Big Tom,
     My magazines are not a cry for help.
They were only a tool to help deter a
bully. They are not needed now anyway.
     I don't have a girlfriend. Fiona is
an imaginary girl.
     I'm glad you stopped the Vietnam War.
Peace and Love,
Thomas Charles Henderson
P.S. ban the bomb
```

And I left the note on the keyboard of his Mac.

My life hadn't had a lot of content till this year. And now that it suddenly had some content, it was being turned upside down and slowly shaken, so that everything got a little mixed up with everything else.

As this process continued after the Fiona party, this weird thing started happening.

Whenever I would try to make a word my slave, that is, when I would use a word from *30 Days to a More Powerful*

Vocabulary, a little image of Mr. Schtuppe's head would pop up in my mind. Like, I'd say "obsequious" and suddenly I'd see a little shiny pink devil-head with lots of ear hair pop up really quickly, spin around, and pop back down again.

I was pretty sure that the little pop-up devil-head was trying to prompt me to mispronounce the word. I rarely ended up mispronouncing them, as it happened, because when you get right down to it, it's kind of hard to mispronounce most words. You have to work at it. How would you mispronounce "obsequious," for example? I guess it would be awb-seh-*cue*-ee-us. But I had to think about it far too long. I mean, I couldn't do it intuitively so that it would flow the way it probably would coming from Mr. Schtuppe. He is a master of his craft and I had a lot to learn. But that's why we have public education, isn't it?

IN THE SHADOW OF THE KNIGHT

The Hillmont High School drama hippies always spend lunch period on this little patch of lawn on the northeast corner of Center Court, over by the Hillmont Knight. The Hillmont Knight is this huge god-awful sculpture made of scrap metal and old auto parts, welded together in what is supposed to be the shape of a knight, which is the Hillmont High School team mascot thing. If you squint and use your imagination, you can just about see how it's supposed to look like a knight, though it's kind of a stretch. The funniest thing about it, though, is that on what is supposed to be the knight's shield, in welded-on letters cut from license plates and old metal signs, it says:

Presentated. A more fitting symbol of Hillmont High School would be difficult to imagine.

So the drama hippies sit in the shade of the Hillmont Knight, leaning against its rusty "legs" or just lying on the grass in the general area. Sometimes they hang their coats on it or do something really funny like put a hat on it. And that's where Sam Hellerman had been when I observed him that first day, "hanging," as he put it, just a little to the left of the Hillmont Knight.

Now, here's something I've noticed about girls, after years of careful observation. They tend to sort themselves into groups of three. There's the hottest one, who is the boss. She dominates and controls the second-hottest one, who is the sidekick and second-in-command, and she instructs her in the art of clothes and sexiness. Then there's a third one, usually chubby or freakishly tall and skinny or otherwise afflicted, whom #1 and #2 both boss around. #3 is a sort of gopher, doormat, punching bag, object of loving condescension, and project for improvement rolled into one.

It's more complicated than it is for guys, where there's a much clearer line between victim and oppressor, and you always know which one you are, and the victims and oppressors never mingle or feign fraternity. In Girl World, #3 is truly friends with #1 and #2, and they do, in fact, enjoy hanging out together. #1 and #2 will help #3 with makeup and clothes, pretending that that will make a difference, and if either of the dominant girls have a boyfriend, they will try to set up #3 with the least attractive of the boyfriend's friends, though everybody really knows that that, like so many of their other #3-related activities, is a (devil-head) charade. Because even though they're sincere about being kind and helpful, there is an undercurrent of (devil-head) malevolence. #1 and #2 love #3, but they're also conscious of how much hotter they are than she is, and they like rubbing it in. #3 resents it deep down but goes along with it because she likes being in a group of friends, which would not otherwise be possible. Eventually, though, the bitterness begins to slip out bit by bit, and #1 and #2 decide #3 is a bitch and that they hate her and end up (devil-head) ostracizing her and replacing her with a new #3. Why don't the #3s all team up and form an anti-1-2 front? I don't know: they just don't.

Anyhow, it happened that the #2 in the subgroup of drama people Sam Hellerman had started hanging out with was Née-Née Tagliafero, the girl who was supposedly going with Pierre Butterfly Cameroon. The #1 in that group was Celeste Fletcher, who was, as drama girls go, pretty much at the top level of sexiness. And the #3 was Yasmynne Schmick, who was very short and whose body shape was almost perfectly spherical. She had a slight black-velvety goth thing going on. Sometimes it's hard to draw the line between goth and fake hippie, I've found.

In fact, this trio, though definitely in drama and thus associated with the whole fake-hippie pretense, was among the least extreme, most tasteful trios of drama girls. They could pass for nonhippies if they wanted to—maybe their hearts weren't completely in it, though they did listen to that awful jam music. They were on the (devil-head) periphery of the fake-hippie drama movement.

Man, I've got to do something about that devil-head situation. Maybe there's some kind of drug they can give you for it.

Anyhow, the Celeste Fletcher trio was closely associated

with the Syndie Duffy trio, which was closer to the center of the drama establishment. Syndie Duffy was quite mean, for a drama hippie. They also had a much looser association, through Née-Née Tagliafero, I imagine, with the Lorra Jaffe group, who were thoroughly normal and thus quite psychotic. It was the #2 of the Lorra Jaffe group who had tried to pull a Make-out/Fake-out on me recently in PE, if I'm not mistaken.

At the lunchtime be-in, Sam Hellerman had been sitting in the shadow of the Knight, roughly in between the Celeste Fletcher and Syndie Duffy trios, and had appeared to be talking to both. I would have given quite a bit to know what the hell they had been discussing. But Sam Hellerman wasn't talking.

Sam Hellerman *had* said I was welcome to "hang" on the lawn during lunch period with him on the drama people's turf if I wanted. I'm sure he said it with solid confidence that I wouldn't take him up on it. Yet I did in fact give it a shot on the following day, more in the spirit of field research than from a sincere desire to be one with the earth.

It was a weird scene, man. Celeste Fletcher was lying on her stomach on the grass facing away from us, raising her head every now and again to tell Yasmynne Schmick to fetch this or that, or to draw subtle attention to Yasmynne Schmick's weight, height, or skin condition with less-than-convincing compassion. Syndie Duffy was lying nearby, with her head in her scruff-grunge knit-cap boyfriend's lap. The boyfriend was half asleep, leaning back between the Hillmont Knight's legs, and Syndie Duffy was sucking idly on his fingers. You could tell her group's #3 was on the way out because whenever the #3 would try to say something, Syndie Duffy would roll her eyes or, with a great show of aggravation, remove the boyfriend's fingers from her mouth and tell her not to be stupid before putting them back in. That's normal 1-on-3 behavior, perhaps, but there was something about the way she was saying it that made it clear it was pretty much all over.

There were some dudes a bit farther down, engaged in a philosophical debate about how high they were now as opposed to how high they were going to get at some future point in time. Everyone over by me was idly watching Née-Née Tagliafero and Pierre Butterfly Cameroon make their rounds, and talking amongst themselves about male and female actors, getting high, *The Music Man,* how LPs sound better than CDs (which I actually agree with), and (did I mention?) getting high. And about Bobby Duboyce, the helmet guy, who, it was claimed, had been seen making out with some unspecified, and grossly implausible, girl in the football-field bleachers. (I was skeptical. Is it even physically possible to do that with a helmet head? But of course I mental-noted the grim fact that, for the sake of argument, even narcoleptic helmet boy was more of a hit with the ladies than I was and filed it away for use in some future flight of self-pity.)

I sat next to Sam Hellerman, cross-legged in my army coat, in silence. I couldn't think of anything to say. The only time anyone acknowledged my presence was when Yasmynne Schmick, for some reason, asked me what I played in the band. "Guitar," I said. Except that I said a few ums and uhs beforehand, stammered a bit during, and had a little coughing fit afterward. I was jumpy. I was doing the ear thing. For some reason, I felt kind of warmly towards Yasmynne Schmick, maybe because of sympathy for her role in life, which really wasn't her fault. But I couldn't talk to these people. My one line in the whole scene, and I had flubbed it.

As for Sam Hellerman, he said not one word the entire time, and no one said anything to him. He just sat there staring at Celeste Fletcher with a faintly stupid expression. He did manage to leave the impression, though, that he was drooling on the inside.

So it was obvious. I guess. Sam Hellerman had the hots for Celeste Fletcher, and for some reason she had decided to tolerate his presence and to allow him to subject her ass to the Hellerman eye-ray treatment for thirty minutes each day. I couldn't blame him for that: it's a nice ass, and I have to admit I was giving it the relatively less dramatic Chi-Mo treatment myself. What she got out of the deal was harder to fathom. It was clear, though, that his deep and tender feelings for her ass were not reciprocated. As to why she decided to tolerate his (devil-head) parasitic presence, who knows? Maybe she was just one of those people who likes having a large (devil-head) entourage and she felt she needed another extra to make the crowd scene look more believable. Maybe her ass needed the positive reinforcement.

All I knew was, Sam Hellerman was no more a genuine participant in the lunch period Grooviness on the Green than I was. Celeste Fletcher hadn't even looked back at him the entire time. It made zero sense.

WE COOL?

I was a little surprised that so much time went by without Little Big Tom acknowledging my peace and love note. It wasn't like him. I'd sent him notes like that before when there had been equally explosive substitute-father/son trouble in the past, and he always responded in some way. Like putting a little Post-it on my door that said "We're cool." Plus, Little Big Tom was almost immediately back to his old self once the conflict had wound down.

I had pretty much decided to pick up the pieces and move on with my life in that particular area when there was a knock on my door that turned out to have come from Little Big Tom's Celtic knot 'n' serpent wedding ring. That was unusual. I mean, that's how he always knocked on things, but when he had something to say to me he would usually just stick his head in and out without warning.

He walked in carrying the weapons-and-tactics magazines in a stack on one upturned palm, like a waiter with a platter of hors d'oeuvres.

He set them down on my dresser and said:

"We cool?" One eyebrow was raised, and his head was tilted and his neck was trained in such a way that he almost looked like he had turned into a question mark for a moment.

"Well," I said, drawing out the word in an exaggerated fashion and making a little motion with my hands as though I were physically weighing whether we were cool or not—mime isn't my strong suit, but, see, I was trying to communicate with Little Big Tom in his own language. Finally, I made a "well, what do you know?" face and said, "We are cool."

He said he had overreacted and was sorry, especially for reading my notebook, but he used way more words than necessary to get that across, and before he was finished he was starting to get a little flustered. I was trying to look at him neutrally while he talked, but the more neutral I tried to look, the less comfortable he seemed to get. Finally, after two half-finished word clumps that were more like automobile accidents than sentences, he gave up trying to get in touch with his feelings and said, in a more familiar tone:

"Some of the things you said the other day have been rattling around in the old brain box. Young men always think they know everything and that old men know nothing, and old men always think the same thing. But maybe the answer could be somewhere in between."

Mmm, deep.

That's what I thought, but what I said was "We're cool, Big Tom." Then I added, uncharacteristically, but because I knew he'd like it: "You're not even that old." I'm shameless.

He looked at me, still expecting something.

I held up two fingers at about shoulder level in a peace sign with what I hoped was the right attitude, slightly sardonic but good-natured.

His mouth crinkled just a bit at the left corner, and he did this little sniffy laugh while shaking his head. Then he rumpled my hair, which was the real sign that he was more or less satisfied with how things had concluded.

"Rock and roll," he said as he went out, sighing just a bit, I think.

LADIES' WEEK?

I was starting to lose track of all of the mysteries. There was Tit's code and the cryptic notes and documents associated with my dad's teen library. There was my adult dad's death. There was Sam Hellerman's unusual behavior. And above all, there was Fiona. I still had the sense that somehow all the puzzles were related and could solve each other if only one were to come undone. I also had the sense that that was crazy. At any rate, I thought about Fiona practically constantly, both as a context within which to experience my horniness and as a puzzle piece. I decided to write down everything I knew about her, imagining that it might be useful one day if I ever gathered my possessions in a satchel, kissed my mom good-bye, and set off on a perilous journey to track her down and discover her secret. Like a hard-boiled detective. Or a hobbit.

I hardly knew anything about Fiona. I sure wished I had paid more attention to what she had been saying while I was ogling her like a sex maniac.

To summarize what I came up with:

Fiona was most likely a junior. She was in drama, acted in plays, made costumes and her own clothes, and was kind of hung up on vocabulary-level feminism but not in any way that mattered practically. She was interested in the occult and the paranormal, though in fact she had no psychokinetic or supernatural powers. She was nearsighted. She liked the Who. She had a boyfriend who was not at the party but who had friends who were. She wouldn't go past second base with anonymous strangers in dark basements; or, the party had coincided with her period (ladies' week, as my mom calls it). She liked to smoke pot.

If she went to CHS, she was known by a name other than Fiona, and dressed and behaved so differently from how she had been at the party that no one who would have seen her at school recognized the description. But most likely she didn't go to CHS. I had assumed she did because she had been at a party with lots of CHS kids, and having the Who shirt and being in drama had made it seem like she had to be one of the CHS drama mods. But that wasn't necessarily the case. She could go to another high school but know some of the CHS drama mods well enough that she would be invited to their parties.

In fact, the Who shirt was the only definite mod-related thing about her, so maybe she wasn't even a real fake mod at all. Maybe the drama people at her high school were all on some other trip (though I don't know what–crochet-core?) and the Who shirt was just random, or worn because she knew she'd be hanging out with CHS drama mods on that particular evening.

There was another reason I had assumed she went to CHS, though. Something in the back of my mind that had been bugging me, though I didn't consciously realize what it was at first: somehow she had known I was from Hellmont.

I had instinctively assumed that she had reached that conclusion because she didn't recognize me from school at CHS, which would have made it obvious. Most kids from Hillmont went to Hillmont High, though a small chunk, from the hills, mostly, went to CHS. No Clearview or Clearview Heights kids ever went to Hillmont, that I knew of–CHS was a much bigger school, and had kids from several towns. What I'm getting at is: if Fiona didn't go to CHS herself, it wouldn't have been at all obvious that I was from Hillmont. I mean, even if she knew a lot of CHS kids, she couldn't have been positive that she could identify every one, especially a random dweeby one, if she didn't go there. She would have assumed I went to CHS, like almost all of the kids at the party, right? She would have said "How's tricks in Queerview?" And I would have said "Homoerotic." And the pop-up devil-he–oh wait, that was before the devil-head started popping up. Those were simpler times.

Now, maybe she had just guessed right, or had mentioned Hillmont randomly. Maybe not, though. But I couldn't figure out how or why she would have known anything about me. Man, maybe she was psychic after all.

So where did you go if you lived in Salthaven but you didn't go to CHS? OMH (Old Mission Hills) possibly. I didn't know a whole lot about the school system out there. I was going to have to do some research. Or maybe she wasn't even from Salthaven or Salthaven Vista. Sooner or later, thinking about all this, everything started to go in circles and I had to take a break.

In my fantasy, Fiona is still a mod, a real one, and she and I are living in a grimy, sweaty gray underground flat in Carnaby Street, London, listening to "Substitute" on a little gramophone. I'm standing in the doorway in a parka and she's on a couch in a houndstooth miniskirt and go-go boots. We're both crying, but I can tell by how she's looking at me through the tears that she wants it. The time, I mean . . .

I woke up the next morning feeling pretty stupid about all that "Fiona must have known who I was all along" crap. Who was I, Miss Marple? Sam Hellerman, please assemble all the guests in the drawing room, and you might want to take the precaution of bringing along your revolver. I rather suspect there may be trouble. Does that mean you have cracked the case, Aunt Jane? Oh my, yes. I have known for some time. People can be very, very cruel. . . .

There was really only one blindingly obvious conclusion here: I was starting to lose my marbles.

I wondered how long this part was going to last. I mean, mooning over the mystery woman, wondering who she was, where she was, what she was doing and with whom, and why she was doing it, walking around feeling like I'd just been punched in the stomach. I was starting to get a little tired of it. Don't get me wrong. I still enjoyed thinking about expressing my horniness in the context of the mystery woman. I did it all the time. And I still tended to feel fairly lovey-dovey and soppy and emotional when I thought of her, imagining what it might be like to be going out with Fiona and doing sweet, ordinary boyfriend-girlfriend things like going to the library and making out, or going to the movies and making out, or ridiculing normal people at the mall. And making out.

Actually, you know what? I'm still not all that clear on what's involved in doing sweet, ordinary boyfriend-girlfriend things. I just assume it's a lot of making out and groping in public, sex in cars, blow jobs in public restrooms, going to movies, eating at restaurants, listening to the radio, arguing about trivia, and—what else? Do you help each other with your homework? Play Scrabble, build models, buy food at the grocery store and cook it for each other, meet at the Rec. Center or at the beach for a game of volleyball with her Nair-commercial friends? Does she ask you which dress makes her look fatter, like Carol does with Little Big Tom? Does she throw a stapler at you and stop talking to you for days when you can't figure out the right answer? Do you share your secrets and deepest fears with one another, or are those subjects still just as weird and awkward and best not brought up, maybe even especially to someone to whom you are constantly, incessantly, relentlessly giving the time?

I only mention it because I have this idea, a dream, really, that part of what it would mean is that the boyfriend is in this little club with the girlfriend where when one is hurt or troubled or being assailed by the cruelties of the world, the other decides not to be on the side of the world, but to join forces with the other member of the club against the world, even if it's frowned upon, even if it's a doomed scenario, even if the world is definitely gonna win. Like you're allies. The last remnant of your people. A Sex Alliance Against Society. But maybe I have it all wrong. It does sound like a quaint, far-fetched idea, now that I've put it in words. And also overly dramatic, if something can be o. d. and q. at the same time.

Nevertheless, Fiona was like that in my mind. What does

133

it have to do with "having sex," as Sam Hellerman might put it if he were in a particularly dainty mood? I'm not all that sure. But I know it's related somehow.

Having made out with Fiona that one time made the issue seem more real. But that was an illusion. There wasn't any difference at all between the idea of being in a Sex Alliance Against Society with Fiona and the idea of being in one with Kyrsten Blakeney. Both notions were remote, impossible, out of the question, preposterous. Both girls were, with regard to me, equally imaginary.

And I was sure, as sure as I was that C. S. Lewis invented Narnia, that neither of them would, in the unlikely event that the option were ever to come up, fail to choose the world. Of course not. I probably wouldn't, either, if the world would have me.

MAKING AMENDS

It wasn't till a couple days after Little Big Tom and I got in touch with our feelings on the occasion of his apologizing for the Stratego Sex Incident that I happened to glance at the stack of deconfiscated weapons-and-tactics magazines on my dresser.

I hadn't noticed it before, but Little Big Tom had put a Post-it on the top magazine. It said "look in the closet." I frowned and slid open the closet door and, well, maybe you guessed it already, but I was totally thrown: there was a guitar case in there with a Post-it on it that said "Merry Christmas in advance."

Damn. Little Big Tom had trouble expressing himself in spoken words, but he was a master of concise communication in Post-it form.

I pulled out the guitar case and opened it. There was a *great* electric guitar in it. I mean, fucking great. Gibson. Melody Maker. Midsixties. Kind of beat-up. The coolest thing I've ever seen or touched with my hands that wasn't attached to someone named Fiona. There was yet another Post-it on the headstock that said "you're on your own for the amp."

Okay, so that might have been one Post-it too many. Even the master of the Post-it communications revolution can overdo it sometimes. But damn. How had he known that that was pretty much my ultimate fantasy guitar? I had no idea. Oh wait, yes I did. Because he had read my notebook. Little Big Tom had done everything wrong and had broken a great many well-established, TV-dramatized, "Dear Abby"–certified rules about parental conduct with regard to respecting people's privacy whenever drugs are not involved, but I've got to say that in the all-important stage known as Making Amends by Trying to Purchase Affection and Trust with Extravagant Gifts, he had really come through.

Maybe it's just the lust for worldly possessions talking, but I think this may have been the first time in my life I was this unsuccessful when I tried to make everything disappear in a cloud of cynicism. I admit, I got a little choked up.

I made a silent vow not to ridicule him without his being aware of it for at least a week.

Having the new guitar made me want to play better, to sort of do it justice, and I started to practice a lot more. Little Big Tom had bought it from a friend of his who had been in some old blues-country-jam band and who now had a guitar repair place, which was the reason it was set up so well and played so easily. According to my mom, Little Big Tom had been planning to get me an electric guitar for Christmas even before the Stratego Sex Incident. He had found out from my notebook that I lusted after a Melody Maker and had felt so bad about the snooping that he had decided to expedite matters and try to scare one up.

This was the nicest thing anyone had ever done for me, and I couldn't forget it. I let a lot of prime opportunities for LBT ridicule slide right by because of it. I knew Little Big Tom could tell that the gift had worked and that I was more positively disposed toward him, because he increased the frequency of his trademark pop-in comments. That was the downside. It was annoying. On the other hand, I didn't mind too much. Why not let him have his fun, too?

Once when I was playing, he stuck his head in and said, "Spanking the plank?" I stared at him. "Uh, no," I finally said, since as I mentioned I was trying to be nice.

But it turns out I was wrong. I *had* been s-ing the p. S-ing the p. used to be a right-on, far-out, with-it expression for playing the guitar, supposedly. I guess when Little Big Tom was a kid, he and his friends used to go around saying "hey, you wanna get together and spank the plank tonight?" and they would be talking about having some kind of opium-den Timothy Leary country-blues-folk-bluegrass-Afro-Caribbean jam session wearing leather vests and velvet pants in an incense-y room that had one poster of Che Guevara and another of Frank Zappa sitting on a toilet, and beads instead of a door.

Supposedly, they also used to call a guitar a "piece of wood," as in "hey, that's a great piece of wood you got there." You know, it's almost like they *want* you to get the wrong idea when they say stuff like that, but knowing Little Big Tom, I'm pretty sure there was nothing going on at these jam sessions but soft drugs, hard-to-follow conversations, and terrible music.

*   *   *

Neither Sam Hellerman nor I had an amp yet, but we continued to practice using the living room Magnavox stereo console. Sam Hellerman figured out how to plug us both in, so he was in the left speaker and I was in the right. He seemed a little put out, strangely. I think he was beginning to see the enormous fake wood–paneled stereo console as his trademark gear and didn't like me horning in on it. He wanted to be the only one to say "yeah, I like to use the Magnavox Astro-Sonic hi-fi stereo console" to *Guitar Player* magazine when they interviewed him about his signature thin, burbly, distorted bass sound. "We never expected Oxford English, Moe Bilalabama on guitar, me on bass and lollygagging, first album *What Part of Suck Don't You Understand?* to be such a big success," he'd say. "But in all modesty, I'd have to say it's that Magnavox magic that always seals the deal. . . ."

In reality, though, Oxford English was off to a pretty terrible start. I mean, the guitar sounded awful through the Magna-V. And it was so hard to distinguish between the bass and guitar that neither of us could tell for sure what we were playing. It was a mess.

Here's how bad it was. We were doing "Don't Play Yahtzee with My Heart." Little Big Tom stuck his head in, tilt-stared at us for a moment as though searching for the right words, gave up, and pulled his head back out. Essentially he had said, in body language, "let's pretend this pop-in never happened, shall we?" If you can't even get a resigned "rock and roll" out of LBT, you're in trouble.

I tried running the guitar through this distortion box I got at Musicville at the mall. The Overlord II. That was a mistake. There was a squeal, and then there was: silence. And I think maybe a smell like smoky toast, though that may have been from something else: it always smells kind of weird around here. The Magnavox was dead.

It's a long way to the top if you want to rock and roll.

THE STAR-SPANGLED BANNER
SUBSTITUTION CIPHER

Now let me try to explain my thinking about the Tit's weird code-parallelogram.

Sam Hellerman and I used to have this code hobby. It began in sixth grade, continued sporadically through junior high, and had even hung on slightly through some of ninth grade, though by that time we were mostly just going through the motions. It was time-consuming and tedious, and, more importantly, we didn't have anything of interest to be all secretive about.

There were different methods, but one we had used pretty frequently was the Star-Spangled Banner Substitution Cipher. What you did was, you chose two words at random from the "Star-Spangled Banner" lyrics. The first letter of the first word would be your "in" character, and the last letter of the second word would be your "out" character. So say your words were "dawn's" and "stripes." You'd write out the alphabet starting with "D" from "dawn's," adding the "A," "B," and "C" at the end; and underneath these letters, you'd write it out again, but this time beginning with "S," the last letter of "stripes." Like this:

D E F G H I J K L M N O P Q R S T U V W X Y Z A B C
S T U V W X Y Z A B C D E F G H I J K L M N O P Q R

You substituted the letters in the second line for the first line's letters in your original text. So in the SSBSC dawn's/stripes cipher, ZNGHITC QAPZTCTN XH RWPGPRITGXOTS QN GTRTHHTH PCS HWTAITGTS WDAADLH would mean "Kyrsten Blakeney is characterized by recesses and sheltered hollows."

All the recipient would need to know to decipher the message was where the alphabet began on each of the two lines. The way we used to do it was by number. "Dawn's" is the eighth word in the SSB, and "stripes" is the twenty-third word. So the key to the Kyrsten Blakeney message would be SSB-F8-L23. We used "The Star-Spangled Banner" because we both knew the first twenty-six words of the lyrics by heart. The "F" and "L" stood for first and last, because sometimes we would vary what letters we would use, so we could have L/F or F/F, or even midword letters that we would identify by Roman numerals: SSB-8iii-23iv. It could get pretty complicated.

Even though the letters of the coded portion of Tit's note were arranged in a neat little parallelogram rather than in one line like normal text, I was pretty sure it was some sort of cipher. It is possible to solve a substitution cipher by trial and error, even without a key, but Tit's message wasn't long enough to gauge the frequency of commonly occurring letters like "E" or "T," which is how you usually begin. Plus, if I was right, he had broken his ordinary coded sentences into fourteen-character clumps, so you couldn't even guess at common words like "the" or "of," though some of the double letters might have provided a clue. There was only one way to decipher it, practically speaking, and that was to discover the key. If it had been based on something they had memorized, like "The Star-Spangled Banner," there was no hope of recovering it. For reasons I'll get to in a second, however, I didn't think it had been memorized. In any case, there would likely have been some indication for the recipient of how the key should be applied, along the lines of the SSB-F8-L23 notation I mentioned. My assumption was that it would be somewhere on the note itself.

At first I thought it might be in the body of the message, which was uncoded, but cryptic, and which indeed made almost as little sense as the cipher. But then I looked at the date. There are only thirty days in June, so the date 6/31 doesn't exist. The original date, 5/31, does exist, of course. Why had Tit scribbled out the five and written a six over it, changing a real date to an imaginary one?

Here was my idea on that:

What if my dad had underlined the passage in *Catcher*, CEH 1960, not because of his deep interest in back rubs, but as a decoding key? It would explain why only one seemingly random passage had been underlined. And if so, there would probably be something on the note that would indicate how the substitution worked, and the date seemed likely. Of course, even if the back rub passage *had* been a decoding key, it wouldn't necessarily have been the one that had been used for this particular message. That was a long shot. Nevertheless, with the Star-Spangled Banner Substitution Cipher in mind, I got out the *Catcher* and started counting words, just to see. I tried a few possibilities, using 5 or 6 and 31, but they yielded only more gibberish.

Then I noticed something: counting letters instead of words, the fifth letter of the passage was "T" and so was the thirty-first. That wouldn't have been any use for a substitution cipher, since the in and out letters would all have been the same. What if Tit had written "5/31" and then changed the five to a six when he realized the 5/31 combination wouldn't work as a key? Sixth letter from the beginning was "H," and the thirty-first was "T. . . ."

Damn. It still didn't work, not in any of the configurations I tried. Yet it seemed too much of a coincidence that Tit would have happened to cross out a date that would not have worked as a key and replace it with one that would, if he hadn't been working from that particular passage. And it explained why there was only one underlined passage, and perhaps also why there were all sorts of other mysterious pairs of numbers scribbled all over the *Catcher*. It was the perfect theory in all but one respect: it didn't work. What was I missing?

THE GIFTED AND THE TALENTED

Meanwhile, though it seemed a bit much with everything else that was going on, I continued to attend my inane, pointless classes.

In Humanities we were still doing The Turbulent Sixties, working on the Peace Collage. There was this big pasteboard "wall" on which you were supposed to glue things cut out from magazines that had to do with the sixties, or peace, or civil rights, or the women's movement, or, well, just about anything at all, really. There was a lot of potential mischief afoot with all that glue, but I managed to avoid getting glued to anything for once.

In part, I believe, this had to do with the Paul Krebs *Brighton Rock* incident. I had been worried about the consequences of the episode, but only a little. Technically, I suppose I had beaten him up, though that had been entirely due to luck and randomness. I still thought of it like he had attacked and persecuted me as usual, even though I "won."

One of the reasons it had been possible to knock him down, and probably the main reason he had given up so easily and resigned himself to whimpering in his own blood, was that he had not expected me to fight back. I never did. I never had. He wasn't on his guard because he had assumed there was no reason to be. He had been shocked out of his normal aggressive mode, and his mind had stalled trying to process the unfamiliar information and finally locked. Plus, I had smashed his head into the gravel very hard and it had to hurt. I guess it was the combination of shock and gravel. And loss of blood.

I had been as surprised by my reaction as he had, but I'm not going to say I don't know what came over me. What had come over me was that in six solid years of being harassed, abused, beaten, ridiculed, humiliated, dehumanized, and tortured by Paul Krebs and his fun-loving buddies, they hadn't ever attacked something I really cared about till they poured Coke on my dad's *Brighton Rock*. There was no way Paul Krebs could have known, but he had picked the wrong fucking book to pour Coke on. I flipped out. I went berserk. I wasn't in control of myself, and he wasn't ready for an attack by a flipped-out, berserk King Dork inflamed by the rage that only grief and (devil-head) filial piety can summon.

If the walkway had been concrete, or even asphalt, the blow to the head would have injured him seriously, maybe even killed him. Then I would have been in trouble. But I doubted it was that serious. The gravel would have absorbed and distributed the impact evenly. As I knew quite well from years of experience, head and scalp injuries bleed a lot and hurt like hell, but they always look worse than they are. The worst you usually have is a concussion, some messy clothes, and a lot of explaining to do. They are easily attributed to accidents. In fact, I have a solid, largely inaccurate, reputation as an absentminded, accident-prone klutz at the Henderson-Tucci HQ, owing to all the times I've said I've fallen off ledges or walked into walls or run into poles.

And I was pretty sure that that was what Paul Krebs would do, as well. I will always think of him as the guy I accidentally beat up, but he would be rather eager to prevent the world at large from knowing him that way. It would hardly have been the first time he had come home from school all bloody, though the fact that this time it was his own blood would have been something of a novelty. But he would keep that part to himself. And he would hate me more than he ever had before, even if neither he nor I had believed such a thing to be possible. I knew I had to brace myself for some kind of retaliation from him and potentially from the other Matt Lynch minions as well, but I was sure it wouldn't become a legal matter. That's what I'm saying.

Anyway, despite that, word did get out around school a bit, somehow. No one said anything to me, but people were looking at me from a distance with a kind of awe. I mean, I was in shock about it myself. These things don't happen, not usually. I imagine most people discounted it as a grossly implausible rumor. Sam Hellerman didn't doubt me, but he said, and I knew he was right, that I would have to watch my back from now on. I was totally used to watching that, though.

It was a measure of just how sick Hillmont High School society is that smashing someone's head to pulp in the gravel by the baseball diamond was such an unequivocal reputation enhancer. But so it was. It had worked for years for Matt Lynch and Paul Krebs and the other normals in their demi-human goon squad. Now, weirdly and in a way that wasn't entirely welcome, it was temporarily working for me. (I had no illusions: the vital element of surprise was only destined to work the one time. But it had worked.)

So maybe that's why no one tried to glue me to anything in Humanities while we were working on the Peace Collage. Someone did, however, glue some stuff from a gay porn magazine on Bobby Duboyce's helmet while he slept peacefully in his seat. Peace indeed.

As for Paul Krebs, I figured he still had a few concussions coming to him. I have heard, though, that if you fall asleep with a concussion you can die, so I was relieved when I learned that he was back in school a couple of days later. And not to be all Bad Seed and everything, but just to be on the safe side I got some new Converse All Stars from the Shoe Mart and threw the old, blood-spattered ones in the shop incinerator on my way back to school. Because you never know.

The day after I attended the lunchtime gathering around the Hillmont Knight, I noticed for the first time that Yasmynne Schmick was in my Advanced French class. She smiled and nodded a greeting as I walked in, which was definitely a new experience for me. I guess my failure to say "guitar" properly had formed a kind of loose bond between us. Which was alarming, in a way. I mean, I wasn't sure I wanted another friend: Sam Hellerman was about all I could handle. She was wearing a tight-fitting purple velvety bodysuit and a lot of silver jewelry. She looked like an enormous Christmas ornament. She was actually pretty nice, though, for a drama goth pod-hippie; maybe the drama hippies weren't all bad after all.

Now, I had started taking French in seventh grade, so this was my fourth year, and even I found it shocking to think how little French I actually knew after three-plus years. True, I knew quite a lot about Jean and Claude and how they go to the movies and eat beefsteak and fruit, and I could tell you all about their other fabulous adventures, though only in the present tense. I was a master of the present tense in French. I guess that is pretty advanced, when you think about it.

I felt a little sorry for the French teacher, Madame Jimenez-Macanally, not only because students would often mispronounce her name so it sounded kind of nasty, but also because it must have been hard knowing deep down that whatever activities may have been going on in that class, the teaching and learning of the French language was not among them. Someone had hit on the idea of asking her to explain the complicated twenty-four-hour French system of telling time at the beginning of each class, just to see how long she would go along with it before cracking. She was determined not to crack, though: she explained the twenty-four-hour system every single day. Whether that was giving in or fighting back is hard to say: you could look at it either way.

The last fifteen minutes of Advanced French is called Advanced Conversation, where the students pair up for advanced, stimulating dialogue. Yasmynne Schmick approached me and said, as near as I could make out: *"Le nez est bête."* The nose is a beast? A little puzzling. Then she switched to English:

"Renée is stupid," she said. "You're actually a pretty nice guy."

Pause. "Really?" I had to assume she was talking about Née-Née Tagliafero. What the hell had they been saying about me?

Madame J.-M. frowned at us. We weren't supposed to speak English in Advanced Conversation. So we continued in French:

"What time is it?" I asked.

"It is 11:05," she replied.

"Thank you very much," I said. "What a shame. If it pleases you, what do you call yourself?"

"I am sorry," said Yasmynne Schmick. "I am hungry. The young girls wear a very pretty dress. They eat and play soccer with the mother and the fathers. My name is Yasmynne. I am four years old."

"Ah, yes," I said. "The young people love to buy discs of

pop music for dancing and for holiday making." I chose my words carefully. "They . . . they . . . my God: they drink beverages. It is true. My two friends Jean and Claude go to the cinema yesterday to view films. What a surprise. They eat. They are flowers."

Yasmynne Schmick nodded. "Thank you very much. I am sorry." Her face clouded over. "There is a match between two opposing teams at the stadium. It is true, is that not correct? Therefore, my little friend," she said quietly and with a sad smile, "all the world very much loves the automobile who calls himself a cat."

"You are correct," I said hopelessly. "I am enchanted. Our little green hat is orange on the head of this very interesting horse."

"Would you like to sleep with me this evening?"

"Thank you, Mr. Roboto."

It was kind of fun. That Yasmynne Schmick was all right.

Later that day, I was on my way to Band, running a little late, when something grabbed the back of my army coat, stopped me short, and almost pulled me to the ground. It turned out to be one of Mr. Teone's large, rubbery hands. He was scratching his butt with the other one. Ugh.

"Henderson," he said. "Henderson."

There was something about the way he said my name that made it sound like a particularly nasty swear word. Wait a minute, I thought: you can't call me that. It's rude.

He told me that he was writing a book on gifted and talented young men and women, and that he'd like to give me an IQ test and interview me with a group of other kids after school on Friday. At his fucking house. I don't think so.

"I can give you a ride in my '93 Geo Prizm if you like," he

said. He was always going on about his '93 Geo Prizm, like it was some kind of cool car or something. What a moron. He reached into his sports-jacket pocket with the butt hand and pulled out this crumpled, grubby, curling fistful of papers. Presumably, this was the IQ test. He poked me with it. And I recoiled in horror.

It was hilarious, though. I had serious doubts that Mr. Teone could write his own name, much less compose a whole book. He had supposedly started out at Hillmont way back as a shop teacher, which I could well believe: he had that air. Then he got some kind of administrative credential and became a principal. So the man had some education. But from what I could tell, he was still more or less functionally illiterate. He looked down at the papers in his butt hand and started to laugh like a maniac.

"No pain, no gain!" he said. "No gain, no pain!" Way to sell your dopey afterschool program to a skeptical student body. Whatever, freak.

Mr. Teone's afterschool Gifted and Talented program might have been of some use as an anecdote factory, but that was about it, and I felt I really didn't need the anecdotes at that price. Not that I ever would seriously have considered participating in something like that, even if it hadn't involved Hillmont High School's most bizarre and unhygienic administrator. I didn't need any more self-congratulatory self-esteem baths and collage-making bees in my life at the present moment. Sam Hellerman had attended one of Mr. Teone's ill-conceived afterschool activities last year, a sort of science fiction club. He never went back. He wouldn't say much about it, except: "he's a deeply weird man." It hardly needed stating.

THE LORD ROCKS IN MYSTERIOUS WAYS

Meanwhile, despite the multifaceted depravity of Hillmont High School, and personal mysteries various and extremely sundry, the band was trying to soldier on. It wasn't easy. I wasn't worried that I'd get in trouble for blowing up the Magnavox Astro-Sonic hi-fi console. It hadn't been used for years and years. Lifting the lid had let loose an enormous cloud of dust. It was just a large piece of furniture from long ago that was used as a thing to put other things on, its original function forgotten. We hadn't even been sure it would turn on.

However, that still left us with two-thirds of a band and nothing to plug in to. (Some Delicious Sky, aka SDS, Squealie on treble and vocals, Sambidextrous on thick bottom and industrial arts, band name squirted on a tanorexic female midriff in white toothpaste, first album *Taste My Juice*.) Because I'm so brilliant, I had blown up the left channel on the stereo in my room, too. I was philosophical about it: after all, a lot of the records I like are in mono. But we were running out of consumer electronics products to abuse in the name of Rock and Art.

Till now, Sam Hellerman and I had done all of our band activities at my house because his parents, even though they were almost never home, came from Germany and were all weird and strict. They specifically disapproved of music, it seemed. How he had talked them into buying him a bass I will never know.

Actually, out of the vast universe of things Sam Hellerman's parents frowned upon, the one they seemed to disapprove of most of all was Sam Hellerman himself. He had to take great care to hide what he did and anything he might be interested in, because if they ever found out about an activity or interest their first impulse was to ban it immediately.

By now so many things were prohibited in the Hellerman household that no one could keep track anymore, and a lot could slide by. Still, Sam Hellerman's peace of mind required that he limit contact with his parents as much as possible, as each enthusiasm stomped upon by the Ministry of Stomping on Enthusiasms represented a tiny missing piece of Sam Hellerman's soul that would probably never grow back. He didn't know whether in reality it would be physically possible for German parent-vampires to suck the rock and roll completely out of the hearts of their defenseless offspring. But he didn't want to be around to find out the hard way.

Nevertheless, Some Delicious Sky had nowhere else to go, for the moment. So we crept into the tomblike foyer of the Hellerman house, carrying our guitars, with a palpable feeling that we were up to no good.

The Hellermans didn't have a Magnavox Astro-Sonic hi-fi console in their living room, but rather an extremely expensive-looking audio setup with all sorts of extra boxes that glowed purply blue. It was always on standby and was never used, as far as I know. Sam Hellerman wasn't allowed to touch it, or even look at it. I suppressed an urge to kick the whole thing over as I tiptoed by, following Sam Hellerman down the hall and into his room.

Sam Hellerman ran the bass through his stereo. As for the guitar: there was this old electronic toy called a Speak-a-matic, left over from remote childhood. When you pushed the buttons, it would play funny sound effects through a tiny speaker. It was shaped like a little cow in overalls, and the speaker was the cow's mouth. When you pressed button #1, it would say: "Moo. What would you like to hear today?" Sam Hellerman had somehow rigged up the Speak-a-matic cow so that I could plug my guitar into it and the sound would come out of the cow's mouth. Well, it sort of did. The sound was rotten and squilchy, and very, very quiet, but come on, how cool is it to be playing a '65 Melody Maker through a souped-up Speak-a-matic cow mouth? That boy is a genius.

Yet I was starting to wonder if it was possible to fashion a crude band out of ordinary household materials. Without amps, I mean.

A couple of practices of that sort were more than enough to demonstrate that rock and roll, like nearly everything else on the planet, was not destined to flourish in the bowels of Hellerman Manor. We had to find another way, I thought.

And, as if directly in answer, Sam Hellerman revealed that he had a plan.

"You know," he said, on the Friday of the second week of his mysterious pod-hippie-dom. "I don't think we should go to the Pep Rally."

I stared at him, with the look that said "Gee, ya think?"

Once a month, the school cancels the period after lunch so they can hold a lengthy Pep Rally in the gym. Sometimes, when it is judged that lunch plus one period is insufficient, they cancel the period before lunch, as well. I wasn't into the idea of two or three solid hours of—what? To be honest, I've never been to a Pep Rally, and I don't know what goes on at one. But I can't imagine it'd be too pleasant. You're supposed to go, but they don't have any way to check, so for anyone not interested in upping their pep intake for the day it's like a little vacation. You just take off. Sam Hellerman's saying "I don't think we should go to the Pep Rally" was like Sam Hellerman saying "You know, I don't think we should use these big rusty nails to hammer our hands and feet to the floor today."

This particular Rally promised to be especially gruesome, as it was billed as a "Cultural Awareness Pep Rally." In a way, it was nice to know that Hillmont's assault on taste and decency was going strong—a predictable world is a manageable world. But that's no reason to participate in the madness, if there's a way to get out of it.

I was a little surprised that Sam Hellerman chose hanging out with me rather than Celeste Fletcher's ass for the precious extended lunch break. But, as I said, Sam Hellerman had a plan, which for once did not involve any of Celeste Fletcher's anatomical parts.

The solution to our amp problem had been under our noses all along, though it took Sam Hellerman's genius to uncover the secret. Ages ago, when the school system had more money and everyone was trying a lot harder to create the impression that Hillmont High School was more than just a clean, well-lighted place for hazing, they used to have a Jazz Band. It is beyond my capabilities to imagine what sort of god-awful "jazz" the Hillmont High band students might have managed to emit in those odd moments when they weren't otherwise occupied in student-on-student abuse. The Jazz Band program had been discontinued long ago, its terrors and cruelties lost in history. (One day they will discontinue all the programs, and that will be a fine day. A world without programs will be just as hard to take, maybe, but at least it will be more honest.)

Some of the Jazz Band paraphernalia remained, however, and it included a couple of amplifiers that were buried behind and underneath several layers of other band-related junk. There was a Polytone twin guitar amp, and a Fender Bassman, which was actually a legitimately cool amp, though I gather from reading interviews with real rock guys that the cool way to use the Fender Bassman is as a guitar amp rather than a bass amp. Anyway, they were better than the nothing we had. And they were free. In a sense.

The band room was normally locked when not occupied, of course, but Sam Hellerman had a key to the main building because he had signed up for a practice room. And he had somehow temporarily rigged the band room door so it wouldn't latch properly when Ms. Filuli, the band teacher, left the building. That boy is a criminal genius.

We had to burrow through quite a few layers, but it didn't take long. The school was deserted; everyone was either at the Pep Rally or skipping the Pep Rally. So no one was there to notice when I picked up the Polytone and just walked out with it. No one even came to investigate when Sam Hellerman wheeled the creaky Fender out of the band room and into the hall, even though its wheels made a squealing sound like I imagine a five-year-old girl might make if someone hung her outside a window by the ankle. Preventing geeks from swiping decrepit school property wasn't high on everybody's list of priorities that day.

We replaced all the band room junk and jumbled and jostled it a bit so it looked pretty much as it had before, kind of like how you would trample on the dirt on top of a grave you didn't want anyone to find out about. Hardly anyone even knew the amps were there in the first place, so we were pretty safe. We left the school grounds and took turns wheeling the Fender with the Polytone on top of it back to my house. I had an absurd feeling of (devil-head) euphoria, like we were on our way.

What finally made us get off our asses and solve the amp problem? Well, there had been another big development, bandwise. Sam Hellerman had taken some time off from his busy schedule of keeping tabs on Celeste Fletcher's ass and had managed to scare up a drummer. An actual drummer. I kid you not. His name was Todd Panchowski, he had a drum set, and for reasons that remain dark to this day, he hadn't flinched at the idea of being in a band with Sam Hellerman and me. Well, actually, he took determined steps to make it clear that he wasn't "in" the band, so maybe that was it. There were other bands he was "in." When he talked about our band (which when we met him was Arab Charger, me on guitar, The Fiend in Human Shape on bass and preventive dentistry, first album *Blank Me*) he would always say we were "jamming," which is less committed sounding than practicing or playing.

The Polytone didn't sound too bad with the distortion box, the Overlord II. Much louder than the cow mouth. The Fender Bassman didn't work when we first plugged it in, but that was just because the tubes were missing. Sam Hellerman had anticipated that and was ready with a new set of tubes that he got from the electronics store. I thought it sounded nice, though I think he was secretly pining for the thin, burbly, distorted Magnavox sound.

We plugged this cheesy microphone from Amanda's mini-karaoke set into the Bassman's second channel and taped it to a bamboo pole from Little Big Tom's gardening supplies, and stood the pole up by sticking it in the red and green Christmas tree stand from the basement. It looked exotic. The mic squealed a bit, and it was kind of hard to get it so that we played all at the same time, but it was loud and we sounded—well, not exactly like a rock band. More like three different rock bands with one member each playing different songs at the same time. But we played "Surrender" and "Cretin Hop," "Fox on the Run," and "Whole Lotta Rosie," sort of, and if our attempt to do my own song, "Wetness for the Prosecution," sounded a bit more experimental than intended, it was still pretty cool in a *Trout Mask Replica* kind of way. Or so I kept telling myself.

This was all happening in the living room of my house. Little Big Tom popped in at one point. He tilted and said something I couldn't hear. We stopped and waited expectantly.

"Living room rock!" he said. I guess I had been hoping for a comment on the song, "I Pledge Allegiance to the Heart." But it was probably pretty hard to make out the lyrics. Plus the mic kept shocking me, so I was shying away from it and not putting a lot into the singing. Living Room Rock was pretty funny, though, and I made a note to self to use it for an album title or something someday. Actually, it was one of the best band names I'd ever heard. . . .

Now, Todd Panchowski was a Christian stoner. That is, he was a stoner who had joined a Christian youth group to deal with his inner turmoil and problems at home and to find guidance and a sense of community. There were a few of those around. The youth group was called the Fellowship. In my experience, despite the cheerful hobbit-evoking name and their (devil-head) ostensible ethical standards, the Fellowship people were just as sadistic and psychotic as any other normal people. Maybe they were nice to each other behind closed doors and reserved their hazing for people of other religions or something. I didn't really know a lot about them.

I don't want to get into the whole stoner classification system, but I should mention that practically every member of the Hillmont student body is technically a stoner, in that they all do various mild drugs continually and are pretty much always stoned to some degree. The difference is that the stoner stoners wear heavy metal T-shirts while doing it. They tend to be nicer to be around than full-on normal people, though, because their ideology includes a self-perceived admiration for social misfits. That part is contrived and not very sincere, perhaps, but in fact they don't hassle me nearly as much as normal people do. I even get points for my ency-clopedic knowledge of firearms and rock and roll history. I'm not one of them, but they don't actively seek to destroy me, and that's a nice novelty.

One more thing: all the psychotic normal people are well aware that there is something weird about dismissing people as "stoners" when the stoners differ from themselves only in the kind of T-shirts they wear and in the diminished ferocity of their attacks on the defenseless. So they prefer to call ston-ers "burnouts." But that's a more appropriate term for teach-ers, if you ask me.

Todd Panchowski was not without his Fellowship-related quirks, as we soon learned when we started to play with him. He was okay with playing our songs, and in fact didn't seem to pay too much attention to the words or music. I guess he was so busy hitting things with sticks that he didn't really have a thought to spare for the content. But there was one song he insisted that we do, and it was kind of an abomina-tion. I guess he had picked up the idea at the Fellowship meetings, where they do God only knows what. What he wanted to do was to play "Glad All Over." (Not the Carl Perkins "Glad All Over." The other one.) Now, I love "Glad All Over," don't get me wrong. But instead of singing "*You* make me feel glad all over," like the Dave Clark Five or the Rezilloes, he wanted it to go "*He* makes me feel glad all over." Like you're singing it about Jesus instead of a hot girl, get it?

I tried to explain to him that "glad all over" had a double meaning, a code meaning, like "giving her the time," and that the song wasn't about how great you feel when you read Paul's First Letter to the Thessalonians. Unless you're weird. It's really about—well, it's like this: boy meets girl, girl shows skin and wiggles, boy gives girl money or fabulous prizes, girl bends over, boy and girl invade each other's personal space, resulting in the propagation of the species and/or a big, sloppy mess. That's what "Glad All Over" is about, a tale as old as time.

Sam Hellerman was more direct.

"You have a crush on Jesus," he said. "But Jesus doesn't know you exist. Is that it?"

Well, no, that wasn't Todd Panchowski's point, although I think there may have been a grain of truth in it concerning what the Fellowship people might have had in mind when they decided to co-opt that particular song for their youth recruitment purposes. There's something weird and sexual about the way some people talk about God–have you noticed?

Those comments could have cost us our drummer right there, but in the end I don't think Todd Panchowski fully understood what we were saying. How can I put this? Todd Panchowski was not exactly a genius. But we didn't need him for textual analysis of the lyrics of pop-rock standards. We needed him to hit things with sticks in a vaguely rhythmic pattern that more or less accompanied our songs, and that was something he could do. Pretty much.

So we did "Glad All Over," just to humor him, and if I was thinking of Kyrsten Blakeney's ass instead of the face of Jesus when I sang it, well, he'd never have to know. In fact, the notion that he was sitting there thinking of the f. o. J. while I was thinking about being glad all over this or that female was amusing enough to make me crack up more than a few times. I don't know why I got such a kick out of that.

Todd Panchowski also wasn't into how often we changed the band name. He thought we should just pick a name and stick with it. He didn't understand that we were still searching, and that the habit of a lifetime of fantasy rocking dies hard.

"What's the name of the band again?" he said, after our second practice.

"Occult Blood," said Sam Hellerman, "Mopey Mo on guitar and vox, me on bass and teleology, you on drums, first album *Pentagrampa*."

"Well, first of all," said Todd Panchowski, "I play *percussion instruments,* not 'drums.' " Second of all, he added, he didn't want to jam with a band with the word "occult" in it. There was some Fellowship rule against it. So he happened to be wearing an I, Cannibal T-shirt depicting a skeletal grim reaper cutting off a nun's head with his scythe. Maybe they hadn't given him the "be nice to nuns" talk yet.

It didn't matter because halfway through the practice I had already decided that the new band name was going to be The Mordor Apes, Mithril-hound on guitar, L'il Sauron on bass and necrology, Dim Todd on drums-oops-I-mean-percussion and stupefaction, first album *Elven Tail*.

MY POOR INEPT PARENTAL UNITS

It seemed as though the smoke from the Sex-Vietnam-Stratego Incident had only just cleared when out of the blue I got called into the kitchen for another family conference. It was the Thursday before Halloween, not too long after our second practice with Todd Panchowski. I passed Amanda on my way in, and she gave me the look that said "you'll never get out of this one, boy." Dear God, what now?

This time my mom was officiating rather than Little Big Tom, though he was hovering in the background. She looked terrible. Her hair was all wild, like it was when she was going through one of her crazy episodes. She was smoking with tremendous ferocity even for her. She looked up at me through her hair with this unreadable but distressed expression on her face. What on earth was wrong?

We stared at each other.

Finally she said, her voice distant and depressed sounding, though also with a little sob, "A lot of kids your age are experimenting with drugs."

I went: "?"

And I'll tell you why I went "?" The first thing my mom did every single morning was to reach to the bedside table for her weed. She couldn't function without it, like some people are with coffee. And even now she had her afternoon lowball, bourbon and soda, no ice, in her hand. And coursing through her veins at this and any given time was a constant stream of about a dozen orally administered tranquilizers and psychotropics and God knows what else–Xanax, Prozac, lithium, Vicodin, Halcion, you name it. The irony was that I was the only person in that room, and probably the only member of the Hillmont High student body, who *wasn't* experimenting with anything. Other than love, literature, rock and roll, and cryptography, I mean.

The notion of these teen drug "experiments" always cracks me up. Like they're in a secret laboratory conducting research on a government grant. As opposed to being in a public lavatory doing lines of crank and holding some poor bastard's head in the toilet till he drowns or till the bell rings, whichever comes first. Well, in a way that's on a government grant, too. What a world we've got here.

My assumption was, of course, that my mom had finally noticed that Sam Hellerman had been raiding her Vicodin supply and had assumed that I was the culprit. Now, if that had been the case, here's what would have happened: I would have looked up and seen Little Big Tom tilting to one side and holding, maybe even rattling, a half-empty medicine bottle, with a concerned yet wry expression. In fact, though, when I looked up, it turned out that Little Big Tom was holding not a bottle, but rather a piece of paper and a little booklet.

It was my lyric sheet to "Thinking of Suicide?" and a copy of the school pamphlet of the same name. I had stupidly left the lyric sheet out after band practice. We had broken out the pamphlet as a visual aid to try to explain to Todd Panchowski why the song was cool. Unsuccessfully, as it turned out, but never mind about that.

My poor inept parental units. Once again, their opening line wasn't the topic sentence, and everyone ended up confused. They were trying to have the suicide talk and somehow got it mixed up with the drug talk.

THINKING OF SUICIDE?

You can put your straightjacket away
I don't plan to kill myself today
Maybe tomorrow, maybe not at all
I'm not ready to make that call

But don't assume that I'm all right
I won't be with my baby tonight
There's no baby, there's nothing there
What baby? I don't care–

Thinking of Suicide? Yeah, that's right.
It's a Thinking of Suicide Saturday night
It's not funny but it's true
I think about suicide when I think about you

So put your E back where you got it from
I don't plan on going to the prom

I know I add up to a figure of fun
But I don't want to be the only one

And there's only one of me
And no one else that I can see
And I'm so tired of trying to
Make believe I'm not dying to, so–

Thinking of Suicide? Yes, I am.
Thinking of Suicide? Hell, goddamn.
It's not funny, but it's free
Do you think about suicide when you think about me?

And if I'm suddenly gone
Then you'll know what's been going on
I'm always thinking
And I never do anything

But,

Thinking of Suicide? Yeah, that's right
Thinking of Suicide with all my might
I have got a history of
Thinking of Suicide when I think about love.

Well, it was a bit better with the music. Not the music as played by me and Sam Hellerman and Todd Panchowski, which was pure (devil-head) cacophony. I mean how it sounded in my head. Maybe you'll have to trust me on that. Anyway, I just thought you should see what my mom had been reading when she flipped out. Plus I'm kind of proud of that song and I'm showing off a little, even though you have to sing "from" a little weird to make it sound like it rhymes with "prom." But actually, that's kind of like my favorite part.

I totally couldn't see what the big deal was. It's a pretty ordinary topic. Not too shocking or unusual. They make a *pamphlet* about it, for Christ's sake. In fact, it wasn't even me in the song. The song had been inspired by the pamphlet girl, as I've explained; and as for those specific lyrics, I had in fact been feeling sorry for myself while pretending to be Yasmynne Schmick when I came up with most of them. But I couldn't figure out a way to explain that to my mom and Little Big Tom without causing even more confusion.

When my mom is in crazy mode it's just not possible to talk to her reasonably. Still, I gave it a shot, trying to make it as simple as possible.

"I'm not on drugs and I'm not going to kill myself," I said. And it was true. I really wasn't. Though I couldn't tell you why not.

No one knew what to say. Then Little Big Tom cleared his throat and filled in some of the background.

My own cleverness had tripped me up. Way back, I had needed to find an excuse for why I never spent much time at home, particularly after school. The real reason was that LBT kind of freaked me out back then, and I felt so uncomfortable with the whole vibe of the Henderson-Tucci household that even the ghastly pall of Hellerman Manor seemed preferable to it. So I invented a series of clubs I was supposed to be in, plausible ones like the Chess Club, Rocketry Club, Monty Python Club, The Middle-earthlings, or the Trekster Gods, and sometimes crazy ones I would make up for my own amusement, like the Caulking and Stripping Club, or the Doorknob Appreciators Society, otherwise known as the Knob-heads. Not that they ever paid much attention to what the clubs were called. My brilliant humor, once again wasted.

Ironically, part of the reason I started hanging out at home more, in addition to the fact that we couldn't do band activities at Sam Hellerman's, was that I had started to warm up to Little Big Tom, even actually almost kind of liked being around him sometimes. But to them it looked like I had suddenly lost interest in all the clubs and afterschool activities. That was a Danger Sign. Then they found the lyrics and pamphlet and that had tipped the whole thing over. I screwed up. And now I was looking at a vast stretch of inept suicide-watch activity from the parental units for some time to come.

"You're not going to like this, chief," Little Big Tom began. What? What could they confiscate in this situation? I was all ears.

"We'd like you to see someone. Just to talk to you and help you work things out."

Out of the three people in that room, there were two in serious need of psychiatric help, and I wasn't one of them. This point would have been lost on them, though, because between them they were already "seeing" a small army of counselors, therapists, psychiatrists, psychologists, analysts, facilitators, and what have you. They thought that was man's natural state. In fact, I was surprised they hadn't tried to force me to go to a shrink long before this, if only in the spirit of trying to provide me with everything they hadn't had as kids.

It was going to be a drag, of course, but as punishments go, I'd certainly had worse.

LINDA'S PANCAKES ON BROADWAY

The following day, Sam Hellerman and I decided to skip PE. The main reason was because we had just started boxing and sometimes that's just too much to take. Sam Hellerman was doing it mostly in solidarity with me. I mean, he didn't really need to, as he had a special talent that made boxing easy for him. But also, he had said, somewhat mysteriously, that there was something important that we needed to discuss, and that he had something to show me. He wouldn't tell me what it was. "Just wait," was all he would say.

There's pretty much nowhere to go in Hillmont except for this place called Linda's Pancakes on Broadway. When all else fails, which is in fact quite often, Sam Hellerman and I end up going there to sit in a booth and drink coffee from these big plastic pitchers they refer to as bottomless cups.

So the state and the school district and the Hillmont school administrators had decided that Sam Hellerman and I would spend second period that day standing in a ring hitting each other, or getting hit by someone else, or watching somebody else hitting somebody else. But instead, at least for this one day, there we were, in a booth at Linda's Pancakes on Broadway, discussing this and that.

Actually, I should explain how PE boxing works. They don't have a real ring. Instead, there's a mat on the floor of the lanai, and everyone stands on the edge of the mat in a kind of human ring while the two poor kids who have to box each other stand in the middle. If one of the boxers gets too close to the human ring, the ring people in that particular area are supposed to shove him back toward the middle. I probably don't have to mention that everybody has to wear the tiny George Michael shorts while this is all going on. It's your basic nightmare.

While the boys are doing boxing, the girls are over on the other side of the lanai doing Rape Prevention, but they'll always come over to watch if there's an interesting matchup, making the whole thing even more embarrassing. There's this pretense, never verbalized without a snicker, that they have boxing to "teach you how to defend yourself." But in reality, it's just a way for a certain type of guy to be able to beat up on a certain other type of guy during class time as well as before and after school.

They're required to stop the festivities at "first blood" (I kid you not, that's the phrase they use). So your best strategy is to try to get hit in the nose and start bleeding as soon as you can and thus spare yourself the rest of the state-mandated beating. Sure, the PE teacher will then lead the class in a rousing chant of "pussy, pussy, pussy" at you, but they're always saying that. Beats getting beat.

Sam Hellerman's special boxing talent was that he got nosebleeds all the time. He was so good at it that he could pretty much start bleeding at will, through the power of his mind. Mr. Donnelly would put him in the ring and roar: "I'm warning you, Hellerman! If you start bleeding before you're hit, there will be hell to pay!" But little Sam Hellerman would just stand there with an angelic look, bleeding away. Mr. Donnelly would glower and yell and turn twenty-three shades of red, but he couldn't touch Sam Hellerman because that would probably have been good for about three or four million dollars, by a conservative estimate. Sam Hellerman's dad is a lawyer, as he makes sure to inform every PE teacher on the first day of class.

The best part, though, is when he leaves the ring to go to the nurse's office and tries to get as much of his blood on as many PE goons and their stuff as he can. I'll say it again: that Sam Hellerman is a genius.

Cutting class wasn't so smart, really, as we'd pay for it later. But sometimes you need a mental health day.

I settled into my side of the booth and looked at Sam Hellerman expectantly. He was cagey, and only seemed to

want to talk about trivial matters rather than this big important thing about which he had called the meeting. Finally, I
just came out and said, "What's the story, Hellerman?"

Now, you have to understand: my day-to-day life was
kind of weird at that time. I was constantly in this frantic,
anxious state, all wound up. I was doing the ear thing more
often than not, and I was hardly sleeping at all. I was spending most of my time thinking furiously about real or imagined
mysteries, many of which, I suspected, could well have no solution. I spent a couple of hours every night working on the
Catcher code when I was supposed to be doing homework. It
would always end in failure, and with my throwing some object across the room in frustration.

Meanwhile, I was having no better luck with the CEH
reading list. *Brighton Rock* was beyond doubt the best book I
had ever read, but I sure didn't know what to make of *The
Journal of Albion Moonlight.* I spent a lot of time "reading" it, but
I never seemed to get anywhere. I couldn't tell you what it was
about or what happened in it if my life depended on it. It's like
this thing was written by a crazy person. Even the printing was
crazy, sometimes tiny, sometimes huge, and sometimes the
sentences and even the words themselves were all out of order.
There was almost half a page with nothing but the word
"look!" repeated over and over again. I don't know anything
about the guy, but whoever he was, I hope he got help.

I was also struggling with the songs for the new band (the
Nancy Wheelers, me on guitar, Sam Hellerman on bass and
Ouija board, first album: *Margaret? It's God. Please Shut Up.*) I
could never get the songs to come out how I wanted. I'd have
a great idea for this brilliant tune where the lyrics and the
melody and the sounds and the arrangement would all com-
plement each other and resolve into a perfect three-minute
encapsulation of a true experience that would play with the

listeners' emotions while simultaneously crushing their skulls. I would start speculating about how it was only a matter of time before they awarded me the Nobel Prize for Rock and Roll, once word of it got round to Sweden. But then I'd actually try to play it or write down the lyrics and it would totally suck.

Finally, there was the Fiona Deal. Fiona seemed more and more distant. I'd spent quite a bit of time riding my bike around various neighborhoods and school areas, scanning all the girls for any who looked even vaguely Fiona-esque. I got nowhere. Eventually, I just dropped it.

I still thought about "giving her the time," of course. But she *had* faded into the background, almost to the point where she was more or less equivalent to all the other imaginary girls whose images I used as masturbatory props. She was as distant as a movie star. Fiona Schmiona. Maybe she went to OMH, maybe she had known who I was, maybe she had been a real fake drama mod, maybe not. Maybe everything she had said was a lie. Maybe I had imagined her. Or maybe she was madly in love with me, and was wandering the earth pining away but could never reveal herself because the Illuminati had kidnapped her parents and had sworn to kill them and detonate a nuclear device they had hidden at Disneyland if she ever made herself known. She was doing it for the children. All of these scenarios were equally plausible. And I have to say I was starting to think I didn't really care too much anymore. That was my attitude.

In view of this, I was floored by what Sam Hellerman said when he finally got to the point.

"I found Fiona."

I dropped my coffee cup.

"She gave you a phony name," said Sam Hellerman, once I had regained my (devil-head) composure and he had stopped laughing–for which I couldn't blame him: I hadn't planned it that way, but the momentary failure of my cup-holding abilities had asserted itself with near-perfect comedic timing.

"Her real name is Deanna," he continued. "And she's a little weird."

He reached into his backpack and pulled out a large red book, which turned out to be last year's yearbook from Immaculate Heart Academy in Salthaven Vista. He opened it to a folded-over page and pointed to a black-and-white picture. There she was: Deanna Schumacher. As I was silently kicking myself for not having considered the Catholic school option as a possible Fiona habitat, he told me what he knew.

Deanna Schumacher was the girlfriend of this guy named Dave, who *was* a CHS fake mod. She had probably made out with me to make him jealous, which was something she was known for doing. She was not a fake mod herself, but rather a generic Catholic schoolgirl, though she was in drama at IHA-SV. She was a little bit psycho and was always doing head trips on her friends and boyfriend. Oh yeah, and by the way: this Dave guy was looking for me and wanted to kick my ass.

She was no longer even in the area. She had moved to Miami with her family just the week before, when her father had suddenly and mysteriously been transferred.

"Miami," I said dubiously. "Florida."

"Or near there," said Sam Hellerman.

I looked at the black-and-white yearbook photo of a dark-haired girl with glasses. She did look a little psycho. The glasses looked about right, though they weren't exactly the same—but people can have different glasses, of course, from year to year. All things considered, she looked quite a bit like the Fiona I remembered, though I don't know if I'd have recognized her if she hadn't been pointed out. My memory of Fiona was idealized and faulty, shaped by the fake fake mod costume and my own fantasies, as I had to acknowledge. In a Catholic schoolgirl uniform she wouldn't, in a sense, have been the same girl. I felt as though I would have been able to pick her belly out of a lineup and to identify what Sam Hellerman would have called her left boobie by touch alone, but maybe not. Girls all have the same parts, basically, and so much of how they look depends on the attitude, expectations, and obsessions of those who are looking at them.

The moving away to Florida part sounded very fake, of course. Maybe Sam Hellerman was just trying to help me "let go" with a little white lie that removed all doubt about her lack of availability. And I appreciated it, I guess. Fiona wasn't real. Whatever. Like I could keep track of all the imaginary girls in my life.

But, see, the truth is, I couldn't quite let go of the idea of Fiona even now that I knew she was fake. Even fake Fiona had a hold on me. I kind of lied about how it was all pure imaginary sex, and how I had stopped daydreaming about a Sex Alliance Against Society with her, even though she was now even more imaginary than she had been before Sam Hellerman showed me the IHA-SV yearbook.

I didn't believe that Miami story for one second, of course. That was just Sam Hellerman trying to be clever and stage-manage my pain, like he does from time to time. He's a born facilitator.

She still lived in Salthaven or Salthaven Vista and went to

Immaculate Heart Academy, Slut Heaven. Of course she did. Except her name was Deanna now instead of Fiona.

Okay. Could there be a future for Deanna Schumacher and me? Well, no. But was it worth continuing to obsess over her anyway? Why the hell not? You know, I could track her down and she would fall for me and break up with her boyfriend and we could go away together. Deanna Schumacher and me, I mean, not me and the boyfriend. And maybe she could even dress up as Fiona for me from time to time. When you think about it, it wouldn't be too different from how grown-up wives dress up in Catholic schoolgirl uniforms for their husbands, except in Deanna Schumacher's case she'd be in her Catholic schoolgirl uniform to begin with and would have to take it off in order to put on the Fiona costume and then put it on again when we were done pleasing each other. Or maybe I could just develop the school uniform fetish myself, so she wouldn't even have to do the fake Fiona thing. I'm sure she'd appreciate that, with her busy schedule and so forth. And you know, once I articulated that thought, I was pretty sure I already *had* started to develop the school uniform fetish. This was promising.

IMBECILE!

Knowing her true identity and where she went to school put the whole Fiona Deal, which had now become the Deanna Schumacher Deal, in a new light. Instead of blindly obsessing and trying to spot her at random, I now knew where to start looking, and it felt like waking up in a new and better world. Sam Hellerman had said I could keep the IHA-SV yearbook– one of his CHS friends had stolen it from an older sister who went there, and didn't care too much about getting it back. I made a note of the name, Wendee Foot, etched in gold lettering on the cover, just in case I needed to contact her for further information. The messages this girl's friends had scribbled in it were pretty hilarious, and that was diverting for at least a while, but other than the photo Sam Hellerman had pointed out, I couldn't find any information on Deanna Schumacher in the yearbook. She wasn't on any teams or in any clubs, not even drama, as Sam Hellerman had indicated. Well, she could have joined this year, I supposed. She didn't even appear to have been in the group class picture–at least, I didn't recognize her if she was.

Once I was back home, just to see, I looked up "Schumacher" in the phone book. No listing. Well, that would have been too easy. I clipped out the little black-and-white photo and put it on my desk, trying to decide if it would be too sad to start carrying it in my wallet. I know, I suck. But you have to give me a break. It was all I had.

I spent the Saturday after the Linda's Pancakes on Broadway meeting staring at Deanna Schumacher's photo, moping, and playing the guitar. The next day was Halloween, and I spent that day doing pretty much the same thing.

When it began to get dark, I broke down and dialed up Sam Hellerman, but he was out. Maybe he was at another CHS party and hadn't invited me this time because he didn't want to risk another Fiona-Deanna fiasco? In fact, I didn't actually believe that Sam Hellerman had gone to a Halloween party, though it was funny to speculate on what kind of goofy-ass costume he would have worn. A month before, I'd have said it was weird that Sam Hellerman hadn't been home, that he was always at home when he wasn't here, but now I just didn't know. At this point it was weird no matter where Sam Hellerman was.

Amanda was out trick-or-treating with her friends. It was a transitional time for her, the last year when trick-or-treating was appropriate, and the first year when all the girls switched from being cats or pumpkins to dressing up as hookers or French maids or slutty celebrities. Little Big Tom had been freaked out by her hoochie mama costume. "Everyone's a ho for Halloween!" she had shouted, and then she had stormed out, slamming the door. Now, that, I thought, is one hell of a song title. I was looking forward to eavesdropping on the family discussion where LBT tried to explain how her Halloween costume was all about disrespect for women and Vietnam, but I knew I would have to wait.

I couldn't think of anything else to do, so I retreated to my room and turned the TV on. Channel two was playing horror movies all night, and *Evil Dead II* had just started. I put on *Rattus Norvegicus,* turned the TV sound down, sat down on my bed, and tried to think of something to do.

I turned to the CEH books, which I had arranged on my desk in a row against the wall, and thought about where to go next with the reading list. I had given it my best shot, but in the end I couldn't make it through *The Journal of Albion Moonlight.* I think the most likely explanation for its existence is that some typesetter wanted to demonstrate all the different typefaces and font sizes and layouts his fancy printing press could do. Back in the days before computers, it must have been pretty impressive. As a story, though, it was a waste of three hundred and thirteen pages. And it told me nothing about my dad. If he went around pretending he was into it, I'd have to say he was one (devil-head) pretentious bastard of a kid. But maybe he tried to read it and didn't get it and gave up on it in frustration just like me. That's how I'd prefer it to have been, but there was no way to know.

I had had an easier time with *Siddhartha,* CEH 1964. It's about this freaky Buddha-wannabe kid, a sort of George Harrison type who wanders the earth looking for enlightenment or whatever. Everybody in the book is all impressed with him, kind of like how the *Catcher* Cult people just love that Holden Caulfield to pieces. Personally, I couldn't really see the attraction, but the book wasn't bad. If *Catcher in the Rye* were a kung fu movie, and HC went up to a mountain to learn some paradoxical truths and some martial arts techniques named after animals from an eccentric old monk, then you'd pretty much have *Siddhartha.* Except they leave out the part where he flies through the air beating up ninjas and finally kills the guy who murdered his family when he was a little kid in the flashback at the beginning: maybe that's in *Siddhartha II.* There were several passages that my dad had marked by drawing lines on the outer margin in pencil, sometimes with question marks and once with a kind of emphatic exclamation point. It made me think of my dad as an intense, yet deep and sensitive, guy.

One corner of a page of *Siddhartha,* CEH 1964, had been folded over to mark the place, which happened to be the best scene in the book, where this sexy girl named Kamala kisses the main guy to reward him for reciting a poem about how hot she is. It reminded me of how Fiona-Deanna had made out with me because she was impressed with my powerful vocabulary, and somehow that felt encouraging. It gave me a feeling of everything coming together.

But there was also, at the top of one page, a spot where the word "help" had been written heavily in pen over and over, so that it had almost pierced through the paper and etched the word into several pages below it. That seemed kind of desperate looking and sad, especially as it contrasted starkly with the serene tone of the book itself. In any other situation, this would have struck me as unremarkable. I'd done the same sort of thing countless times in my notebooks. But because it had been written by my dad, however long ago, it was simply excruciating to look at. I would never know what had caused him that kind of distress, though I suppose he had found comfort in *Siddhartha,* which was yet another thing I probably would never quite understand all the way. I shook the thought out of my head.

Well, at least *Siddhartha* was short, which was the way to go when choosing books from the CEH library. I decided the next one would be *Slan,* CEH 1965, which was short as well.

Evil Dead II had ended, and channel two was about fifteen minutes into *Blood on Satan's Claw.* I let the last couple of songs on *Pink Flag* play out, and then put on *Black Rose.* I carefully replaced *Siddhartha* in its slot amongst the other books, feeling a bit solemn as I always did when handling them. Then I stood there staring at them for a while. Something was bugging me. Something about the books . . . Many of the titles would make great band names. I had always thought that one of the best potential band names among them was *La Peste,* CEH 1965, a book I hadn't even considered trying to read because it was in French, and I was pretty sure it would be too tough for me, despite my mastery of the present tense and telling time in the twenty-four-hour system. But obviously, my dad had been able to read French all right, if this had been among his books. I couldn't imagine reading a whole book in French. The educational system must have been quite a bit better back then, I thought, before they decided to adopt the collage 'n' *Catcher* curriculum.

Now, if this were a murder mystery, and I were a weird Belgian guy with a big mustache, this is the point where I would suddenly stop dead, drop my tiny glass of chocolate liqueur, and say something like "But no! But I have been an imbecile! *Imbécile!*" And then you'd have to wait another fifty pages or so to find out exactly what the hell I had been talking about. But I won't do that to you.

The salutation of Tit's note had been *mon cher monsieur,* "my dear sir" in French and kind of a standard French way to start a letter. I hadn't thought too much about it before. But the thought that struck me while I was standing there in front of the books, looking at *La Peste,* CEH 1965, and listening to Thin Lizzy was: what if *mon cher monsieur* hadn't been a real part of the note, but rather part of the key, like the scratched-out and corrected date?

Well, that was it. Tit had been very, very complicated about it, though and even with the key from the *Catcher* I almost didn't realize I had cracked the code. But after a lengthy scribbling session, I pretty much had it. The salutation was indeed an indication to the recipient that the coded message would be in French. Tit had left out the punctuation and accents, regrouped the characters in strings of fourteen, *and* recopied the resulting coded message backward before arranging the fourteen-character clumps underneath each other—man, those boys must have had a lot of time on their hands.

It decoded to:

"J'ai vu MT hier soir et je l'ai ramonée sec. Détails à suivre. Vas-tu aux funerailles? J'aimerais meiux être ligoté et fouetté."

At first, though I recognized it as French, I wasn't able to figure out exactly where all the accents and spaces and punctuation went, though it helped that the capital letters had remained in the code-parallelogram. The word *mieux* had been misspelled. As I've said, despite three plus years of study, French wasn't my strongest suit. But I was highly motivated.

In the end I had to ask Madame Jimenez-Macanally a few discreet questions at school the next day, but eventually I was able to punctuate and translate it.

The first line threw me a bit because of the verb *ramoner,* which I'd never seen before but which grabbed my attention as it would any Ramones fan. According to the dictionary, it literally means "to scrub out or vigorously clean a chimney." Here, though, it was clearly being used as a sexual metaphor. To ramone someone dry, as Tit's sentence had it, is to, well, you know—do I have to draw a diagram, folks? It couldn't have had anything to do with the actual Ramones—unless that's where they got their name or something?

Anyway, the whole thing translates, roughly, as:

"I saw MT last night and I ramoned her dry. Details to follow. Are you going to the funeral? I would rather be tied up and whipped."

I learned more French translating those sentences with a dictionary and a grammar and a weird conversation with Madame Jimenez-Macanally than I had in three-plus years of Jean and Claude, I can tell you that.

November

THE FESTIVAL OF LIGHTS

I can't even begin to describe how hard it was to refrain from mentioning the *Catcher* code to Sam Hellerman on the way to school the next day.

He was in a buoyant mood when I met him at the usual corner. He wanted to discuss his new theory:

"Just think what a better world we would have," he said, "if David Bowie had never met Brian Eno. That was the worst tragedy of the twentieth century."

"Really?" I said.

In fact, I disagreed rather strongly with this, but my mind was on other things, and, to be honest, Sam Hellerman was getting on my nerves. Who wanted to think about Eno and Bowie when there was a Deanna Schumacher and a *Catcher* code on the menu? I didn't even bother trying to ask him where he had been on Halloween night: I knew he'd only lie, which would demean us both. Plus, I still had some questions to ask Madame Jimenez-Macanally about the French text before I could be totally sure what the message said, so I was preoccupied. I gave him the silent treatment for most of the way. But I doubt he noticed: it wasn't too different from how things were when I was not giving him the silent treatment.

I found Madame Jimenez-Macanally in her classroom during Brunch and asked her my questions about accents, punctuation, funerals, ramoning, and being tied up and whipped. She had more questions about my questions than I thought necessary or polite, and she was giving me a peculiar look the whole time, but I ended up getting what I needed. Then, when class started, I'd catch her staring at me from time to time with this mystified expression.

"Mack Anally has a crush on you," said Yasmynne Schmick, noticing.

That was kind of funny, but I had other concerns. Because Madame J.-M. and I were basically in the same mystified boat. The "solved" puzzle was still a puzzle. What the hell did it mean?

Now, the school calendar for November is dominated by this thing called "Homecoming." I'm not all that clear on it, but I know it involves a football game, a "Rally," and a dance, plus a slew of other pointless and embarrassing activities intended to promote the whole thing. It's nothing to do with me. They always decorate the Hillmont Knight with flowers and blue and white ribbons. And this year, they had signs up everywhere trying to stoke excitement over Spirit Week: "Come See the Spirit Towel!" Even if I knew what the hell the Spirit Towel was, I don't think I'd tell you: I'm pretty sure we're all better off not knowing.

I have my doubts as to whether even the full-on normal people cared very much about Homecoming or Spirit Week, to be honest. But definitely no one in my world (which I have to concede now included not only Sam Hellerman but also, by extension, the drama hippies) had the slightest interest in any of this stuff, other than to mock it. Yasmynne Schmick, who had by now become my regular Advanced Conversation partner, had said: "I can't help it, Moe—I'm obsessed with the Spirit Towel." Which I thought was pretty funny, actually.

But with the announcement of the Spirit Week activities came some more interesting and surprising news. The Hillmont powers that be, for reasons that remain unclear, had decided to hold a "Battle of the Bands" instead of a Pep Rally for December. Well, first they called it a Battle of the Bands, but someone objected to the word "Battle" as being too competitive. Which is hilarious, because "Battle" is far too gentle a word to use to describe the game of survival of the most psychotic that is the soul and essence of Hillmont High School and that would have made Charles Darwin himself weep and wish he'd never invented a theory to elucidate it. Some things are better left unelucidated, he would have said, and it would have been hard to disagree with him.

So anyway, they changed the name to "Convergence of the Bands," and then to "Convergence!" because they didn't want to restrict it to bands. Then, and why I'll never know, they changed the name to "Festival of Lights." But essentially we were looking at your basic high school talent show. It was going to happen during fourth period–lunch–fifth period at the end of the second week of December, six weeks away.

"Green Sabbath should totally try to get on this," said Sam Hellerman, during one of his increasingly rare appearances in my presence instead of in the shadow of the Hillmont Knight and Celeste Fletcher's ass. He was talking about Green Sabbath, of course, Monsignor Eco-druid on guitar, The Grim Recycler on bass and industrial sabotage, Todd "Percussion" Panchowski on drums, percussion, acoustic and semiacoustic drums, cymbals, tambourines, cowbells, chimes, gongs, toms, shaker eggs, bongos, stick clicks, wood blocks, percussion, percussion and more percussion. First album *Our Drummer Is Kind of Full of Himself.*

I looked at him dubiously. How could we ever get on it? You had to submit an audition tape to this group of normal students supervised by Mr. Teone. A tape of us actually playing, I was pretty sure, would automatically disqualify us, maybe even permanently, from playing anywhere, even with a more sympathetic panel of judges. Anyway, it sounded like a Festival of Insufferable Tedium and Aggravation to me. Did we even want to get in on it?

"We do," said Sam Hellerman, "and we can." And he

gave me that "leave it to me" look. So I figured he had a plan.

At the time, I found it difficult to see how any good could come of such a thing. And as it turns out, I guess I was mostly right.

DR. HEXSTROM

My first "therapy" appointment was also during that first week of November. My mom insisted on driving me there, even though I wanted to ride my bike. That was to make sure I wouldn't duck out, which was a valid concern. She checked me in with the receptionist but didn't stick around to see the shrink with me–maybe that was against the rules or something.

The psychiatrist was Dr. Judith Hexstrom. My plan had been to give her the old freaky-youth-genius treatment and try to unnerve her with silence and unreadable facial expressions. I was thinking maybe if I could convince her I was legitimately crazy I could at least get some medication that I could give to Sam Hellerman for a Christmas present. It didn't work out that way, though.

For one thing, to my surprise, I kind of liked Dr. Hexstrom. She wasn't young or pretty, but there was something about her face that I liked, even though it was my considered opinion that her whole profession wasn't much more than a shameless racket. And she was by far the most intelligent adult I'd ever talked to.

Here's how sharp Dr. Hexstrom was: I happened to mention Mr. Teone's "naked day of zombies" comment, as an example of his bizarre behavior and of how weird normal people can be. "Pretty strange, huh?" I said.

"Not really. If you were wearing that shirt."

I looked down at my T-shirt, then raised my head and gave her the look that says "how so?"

Dr. Hexstrom said: "*Neca eos omnes. Deus suos agnoscet.* It's Latin for 'Kill them all, and God will know his own.' From the Middle Ages, the Crusades."

Damn. I *had* been wearing my "Kill 'em All" shirt that day, and he had made me turn it inside out. And Dr. Hexstrom's phrase did sound kind of like what Mr. Teone had said, allowing for his speech impediment. It made more sense than "day of suicide-osity," anyway, though I'd still classify it as a bizarre episode, especially with all that laughing.

I looked at Dr. Hexstrom, and my look said: "how the hell did you figure that out?"

Then, when she didn't respond, I said, out loud, if I remember correctly: "How the hell did you figure that out?"

"It's well known," she said imperiously.

It's well known. Not by me it wasn't. I'm not sure she was able to pick it up, but I gave her the look that said: "well, ladi-da."

I had expected Dr. Hexstrom to plunge into the suicide thing right away, but instead, the first thing she said was, "That's an unusual book."

She was talking about *The Doors of Perception,* CEH 1966. I know I said that the next CEH book on the reading list was *Slan.* I had started it, and it was pretty cool. It was about this freaky kid whose dad is dead. He and his mom are members of a mutant alien species called slans that have telepathic powers because of tendrils on their heads, which they try to disguise by hiding them in their hair-dos. But the normal people still pursue them and try to exterminate them. They got the dad already when the main slan was a little kid, and they get the mom, too, right at the beginning of the book. I could totally relate.

But there had been a change in plans since I solved the *Catcher* code and gained a new interest in underlining, so I put *Slan* aside temporarily. Only two of the books had a whole lot of actual underlining: *The Doors of Perception* and *The Naked and the Dead*. *The Naked and the Dead* was the one that had been inscribed only CH with no date, so I wasn't even sure it belonged with the others. However, it was the one where the markings had seemed the most codelike. There were individual words underlined, sometimes very insignificant ones like "of" or "very"; some were circled and sometimes only parts of words were underlined or circled. If there was an encoded message in there, though, I couldn't find it. And I had spent hours and hours trying.

I had originally shied away from this book because I was worried it had to do with the Grateful Dead and nudity, and, well, let me put it this way: if you can imagine a more alarming combination, your imagination is quite a bit better than mine. Then I realized it was about war, and it was more like naked people and dead people, two of my favorite subjects, so I thought I'd give it a try.

Now, this book was by a guy named Norman Mailer, and he was a piece of work. You know how Holden Caulfield said "giving her the time?" Well it was the same with Norman Mailer. He said "fug." I kid you not. Like "this is a fugging nightmare!" or "go fug yourself." You know, it's no wonder everyone was all crazy and weird in the sixties, if everything was being run by prissy grandma types like Holden Caulfield and Norman Mailer.

In the end I couldn't take much of *The Naked and the Dead,* and I put it aside for later. It wasn't like it was even a real CEH book anyway. I went for *The Doors of Perception* instead, because it had a lot of underlining, too, though admittedly it didn't look very code-y.

The Doors of Perception is about this guy who takes a lot of drugs to try to see what it's like to be a crazy person. It's kind of interesting, but the guy is pretty full of himself and a bad writer, too. He seems to forget what he was going to say around halfway through many of his long, complicated sentences, and then he tries to cover it up by spattering the page with highfalutin words that I swear he just made up. *30 Days to a More Annoying Vocabulary.* If Holden Caulfield were to read it, he'd say something like "Gee, Wally, that's swell and junk, but I feel all crumby on account of how it's so phony and all."

Still, I got a kick out of watching the drug guy try to pretend he was doing his drugs for some noble purpose rather than just indulging himself and getting high and trying to show off how with-it he was. It's cool if you want to do drugs, but if you go around claiming it's like discovering Antarctica or curing cancer you're not fooling anyone but yourself.

Believe it or not, that's pretty much what Dr. Hexstrom and I talked about, and she even kind of seemed to see what I was getting at. She was the only adult I had ever met who was *Catcher* aware but not necessarily *Catcher* devoted. She said she thought HC needed medication, and we had a good laugh about that one. She was all right.

Dr. Hexstrom was very interested in the CEH reading list, which I hadn't intended to tell her about, but somehow I couldn't stop myself in the end. I didn't mention Tit or the *Catcher* code, of course, but we did talk a lot about *Brighton Rock* and even a little about the guy I accidentally beat up (though I downplayed it a bit and left out most of the blood, in consideration of the sensibilities of my audience). It was nice to talk to someone about a book without being worried that they would make you copy a page out of it, even though it probably wasn't going to cure my unspecified mental problems and even though I very much doubted it would turn out to be worth a hundred and fifty bucks.

I think it was the most I'd ever spoken out loud in one sitting, and in spite of myself, I actually had a pretty good time. In fact, we never made it to the suicide thing. It was just like on TV. She said, "I'm sorry but I'm afraid our time is up." I doubt she was actually all that sorry, but I kind of was.

SISTERHOOD IS POWERFUL

Remember how the world came loose from its hinges and the fabric of reality began to unravel thread by thread and the space-time continuum got all chopped up and out of order all of a sudden? Well, that was just a passing thing.

What I'm getting at is, after weeks of transgressions against the established norms of dating mandated by international law, Née-Née Tagliafero abruptly ditched Pierre Butterfly Cameroon, bringing to a close one of the most curious episodes in Hillmont High School history. She started going instead with an eminently normal slow-witted alpha sadist named Mike Moon, who promptly proceeded to beat the hell out of Pierre Butterfly Cameroon in the parking lot before first period, to the evident amusement of a small crowd of onlookers and with the apparent approval of sweet little Née-Née as well. Like I said, back to normal. WAGBOG.

Sam Hellerman's stint of spending every single lunch period with the drama hippies also abruptly ended on the same day: he met me at around locker 414, like in the old days, just as if the intervening weeks hadn't even happened. And, you know, maybe I should have spotted it sooner, but there were just too many coincidences in bloom in and around this particular patch of the Sam Hellerman garden.

We were in the cafeteria. I was staring at Sam Hellerman with the question on my face, and he knew what the question was without my having to say it out loud. His earlier evasiveness had evaporated, and he actually seemed in a pretty good mood, though I didn't know why yet.

"There's some stuff I haven't told you," he said, as though that were something I didn't already know.

Then Sam Hellerman began to tell the following story:

It seems that the Celeste Fletcher trio, along with the Syndie Duffy group and a few others as well, had this kind of club that they called the Sisterhood. (I know—I'm eye-rolling and gagging, too.) They had a lot of complicated activities and rules and procedures, but the one that concerned Sam Hellerman was this game called Dud Chart. Or, I guess it was more like a contest. The name comes from this board game for girls called Mystery Date, where you would open a door in the middle of the board and the guy behind it would either be a dream, meaning a Greg Brady–looking guy with big fluffy sideburns in a purple velvet tuxedo, or a dud, meaning a guy who pretty much looked like Sam Hellerman and me. It was pretty kitschy retro popular. I think Mystery Date was even the theme of one of the proms last year.

In Dud Chart, they had this chart of all the dorky, nerdy guys in school, and the object was for each girl to score points on the chart by flirting with them or making out with them in various ways. Like you'd get a certain number of points for flirting, for kissing, for getting to different bases, or for walking around like Née-Née Tagliafero did with Pierre Butterfly Cameroon, which had had one of the highest point values because it was so public. But it all had to be in public to some degree so it could be observed and documented. Different guys had different point values: the less desirable the guy, the higher the score. It was originally supposed to be just flirting and making out, but like a lot of dare-type situations, the stakes escalated as the game went on.

"So basically," I said, "you're talking about an institutionalized Make-out/Fake-out."

"Pretty much," he said, a little curtly, and continued to explain the system.

I supposedly had a pretty high point value, mostly because of the now-famous PE Rape-Prevention balls incident, which had made a big splash. Bobby Duboyce was near the top, too, because of his helmet. But here's where Sam Hellerman came in. Celeste Fletcher, hoping to gain unfair advantage over the other girls, had hired Sam Hellerman as a kind of consultant. He pretty much knew everyone on the chart, and had all sorts of information about them that might be useful, and might even, she thought, be able to help set some of them up. Sam Hellerman's stipulation was that she use her influence to keep both him and me off the chart and out of the game, which she had somehow been able to do. I said a silent prayer of thanks: my life definitely didn't need another formal humiliation ritual.

They had planned to do some kind of splashy announcement of the results at one of the pep rallies. I don't know, maybe passing out a zine with all the scores, or posting the chart? That's just a guess. It didn't actually happen because before they could complete the game Syndie Duffy had had a big falling-out with Lorra Jaffe. I don't know the details, but the whole Sisterhood had basically collapsed in a shambles of infighting and scheming against one another, and Dud Chart had been forgotten in the excitement. Lorra Jaffe had focused her energy on trying to destroy Syndie Duffy instead of winning the relatively inconsequential make-out-with-dorks contest, and everyone else had followed suit.

It's pretty hard to keep these elaborate schemes going for too long, though they can sometimes coast along on their own for a while. Meanspiritedness is powerful. I have no doubt that Née-Née Tagliafero's team would have won, though. The Pierre Butterfly Cameroon gambit had been so spectacular that it was still being talked about several towns down the strip months later.

In the end, the Dud Chart fiasco was an object lesson in how getting involved with normal people, if you're not normal yourself, or even if you're subnormal/drama, is always trouble. You start by allowing your own world to be corrupted by their warped values, and then you gradually start using their sadistic methods and eventually end up adopting bits of their sick ideology. And even then, when you have become just like them, they will eventually turn on you anyway. Normal people are savage beasts. Even Sam Hellerman hadn't been immune: he sold out his people, though the corruption thankfully hadn't been deep enough to induce him to betray the sacred bonds of alphabetical order. It's sad. I imagine some of those girls at least had been decent, nice people before they were infected with normalcy by exposure to Lorra Jaffe. Maybe not, though.

I *was* impressed by the deal Sam Hellerman had managed to get for his services as Celeste Fletcher's Dork Consultant. Two full bottles of Percodan (from her dad's pharmacy), a half-bottle of Valium (from her mom's night table), twenty dollars, and a blow job. No way did I believe the blow job part at first, but he looked so serious and, um, pleased with himself while he was saying it that I even almost started to believe it. Or maybe I just wanted to believe that there were circumstances where it was conceivable that a

Sam Hellerman could get a blow job, even an insincere one, from a Celeste Fletcher. And if you are under the impression that I was not burning with envy over said insincere blow job, I can assure you that you are quite mistaken.

According to Sam Hellerman, anyway, Celeste Fletcher had been a Sister of her word despite the cancelled contest. But she had held out till the end of the term of the deal before delivering the i. b. j. as a kind of final payment, which partly explained his searching looks in her direction out there on the lawn (he had been keeping an eye on his business interests, among other things) and his seeming indifference now that the transaction had been completed. On learning this, it occurred to me that oral sex would probably have been worth a lot of points in their game and that maybe Sam Hellerman *had* been in the running for the Make-out/Fake-out after all without his knowledge. Or maybe he had known, but they hadn't known he'd known. Sometimes it's hard to tell who's faking out whom in the battle of the sexes. It hardly matters, though. A blow job is a blow job. Or so I am given to understand.

The Hellerman/Fletcher eye-ray/ass phenomenon had been pretty spectacular, though, and I still wasn't sure, so I asked one last question: was it all just business, or did he really have the hots for Celeste Fletcher?

"Henderson," he said, as he does when he wants me to know he's being serious, "I have the hots for everyone."

I could see his point.

COINCIDENCES WILL DO THAT TO YOU

Meanwhile, it was time to reassess the *Catcher* code. There wasn't any direct evidence that the note had in fact been addressed to my dad, but it was a fair assumption. So my dad had had a friend, a Sam Hellerman–ish figure, named Tit, and they used to give each other coded notes. Probably there had been many, many other such notes, because such elaborate methods only develop over time, and not if you're just dabbling. Each of the scribbled dates in the *Catcher* had potentially been keys to notes that were now lost. The note preserved in *A Separate Peace* was, I was guessing, a tiny remnant of a vast body of other coded notes, like a dinosaur's fossilized rib. The more bones you find, the easier it is to imagine what the dinosaur might have looked like when it lived. If you only have the one rib, it's harder, and the results will be sketchier. More notes would have made it easier to see the total picture of my dad and Tit and their world, but I only had the one note to go on. It was clear, though, that it was a pretty weird world.

I knew right off the bat that the picture was going to be distorted, but that didn't prevent me from asking some questions. What kind of things did they encode? It appeared that they were in the habit of discussing more important, meaningful matters than Sam Hellerman and I ever had when we were playing our code games. Our coded messages were entirely trivial. For my dad and Tit, it was all about sexual conquests and dead people, neither of which had ever figured prominently in my and Sam Hellerman's lives, though I guess Sam Hellerman was showing some promise in the former category. Moreover, I got the impression that Tit and my dad weren't doing it just for fun but because they really didn't want anyone else to read what they were writing.

I could understand why the sexual stuff was coded: in the sixties, everybody was all uptight about sex, and I bet you would have got in trouble for writing about how you had ramoned someone. But there was something odd about the fact that "the bastard is dead" had not been deemed worthy of being encoded, but "are you going to the funeral?" had been. Or maybe the bastard who was dead wasn't the same dead guy they were having the funeral for? Or maybe "the bastard is dead" is some quotation, like the Superman reference, that I wasn't aware of. It could have been sex again, though. The being tied up and whipped thing, I mean, though that's just an expression, too, in a way.

Tit's question, however, had an answer. I had no doubt that my dad had in fact gone to the funeral. The date on Timothy J. Anderson's funeral card from *The Seven Storey Mountain* was March 13, 1963. It didn't square with the date on the note, but of course that wasn't a real date; and "3/[something]/63" had been written in the *Catcher*. This pretty much had to be the funeral Tit had been asking about. Funerals don't come up that often in a fifteen-year-old's life.

So Timothy J. Anderson was dead, whether or not he had been "the bastard," and my dad had gone to the funeral. He had had a book with him at the time, as always, and had put the memorial card in it, and maybe used it as a bookmark. There wasn't much information on the card, just the date, a generic-sounding quotation from the Bible, and the location: St. Mary Star of the Sea in San Francisco. The other card in *The Seven Storey Mountain*, from Happy Day Dry Cleaners with One-Hour Martinizing, had no date, of course, but it happened to be located in roughly the same neighborhood as the church, if I wasn't mistaken. All that proved was that he attended the funeral and visited the dry cleaners in the same neighborhood during the period when he was reading *The Seven Storey Mountain*. I knew my dad had grown up in the city, but I didn't know where–I note-to-selfed that I should find a way to ask my mom discreetly.

I hadn't quite finished *The Doors of Perception* yet, but it was clear that *The Seven Storey Mountain* was the book I should be reading, even though it looked kind of boring. I picked it up to flip through it and almost dropped it in surprise, because the title page had a quote from the Bible, and it was the same one that had been printed on Timothy J. Anderson's funeral card: "for I tell you that God is able of these stones to raise up children to Abraham."

It kind of made me shiver like when you're afraid of something spooky. Coincidences will do that to you.

THE ART ENSEMBLE OF CHICAGO

If we were really going to be in this Festival of Lights thing, we had our work cut out for us. We didn't sound—what's the word I'm looking for? "Good"? Yes, that's the one: we didn't sound good. We had grand ambitions but limited talent and finesse, and we had less than six weeks to get our act together.

Nevertheless, choosing the band name, stage names, credits, and first album title for your first performance during a midday talent exhibition in the high school auditorium are some of the most important decisions in a band's career, and we gave them a great deal of thought.

Eventually, we settled on Balls Deep, Comrade Galhammer on guitar, Our Dear Leader on bass and embroidery, the Lonely Dissident on Real Fancy and Important Percussion, first album *We Control the Horizontal*. We were going for a kind of communist guerilla/seventies porn vibe. If we had had the time or ability we would have grown mustaches and chest hair. That wasn't possible, but we did have big medallions and little blue Chinese hats with red stars on them from the surplus store, and these huge white shoulder holsters that looked great with the black mechanic's jumpsuits we got from the St. Vincent de Paul. I swiped Little Big Tom's Che Guevara T-shirt, which looked pretty cool when I unzipped the jumpsuit down to Che's cute little chin and positioned my medallion over his nose.

Amanda, who has a lot of artistic talent, even painted us a big banner, following Sam Hellerman's specifications, though I think she put a lot of herself into it, too. It was very seventies, with some silhouetted figures in educational kama sutra poses along the bottom, and a big AK-47 on either side.

"You'll never get away with this," she said, and I supposed she was probably right. It did look great, though.

Sam Hellerman's idea for the audition tape was simple: just make a tape of a real, harmless band and put our name on it. Well, not our full name. We were going to be B.D. till the day of the show. We ended up putting some of Little Big Tom's bland elevator rock on the tape.

I felt bad because Little Big Tom came in while we were making the tape and was like over the moon because he thought we were interested in his music. We had to humor him and listen to him deliver around six hundred speeches about fusion and the Art Ensemble of Chicago and Chicano and Latino influences on pretentious jazzy pseudorock. I think it was probably the happiest I'd ever seen him. And I also felt bad about the fact that after he left we kind of made fun of the funny way he said Latino, like he was the Frito Bandito or something. I felt bad, but I did it anyway, because I'm only human. I was ashamed of myself and depressed afterward, though, which is human, too, I guess. Being human is an excuse for just about everything, but it also kind of sucks in a way.

Now that we had laid the groundwork, all we had to do was try to convince Todd Panchowski to show up to some practices for a change. Sam Hellerman said he'd get right on it.

A WEIRD, WEIRD THING

I was scheduled to visit Dr. Hexstrom's office every Tuesday for the foreseeable future. In our second session, during Spirit Week, she continued to talk to me about books and my dad's teenage library, never even bringing up the suicide thing. Or rather, I talked about the books. Strangely, I was doing most of the talking. Usually my role in a conversation is just to stare at the other person till they lose track of what they're trying to say and eventually give up. But with Dr. Hexstrom, it was almost like these roles were reversed. Sometimes her facial expressions would communicate things like "oh, come off it," or "I see what you're getting at," or "I have no idea what you're talking about right now." Other times her face would be like that of a blank, unreadable mannequin head.

I wasn't used to this role, and I was embarrassed by how I sounded when I tried to speak like that. In my head, my thoughts always sound so good and persuasive and witty and well constructed, even when I'm confused about something. I can be addled, or totally lost, or even feeling crazy, but I usually have at least some confidence in my ability to describe the confusion, even if I don't have any idea what the hell I'm doing. Out loud, though, it's a mess. I sound like way more of an idiot than I like to think I am. I'm worse than Little Big Tom. It was only because I liked and trusted Dr. Hexstrom so much that I could handle the humiliation—I would have run from the room screaming if anybody else had been there.

Anyway, as I explained to Dr. Hexstrom during our second ride on the funky mental-health express, the main guy in *The Doors of Perception* really is an ass. At one point, he picks up *The Tibetan Book of the Dead,* opens it at random, and finds great significance in this quotation: "O nobly born, let not thy mind be distracted." Mmm, deep. I guess if you're on drugs all the time, and if you're confident that everyone will be all impressed by the fact that you're o. d. all the t., and if you make sure you get in at least one mention of *The Tibetan Book of the Dead*, you can get away with scribbling down any old thing, and pretending it's a book. And everyone will just go along with it. Or it was like that in the sixties, anyway. The *Doors of Perception* guy is a Little Big Tom type, only much less loveable. You get lost in one of his convoluted sentences and you may never find your way back again: just light a signal fire with a couple of otherwise unattested adverbs and hope the rescue squad notices you and sends in a helicopter to fly you out. The book is short, but it took what seemed like several lifetimes to be over, and when it finally was over I felt as though I had just been informed that I didn't have terminal cancer after all. There was another "book" in the same volume called *Heaven and Hell*, but I was confident that this guy would have nothing to teach me about hell that I had not already directly experienced while slogging through *The Doors of Perception*, so I decided to give it a miss.

The Seven Storey Mountain started off slow, but at least you could tell it was about something real, not just some poseur showing off. The main reason I started reading it was to see if I could figure out if there was a reason why the funeral card and the book shared the same scriptural quotation. So far I couldn't tell about that, but the book was strangely absorbing. It reminded me of *Slan*, a bit. It's about this weird, slightly freaky kid whose mom is dead and whose dad is this crazy artist. He reminded me a little of me, too, to be honest. Well, he's not quite as freaky as me or the slan kid, maybe, but I could tell his true freakiness was scheduled to come out later, since he drops a lot of hints right from the beginning that he's going to end up becoming a monk at the end. That sort of blows the suspense, though maybe the excitement is all in how he ends up getting there—the best stories are sometimes like that.

I hadn't even known they still had monks outside of D and D, kung fu movies, and heavy metal albums. But I have this weird interest in priests and churches and that sort of thing because the seventh-grade aptitude test and my derogatory nickname set me up for it. I don't know if it has occurred to you, but I couldn't help thinking that maybe the dim but well-intentioned social engineer who had designed that aptitude test had read *The Seven Storey Mountain* and incorporated it into the test, so that when I answered questions indicating that I was a weird, slightly freaky kid with one parent missing like this slanlike monk-to-be character, the test said "ding! Clergy!"

If that's the case, I bet the *Seven Storey Mountain* guy never dreamed that his book would set in motion a process that fifty years later would cause a fourteen-year-old rock and roller in suburban California to have as his derogatory nickname an abbreviation for Child Molester. Or maybe he knew all along that that's what would happen. And wrote the book anyway, the bastard.

So I had to explain to Dr. Hexstrom about Chi-Mo in order to talk about my *Seven Storey Mountain* theory. I could tell she didn't believe me at first, but then I could tell she did. She seemed pretty taken aback by it. I can see why. It's a weird, weird thing.

NATURE'S MARVELS

We had known it was coming, and eventually it did, the day after my second Dr. Hexstrom session. To pay us back for skipping boxing to discuss Deanna Schumacher at Linda's Pancakes on Broadway, Mr. Donnelly decided to subject Sam Hellerman and me to this thing they call a "grudge match." That's when they put two best friends in the ring of sub-human PE students. There's this theory that such fights will be especially vicious and entertaining because of the fighters' long history with each other and because they're more likely to react with indignation when attacked by one another. "Grudge match" doesn't seem like the most appropriate term for it, but that's what they call it, being psychopathic semi-literates with vocabularies that are, let's face it, not all that powerful.

This is the sort of thing that gets everyone really excited around here. The girls took time off from Rape Prevention to crowd around and watch. The normal guys in the class even pushed pause on their "who you callin' faggot, homo?" tape loop. Which rarely happens: this was a big occasion. Mr. Donnelly cranked up his facial hue till he was approximately the color of ketchup and opened the proceedings in the usual way: he made us touch our gloves together, bellowed "Don't bleed till you're hit, Hellerman! I mean it!" and trotted back-ward to the corner of the mat. Then he shouted, as he always does: "Commence!"

Well, it was a dumb idea, of course, because everyone knew that bleeding before he was hit was precisely what Sam Hellerman intended to do, and that I wasn't going to hit him anyway. In other words, there wasn't destined to be much dork-on-dork drama, and the crowd was going to be disap-pointed. But in fact Sam Hellerman just stood there for a long while, staring at me. I shot him a puzzled look, and everyone shifted a little uncomfortably, as mystified as I was. I was al-most starting to wonder if something had snapped inside his brain and he really intended to go through with "boxing" me, but then I realized what he was up to. He was trying to stall as long as possible, knowing that once he and his sponta-neously bloody nose had finally pushed off to the nurse's of-fice, I might still have to face another opponent. I doubted he'd be able to stall long enough, but I appreciated the ges-ture. I focused my mind on my own nose as though it were Fiona-Deanna's candle, but try as I might, I just couldn't make the blood flow Hellerman style–that's why I don't call myself a hypnotizer.

The crowd started the customary chant of "pussy, pussy, pussy," though some were saying "kill, kill, kill," which was ludicrously wishful thinking, under the circumstances. Some of them started trying to shove us farther into the ring toward each other. Mr. Donnelly, his face now throbbing and glow-ing and looking just a bit like a Lava lamp, was still shouting, "Commence! Commence!"

It was at this point, amidst all the shoving, that someone successfully "pantsed" Sam Hellerman. That is to say, some-one grabbed his gay little blue and white George Michael shorts by the hem of each leg and yanked them down, so that he was standing there with the g. l. b. & w. GMS's around his ankles, looking extremely ludicrous, wearing nothing but his Boogie Knights T-shirt and his rather ill-fitting jockstrap. A wave of giggling from the Rape Prevention girls swept the room and shook the rafters. I was glad it wasn't me they had pantsed, not least because of that whole ball-spotting thing, but my heart really went out to Sam Hellerman, especially since he had only been standing there in pantsing position in the first place out of kindness to me.

I don't know if you've ever been in Sam Hellerman's sit-uation, but if you have, you probably already know how dif-ficult it is to pull up any gay little George Michael shorts that may happen to be resting on the floor around your ankles while your hands are encased in boxing gloves. Try it if you don't believe me. It's very hard to get a grip. Sam Hellerman, poor guy, gave it a shot, though, exposing himself to even more indignity as he did so. That was enough for him: he looked up at Mr. Donnelly with a transcendent kind of hatred and opened the floodgates. He even leaned his head back so that the blood bubbled up from his nostrils like lava. Mount Hellerman. It was very impressive.

The crowd recoiled and seemed to hesitate between disappointment and disgust, finally settling on the surly, vapid bewilderment that is pretty much the normal person's natural state. The vein just under the surface of Mr. Donnelly's shiny burgundy forehead slithered like a shrink-wrapped lizard, and I almost thought he was going to say something like "curses, foiled again!" But he didn't say c., f. a. Rather, he sputtered inarticulately and turned his attention to me, a snake eyeing a tasty rodent. Fortunately, I was saved once again through the agency of the solid, dependable Mount Hellerman, which even in the midst of a major eruption had the presence of mind to pull the fire alarm on the way out. It was at best a temporary reprieve, but it was almost worth whatever consequences lay ahead to have the opportunity to witness Mr. Donnelly's face turn from a light burgundy to a hitherto unrecorded shade of deep magenta. One of nature's marvels.

A BROOD OF VIPERS

One thing was certain: the mysteries and puzzles in my life were percolating with more oomph than they ever had previously. Yet I had the distinct impression that I wasn't getting anywhere with them. At any rate, I now had two people to investigate: Deanna Schumacher, the fake Fiona, and Timothy J. Anderson, the dead bastard. If he *was* the dead bastard. He probably was. How many dead people could there be in this thing?

Things were pretty much back to normal between Sam Hellerman and me since he had come clean on the Dud Chart situation. I had hesitated a bit out of lingering resentment, but after he got pantsed in boxing for my sake I relented and decided to let him in on the *Catcher* code, mostly because I was so pleased with myself for having cracked it and I couldn't think of anyone other than Sam Hellerman who would be at all impressed by it. And he *was* impressed, though he claimed he would have easily spotted the French angle–maybe he would have, though I doubt it. I wasn't planning to include him in the fake Fiona arm of the investigation, but he was totally on the Anderson case and insisted we go to the library the minute I showed him Tit's note.

The first thing we did at the library was to use a concordance to look up the biblical quotation about stones and children and Abraham. Sam Hellerman knew how to do that because of his long years of experience as the son of weird German vampire religious fanatics, I guess. It was from Matthew 3:9.

The chapter was kind of hard to understand. John the Baptist is telling some authorities (he calls them a "brood of vipers") that they aren't as powerful as they think they are, I believe.

Sam Hellerman thought it was a more or less generic "question authority" message. "Maybe they were trying to say that this Timothy J. Anderson was some kind of rebel."

He had a point about the Q. A. theme, though it seemed to me there was also a warning of an impending swift and terrible revenge: it reminded me of the movie *Carrie*. J. the B.

was saying, in effect, "Okay, guys, just keep dumping buckets of pig blood on introverted girls at proms, and see what happens—you have no idea what you're playing with here."

I was doubtful that the actual meaning of the quote would have much to tell us about Timothy J. Anderson's character, though. It could be a question authority message, but it could also be about the generic power of God, or about the difference between earthly and spiritual reality, you know, stones versus heaven, earth as opposed to air. It could be all of them at once, or none of them. I hadn't read enough to be sure, but I think the *Seven Story Mountain* guy was getting at the rocks/air thing; plus maybe he was thinking of the stone walls of the monasteries and cathedrals of Europe, which had inspired him as a child and which, I assume, were intended to foreshadow his eventual monk-ization. Who knows? The *SSM* guy chose it for whatever reason he might have had; maybe Timothy J. Anderson or his survivors had chosen it because they were under the influence of that book, or maybe for some other unrelated reason. All I'm saying is that as far as the content goes, the epigraph and the epitaph might as well have said "Have a Nice Day" or "I Heart Cats" for all the difference it would make. You can make something mean anything you want. And you can spend a great deal of time and effort choosing your words and allusions and quotations carefully and hardly anyone will even notice or get it anyway.

But, as usual, while I was giving myself this stern lecture on the meaninglessness of the data we'd just uncovered and how communication is pointless and we're all doomed, Sam Hellerman was noticing the interesting part. I was jolted out of my daydream by the sound of his finger hitting the page of the Jerusalem Bible that lay open on the library table.

"Look," he said in a library whisper.

I went "?" but I soon saw what he was getting at. Right after that quotation comes a kind of threat to the brood of vipers, a variation on the notion of clearing out dead wood:

"Even now the ax is lying at the root of the trees; every tree therefore that does not bear good fruit is cut down and thrown into the fire."

If he is talking about the vipers, that's kind of a mixed metaphor, if I'm not mistaken, but who am I to criticize John the Baptist on stylistic grounds? I'm sure it sounded very convincing at the time. You probably had to be there. Anyway, Tit, remember, had written in the uncoded part of his note: "The bastard is dead. Thrown into the fire."

That sounded like it could possibly be a reference to the biblical passage, though it could also be coincidental. I couldn't decide. But if it was an allusion, this passage from the Bible arguably linked Tit, Timothy J. Anderson, my dad, and the *Seven Storey Mountain* guy. I wasn't sure how, exactly, or what it meant. Maybe it was a common, standard quotation that was used all over the place, though. And maybe "thrown into the fire" was just something people in the sixties used to say whenever a bastard died. You never know.

The Bible passage brought to mind my first response to the note, the *Rosemary's Baby*/Black Sabbath–influenced idea that it had something to do with burning witches. Was there something in that after all? I mean, maybe Tit was implying that Timothy J. Anderson had been some kind of heretic, through a (devil-head) oblique and maybe ironic reference to a biblical text about burning trees and vipers and questioning authority? I really wished I knew more about history, religion, the Bible, witches, the sixties, and so forth. My Academic Achievements were second to none, yet somehow I instinctively knew I wasn't going to solve this particular problem by making a collage or appreciating ethnic food or putting on a skit. In fact, I felt severely handicapped by my lack of knowledge in general, which is not something that comes up very often in my day-to-day life. Or more likely it comes up all the time without my realizing it.

We had discovered something potentially meaningful, yet I didn't get much satisfaction from it. Part of that was because solving one puzzle had simply opened a new set of puzzles, and vaguer ones at that, and I was more confused than ever. But mostly, it was because the whole thing gave me an uncomfortable, creepy feeling. Tit's note was creepy. The Bible passage was creepy. It wasn't what I had been going for with this cute little hobby of trying to investigate my dad's teenage life through clues he had inadvertently left behind. I looked down at all of our research materials spread out on the table: *Catcher*, CEH 1960; the note from Tit; *The Seven Storey Mountain;* the Jerusalem Bible; the concordance; my French dictionary; my various notebooks—I could almost see and feel them morph from charming-exhilarating-profound to sordid-depressing-pointless. For some reason the phrase "brood of vipers" kept echoing unpleasantly in my head. I had this idiotic notion that the materials spread out on the table formed a kind of picture of the world, and that it wasn't a picture I particularly cared for. And my dad's role in this picture was maddeningly dim and indistinct.

I had once again been distracted from the investigation by my own fantasies and emotions. Not Sam Hellerman, though. He was a bespectacled teenage research machine, the dork Woodward and the geek Bernstein rolled into one diminutive, socially inferior package, loading the archives of the *San Francisco Chronicle* into the microfilm viewing machine.

I tried to shake the vipers out of my head. It seemed to

me that the way to approach the *Seven Storey Mountain/*
Timothy J. Anderson problem was not so much through trying to understand the meaning of the text itself but through
thinking of the quotation as a kind of object, an accessory. I
wear a "Kill 'em All" shirt and it pegs me as a Guns-and-
Ammo guy, even if I don't literally want *everybody* to get
killed and sorted out by God. Sam Hellerman's black high-
tops put him in this category made up of the kind of people
who wear Converse All Stars; and if you notice that I, too, am
wearing black high-tops, you could conjecture that I might
have more in common with Sam Hellerman than just shoes.
Perhaps, I thought, it's the same way with quotations from
the Bible as it is with shoes. So this freaky monk character
has Matthew 3:9–11 on the title page of his book; Timothy J.
Anderson had it on his funeral card. Maybe Timothy J.
Anderson was a freaky monk, too. Clergy.

I had been thinking along these lines for a couple of days,
since the Dr. Hexstrom session I described above, when I explained to her about how I ended up being called Chi-Mo.

Now, one thing you have to understand is that my conversations with Dr. Hexstrom involved very few spoken
words. We had quickly reached the point where a great deal
could be communicated through a series of facial expressions
and meaningful looks. It would have looked a bit like telepa-
thy to an outside observer, probably, though it wasn't. We
were like two slans, that Dr. Hexstrom and me.

She got the ball rolling, as usual, with a question: "So, in
view of that, how do you feel about your father being Catholic?"

My look said "how do you mean, Catholic?"

She gave me a pretty complicated look, which basically
meant "what part of Catholic don't you understand?" but also
implied "come, come, now, you're a bright boy–surely such
an obvious fact cannot have escaped you?"

Well, she was right, of course, as I realized when I thought about it. We had never gone to church as a family, that I could recall, and I don't remember there being any talk of my dad's going to church on his own, either. But my dad's funeral had been in a Catholic church and he was buried in a Catholic cemetery, or rather in a Catholic marble filing cabinet for dead people. When I brought it up to Amanda later on, *she* looked at me as though I were as dumb as a bag of dry leaves and said of course he had been Catholic. She even knew the names of the Catholic schools he had attended: Queen of the Universe grammar school and MPB College Preparatory. That's what I get for spending so much time in my own world. Humiliating ignorance of the obvious.

I guess I'd always figured my dad had had the same religious views as my mom. She thought organized religion was for unsophisticated simpletons. She wanted everyone to be "free-thinking" instead. So she embraced "spirituality," which pretty much meant whatever happened to turn up in the Body and Spirit section of her organic cooking magazines.

I'm not any religion myself, but for the record, I'm pretty sure I do believe in God. It's just a feeling I have. I can't prove it, but since when are you supposed to prove a feeling? God is the only situation where they expect you to do that. (Though I have to say, the universe seems so flawlessly designed to be at my expense that I doubt it could be entirely accidental.) Even if I didn't believe in God, though, I'd probably say I did just out of spite. To irritate people like my mom who think believing in God is tacky and beneath them. They're wrong about everything else; chances are they're wrong about that, too. Plus, God embarrasses people. Which I totally enjoy.

Anyway, I couldn't see how my mom could have handled it if my dad had been a full-on Catholic. She would have spent so much time ridiculing him that there wouldn't have been any time left to ask which dress made her look fatter. Maybe, in fact, this method of avoiding that topic was the key to a successful marriage, but I couldn't quite picture it.

I must have been looking puzzled, because Dr. Hexstrom's face once again went: "you're a bright boy–this is not really all that hard to get." Then she added, in words, "many of those books are books Catholics used to read in the sixties."

My look said: "*Catcher* and *Slan* and *The Doors of Perception*? Surely not."

Her look was once again complicated: "some of the books are books young people read in the sixties," it said patiently, "some are books Catholics read in the sixties, and some are books sixties people read in the sixties. Ergo: your father was young and Catholic in the sixties."

"Plus," she added in words, "your mother told me."

Well, that seemed like cheating, but there was no arguing with it. My inclined head said, with what I hoped was a touch of class: "Touché."

So back to the library research session with Sam Hellerman: there I was thinking about all this Catholic stuff, my nickname, and the notion that the stones/Abraham quote might be something Catholic clergy tended to associate with themselves. And I had pretty much reached the conclusion– in fact, I had little doubt–that what we were dealing with here was some kind of pedophile priest situation.

Timothy J. Anderson was a clergyman who had molested Tit and maybe others, maybe even my dad–a weird thought indeed. Tit and company had finally risen up to take some kind of elaborate revenge. Poisoned the Communion wine. Pushed him out of a bell tower. The bastard was dead at last, thrown into the metaphorical fire, as such a man was surely going straight to hell. Tit had hated him so much that he hadn't even considered going to the funeral, but my dad had gone for some reason. To view the body, to make sure the b. was d.? Did such things ever really happen? Presumably so: if it can be thought, it can be done.

So when Sam Hellerman called me over to the microfilm viewer, I was expecting to read an obituary from around 3/13/63 noting the death (under mysterious circumstances, perhaps) of someone by the name of Brother Timothy J. Anderson.

"It's a monk, right?" I said. "A dead monk. Possibly poisoned."

Sam Hellerman stared at me.

"What in God's name are you talking about?"

"Or a priest, a bishop, something like that." I started to explain my theory, but he was already shaking his head.

Because here's what he had found in the archives, or rather, what he hadn't found: there was no obituary or death notice for anyone by the name of Timothy J. Anderson anywhere around that date.

"Priests," he said, "are prominent members of the community. There's no way a death like that wouldn't be in the paper."

I could see that he was probably right. Yet the card pretty clearly indicated a funeral in San Francisco at the time. Had the listing been suppressed because of the scandal? But if there had been a scandal, if the story was "out," we'd have seen huge headlines about "Altar Boy Avengers" or something. (Which is not a bad band name, as Sam Hellerman replied when I mentioned it.) Anyway, I'm pretty sure that sort of thing is usually dark and secret and behind the scenes and only comes out after everyone involved has had years of therapy and/or Alzheimer's.

Nonetheless, Timothy J. Anderson, whoever he had been, had clearly lived and died somehow. There were presumably official death records other than newspapers that could be checked somewhere, though the very thought filled me with fatigue and dread.

A moment earlier everything had seemed to fit together neatly, if distastefully. Now nothing fit, but the distastefulness remained. We tried looking up Timothy J. Anderson in every local reference book we could find: no result, not even close. Well, we could call up all the Andersons in the phone book to ask if any of them knew a Timothy J. who had died in 1963. Yeah, right.

"I'm sorry, dude," said Sam Hellerman, because we had started to say dude recently. "He doesn't exist."

CONNECTIONS

Tracking down Deanna-Fiona was going to be a snap compared to figuring out the deal with Timothy J. Anderson, and not just because she wasn't dead. But the prospect filled me with terror because it would involve more speaking out loud than I liked even under normal circumstances, and these circumstances would not be normal. There were no listings for any Schumachers in Salthaven, Salthaven Vista, Old Mission Hills, Rancho Sans Souci, or any of the surrounding towns. But every year Immaculate Heart Academy puts out a booklet called "Connections," which has contact information for all the students. Hillmont has a similar thing, called "What's the Buzz (Call a Knight!)," and as I realized after I had thought about it a bit, there was a pretty good chance that I already had a copy of last year's edition of IHA-SV's "Connections" somewhere in my room.

Mrs. Teneb, my mom's nondiminutive female actor friend, had a daughter who went there, and last year there had been some talk of trying to stimulate my nonexistent social life by encouraging me to get in touch with some of the IHA-SV girls. The pretense had been my imaginary Monty Python/Dr. Who club and Susye Teneb's hugely implausible claim that there was a group of geek girls who had a similar club at IHA-SV. No doubt that myth had its origin in some feeble practical joke attempt by Susye Teneb, but names had been underlined and the book solemnly received and eventually ignored, thrown in the corner with all the other junk in my room.

It took a while to dig it out, but when I did, there she was: Deanna Gabriella Schumacher, 1854 North del Norte Plaza Circle, Salthaven, with a phone number and everything. I had trouble whacking up the nerve to call, though, and I kept putting it off and making excuses for why it might be better to wait. Because this was really it. Make-or-break time for the Fiona-Deanna Deal. I wanted to know what would happen, but I was scared at the same time. The library research session had filled me with a kind of resolve, though, and I decided to give it a shot that night.

Holden Caulfield, when calling his various preppie girlfriends, would always say he planned to hang up if the parents answered. I told myself that's what I'd do, too, even though I knew she would probably have her own phone. In the fifties, no one had their own goddam phone and all, as HC would have put it. In other words, modern communications technology and the higher standard of living had made things more convenient and less convenient at the same time.

I almost couldn't bring myself to dial the numbers, I was so nervous, and I had no idea what I would say. I got an answering machine that said "Didi's phone, leave me a message." Hanging up on the machine was like Holden's hanging up on Jane Gallagher's highfalutin parents. I was doing okay in the grand tradition of calling up girls and not knowing what to say and then hanging up without saying anything. Mr. Schtuppe should give me extra credit or something.

The effort had taken a lot out of me, though. I was feeling a little faint and peaked. It was six-forty-five. I decided to try again in twenty minutes. I poured the rest of my Coke down the drain and poured some of my mom's bourbon into the empty can. Because I needed some help, man.

The fourth time I tried Deanna Schumacher's number, the answering machine message had been changed to "Look, asshole, I screen, so if you don't leave a message there's no way you'll ever find out if I would have picked up."

Off to a good start. So after the beep, I said, haltingly, "This—this message is for Deanna Schumacher—" I pronounced it shoe-mocker. But the phone was suddenly picked up and a female voice said, "Skoo-macker."

"Skoo-macker?" I repeated.

"Skoo-macker," said the voice.

"Really?"

I realized the conversation was going nowhere, and I decided to suspend my disbelief about the whole Skoo-macker thing. She was the Schumacher expert around here. "This is she," the voice was saying with charm-school precision. "Who, may I ask, is calling?"

"Oh. This is, um um Tom Tom Henderson." The "um um" is where I momentarily forgot who I was. I was starting to say, though with perhaps a bit less suavity than I had planned, that we had met at a party in Clearview Heights last month, when she broke in:

"Tom-Tom?" she said. "Is that Moe Henderson? Chi-Mo Henderson?"

That about covered it. So she *had* known who I was. Not surprising, if she knew Susye Teneb.

"Oh. Yes. We met at a party—"

"How nice to hear from you. What can I do for you, Tom-Tom?"

"Oh. Well, we met at a party—"

"What?" She was determined not to let me deliver the rest of my suave "we met at a party" speech. She was quite the conversationalist.

I decided to ignore her interruptions and charge ahead, so I explained that we-met-at-a-party-in-Clearview-Heights-last-month, and tried to make it quick so it would fit in the brief space before she burst out with another interruption. I just about managed it, too, and I think the information finally penetrated, because her next question was quite to the point.

"And?"

Well, that was a tough one. So many different things could follow that "and." *And*, I don't know if you remember, but we made out on the couch when a telekinesis experiment went awry. *And* you wouldn't let me go down your pants, going "my tits, my tits" instead, and I was wondering whether that was because of ladies' week or was there some other reason? *And* you asked about my band's gigs, and, well, it just so happens that we're playing at the Festival of Lights in a few weeks, maybe you'd like to cut class at IHA and come? *And* I look fondly upon the special moments your left breast and I spent together, and I'd welcome the chance to pick up where we left off and get to know the rest of you better. *And*, though I doubt it's something people generally say about just anybody whose nipple they happen to maul in a dark room at this or that fake mod stoner party, I have this dream where we're imaginary boyfriend-girlfriend in a Sex Alliance Against Society. . . .

None of those answers to "And?" would have fit into one of Deanna-Fiona's pauses, I knew that, and most of them would have come off weird over the phone. So I said, as quickly as I could:

"I think we have some some matters to discuss, but I'd rather not do it over the phone. Maybe we could get together some time at your convenience if that would be be copasetic." Devil-head. Boy, did I ever feel like an idiot.

"You're so *professional*," she said, giggling. I'm not sure what she meant, exactly, though it sounded sarcastic. I guess she wasn't stoned enough to be quite as amused by my virtuoso devil-headedness as she had been at the party. Then she said: "Are you asking me out, Tom-Tom?"

Was I? "Oh," I said. "Oh. Um. Well. I mean . . ."

"You know, I have a boyfriend."

"Right. Dave."

"Tim."

"Tim?"

"Tim."

"Really?"

"Really. I think I would know."

I could sense that this fascinating conversation was drawing to a close, and I was trying to figure out a way to slip in a quick "well, nice talking to you, bye now," to make her hanging up on me seem a bit less embarrassing, when she said, to my astonishment:

"Well, maybe you'd better come over, then."

WHAT HAPPENS WHEN YOU NEED TO GET TO SLUT HEAVEN AS QUICKLY AS POSSIBLE BUT YOU CAN'T DRIVE YET

Deanna Skoo-macker's directions to her house had been from the freeway, so she had assumed I'd be driving. I wish.

Salthaven is several towns away, near the bay, clear on the other side of Rancho Sans Souci. I figured I should give myself at least an hour to get there on my bike, just in case I got lost or something. So I said I had some things I had to do first, but that I could probably make it by around nine.

"Okay," she had said, "but I turn into a pumpkin at ten-fifteen."

Right. These modern girls and their mysterious ways. Best not to ask. They're either going to explain things or they're not, is how I look at it.

Since the whole "Thinking of Suicide?" debacle, I was supposed to tell Little Big Tom and Carol where I was going every time I left the house. Maybe they thought I'd slip up and say "well, Mom, I'm off to jump off the Golden Gate Bridge—oops! I mean . . . ," and then they'd know to withhold their permission and avert a great American tragedy. In fact, though, I was finding that playing D and D at Sam Hellerman's house was all the excuse I ever needed.

"Slay an orc with a lightning bolt for me!" said Little Big Tom as I headed out the door.

Now, you're going to think I'm nuts, but I spent quite a bit of time during the ride over to Salthaven thinking about Timothy J. Anderson and Tit. I mean, I was wild with anticipation over the reunion with the elusive fake Fiona; and I was still reeling from the surprising conclusion to my inept attempt at telephone communication. "You'd better come over, then." Sounded pretty fucking promising. Great song title, too.

But while one part of my mind was picturing Deanna Schumacher naked, seminaked, outfitted in fake mod and schoolgirl fetish gear, tied to a pole, sitting on a motorcycle, and so forth, another part of my mind was trying to figure out why *The Seven Storey Mountain*, CEH 1963, had contained a funeral memorial card for a funeral that didn't appear to have occurred, for a person who didn't appear to have existed.

If the card wasn't a funeral card, I couldn't think what else it might have been for. It was very much like the card for my dad's funeral, except that it contained a lot less information and no photo. There was a cross on one side; the quotation, date, and location were centered on the other. It didn't seem like very good printing, and the amateurishness was one of the reasons it looked so creepy and disturbing. But assuming it *was* for a funeral, why had there been nothing about it in the newspaper? The church would probably have a record of it somewhere, as would the city or county. I'm sure it was possible to track it down, if I had the energy and inclination.

Did I? I was starting to realize that Tit's code and the mystery of Timothy J. Anderson, as exciting as it had seemed at first, had been distracting me from what I really hoped to learn from all this. I found I didn't really care all that much about Timothy J. Anderson. What I really wanted was to get an idea of who my dad had been, the kinds of thoughts he had had, the kind of world he had inhabited, things that were still dark to me. I had started out with a simplistic, unquestioned caricature of my dad, the Charles Evan Henderson I had known as an eight-year-old. Now I didn't even have that. Tit and Timothy J. Anderson had crowded my dad out of the picture. I realized I had been looking at the memorial card as a kind of sign from beyond, which was pretty nutty. What had I been thinking?

Maybe there was no real message: kids do bizarre things and construct elaborate games to drive away the boredom. Tit could very well have been playing some nonsensical game with no relation to actual reality, and I was just falling for it decades later, very much like how Little Big Tom misread the Talons of Rage fantasy blades, or how my mom had misread

"Thinking of Suicide?" It was weird to think that I was playing the role of the Clueless Adult from the Future, but maybe I kind of was.

The whole thing left me with an empty, lonely feeling. I did know one thing, however: I didn't much like Tit. There was something nasty about his note and about the fact that he had taken such care to encipher part of it, and had a sort of–what? Gleeful? Yeah, a gleeful, flippant attitude, when the subject matter was pretty somber. And including the ramoning boast in the same breath as the reference to the funeral and to being tied up and whipped–well, this Tit was clearly a weird guy.

Then again, there was Deanna-Fiona's sexy stomach and her "maybe you'd better come over, then" to look forward to and be nervous about. Why was I obsessing over Timothy J. Anderson? Under the circumstances, it was a crazy thing to do. I got a bit lost in the (devil-head) labyrinth of plazas, terraces, caminos, lanes, vistas, circles, and courts, but I finally made it to North del Norte Plaza Circle in Salthaven with nearly an hour to spare before Deanna/Fiona's pumpkin meter was set to run out at ten-fifteen.

As directed, I "parked" before I reached the Schumacher residence (hiding my bike in some bushes a couple of houses down) and walked as quietly as I could down a path running alongside the house. When I reached the side door, I tapped lightly. And I was pretty freaked out by what I saw when the door opened.

FOX ON THE RUN

I was in a kind of daze as I followed Deanna Schumacher through the door, down a dark hall and some stairs, and into a basement bedroom. Because as soon as I saw her, I knew that this was not, in fact, the Fiona of the fake-mod party. She was much shorter, and kind of chunky, though not chunky in a bad way—she was actually pretty sexy and curvy, to be honest. My Fiona had been taller and much skinnier. Even allowing for the headiness of the moment and the mists of memory, there was just no way you would find anything like the Fiona stomach underneath Deanna Schumacher's loose, untucked blouse. No way.

I just stood there in Deanna Schumacher's room, not knowing what to say. Now, I feel safe in assuming that that's what I would have done in any case. But if I had had my Fiona standing in front of me, it would have been a different type of speechlessness. How had this mistake, if mistake it had been, come about? Somehow all roads led to Sam Hellerman in that line of inquiry, and for some reason I wasn't really in the mood for thinking about Sam Hellerman at the moment. So I examined Deanna Schumacher and tried to shift gears, in a dilemma I never imagined I'd have: what do you say to a girl you have never made out with at a party while she was in a fake-mod costume but who has nevertheless invited you to a secret tryst in her bedroom without realizing that you thought she was someone else? We had not, as it turned out, met at a party. And we did not, accordingly, have any matters to discuss, like I had said. Not really.

She wasn't wearing a school uniform like I had expected, but she did have on a pretty short skirt over bare legs and the loose blouse I mentioned. She was actually quite pretty, in a mousy/nerdy way (which I found I really liked). The glasses were sexy, and she somehow managed to keep her mouth slightly open at practically all times. It was just naturally that way, I guess. Naturally hot.

"Take off your coat and stay a while," she said.

I threw my army coat on the floor, and then felt a bit embarrassed when she immediately scooped it up and put it on a chair.

She asked how my mom and Amanda were doing. The fact that she knew so much about me and my family would have been pretty spooky coming from the real fake Fiona, but coming from the fake fake Fiona it didn't have the same effect. And while I had been walking in and planning my dialogue and checking out her legs and so forth, I had also put two and two together and realized that not only must she have known Susye Teneb, but also that there had been a Didi a grade ahead of me at McKinley Intermediate, and that this was probably her. She must have gone on to Immaculate Heart Academy rather than public high school, which happened sometimes, especially with delinquent or troubled girls. So her knowledge of the Henderson family and my nickname wasn't all that surprising.

"I never got to say," she said, suddenly very serious, "how sorry I was to hear about your father." I was stunned, both by the unexpected condolences and by the even more unexpected grace with which she offered them. "My father was with the Santa Carla coroner's office, and he speaks very highly of him." Stunned. Again.

I still hadn't said a word. She motioned me over to sit next to her on the ruffly, frilly bed.

"Thank you," I said, meaning thanks for being sorry to hear about my dad, and also for letting me sit on her bed next to her. The silence that followed could be seen as respectful, excruciating, peaceful, tortured, uncomfortable, exciting, tense, or divine, depending on how you looked at it.

"What have you been up to, Tom-Tom?" she eventually said.

"I'm in a . . . band," I said. "A band." And even though the current band name, Balls Deep, had been fixed at least till after the Festival of Lights, the habit of a lifetime asserted itself. "Super Mega Plus," I added. Me on guitar/vox; Sam Hell on bass, prevarication, and procuring young girls under false pretenses; Brain-Dead Panchowski on irregular timekeeping; first album *A Woman Knows*. But I didn't say that last part. "We're playing at lunch lunch at Hillmont in a few weeks."

"Lunch-lunch?" I was getting a little tired of that joke, to be honest. Then she said: "Tom-Tom the rock star. Look at you." I'd rather you didn't, actually. Then, I kid you not, she said: "You're so cool." Well, I mean: certainly not. I couldn't sort out the sarcasm from the politeness from the sincerity. There was a tiny bit of sincerity, I thought, wasn't there? Maybe not. Maybe it was all politeness. She was a very, very polite young thing. Even her mockery was kind of polite.

She grabbed my wrist to look at my watch, and I thought she was going to go all Dr. Hexstrom on me and say "I'm sorry but our time is up," but then she suddenly turned around and straddled me and after shooting me an unreadable look leaned in and started to lick my lips. I was, again, taken aback, but I knew what to do. Or I thought I did. This time, the kissing part was going much better, but when I reached beneath her blouse and located her left breast just under the front of her bra and started to squeeze it Fiona style with my nails against my palm, so it went nails–upper nipple–bra–palm, she squirmed, and not in a good way. And when I tried it again, she twisted away a bit, and I paused and made a note to self: not all girls like the nipple thing. Check. She hadn't been too fazed, though, and she continued the kissing, which was a lot sloppier and–what? Wild? Yeah, wet and wild. Sloppier, wetter and wilder than it had been with Fiona, anyway. I hadn't known there were so many variations.

So my right hand had been rebuffed, but I reached up

with the left and placed it neutrally yet with reverence on the other breast, which felt very nice. See, I figured I'd let the right one cool off for a while. I moved my rebuffed hand down to her thigh and then started sliding it up toward her butt, while we were both still slobbering on each other's faces, her tongue ring clicking occasionally against my teeth. Then, feeling no resistance, I slid my fingers up even farther. I don't even know how to describe what that felt like; there isn't anything remotely like it to compare it to. Let's just say it was really, really nice.

She leaned back and laughed just a bit with that open-mouth thing she did and said, "You really know your way around a girl."

Now, *I* had to laugh at that, because it was so, so, so not true. Probably just more politeness. They grow 'em up sweet and well mannered in the Catholic church, I can tell you that right now.

What happened next was: she stopped kissing me, leaned back, snatched my wrist to look at my watch, and then looked at me. My return look said "what?" but I was prepared to be shown the door at any moment.

"I wouldn't mind," she said finally in a matter-of-fact tone, "giving you some head." Well, I guess she could tell I wouldn't mind it all that much either, because she added, "Why don't you get in the bed?" And she leaned over and pulled back the Holly Hobbie bedcover.

I scrambled back quickly, not knowing exactly how what was going to come next would end up coming, or even knowing what that would be with much specificity.

"With your pants on, huh?" she said. "Well, that's different."

Too late, I realized I had committed some horrible (devil-head) faux pas. I quickly got rid of my shoes and slithered out of my jeans and sat there in my U.S. Army shirt and white

BVDs leaning against Deanna Schumacher's headboard. It had a horse on it. I looked pretty stupid, I'm sure, and I'm not surprised that Deanna Schumacher started snickering a little bit. "You've got to get some boxers," she said.

What she did then was kind of weird, or I thought it was weird. She put her glasses on the pillow next to me, slid under the sheet, and put it over her shoulders like it was Superman's cape or something; and then she moved the sheet so that it was over her head, too; and then she kind of swooped down and the official blow job part of the program began. I wasn't really in a position to complain, but the sheet was kind of a bummer. I wanted to watch, to see what it looked like, as I had been fantasizing about this precise scenario since time immemorial and I was pretty interested in how the reality would match up to the pretend images and the porn. She clearly didn't like being observed while she worked, however. She also wasn't very into having a person's hands on her head during this operation, even though I couldn't help putting them there anyway, just a bit. That wasn't a deal-breaking faux pas, though. I realized, with a bit of a shock, that even King Dork, the (devil-head) embodiment of the faux pas, hadn't committed a deal-breaking faux pas the whole time. Maybe, in the end, there weren't any deal-breaking faux pas in this situation. I didn't have a lot of data at my disposal, you understand.

It was great. It really was. But I was also very aware of the ticking pumpkin-meter, and it made me nervous and distracted. Yeah, that was probably it.

At one point she leaned up, the sheet around her face like a–what's it called? Babushka, I think. But she didn't say "matchmaker, matchmaker, make me a match." What she said, in a hurried whisper, was:

"We only have around ten minutes left, Tom-Tom."

"Okay, okay," I said. It was nice to get the reminder, though hearing her say it made me even more nervous. However, I wasn't going to let this one go. It was my big chance. I concentrated and replayed my memory of the episode with the real Fiona in my head, as I had done hundreds of times before, and it relaxed and excited me at the same time as it always did. We were back on the right track. And it wasn't long before I was feeling glad all over, believe me.

Then she emerged from her little sheet fort, leaned up, and pulled my hair back from my face so it was flat on top of my head, staring at me up close from above for what seemed like quite a while, despite the still-ticking clock. Then she said:

"My boyfriend gets off at ten, and he's going to be here any minute, so you're going to have to get out of here. Don't"–she paused–"Don't, um, please don't–" I could tell she wasn't sure how to ask me not to tell anyone about what had just happened. It was the only time during the whole episode where she seemed less than perfectly composed and all-knowing.

My look said "oh, absolutely not. Absolutely not. Your secret is safe with me." But she was no slan, so I added, out loud, "Don't worry–I won't tell anyone. Promise." She smiled, and then leaned over and kissed me softly and lightly on the mouth. A hefty twenty-four words and a couple of urgent inarticulate spasms had escaped my lips during the whole affair, but I couldn't help adding another four words in spite of myself. "You're very pretty, Deanna." And I meant it, too. I suddenly realized that she kind of reminded me of the "Thinking of Suicide?" girl from the pamphlet, which really pushed my buttons. But Deanna Schumacher didn't seem too interested in discussing the matter any further at the moment.

Maybe "you're very pretty" was laying it on too thick. It's really hard to know.

She said she was going to have to run upstairs to brush her teeth. Straightening up the place for the next customer, I guess. "It was very nice seeing you again, Tom-Tom, after all these years," she said, back in her well-mannered element. "Say hello to your mother and sister for me. Maybe you could come by again sometime. . . ."

I was very, very proud of myself.

On the way home, I was singing "Glad All Over," "My Baby Loves Lovin'," and "Yummy, Yummy, Yummy," at the top of my lungs as I rode through the near-deserted streets. When I did "Fox on the Run," I tried to sing the "I" loud enough that it would echo, "I . . . I . . . I . . . ," just like on the record. And it kind of almost did.

THE FOG OF DEANNA

Believe it or not, it didn't hit me till I woke up the next day that Deanna Schumacher was not only a confusing sex kitten I had never made out at a party with, but also the daughter of a man who had known my dad and worked with him in some capacity. In other words, he was a potential source of information about the circumstances surrounding his death. Somehow I knew it wouldn't be easy to engage Deanna Schumacher on that topic—nothing was easy when it came to talking to her. But I resolved to give it a shot sometime, if I ever had the chance.

Here's how I knew I was starting to fall for Deanna Schumacher: I began to take time off from trying to psychoanalyze her and from replaying the mental video of our "date" and from splashing around in a pool of self-pity and instead started writing love songs about her. "I Wanna Ramone You," for example:

> *I wanna ramone you*
> hier *and* ici.
> *I wanna ramone you*
> là *and* aujourd'hui.

> *If your boyfriend's been postponed*
> *and if we won't be chaperoned*
> *and if you wanna get ramoned,*
> comment? *come on, come on . . .*

There's more where that came from, but it should be enough to demonstrate: I am a Romantic Genius, and a Dreamer.

I was still scared to call her, though. In fact, it took me a couple of days to get up the nerve even to dial Holden Caulfield style—that is, with the intention of hanging up. Our secret date had been on Thursday, Veterans' Day. I stalled on Friday. I took the weekend off. Then I took a deep breath on Monday and picked up the phone with steely determination. I needn't have bothered with the s. d., however. Her answering machine was full, and I couldn't have left a message even if I tried. I hadn't realized that it was possible for frustration and relief to come in the same box, but it did. Maybe her family had gone out of town for a long weekend. So who had been leaving all those messages on her machine? That thought drove me crazy and made me cry, though not quite literally.

She could have gone away with her boyfriend—Tim, was it?—instead of with her family. Or perhaps the boyfriend had gone along on the family excursion. Maybe they were riding in the backseat of the family car surreptitiously groping each other underneath a blanket. Maybe they were ramoning right now. I was starting to feel a little jealous of Ted, or Dan, or whoever. In fact, I thought I might be starting to hate him. But I squelched that thought. There was no future in that line of thinking. And I was impressed with my own maturity for realizing it. The whole thing was very adult and sophisticated.

I had settled into a comfortable pattern of dialing and being informed by a robot voice that the machine was full, which I did several times a day, causing some turmoil in the household because Amanda thought of the phone as her exclusive property. So I dropped the phone in shock when, on Thursday evening, I heard not the robot voice, but the voice of my imaginary girlfriend saying "Didi's phone, leave a message." I picked the phone off the floor without being able to think of anything to say, but it was too late anyway, so I had to dial again, once the dial tone came back on. Then it was busy. In its own way, this unexpectedly retarded attempt to make a phone call was like a little Hitchcock film: all suspense and delayed gratification with plot twists and multiple false endings. I waited ten minutes and dialed again, and waited another ten minutes and dialed again, thinking that I would not be too surprised if it were answered by a mysterious German-accented voice asking me if I had the formula and telling me to wear a red carnation and come to the Oberausterplatz. But no. "Didi's phone, leave a message."

I took a deep breath. "This message is for Deanna Skoo—"

Deanna Schumacher picked up the phone, and she didn't mention the Oberausterplatz.

"Jerk."

I didn't know what to say. Finally she said, "Hello? Hello? Are you there?" I cleared my throat and said that I was there, and that I had been trying to call–

"Jerk," she repeated, breaking in.

We were back where we started.

"I've been trying–"

"Whatever," she broke in. "I don't mess around with just anyone." Now, how I was supposed to know that was a little unclear: it seemed to me, on the evidence, that her criteria in that regard were in fact rather broad. "I'm not used to being ignored," she said, "and, in case you're wondering, I don't have any trouble getting dates."

I'm sure you don't, I thought. It's the phone conversation afterward that you seem to have not quite gotten the hang of. But I doubted this was the right answer, so what I said was: "I've been trying–"

"Well, I've been away."

"–to call–"

"What?" It struck me that despite all the "this is she" and "say hello to your mother" stuff, she was a lot less polite on the phone than she was when she was offering to give you an illicit blow job in the fifteen minutes before her boyfriend arrived. Did she ever let anyone finish a sentence?

"I've-been-trying-to-call-you-but-your-machine-has-been-full," I said as quickly as I could. And I almost got to "your" before she broke in: "I've been away—are you deaf? My machine was full." I was at a loss, and I almost hung up. But then, her voice softened.

"I'm glad you called, Tom-Tom. I was beginning to think you had used and forgotten me." Now there was a teasing tone. How many personalities did this girl have, anyway? I realized there would be no point trying to puzzle out how being unable to leave a message on someone's answering machine because they have been away from home for four days counts as ignoring them. Or why she was going all *Fatal Attraction* on me when I was the one who was supposed to pretend I didn't exist for the preservation of her real-life serious nonimaginary relationship. We were in boy-girl world, or we sort of were, where logic is optional. I was learning a lot.

Really, I was just glad to hear her voice, even if I had no earthly idea what the things it was saying were intended to accomplish. Or rather, I liked hearing the nice voice. The mean voice was harder to take. But she also confusingly used the nice voice to tell me that her boyfriend was a very jealous, unstable person who had rage issues and that all she would have to do is tell him about me and I'd be dead almost instantaneously. Also to say: "If my father found out how you took advantage of me, he would bash your fucking head in and you'd go to jail for twenty years." I doubted she was right about the specifics there, but I got her point. But then she laughed, as though she had only been kidding, and told me, in the softest, most feminine manner, that she was glad I called. At one point she got really quiet and said that sometimes she hates who she is and feels there's no way out, and she sniffled like she was trying to hold back the tears. But just as I was starting to say I totally understood what that felt like, intending to offer some words of comfort and encouragement, she just started laughing.

"Are you okay?" I said, after a confused pause.

"What's that supposed to mean?" she said with a kind of venom in her voice. "You're the one who can't take a joke." She had been making fun of my attempt at a cool and dignified (devil-head) demeanor, I guess.

Sam Hellerman had been wrong about Deanna Schumacher in every respect but one: she was kind of a psycho freak.

Now, what you have to understand is that the whole time, Amanda was standing in the doorway glowering at me and chanting "get off the phone, get off the phone" with ever-increasing volume. And Little Big Tom and Carol had crowded around to observe the novelty of clumsy little Chi-Mo trying to talk to a female. It was hard to concentrate, and I was nervous enough to begin with. So I can't rely on my interpretations of Deanna Schumacher's words or the awkward pauses between them or the tone of her voice. In warfare there's a thing called the "fog of war" where everything around you is confusion and chaos and no one is able to see the big picture till it's all over, and even then everyone has a different memory of it. It was like that. The Fog of Deanna. Somehow, though, amid the confusion, it was established that she wasn't being ignored, at least not by me, and that she didn't really intend to go through with any orders for my execution, though I still got the impression that she was mad at me somehow. She kept saying "I'm glad you called," though, which was a good sign. I truly had no idea what was going on, but it was beginning to dawn on me that having no idea what's going on is a more or less defining part of the whole coupling process.

Somehow it became clear that no one in this situation would mind all that much if I were to visit again. At least, that was the conclusion I reached when she said that Mondays and Thursdays were best, as that was when her boyfriend worked late. Okay, I'm game. "Don't disappoint me," she added, which I knew was from a movie, but I forget which one. Then there was an operator-assisted emergency break-through on the phone from one of Amanda's friends.

"I'll have to call you back," I said, and she said, "Whatever, Tom-Tom," in her pissed-off voice, and then she switched to the polite voice again and said, "Be sure to tell your mother and sister hello from me." I was going to say something like "Okay, then," but she had already hung up.

I know I said I was going to call her back, but I honestly didn't know if I could take another one of those chats anytime soon. Amanda pounced on the phone as soon as I set it down. My mom was laughing and smoking, asking who I had been talking to in a teasing tone that was eerily similar to the one Deanna Schumacher had employed to ask if I had used and forgotten her. And *she's* the one who claims not to want me to attempt suicide. I'll never understand women, no matter whose mom they are.

Little Big Tom tilted his head and said, "Mojo working!"

I resolved to take the GED and emancipate myself as soon as possible, just so I could safely use the phone again. But I think you have to be sixteen.

I ended up visiting Deanna Schumacher again the following week. It went pretty much the same way as before—a psychotic conversation, followed by making out, ending in a blow job. We had some more time left on the pumpkinometer this time, so I decided to risk it:

"So your father's a Santa Carla cop."

"Peace officer," she said absently. She was straightening up the room. "Or he was. Not anymore."

"And he knew my dad, you said."

"Yeah, I told you that already. Can't you shut up about my father for five minutes?"

That was about all I had the strength for. Something about her tone told me I wasn't going to get too far with this line of inquiry.

When we switched to other topics, things went better. I mean, I learned some interesting things about Deanna Schumacher. She liked to talk about herself, though she wasn't all that interested in hearing a person's comments in reaction to her statements, which seemed intended primarily for effect.

"One thing you have to understand about me," she said, "is that I'm totally into Stoli." Ah, I thought—the relationship deepens. She also said at one point that she "likes girls" even though she was mostly into guys.

"Is that a Suzi Quatro–Joan Jett kind of thing?" I said. She had no idea what I was talking about, but I had a feeling she didn't really care what I had to say on that or any other matter. It was just part of her general method of trying to overwhelm me with confusing data and erratic moods and to keep me just a little off-kilter at all times. It was working, too. I never had any idea what she was thinking, whether she was glad to hear from me, whether she had lost interest in me, or anything. The Fog of Deanna was exhausting.

The coming Thursday was Thanksgiving, and I knew I couldn't call or visit on that day, which worried me a little. How was I going to make it through a whole week without any contact? I was already walking around with that punched-in-the-stomach feeling almost all the time, unable to eat or do much of anything, and I knew it would only get worse.

Then something happened that made even the Fog of Deanna look comparatively easy to navigate.

POINT-BLANK AT YOUR OWN RISK

It was my fourth session with Dr. Hexstrom, the day after my second Deanna Schumacher experience.

I have to admit, my interest in *The Seven Storey Mountain* was dwindling. It was pretty slow going, and I already knew the ending, which is that the guy ends up deciding there's more to life than fast times and goes into a monastery. Plus, there's this part where he starts heaping praise on the *Doors of Perception* guy, so I was kind of disappointed in him. It's weird how all these guys seemed to know each other. There was even a quote on the cover of *The Seven Storey Mountain* from the *Brighton Rock* guy, saying something like "the best way to read this book is with a pencil," whatever that might mean. It must have to do with their all being weird Catholics.

But maybe there was more to that guy than *The Doors of Perception* indicated. I made a promise-to-self to try one of his other books—maybe they weren't all poorly written, self-important, desperately trendy drug memoirs. Not that I had much time for that at the moment: what with the Timothy J. Anderson investigation, band practices, learning to mispronounce vocabulary words from *Catcher in the Rye*, psychoanalyzing Sam Hellerman, being on the receiving end of secret sheet-covered Catholic-schoolgirl blow jobs *and* of inept parental suicide prevention schemes—well, I was a busy man these days. So I set *The Seven Storey Mountain* aside with *The Naked and the Dead* to finish later, and boldly started on *La Peste,* CEH 1965. But it took me around two hours to translate the first page, and even then I wasn't too clear on most of it, so I put that aside, too, and decided to pick up *Slan* where I had left off, where the freaky slan kid wakes up to find he's been chained to a bed by this creepy old lady. In a way, *Slan* was a lot like *The Seven Storey Mountain* or *Siddhartha* with all the religious stuff taken out. Same basic idea. Kind of an improvement, if you ask me.

Now, as much as I enjoyed discussing slans and monks and drugs with Dr. Hexstrom, I wanted to try to steer things in a different direction for this session. Basically, I just decided to point-blank her on some questions I was tired of wondering when we were going to get to. And because I knew that a Hexstrom could be kind of hard to steer sometimes, I wrote them down on a sheet of paper and handed it to her when I walked in.

```
a) When are you going to get it over
with and put me on medication so that my
brain chemistry will match everybody
else's brain chemistry and there will be
no reason for further strife and
unpleasantness and we can all die happy?

b) Why do you think my mom freaked out
over my song about how Yasmynne Schmick
hadn't decided whether to commit suicide
just yet? When are we going to get
around  to discussing that? And what did
you think of the song? Not bad, huh?

c) Do they have to put a notice in the
paper when someone dies, or is it
optional?
```

I hadn't meant to put (c) there, but I wrote it without thinking and decided in the end not to cross it out. I almost added another question, too, for my own personal information, about what base oral sex counts as, but thought it might be better not to get into it. As for (c), though, maybe Dr. Hexstrom would have some ideas.

She did, though she gave me a funny, Jimenez-Macanally–esque look and wanted to know why I was asking. I showed her the Timothy J. Anderson card and told her how we couldn't find any funeral notice in the paper on or around that date.

"I don't think you *have* to put a death notice in the paper unless there's some legal reason," she said, "such as if there's no will. I'm not a lawyer, so don't quote me. But a funeral notice or obituary is usually done to make sure that everyone who might be interested knows and can make plans to attend."

"So if you didn't list it in the paper, it would be because you didn't want anyone to know it was happening and didn't want anyone to attend? Because you wanted to keep it quiet?"

She gave me the look that said: "don't be so melodramatic."

"Or maybe," she added aloud, "because you couldn't afford to pay for an announcement." Well, the card did look a bit on the cheap side. Or perhaps the whole thing had just slipped their minds. You can forget to do a lot of things when someone dies.

She gave me a look that said: "why are you so interested in this Timothy J. Anderson anyway?" I told her that the card had been in one of my dad's books and then gave her the look that said: "I feel like I don't know anything about my father or who he was or what he was like, and I'm grasping for any clue, no matter how trivial or far-fetched or even delusional." Well, it was true.

She eyed the card dubiously. "Why are you so sure it's from a funeral?" she asked.

Because it looked a bit like my dad's funeral card. And because of Tit's note, of course, but I was keeping Tit's note to myself, so I couldn't mention that. Dr. Hexstrom said she didn't quite know what to make of the card. Usually, she said, they put more information on them, like the dates of birth and death. The single date was hard to interpret. She also pointed out something about the card that I hadn't noticed, which was that the left edge didn't look quite the same as the other edges. It had a slightly different color and was perhaps less evenly cut. I could see what she was getting at, and I couldn't believe I hadn't noticed it before. Once it was drawn to my attention, however, it really did look like it had been cut off, like it had originally been the front face of a folded-over card. What had been on the other side? Presumably more information, like the dates of birth and death and so forth. And what had happened to it?

She added that they also make cards like that for memorial services or masses that could be held long after the death or funeral, sometimes years later, and that cards of that kind can commemorate other important events that may not even be deaths. I hadn't realized any of that. So even if it was for a funeral, it was possible that Timothy J. Anderson died earlier, maybe even much earlier than 3/13/63, and that we hadn't searched early enough for the obituary. Tit's note had mentioned a funeral, but the date was fake, and it could have been from any time. And it may not have even been a funeral. In which case, Timothy J. Anderson was not the dead bastard. If not, who the hell was the d. b.? Man, these (devil-head) retrospective investigations into a deceased parent's personal effects can suck the life right out of you. My brain was starting to hurt. I sighed heavily, and so did Dr. Hexstrom, just a bit, unless I'm mistaken.

"Now (a)," she said evenly, pointing to the note. "I'm still not sure you need that kind of medication." And I was sure she was right: the kind of medication I would need was not a straightforward issue, and it might take years to figure out. Maybe that medication hasn't even been invented yet. Well, let me know when you've got it. I'll be right here.

Then she pointed to (b) and said she had found the suicide song very interesting. I resisted the urge to ask which part she liked best. Maybe we could cover that later. For now,

I really wanted to know about my mom's freak-out. Had she said anything to Dr. Hexstrom to indicate where the hell she had been coming from, or why this, out of all the Chi-Mo freakiness over the last four to six years, had been the thing that finally spurred her to send me to a shrink?

Dr. Hexstrom said nothing but gave me a familiar look, the one that says: "come on, Tom, you know better than to play innocent–you know perfectly well what's going on here."

So we were back in slan mode, were we? Okay.

I gave her the look that said: "the fuck?" And her look said: "I'll ignore the rude choice of words, as you're clearly under some type of strain, but you can stop pretending you don't know."

"What?" my look said. "What? What do I know that I'm pretending not to know?" Except I must have said that last part out loud, because she coughed and said, in words:

"You're pretending you don't know that your father committed suicide."

"The fuck?" I said, out loud I think, standing up. It was a car wreck, murder or manslaughter. The *San Francisco Chronicle* had said so. My ears were ringing and I was feeling dizzy and seeing the weird liquid kaleidoscope like when I had accidentally beaten up Paul Krebs. Part of me was wondering whether I was going to end up accidentally beating up Dr. Hexstrom, too, when the liquid kaleidoscope swallowed the rest of my mind and I kind of lost track of things.

I knew I hadn't been unconscious for long, because when I came to there was still time on the clock. I had fallen back into the chair, and it was possible that my blackout had been so brief that Dr. Hexstrom hadn't realized it had even happened. I could tell she was taken aback by my reaction, though, blackout or no. We stared at each other, trying to work out who knew what, who was mistaken about what, and who was lying about what. I concluded she really believed that my dad had killed himself, and had also believed that I had known, and that she was shocked to learn that the idea came as such a spectacular surprise to me.

Was she right? Well, that was really two questions. Question one: was she right that I ought to have known about the supposed suicide, or that I did know but was pretending not to know? Lying to myself? I've learned I should never be too sure about such things. I hadn't known about the Catholic thing, though I should have—it was obvious enough that even Amanda had known all about it. If I were to ask Amanda about the suicide thing (which I would never in a million years do, but still), would she look at me like I was dumb as a cup of melting ice and say "no duh?" Well, I can't speak for Amanda, but a quick, ruthless self-examination indicated that my ignorance was genuine. I truly had not "known" about the suicide, nor even considered it as a possibility.

The second question was, was the suicide story itself true? It didn't seem possible. I had read all about it in the paper, and even though there had been details missing, the car crash had definitely happened. If my dad had killed himself, he would had to have done it in the car before the hit-and-run. How likely was that? Maybe someone had intended to murder him and just hadn't realized that the guy in the car was already dead by his own hand? Or someone had known he had killed himself and had crashed into the car to make it seem like an accident? Or my dad had deliberately placed himself in a position where he knew he'd be crashed into, as a roundabout suicide method? That sounded really crazy. I realized I should probably go back and read those articles again: since I did the research at age ten, I'd had four whole years of being disappointed by my fellow man and having this and that illusion shattered, which had resulted in a firmer, or at least less inaccurate, grasp of reality, presumably. Maybe I'd read things differently now.

Of course, everything Dr. Hexstrom knew about me and my family history came from my mom and from me, filtered through her own (admittedly impressive) knowledge of the world and corrected by her equally impressive powers of deduction. I had exaggerated and left out details and tried to make myself look better and/or worse than I actually was all over the place for various personal reasons. Her view of my world based on my account was wildly inaccurate, except in those areas where her own common sense corrected the picture. But she hadn't gotten the suicide thing from me. So either my mom had lied to her deliberately for some unfathomable reason, or my mom genuinely believed, rightly or wrongly, that the suicide story was true. Since it was the better explanation for her freak-out over the song, I had to conclude that the latter was the case. She liked to exaggerate and fabricate things for melodramatic purposes, but she wouldn't do that to someone to whom she was paying a hundred and fifty dollars an hour to cure her son of individuality. Would she?

These thoughts took a lot less time to think than it just took to describe them. When I finally spoke, I was almost incoherent. The questions I was able to get out were, how did my mom know about this when everyone else seemed to think it had been a hit-and-run, and why had Dr. Hexstrom believed her, a known liar.

"She said he left a note," said Dr. Hexstrom, but then seemed to think better of continuing. "I need to speak to your mother about this. And our time is up."

She wouldn't let me leave on my own, though. She insisted on calling Little Big Tom to pick me up. I spent the ride home in a daze, thinking about my dad's alleged suicide note and how I'd have to do some Little Big Tom–style snooping to try to locate it amidst Carol's stuff. If it really existed.

A BETTER CLASS OF LIE

I was starting to wonder how anybody knows anything at all about anything. All sources are suspect.

Even if I were to find this supposed suicide note, chances were it would be inconclusive, too. "Dear Honey, I have decided to end it all," it would say, and there would be no proof that he was talking about his life as opposed to eating red meat or subscribing to *TV Guide*. On the other hand, I suppose a wife would know. One thing *I* knew: asking her about it would serve no purpose. God help Dr. Hexstrom if she really planned to go through with trying to talk to her about it. I was sure the good doctor had encountered quite a few crazy people in her day, but my mom was in a category all her own.

I was starting to realize the extent of the problem here: everyone is always lying to each other, and even when they're trying to tell the truth, it can still be misleading or wrong. In fact, it almost always is wrong from at least one angle. I mean, in a way, the truth is really just a better class of lie.

And then there was Fiona. She was still at large, whoever she was. The Deanna Schumacher episode, pleasant and mind-blowing as it was, hadn't changed that. Sam Hellerman had stated categorically that Fiona was Deanna Schumacher dressed up as a fake mod, which was plausible, but which hadn't been the case. He could have simply been mistaken, misled by his CHS friends. On the other hand, it was possible that he had known and had been lying, for obscure reasons of his own. Had he been trying to help me get over my Fiona-related pain and longing by providing me with a fake fake Fiona to focus on, feeling fairly certain I wouldn't end up putting his story to the test by tracking her down and going over to her house for some illicit oral sex? (A safe assumption: I still couldn't quite believe it myself.) Or maybe Sam "the Matchmaker" Hellerman had known all along that I would follow up on the Deanna Schumacher lead and had intended for us to get together? Maybe the Deanna Schumacher blow job had been a gift from Sam Hellerman unto me, in return for my years of faithful service to the Hermetic Order of the Alphabet. Maybe Deanna Schumacher had been in on the scheme, as well.

All I knew was that Sam Hellerman always had something up his sleeve. He had a plan for the band. He had a plan for me. He had a plan for everybody, and he would only let you in on what he felt you needed to know.

I suppressed the urge to point-blank him on it as I had done with Dr. Hexstrom. He would come up with an explanation that would be just as plausible as the others (in other words, just barely—but I would want to believe). Or he would refuse to say anything and subject me to the dread power of his overwhelming, wordless sarcasm. Fearing more Hellerman eye-ray treatment than I felt I could handle in my confused and enfeebled state, I decided to hold off on the point-blanking, at least till after the Festival of Lights. We still had a lot of work to do to get the band ready for the show, and, as I had learned the hard way when the whole Fiona business began, a disgruntled, sarcasm-soaked Hellerman is in many ways worse than no Hellerman at all. I had to keep the band together at least till the show, which was only two weeks away. I was grateful to the school schedule for providing me with a reason to postpone my decisions for just a bit longer. That's all a man ever really wants, in any case.

December

THE RODENT ROLE

The first two weeks of December were a bit surreal and went by in a kind of blur. Mr. Schtuppe was trying to time *Catcher in the Rye* so that we finished the reading and brain-dead assignments on the last day before the Christmas break began on the twentieth. We were already almost to the end, so the reading had slowed to a crawl. I imagine we copied down and used in sentences and mispronounced practically every word in the book several times, including "the" and "and." I spent a lot of time, in and out of class, engaged in an unspoken stream of questions that, if spoken aloud, would have been totally incomprehensible to anyone but me: "What's the deal with Tit? Who was MT? Did Tit really ramone MT? And what about the Dead Bastard?" On and on.

As for Deanna Schumacher, she and I were engaged in a deadly game of cat and mouse, with me in the rodent role. We were okay when we weren't talking, but practically every conversation was more or less a train wreck. The hardest part for me was her cold-and-distant routine, which she could turn on and off at will. It drove me crazy not to know what she was thinking about me, and there was never any point in asking–that would only spark a contemptuous kind of laughter. I knew the proper strategy was to act just as indifferent as she did, to try to keep her guessing, as well. But it was beyond my capabilities. I always broke down and revealed my anxiety in the end. Then she would pounce.

My third visit to her house, on the Monday after the Thanksgiving weekend, had gone pretty much like the previous episodes. She telephoned shortly after I got home, and I was all excited because that was the first time that had happened, until I heard what she said.

"You know, this really isn't working out for me. So, be

seeing you in all those old familiar places." And she hung up. I tried to call back, but her phone was off the hook. Anyway, she would have been with her boyfriend by that time anyway. The bastard.

I spent the rest of the night in a kind of agony, saying to myself over and over, "Don't call, don't call, don't call. . . ." Then when I would finally break down and call, it was busy anyway. Johnny Thunders was singing "You Can't Put Your Arm Around a Memory" on the stereo, or rather, I guess I should call it a mono, since it still had one blown channel: for the first time, I really felt I understood what he was getting at.

The next day I was a zombie. I felt the estrangement physically, as though sharp objects were embedded in my chest, slicing me up, and, not coincidentally, making me feel like a total idiot as well. Then when I got home from school, there was a note from Amanda on my door: "phone call, some chick, said don't worry and everything will be OK." I was suddenly ecstatic, till I realized that "everything will be OK" could be read in different ways. And I wasn't sure I would be all that pleased if things were Deanna Schumacher's version of okay.

Of course, I had other things to obsess over besides Deanna Schumacher and Timothy J. Anderson. There were just too many explanations for my dad's death floating around. It couldn't possibly have been murder *and* an accident *and* suicide. Any scenario I could come up with to explain why people seemed to think it could was preposterous. I didn't have much to go on, but if the deeply engraved "help" in *Siddhartha*, CEH 1964, was any indication, my dad had had something of a history of feeling overwhelmed and desperate. Most kids do. But I guess it can continue when they grow up. *The Crying of Lot 49* also had the word "help" written on it. I had thought it referred to the Beatles song, but if it was the same kind of help as the *Siddhartha* one, maybe there was a pattern there. It didn't square with my memory of him, but if he had been a habitually depressed person, my mom would have known. Perhaps this knowledge and an ambiguously phrased note had convinced my mom that it had been suicide despite the evidence to the contrary. It certainly wouldn't have been the only time my mom had believed something illogical or unsupported by the facts. On the other hand, she could just have been lying. I really couldn't say.

We had been working pretty hard to get the band ready for the Festival of Lights. We weren't sounding too bad. It was still pretty rough, but in our better moments, we sounded kind of like Buddy Holly meets Thin Lizzy with a punk rock sensibility and a slight psychedelic edge, like UFO playing Velvet Underground songs or something. Or so I told myself. When I said as much to Sam Hellerman, he sniffed and told me I was "trippin'." Well, at least we were getting better at playing at the same time as each other for most of the song, which was a big improvement.

RYE HELL

The title of *The Catcher in the Rye* comes from a misquoted poem by Robert Burns, which Holden Caulfield elaborates into a mystical fantasy about saving children from falling off a cliff. There are all these kids playing in a field of rye, and he stands guard ready to catch them if they stray from the field. A lot of people have found this to be a very moving metaphor for the experience of growing up, or anxiety about the loss of innocence, or the Mysterious Dance of Life. Or any random thing, really.

To use HC's own terminology, it has always seemed pretty goddam phony and all to me. Fantasies about Jane Gallagher's preppie ass? Check—even I have those. Fantasies about twisting yourself into a tortured symbol of the precious authenticity of youth? I don't think so. It's the kind of thing you'd make up to impress an AP teacher. And the AP teachers are duly impressed with it, of course. Suckers.

The brilliance of it, though, is that the people in the *Catcher* Cult manage to see themselves as everybody in the scenario all at once. They're the cute, virtuous kids playing in the rye, and they're also the troubled misfit adolescent who dreams of preserving the kids' innocence by force and who turns out to have been right all along. And they're *also* the grown-up moralistic busybody with the kid-sized butterfly net who is charged with keeping all the kids on the premises, no matter what. Somehow, they don't realize you can't root for them all.

Say you're a kid in this field of rye. You try to find a quiet place where you can be by yourself, to invent a code based on "The Star-Spangled Banner," or to design the first four album covers of your next band, or to write a song about a sad girl, or to read a book once owned by your deceased father. Or just to stare off into space and be alone with your thoughts. But pretty soon someone comes along and starts throwing gum in your hair, and gluing gay porn to your helmet, and urinating on your funny little hat from the St. Vincent de Paul, and hiring a psychiatrist to squeeze the individuality out of you, and making you box till first blood, and pouring Coke on your book, and beating you senseless in the boys' bathroom, and ridiculing your balls, and holding you upside down till you fall out of your pants, and publicly charting your sexual unattractiveness, and confiscating your Stratego, and forcing you to read and copy out pages from the same three books over and over and over. So you think, who needs it? You get up and start walking. And just when you think you've found the edge of the field and are about to emerge from Rye Hell, this AP teacher or baby-boomer parent dressed as a beloved literary character scoops you up and throws you back into the pit of vipers. I mean, the field of rye.

Sound good? I'm sorry, but I'm rooting for the kids and hoping they get out while they can. And as for you, Holden, old son: if you happen to meet my body coming through the rye, I'd really appreciate it if you'd just stand aside and get out of my fucking way.

HOW NORMAL PEOPLE TRIED TO KILL ROCK AND ROLL, AND HOW ROCK AND ROLL CAME BACK TO BITE THEM ON THE ASS

When the day of the show arrived, I was pretty surprised at how many other rock bands there turned out to be at Hillmont. We were on last out of four bands, according to the schedule. Everyone who was in the Festival of Lights was allowed to take third period off as well, to set up. So there we were in the auditorium standing around checking each other out while the three sullen drummers were off to the side, grumbling and swearing under their breath about how no one was helping them set up, and mumbling that they played percussion, not just drums. There were three rather than four disgruntled percussionists because Todd Panchowski was in two of the bands, ours and Alter of Blood. Actually, to judge from the retarded flyers they had made, their official name appeared to be Alter of Blood (Formally Black Leviticus). I supposed they were Christian metal, though they could have been just plain old metal. Hard to tell sometimes.

It was easy to tell, though, who was in either Alter of Blood or Karmageddon, as they were the heavy-metal stoner types. By process of elimination, I guessed that the remaining band, Radio Free Atlantis, had to be made up of one stoner drummer, two goths, and two normal people. Everyone had better amps than us in terms of quality, but Sam Hellerman had them all beat in terms of coolness. He had purchased an old and extremely large nonfunctional Magnavox hi-fi stereo cabinet from the St. Vincent de Paul for twenty bucks and had replaced the insides with the electronics and speakers from the Fender Bassman. Okay, so Sam Hellerman and I were the only ones there who realized how cool it was. We're used to it. One day they'll wake up and realize that we were right about everything all along. Now, though, they were just standing there laughing at my guitar, which was, unbeknownst to them, by far the coolest and most valuable thing in the room. But I admit: it certainly didn't have uber-super-mega-quadruple-distortion pickups like everybody else's guitar.

The hippie-ish drama teacher (Mr. Malkoe, but he wanted you to call him Chet) was in charge, because it was "his" auditorium we would potentially be trashing. The third-period drama class, those who were still there, including Celeste Fletcher, Syndie Duffy, and assorted boyfriends and minions, were all sitting in the back, laughing and "getting high," I suppose. "Chet" had an easygoing manner on the outside, but inside he was an auditorium Nazi. He immediately confiscated our Balls Deep banner, just as Amanda had predicted. I tried all the usual tricks (calling him "man," saying I was glad he stopped the Vietnam War, flashing him the peace sign). But despite his obvious admiration for Little Big Tom's Che Guevara shirt, he had pretty much seen it all and positively would not be sweet-talked out of his fascist freedom-of-expression-crushing banner ban. So the banner was history. He also forbade everyone from setting anything on fire. I saw a little light grow and die in Sam Hellerman's eyes: even if he hadn't been intending to set anything on fire before, he certainly was indignant at the prohibition now. "What might have been," his eyes seemed to say.

"Wait till the revolution comes," he whispered. "Chet Guevara will be the first against the wall." And I could see his point, Matt Lynch notwithstanding.

Only Radio Free Atlantis, the first band, got to soundcheck, which they finished doing just as the small chunk of the Hillmont High School student body that hadn't decided to skip the "festival" and take off began to filter in. I was impressed with how RFA sounded. And when I say impressed, I mean that in the sense of "extremely bummed out." How come we couldn't sound like that? Maybe it was all in the PA.

So they started playing for real, and as I said, sonically it was relatively awesome, much better than any sound we were ever able to produce in my living room. The bass player (one of the goths) was even pretty good. They couldn't play together very well, but it's not like we could, either. I wasn't sure what they were going for. At first I thought they were doing a kind of Cocksparrer/Sham 69 sort of football-chant punk rock. Then, to my even greater surprise, I figured out that they were going for a Smiths-y kind of thing. In fact, I soon realized that their whole set list was made up of punky Smiths and Cure and Joy Division covers, though many were so ineptly executed that it was hard to tell without a great deal of structural analysis. I don't know if the punkiness was intentional or not, which is a common enough situation. Now, the irony was that the singer was Dennis Trela, who was among the most sadistic alpha psychos the normal world had to offer. In other words, he was a major player in the nation of perpetrators: he and his evil superbitch girlfriend had been responsible for half of the suicide attempts, nervous breakdowns, and eating disorders in the greater Bay Area. It's guys like Dennis Trela who made the Smiths and the Cure and Joy Division necessary in the first place. I had thought normal people and that sort of music were mutually exclusive, but I guess I was wrong. It's a funny world.

The nonband acts were scheduled to go on during the setup times, so while Karmageddon were setting up, this guy named Ben was doing an extremely ill-advised tap-dancing routine to "Singin' in the Rain." My guess is that he had lost a bet. But you just can't tap-dance in front of an auditorium full of normal people and expect them not to take the bait. I heard this sound that was at once familiar and strange, the sound of around a hundred people pretending to cough and saying the word "homo" at the same time. There was also some loud fag-oriented heckling, chanting, and whatnot, which the crowd continued for some time after Ben left the stage. Fortunately, when you have amps and so forth, you can drown out the heckling. That's what I was counting on. But hell, Ben got more of a response than Radio Free Atlantis had. You could look at it that way.

Both of the other bands were Black Sabbath–y, whether they realized it or not. Alter of Blood did their Christian Black Sabbath songs at normal slow speed, while Karmageddon sped their evil Black Sabbath songs up to a blur, so that they sounded like a malfunctioning piece of machinery. Both lead singers were trying as hard as they could to impersonate the Cookie Monster, and both guitarists played variations on "Flight of the Bumblebee" during the entire set without stopping, even between "songs." Fortunately for Alter of Blood, the guitar-o-technics drew attention away from the fact that

Todd Panchowski was finding counting to four a bit beyond his grasp. I envied them for that, at least.

Sam Hellerman pointed to the Alter of Blood guitarist as he let loose volley after volley of hammered-on and pulled-off hemisemidemiquavers. "Go tell him he missed a note," he whispered. I almost spit my Coke all over my Che Guevara shirt.

I must admit, as our turn approached, I was getting pretty nervous, especially when I noticed Deanna Schumacher, along with around three or four other girls in IHA-SV uniforms, creeping into the auditorium through the side door. I tried to catch her eye and wave to her, but she pretended she didn't notice. Oops, I realized. I was supposed to act like I didn't know her, especially in front of her friends. I tried to wink, but I'm no good at winking, so I just mouthed "gotcha," but she pretended not to notice that either.

Of course, that "gotcha" was dubious in every sense.

The main reason I was so taken aback by the Skoomacker factor was that I had recently broken down and tried to call her on an unauthorized day. I suppose I had been hoping for a little "I'm so glad you called" action and for a feeling that I had more or less made it through the maze after all. As it turned out, though, here's what happened:

She picked up the phone without screening and, when she realized it was me, said, "My boyfriend's here right now, and I'm sure he's wondering who's calling me at this hour. You want to talk to him?" I quickly hung up and went searching for a place to hide till I was done hyperventilating. I guess the Monday/Thursday schedule was there for a reason. I had reached a dead end and was still in the pseudorelationship maze after all. Yet now here she was, cutting class at Immaculate Heart Academy to see my band play. Or maybe it was her lunch period and they had open campus.

Now, if they ever make a TV movie called *The Chi-Mo Story*, they'll probably try to present our performance at the Festival of Lights as a grand triumph of the underdog, a tribute to the noble spirit of the alienated and abused. We shamed and changed society. Because we three claimed our freedom, all are free. Hooray for us. In fact, our set did have a pretty significant impact on Hillmont High School society, but it was mostly negative, and entirely by accident. And it wasn't a triumph. In fact, it totally sucked.

The first thing that went wrong was that unlike in movies and afterschool specials, where the sound would have been done by sympathetic people from the Math Club or something, the people in charge of the PA were totally normal guys, so they were psychotic and hate-filled and wanted us to die. And they wouldn't let us use the PA. Or rather, they wanted a hundred dollars for the PA and fifty for the lights. I'm sure they hadn't tried to charge the other bands, but they weren't interested in arguing on that basis. Clearly, we didn't have the money, and we had to resolve the issue quickly. The act before us was a normal backward-baseball-hat guy who was "rapping" to a backing track about how he had ramoned everybody's mother or something. He was deeply into his second appalling minute and we knew it would end soon and we would be on. But the normal PA guys wouldn't budge on the hundred and fifty bucks.

Sam Hellerman did a little Ronald Reagan voice and said, "I paid for this microphone," which I thought was funny but which didn't go over so well with the normal PA guys.

"Oops," said one of them, and knocked Sam Hellerman's Slurpee into his chest, all over his lovingly hand-lettered "Mao Is Murder" T-shirt. Sam Hellerman got that familiar "I'm totally gonna bleed all over this guy" look on his face, but he restrained himself and started to wheel and deal with them instead. In the end he got them to rent him one microphone and to turn on two lights for fifteen bucks, which was all we had on us.

We had to work quickly, but we knew what to do. I found a hand truck backstage and duct-taped Amanda's karaoke mic to the handle, while Sam Hellerman taped the rented microphone to one of Todd Panchowski's unused cymbal stands. Todd Panchowski wasn't too pleased about that but allowed it, presumably because he was worried that otherwise Sam Hellerman might be tempted to express his disappointment by bleeding on his drums—it wasn't like it hadn't happened before. Although the stand was pretty short, it was about Hellerman height after its legs had been taped to the seat of a metal folding chair. In fact, since he had to slump so far to reach the strings of his low-slung bass with the fingers at the end of his half-dislocated right arm, he still had to tilt his head up Lemmy style to sing into the mic after all. My mouth was level with the taped-on karaoke mic if I lowered my body by spreading my legs wide enough. It almost worked.

Sam Hellerman, true to form, had brought along an XLR-to-quarter-inch adaptor, so we were able to plug both mics into the Frankenstein Bassman/Magnavox amp, just like at home. Living room rock. Live. In concert.

The fake rap guy finished, saying how he had "mad love" for his "hood" and "da funk," and wanted to "shout out" to his "homies" about how he had nine millimeters for "they ass" and wanted to put his "gat" to "they dome" just as we were ready to go. It was more like an abortion than music, but he got a wildly enthusiastic response from the crowd. Well, we're all pro-choice out here in Hillmont, after all.

I hadn't meant to, but it turned out that here I made what I guess you'd call a fateful decision. I was standing at the taped-on mic thinking about how Amanda's banned banner had really been the best thing about Balls Deep, and how Sam Hellerman's costume had been ruined and how Todd Panchowski had refused even to consider wearing his, and how everyone else got to use the PA without paying, and how nobody was ever going to understand the seventies porn/communist guerilla concept, and how I was tired of the name anyway, and how I would never know why my dad was dead, and how I really hated all normal people with every fiber of my being, not only because of the PA and Sam Hellerman's Slurpee, but because of Charles Evan Henderson's *Brighton Rock* and Bobby Duboyce's helmet and Yasmynne Schmick's pain and suffering and everybody's *Catcher in the Rye* hypocrisy and Mr. Donnelly's cruelty and Matt Lynch's sadism and Mr. Teone's idiocy and so many, many other things, including pretty much everything that had ever happened to me or that I had ever seen happen to anybody else. So as the student body's white rap/poetry slam euphoria started to fade, and they gaped at us and several of them started trying to instigate a "you suck!" chant, I positioned my mouth about an inch from the karaoke mic (so I wouldn't get shocked too bad) and—well, I think right up to the end I had intended to say, "hi, we're Balls Deep." But instead, what came out of my mouth was:

"Hi, we're the Chi-Mos." Then I didn't know what to say. Sam Hellerman stared at me, but he quickly recovered.

"Yeah!" he yelled in a high-pitched Paul Stanley voice, with a surprising degree of (devil-head) bravado, under the circumstances. "All right! We're the Chi-Mos! That's the Reverend Chi-Mo on guitar! And I'm your Assistant Principal Chi-Mo on bass and being aware of my own mortality, and back there we have Chi-Mo Panchowski on percussion and counting to four! Well, close enough, anyway! This song's called 'I Saw Mr. Teone Checking Out Kyrsten Blakeney's Ass'!"

Now, what was supposed to happen next was that Todd Panchowski would count off with four stick clicks and we would launch into the song. And that would have been pretty cool. But what actually happened was that Todd Panchowski just sat there for a while. Then he took his little towel and wiped off his face. Then he stood up and adjusted his drum seat. Then he raised his sticks in the air and twirled them around. Then he bent down to pick up the stick he had dropped. Then, around four hours later, he finally did the count-in, except that he did only three not-quite-regular clicks and started a beat ahead of the rest of us. Well, he always did have a hard time remembering what comes after three. And here's a valuable lesson I learned that I will share with anybody who may want to try to have a band one day: the fewer songs you have the drummer start, the more chance you'll have of getting to do more than a couple of them in twenty minutes. Have them start with the guitar instead. Trust me.

I have to admit, our "music" was, in its own way, no less abominable than the white rap thing had been. Most of what we had accomplished in all those practices just evaporated under the pressure of the "gig." The Hillmont student body were unimpressed, and not even moved enough to join in the "you suck!" chant that a few optimistic psycho normals kept trying to start. I think the crowd had realized that the most disheartening thing they could do in this situation was to gape in silent, stunned bemusement. They weren't wrong about that, either. I don't know how real bands manage to have three or more people all play the same thing at the same time—it was clearly beyond our capabilities. I kept getting shocked by the mic, so around half of the lyrics were lost, though without the PA I doubt anyone could tell one way or another. Meanwhile, we had these long, uncomfortable pauses between songs because of Todd Panchowski's misguided attempts at reverse showmanship. It was a disaster.

"Yeah, I hear somebody say keep on rockin'?" said Sam Hellerman after we had finished the first tune. Now, this world is vast and complex, full of ambiguity and uncertainty. But if there was one thing in this muddled, crazy universe that was absolutely clear and beyond debate at that particular moment, it was this: Sam Hellerman had not heard anybody say keep on rockin'.

The best thing we had going for us was the song titles, many of which got a laugh when Sam Hellerman announced them. We did "Mr. Teone Likes 'em Young" and "Are There Hippies in Heaven (and If So, Can We at Least Confiscate Their Patchouli, 'Cause Otherwise I'm Definitely Going to Hell)?" We also did "I Wanna Ramone You," which only I knew was in honor of Deanna Schumacher, and "Glad All Over," which Sam Hellerman introduced by saying, "This song is about the face of God."

Fortunately, our songs were very short. But we still had to cut quite a few because of Todd Panchowski's delays, which were driving Sam Hellerman off the deep end. He kept looking back at the drum set, begging him with his eyes to start the song already. Plus, while Sam Hellerman was trying to introduce the songs with his clever little shrieked speeches, Todd Panchowski would just hit drums randomly, or practice his paradiddles on the snare. It was distracting, and I didn't blame Sam Hellerman for being annoyed.

Our big finale was supposed to be "The Guy I Accidentally Beat Up," the lyrics of which were just Paul Krebs's name repeated over and over, ending in a wall of instrumental psychedelia during which we were supposed to chant "Freak out, freak out. . . . " Sam Hellerman announced the song as best he could, trying to shout over the paradiddles, and waited for Todd Panchowski's irregular count-in. He looked back after a while and saw TP standing on the drum seat with his arms raised for some reason. He'd had enough. He gave Todd Panchowski the most intense, most devastating eye-ray treatment the world had yet seen. Todd Panchowski flipped Sam Hellerman off, threw his sticks at him and stormed off the stage. Oh, well, it really wasn't working out between us anyway.

So we did "The Guy I Accidentally Beat Up" without drums, but we skipped the actual song and started from the outro because we were running out of time and the audience was leaving. Sam Hellerman started bleeding from his nose, making sure that he thoroughly soaked the rented microphone. I put my guitar against the amp and turned it up all the way to cause as much feedback as possible, and then we knocked the drums over and tore the Magnavox apart by hitting it with the drum hardware. Sam Hellerman was on the speakers, jumping up and down, blood flying, hitting the Magnavox with a cymbal stand till it stopped making noise and was in several pieces. I was kicking the drum set, which soon was little more than a pile of rubbish. We were definitely going to have to find a new drummer after this. Todd Panchowski's main qualification had been that he'd had a drum set. And he certainly didn't have one of those anymore.

The set, and the Festival of Lights, finally ended when "Chet" and a few others pulled us away from the wreckage and switched off the Polytone. Sam Hellerman, who had been rolling in his own blood screaming what sounded like "yay-uss" over and over, had to be physically restrained by no fewer than three thoroughly confused goons. The students, who had been hurrying toward the exits when the destruction began, had all stopped dead in their tracks to stare and remained frozen for some time. They didn't know what to say—even "you suck!" must have seemed inadequate. There was total silence, and for probably the first time in my Hillmont High School career I could hear myself think. It was nice, though the thoughts weren't.

TOTALLY CALLABLE

We didn't win the battle of—I mean, the Festival of Lights. The "yo mama" guy did. Everyone had hated the Chi-Mos. But we had made an impression, albeit a negative one, and it was the kind of thing people talked about, which is what everyone did for the rest of the day and well into the following week.

Sam Hellerman had printed up a zine with the lyrics to all the songs on the set list plus several others. It had said "Balls Deep," of course, but as he stood at the main exit handing them out, he wrote "The Chi-Mos" at the top of each one in Sharpie, so it looked like "Balls Deep" was just the title. It proved to be a pretty popular item because of its populist anti-Teone message, and he ran out quickly, promising to go over to the Copymat to make more as soon as possible.

I was kind of in a daze standing by the stage when Deanna Schumacher came up and whispered, "Thanks for hanging up on me, ass." (It didn't matter what I said before I put the phone back on the hook: she always claimed she thought I had hung up on her.) But then she said, "Nice show, sexy," in a voice that didn't sound all the way sarcastic and handed me a note, sneakily rubbing my palm with her finger as she did it, before running off to join her friends, who were on the way out. The note said: "Thanks for rawking my world. I'm totally callable Mon/Thur from 6 to 10 if you're into it," and it was signed with a heart and a big "D." And next to the heart it said "slurp." I kid you not.

Cleaning up after our set had taken longer than anticipated, so I was late for sixth period. I stopped in to the otherwise deserted boys' bathroom, and Mr. Teone ambled in.

Now, Mr. Teone's office is located just across the corner from the boys' bathroom at the southwest corner of center court, so he can see its door from his desk through the mirrored plate glass, though you can't see him looking. When he has some important matter to discuss with a student in an unofficial capacity, he'll wait for his moment and try to meet him in the bathroom for an informal chat. I don't know who takes care of the girls' bathroom in that corner of center court. Not Mr. Teone, surely, but, hey, you never know.

I had never been a participant in one of these secret meetings, but I had walked in on them. When someone walks in, Mr. Teone abruptly ends the meeting and growls something like "keep your nose clean!" Then he'll zoom out, but as he leaves he'll say to the interloper: "that goes double for you, Henderson!" Well, he only says Henderson if the interloper happens to be me or someone else with my last name. Obviously.

But for the first time, I wasn't the interloper. I was the main guy.

"Well, well, Henderson," he said, standing a couple of urinals over from me, "you and your stunt you boys pulled has a great deal of folks around here pretty steamed."

I gave him a look that said: "well, if I interpret your tortured, semiliterate syntax correctly, my only comment is that all great artists are misunderstood in their own time."

He stepped away from his urinal, which was kind of scary, but it turned out he was fully dressed and buttoned up. Thank

God. I gave up trying to pee and buttoned up as well. I can't do that with anyone else in the room, especially Mr. Teone. He was holding his reading glasses to one eye and squinting at a copy of Sam Hellerman's song zine.

"Chi-Mos," he said slowly, but he pronounced it, Schtuppe fashion, "chee moss." "Mind telling me what that's supposed to mean?"

Now, I had been in many ironic situations before, but none of them had quite prepared me for this. I mean, here was a leading figure in the normal hierarchy, a high-ranking official representative of the Perpetrator Nation, asking me to explain the meaning of the derogatory name foisted upon me by their own sadistic test several years ago and used against me as a weapon by their lower-ranking minions ever since. I snorted. How quickly we forget.

"It's the plural of 'chy moe,'" I said, correcting his pronunciation. "It stands for 'child molester.'"

He continued to squint at me. "Where are you getting this stuff?" he said.

I stared at him with a serious look, the look that says only a (devil-head) philistine asks an artist where he gets his ideas. Then I laughed a little, because, you know, sometimes I crack myself up.

"Now listen to me," he said suddenly, his red face a match for that of any PE teacher, his voice a (devil-head) histrionic stage whisper. He tapped the zine with his finger. "This crap . . ." He trailed off. "I don't know who you think you're dealing with, but watch your step, Henderson. Keep your nose clean!" Well, I could understand why he didn't like the lyrics to "Mr. Hitler, Mr. Stalin, Mr. Teone," but this was a bit over-the-top. He was still whispering, but it was loud, kind of like yell-whispering. His face was throbbing red, and drops of sweat were spattering from it in all directions. Yuck.

Enter the interloper, who happened to be Syndie Duffy's floppy fake-hippie boyfriend.

"You remember what I said," said Mr. Teone. "Don't be an a-hole." And then, as he stormed out: "And that goes double for you, Shinefield!"

"Dude," said Shinefield, after Mr. Teone left. "Radical show!" Pause. "Really?"

"Insane," he said, which I took to mean "yes, really." Then he added: "What did Teone want?"

"He was just advising me not to be an a-hole."

"Yeah," said Shinefield. "Me too."

I felt a strange sense of well-being. Here was the only conversation I'd ever had in the boys' bathroom that hadn't consisted of introductory remarks to an eventual attempt on my life. In fact, I was trying to think of another conversation I'd had anywhere with anyone other than Sam Hellerman or Dr. Hexstrom that hadn't been at my expense, but I was drawing a blank. So this is what it's like, I thought. Going to the bathroom would never be the same again. As I was soon to learn, though, suddenly becoming a quasi celebrity doesn't necessarily mean that attempts on your life cease to occur: they just tend to move to venues other than the boys' bathroom. Still, it was progress, any way you sliced it.

"Rock on, Chi-Mo!" Shinefield called out as I left, and I didn't really mind the nickname all that much.

A DR. HEXSTROM-ECTOMY

When I got home from school that day, Little Big Tom took me aside and told me that my mom had had a falling-out with Dr. Hexstrom and that they were looking for another therapist for me. I'd expected this. My guess was that they wouldn't actually get around to finding another doctor, and that that would be the end of the experiment in Chi-Mo modification unless I did something major like set something on fire or killed somebody.

A little later on, I talked to Amanda, who said that as far as she knew, suicide prevention hadn't even been the main thing on Mom's mind with the psychiatrist plan; she had just been hoping Dr. Hexstrom would give me some pills and set me on the road to being more normal and maybe then I'd go out for sports or something. But in their meeting, Dr. Hexstrom had told her that she was the problem, not me, and suggested that she come in with me for some family-type counseling, because she needed help. My mom fired her on the spot. Well, good old Dr. Hexstrom. Not that I would have gone along with the family counseling thing. That sounded like a nightmare. I was going to miss talking to her, but oh well. Maybe it's my destiny to remain a non-normal, unmed-icated and uncorrected eccentric with no one interesting to talk to. It would figure.

"Did you know Dad killed himself?" I asked, after a brief struggle to remain silent. To my surprise, for once she didn't give me the look that says "you're as dumb as a freeze-dried coffee crystal."

"That's what she thinks," she said. "I don't know. She thinks a lot of weird things."

"She told Dr. Hexstrom he left a note."

"I know," she said. "I've looked for that note. There is no note."

So while my mom had been telling me a story about how my dad had died in a car accident, she was also telling Amanda a story about how he had killed himself. Or more probably, she was just being her crazy self, oblivious to both of us, and we had sensibly assumed that whatever she was implying had to be wrong. It's just that Amanda and I had accidentally drawn different conclusions about which fake story was being implied. Who knows who was right?

Amanda had started to cry a little. I felt bad for bringing it up, as I'd known I would.

"I don't care how it happened," she said. "I just wish it didn't happen."

She had the right idea, of course. I put my arm around her kind of awkwardly, and she put hers around my neck and squeezed really hard, still sobbing. I almost joined in, even though she was doing enough crying for both of us. All the reasoning and investigating in the world were never going to bring him back. Part of me still wanted everything to make sense, but the biggest part of me realized that Amanda was right and that that was an impossibly high standard.

IS THE RELATIONSHIP STILL IMAGINARY IF YOU CAN MAKE EACH OTHER CRY?

On Saturday afternoon, the day after the Festival of Lights, I walked into the kitchen to find my mom waiting for me with that familiar family-discussion look on her face. Little Big Tom wasn't there, though, which was pretty weird: he lives for family discussions. I expected we were going to be talking about psychiatry and suicide and sports, that sort of thing, and I braced myself. But she wasn't looking all that disturbed or crazy–she was more like bemusedly exasperated, if I read her body language correctly. You never could tell with her, though.

"I've been on the phone with Marjorie Blakeney all morning," she said. "Kyrsten was very upset by your little poetry booklet. Everyone has been teasing her. She locked herself in her room and hasn't stopped crying since yesterday. So . . ."

I hadn't noticed before, but my mom was holding a copy of Sam Hellerman's zine—one of the new ones that he had printed up that said "The Chi-Mos" instead of "Balls Deep." The cover had a big picture of Mr. Teone and the title was "Never Again." Carol moves in mysterious ways. I didn't even have one of those yet.

I shot her my best "you're losing me, sweetheart" look. I mean, "Callipygian Princess" is really just a heartfelt celebration of feminine beauty, and "Shake It Like You Mean It" doesn't even mention her by name. But she had the zine open to "I Saw Mr. Teone Checking Out Kyrsten Blakeney's Ass," and I guess it wasn't too hard to fill in the "so." Who knew Kyrsten Blakeney would have such a thin skin? She had to be used to people checking out her ass, but maybe she just blocked Mr. Teone out of her mind when the subject of ass-gazing popped up. I mean, that's what I would have done. But here it was in unavoidable black and white. Now, I had meant that song as a righteous indictment of Mr. Teone's (devil-head) iniquity, but I suppose I had also accidentally robbed Kyrsten Blakeney of the peace of willful ignorance and forgetting. I knew how that felt, I really did, and I genuinely felt bad about it. It was a bit of a stretch, but I made a quick attempt to feel sorry for myself while pretending to be Kyrsten Blakeney, and it even kind of almost worked in the end: that is, the resulting song "Up for Grabs" ended up being one of my few good girl-point-of-view tunes when I finally got around to writing it.

But that was long after all the stuff that I'm about to explain happened. At the time I just said, "I didn't mean to hurt Kyrsten Blakeney's feelings." Then I couldn't help adding that the callipygous among us have a certain responsibility as public figures. My mom just stared at me in incomprehension, which I suppose was the reaction I wanted. I don't even understand what motivates me sometimes. She finally said she thought it might be nice if I apologized. So while she lighted up a Virginia Slims 120, I tore a sheet from my notebook and quickly wrote:

```
Dear Kyrsten Blakeney,
    I apologize for mentioning your
callipygousness in the context of Mr.
Teone, and for immortalizing it in song.
That was inappropriate. I see that now.
But you should probably get used to the
idea that one of your roles in life will
always be to inspire devotion and poetry
among the dreamers, even though I can
see how in a certain way that can be a
pain.
    Anyhow, I am very, very sorry. Please
don't develop another eating disorder on
my account. It's really not worth it.
Sincerely,
Thomas Charles Henderson
```

I was folding it up, but my mom was holding out her hand, so I gave it to her. After she read it, she refolded it and put it in the Chi-Mos zine. Then she said, in a wry manner I hadn't really thought her capable of, "maybe you'd better leave the apologizing to me after all."

That seemed to wrap it up, but Carol had more to say. She asked me what Chi-Mo meant. I told her it was a fond name that the other kids had given me just to show how much they loved and cared for me. She didn't believe me, but she wouldn't have believed the truth, either.

"Well, I've also been on the phone with Tony Teone," she said, after a brief pause. "He's also very upset by your little booklet. So . . ."

I almost didn't realize who she was referring to. Then I did, and I snort-laughed uncontrollably. Tony Teone? *Tony Teone?* Fully retarded. She misinterpreted the laughter and looked at me sternly. "You really hurt his feelings."

Now, this was too much.

"Mr. Teone," I said carefully, "is a devil-head maleficent, depraved, iniquitous, sadistic blackguard." Except, in excellent Mr. Schtuppe style, I said "mal-efficient." I was finally getting the hang of the mispronunciation thing. The trick is to make the mispronunciation have a totally different meaning from the correctly pronounced word. My education was finally starting to bear fruit.

She stared at me. "A devil-head, inefficient, black—uh, what?" Okay, I hadn't intended to say "devil-head" aloud, and I could see why she was confused.

"Look," I said, trying again in words she would be sure to understand. "Mr. Teone is a bad, bad man. The font of all evil."

"He has always felt warmly toward you," she said. "He had a lot of respect for your father."

The fuck? I told her about Mr. Teone's constant ridicule and abuse, the sarcastic salutes, and so forth. "Yeah," I said, "he's the devil-head embodiment of warmth and respect. A real swell guy. No way I'm apologizing to him."

"Well, they were in the navy together," she said, and I had to admit, though reluctantly, that that kind of could account for the saluting thing. And maybe the "say hi to your father" had been a retarded attempt to say "pay my respects when you visit the cemetery"? I had to concede that it hadn't, perhaps, all been sarcastic. When you think about it, it's kind of hard to pull off Respect without everybody assuming it's Sarcasm. It just is. But while I was considering this, my mom was still talking. "... they were very close, the two of them. So ..."

I was trying to fill in that so when a weird thought struck me. "Mom, do you know Mr. Teone's middle name?" I asked, but I already knew the kind of answer I was going to get.

"Yeah, it's Isadore," she said. "And it's actually kind of funny. Because of his initials, everyone always used to call him Tit." She giggled, and under other circumstances I would have found that cute.

Tony Isadore Teone. Well, ramone me with a Mosrite.

BEYOND GOOD AND EVIL

So Mr. Teone was Tit. A middle-aged Tit, rather, just as my dad would have been a middle-aged CEH had he lived. It was really hard to imagine that in 1960 my dad's best friend had been a twelve-year-old version of Mr. Teone. On the other hand, how did I know what was hard or easy to imagine? I hadn't known my dad then, and, as was constantly being brought home to me, I hadn't known him very well even when the two of us had happened to be alive at the same time. Maybe he and Tit were two peas in a pod, just as evil as each other. Or maybe Mr. Teone had once been sweet and delightful, an all-around great guy and a joy to be around as a child, only turning evil later on. But no, Tit was evil by at least 1963. The coded note proved that. I loved my dad and trusted that he hadn't been evil but had merely associated with at least one guy who happened to be evil, which wasn't quite so bad. Because you have to believe in something. Don't you?

I was also having some trouble squaring the clever young Tit, who could write codes in backward French and manipulate biblical quotations to his own nefarious ends, with the fat, dumb galunk he had apparently become. But people degenerate as they get older, and anyway, it was possible that Mr. Teone wasn't quite as dumb as he looked. He knew Latin, after all, though that could simply reflect the fact that he had gone to school back when they still taught you things other than how to make great collages. It wasn't a matter of intelligence, really. Evil was the common thread here. And maybe the obesity, too. Poor, dear little MT, I thought. Something told me we weren't talking about top-quality ramoning here.

A thought struck: what if Mr. Teone wasn't evil after all? What if he turned out to be a Disney-ish figure, unjustly maligned at the beginning, who would eventually be revealed as a kindly soul with an important message to impart? "Son, your old man wanted you to have this," he'd say, waving some object or other, a sword or a curious gold coin. "But I had to wait till I knew you were old enough to understand. Fortunately, you passed the test. Oh, you didn't realize you are descended from kings? Well, you are, and it's time to claim your rightful place." Descended from kings? Oh my God, it all fits. "I'm terribly sorry," he'd continue, "about the hazing, the mockery, the torture, the permanent psychological and emotional scars. We had to do that so you wouldn't suspect the big surprise party we've been planning for you."

Somehow, I couldn't see it. I had to stand by my instinct that Mr. Teone was a bad guy, the apex of a pyramid of despicable, sadistic normal psychos who wanted me and Sam Hellerman dead. I never really doubted it. The fact that he had known my dad just made his evil a bit more complicated, that's all.

That said, I realized that Mr. Teone would have answers to many of my questions, if only I could figure out a way to ask them. I was still sitting in the kitchen, thinking things over. My mom got up and I could hear her footsteps as she walked over to the living room. Then I heard some shuffling, followed by another little burst of giggling: and I knew she had just looked up "callipygian" in the dictionary.

I took out a sheet of paper and wrote another note:

Dear Mr. Teone,
    In light of recent events, I feel there are important matters we need to discuss. These concern materials among my deceased father's effects which you may be in a position to elucidate.
Please contact me at your earliest convenience to arrange a meeting so that we can discuss these issues and, I hope, come to a satisfactory arrangement.
Best wishes,
Thomas Charles Henderson

I put the note in an envelope and put the envelope in my backpack. Then I went into the living room. My mom was sitting on the couch, reading the Chi-Mos zine and looking up words in the American Heritage dictionary.

"Mom, was Dad really in the navy?" I asked.

"Yes, he was," she replied absently. "For three years."

And then, since I was on a roll, I dared to add, "and did he really commit suicide?"

"I'm sorry, baby," she whispered. I had a sort of feeling that she meant that as a "yes, but let's say no more about it." But it could just as easily have meant "no" or "maybe," or perhaps "decline to state." I tried one more.

"Can I see the note?"

"No."

Well, that answer seemed to imply that there *had* been a note, but I remained unsure. I was ready in case she started to flip out, but she didn't. She looked pretty sad, though, and there may have been tears in her eyes; but there were almost always tears in her eyes. So I just went over and kissed her on the cheek.

I left the room in silence. I was going to leave it at that, but then something came over me, and I reversed course and went back in and approached the couch.

"Why can't you be straight with anyone?" I said. "You tell everyone different things and you keep the truth to yourself."

She looked up, surprised: it was a very uncharacteristic outburst from me. Then she said, quietly, "I'm sorry, baby." This time I knew what it meant. It meant she didn't know why she couldn't be straight with anyone. She touched my arm, and it was the most affectionate thing I'd had from her in a long, long time.

UNCLE TONY

On Monday morning, it was already clear that our performance at the Festival of Lights had had an impact on Hillmont High society. Sam Hellerman's new version of the lyrics zine was quite popular. He was selling them for two dollars apiece, and he already had over a hundred dollars by the end of first period. It was a good thing, too, because Todd Panchowski's parents were reportedly planning to sue our parents' asses over his wrecked drum set: we needed the money. At this rate–well, I couldn't quite calculate how many we'd have to sell to cover a drum set and legal costs and still maybe have enough left over so that my share would be at least a hundred and fifty dollars so I could schedule my own appointment with Dr. Hexstrom. Because I really wanted to discuss Tit with her, after all that had happened.

Anyway, our band had sucked and had been hated by one and all, but the zine was a hit. A couple of kids in homeroom even asked me to autograph their copies. (I noticed, though, with a slightly guilty pang, that Kyrsten Blakeney was absent. Or I think that's what that pang was.) It wasn't like suddenly everyone wanted to be our friends or anything. Well, Shinefield, Syndie Duffy's fake-hippie boyfriend, did seem to want to be friends. When I passed him in the hall he said, "Chi-Mo!" and put out his fist, which I dodged by force of habit. But he was only trying to do the hipster patty-cake secret-handshake thing, where you touch fists, then touch them again with one on top and then the other on top, and then snap your fingers and say "my brother" or something. I don't really get how to do it, so I gave him the Vulcan "live long and prosper" sign instead, which was just going to have to do.

Other than Shinefield, the general public still gave us a wide berth, and most of them probably wouldn't have considered being seen doing the hipster handshake with either of us. But it was a bit like when I had accidentally beaten up Paul Krebs. Somehow we had inched up the scale. We had produced useful materials and provided a needed service. Laughter at Mr. Teone's expense was in the end more valuable to society than strict enforcement of the pecking order.

Speaking of which, after homeroom that morning, Mr. Teone once again accosted me in the boys' bathroom. If I still harbored any hope that there was in the offing a Teone-related surprise party in my honor, it quickly sank, killing all on board. His transformation from pudgy, freakish, administrative buffoon to terrifying PE teacher–ogre had reached yet a further stage. I mean, his face was the color of sweet-and-sour sauce and a vein in his neck was throbbing to the beat of a dance track that it alone could hear. I almost didn't recognize him. He looked like a less flat-chested Ms. Rimbaud.

"God damn it, Henderson!" he whisper-roared. "What in hell you think you're trying to pull?"

"I'm sorry I hurt your feelings," I said deliberately, "but I believe my right to satirize you, as a public figure, is protected by the First Amendment."

He ignored the legal argument. "What we need to establish," he continued, his damp, vibrating, PE-teacher face a revolting inch or so from mine, "is where you're getting your information."

I reached into my backpack, pulled out my *Catcher in the Rye*, CEH 1960, and looked at him meaningfully, sure he would recognize it. But I was wrong.

"Yes, yes, yes," he said impatiently. "A timeless classic. I used to carry one around with me when I was your age and it changed my life and society. Now cut the cute stuff–" I kid you not, he said "cut the cute stuff." Despite the vibrant, Technicolor facial hue, this was pure black-and-white B-movie dialogue.

"Look," I said, when it was clear that he hadn't been able to come up with a way to end that sentence about the cute stuff. "Don't you think you ought to be a little less unpleasant toward me, considering everything?" It seemed reasonable, given that we were two people separated by a common relationship with Charles Evan Henderson's copy of *Catcher in the Rye,* and I said it as politely as I could. He didn't take it that way, though.

"If that's supposed to be a threat, let me assure you: you are fucking with the wrong guy."

A weird thing to say. From a deeply weird man.

He didn't even wait for an interloper before he stormed out. "Keep your nose clean," I called out helpfully, but I don't know if he heard.

I walked past his office on my way to first period, then doubled back, took the note I had written on Saturday out of my backpack, and slid it under his door. Maybe he would be more reasonable when he'd had a chance to cool off. And maybe then we could have a more productive discussion, with our pants on, in neutral territory, say at Linda's Pancakes on Broadway, rather than in the boys' bathroom, though it would still be a weird scene. I'd even be willing to apologize for my rude lyrics, given the right conciliatory gesture. And he would tell me all about my dad and their carefree youth together, and the turmoil of the Turbulent Sixties, their hopes, their dreams of sailing away to sea to find the answers to their souls' mysteries. Maybe he'd even reveal his softer, human side, and I'd realize that he wasn't such a bad guy after all, just misunderstood. The wounds wouldn't heal instantly. There would have to be time for reflection, for honest soul-searching, for letting go. But bit by bit, we'd learn to laugh again. "You know, you remind me a lot of your old man," he'd say from time to time, with a twinkle in his eye. I'd start referring to him as Uncle Tony. And then Mr. Teone would finally explain the whole story behind Timothy J. Anderson, CEH, the dead bastard, John the Baptist, and *The Catcher in the Rye.* Not the most solid plan, perhaps, but it was worth a shot, and anyway, I couldn't think of an alternative.

NERD BLOOD

I missed out on a lot of what happened next and had to have it explained to me later, for reasons that will become clear in a minute. I still have some numb spots on my head from the experience, though they tell me that some of the nerve tissue may well end up growing back over time. We'll see.

Anyway, looking back, I suppose it hadn't been the smartest idea to end our set with "The Guy I Accidentally Beat Up." The Paul Krebs–Matt Lynch people had been looking for a discreet, plausibly deniable way to wreak vengeance on me ever since the *Brighton Rock* incident. What am I saying? They had been looking for d., p. d. ways to w. v. since they first became aware of my existence around the third grade. And finding them, too. But that song, not to mention its inclusion in a bestselling publication–by second period, Sam Hellerman had unloaded another forty copies–had invited immediate retaliation. Sam Hellerman thought the conspiracy went all the way to the top, at least up to Mr. Teone himself, who of course had his own reasons to wish me ill, despite my magnanimous decision to give him the tentative benefit of the barest doubt. I don't know about that, but Mr. Donnelly had certainly been in on it to some degree. If we could prove even that, Sam Hellerman promised, the lawsuit could bankrupt the school system, which was a nice thought. But I doubted it could be proved. Their plan wasn't particularly brilliant, but it was elaborate and involved several actors, all of whom were responsible only for their individual parts. It did the job.

Sam Hellerman had just been sent to the nurse's office, having once again used his magic bleeding nose to end a boxing match before it began. Mr. Donnelly had slated me to box Mark McAlistair next. Mark McAlistair was one of the lower

Matt Lynch minions, no more than a gopher, really, but he had clearly committed some transgression because he was the fall guy in the scheme. Soon after our match began and everyone had begun the usual chant of "pussy, pussy, pussy," someone tripped me, and Mark McAlistair, as instructed, fell on top of me and pinned me down while a couple of accomplices in the "ring" stood on my wrists and knees. Then he removed his right glove and hit me on the back of the head with his ungloved fist repeatedly as hard and fast as he could. That was really against the rules, but Mr. Donnelly pretended not to notice at first. Then, when I was already seeing stars and starting to fade, he yelled, "What the hell are you doing, McAlistair?" and pulled him off me. Then he sent Rich Zim, another Lynchie, to escort me to the nurse's office. On our way there, while I was still more or less in a daze, Rich Zim led me past the band room where a person or persons unknown stepped out while we were passing the door and brained me on the back of the head with a brass instrument. I lost consciousness completely at that point. I think they may have kicked me in the ribs a bit while I was out, judging from the feeling when I came to. At some point, though, Rich Zim and another guy carried me to the nurse's office, banging my head on lockers and posts and doors and dropping me on the ground all along the way. At least, it felt that way when I assessed the damages after the fact. They did just about everything except beat me with a bag of oranges. And maybe they did that, too, for all I know.

The whole thing could then be blamed on Mark McAlistair's gloveless punches. That was the plan, anyway, as near as I could figure. At any rate, Mark McAlistair was toast, and was headed to some sort of facility for delinquents that would be even harder to take than Hillmont. I felt a little sorry for him, as he was only a pawn. But he should have known better than to sign up with a pack of depraved normal people, who didn't care whom they sold out as long as it meant a chance at a couple more drops of nerd blood. Savages.

So I ended up with a concussion and some skull fractures, and I had to spend the next few days in a hospital so I wouldn't fall asleep and die. I didn't die and life went on, but for a while there I wasn't around to observe much of it. It takes more than a blow from a brass instrument to kill King Dork, apparently. Who knew?

It turned out I needed surgery because of some nerve damage. I was told that the surgeon was very good, but that there was a possibility that I was going to have some permanent numb spots on my scalp. That didn't seem so bad, though part of me wished there was some way that I could have some numb spots *inside* my head as well as outside. They supplied that on a temporary basis, anyway, which was nice. For a while there, I had feared that Hillmont was going to end up with another helmet guy on its hands, but fortunately it wasn't going to come to that.

I have no recollection of the operation. Afterward, they moved me to a recovery room on a different floor, which I shared with this guy named Mr. Aquino. We were separated by a curtain: my side was by the window, while he had the door side. I don't know what was wrong with him, but whatever it was, it resulted in a steady stream of moaning from his side of the curtain. After I got used to it, I took it in stride and didn't really notice it anymore. But when anyone approached the door, the volume would increase, and if someone actually entered our room, he would break into a kind of hysterical wheezing. It was like an alarm system. When Mr. Aquino "went off," I knew someone was about to enter, which was useful. I always had a few seconds to compose myself before entertaining guests.

More people came through that door and over to my side than you might imagine. My recollection is fuzzy, partly because of deluxe pain medication that would have quite literally made Sam Hellerman drool and partly because the whole situation was so disorienting. I gradually learned what had happened at Hillmont High in the aftermath of the Festival of Lights by piecing together accounts from various sources. But now I can't quite recall which parts were explained by visitors, which parts I read about in the paper or saw on TV, and which parts I figured out afterward by putting two and two together.

The school ended up banning the Chi-Mos zine, which only made it more sought after, of course: Sam Hellerman had added a sticker that said "Banned in Hillmont" and had been able to raise the price to three dollars. Some of the punky kids, Sam Hellerman said, had even started showing up to school with "Chi-Mos" written in Wite-Out on their jackets and bags. We were famous.

Mr. Teone had left for lunch on Monday and never came back. After he had been missing for two days, they entered his house to investigate and found–

Well, let me describe how I first heard about it, in a fuzzy hospital conversation with Sam Hellerman. He had just told me about the mysterious disappearance of Mr. Teone and about how the cops had searched his house. Then he fell silent, lost in thought.

"What's on your mind, Hellerman?" I said, after a while.

"Oh. I was just thinking about whether Budgie really was a part of the new wave of British heavy metal."

"Really?" I said. What the hell was he talking about? Of *course* Budgie was a part of the new wave of British heavy metal. The question was, what were we doing talking about who may or may not have been a part of the NWOBHM at a time like this? "Now, in the case of Ethel the Frog . . . ," he began. He was just toying with me, though.

"I suppose you want to hear about Tit's Satanic Empire?"

Which of course, as I immediately realized, was exactly what I wanted to hear about, though I hadn't been able to find the words.

What the police had found at Mr. Teone's house was evidence of this high school–oriented pornography operation. Much of it had been removed or destroyed, but what was left supposedly included a large number of videos of Hillmont High School students from the past ten years, ramoning each other like crazy and doing God only knows what else.

As usual, Sam Hellerman seemed to know more about the situation, especially at that early stage, than the newspapers, the TV, or anyone else. But word got around pretty quickly, even though the details were murky. As always seems to happen whenever anything scandalous occurs in Hillmont, a group of parents and community leaders had decided that it all had to do with a powerful Satanic cult. Satanists, they believed, were turning Hillmont teens into mixed-up zombies and using them in their pornographic rituals. Parents were already taking their kids to be deprogrammed and hypnotized by therapists who specialized in recovering buried memories of Satanist porn-abuse. Mr. Teone had been smart to skip town; by the end of the week, there would be enough recovered-memory evidence to convict him several times over even without the videotapes. Now, I'd be the last person to deny a Teone-Satan resemblance, but that part of it seemed pretty far-fetched to me. I mean, a real Satanic conspiracy could probably have come up with someone better than Mr. Teone to handle the teen porn angle.

Anyway, Mr. Teone had been selling and trading the pictures and videos to similar operations overseas, which made it a very serious offense. His method appeared to be to recruit accomplices from within the student body, who would help to sign up friends and younger siblings to act in the videos; then, when the accomplices had graduated, the younger kids would "move up" and become the recruiters. He managed to keep everybody on board through a combination of rewards, punishments, perks, and intimidation; supposedly he even had a profit-sharing scheme for the "senior" student associates. They had really been raking it in, too, by all accounts. I thought of Mr. Teone's afterschool programs—it sure gave a new meaning to the word "gifted," not to mention "talented." Once again, I found myself wondering whether Sam Hellerman knew even more than he was telling about the whole situation. It wouldn't have surprised me one bit.

The subject of who had been involved was of course a big topic of conversation at school. The Hillmont student body was now divided into two groups: those who desperately wanted to see those tapes and those who claimed they wanted to see the tapes but were secretly hoping the tapes would never leak out because they were in some of them. I also had an inkling of which of the two groups Kyrsten Blakeney probably belonged to, and I felt a bit sad for her. And also just a bit interested, though I know this doesn't reflect particularly well on me, in viewing her tapes, just for my own personal information.

I glanced up at Sam Hellerman, and I knew that if anyone could manage to get hold of them, he could, and I was pretty sure he was thinking something similar. If he didn't already have a complete set, numbered and cross-referenced and neatly displayed in a little cabinet over at Hellerman Manor. You never knew with that guy.

I suddenly had a weird thought. What if Mr. Teone and company had wanted to make a "Hot Girls Do Geeks" video series for the specialized European fetish market? It wouldn't have been hard to do with the cooperation of certain key people and some hidden cameras and so forth.

So I asked: "Was Dud Chart part of Tit's Satanic Empire, too?"

Sam Hellerman looked startled and kind of peeved, as he usually did when the subject of Dud Chart came up.

"Oh, no," he said. "No—they had nothing to do with each other."

I wasn't totally sure I believed him, though. I never am.

According to Sam Hellerman, one of Mr. Teone's most trusted minions had been Matt Lynch, who had started at the bottom, recruited by his older brother, and had gradually moved up in the organization. I hated to admit it, but Matt Lynch's promotion to Hillmont High Satanic Pornography Monitor (after his brother had graduated) had occurred around the time I had adopted my gun-freak strategy of Matt Lynch deterrence. Maybe he hadn't been fazed by the gun stuff after all, as I had thought, but had just had other things on his mind by that point. All I knew was, if I had endured Little Big Tom's devil-head sanctimony *and* worn that blessed army coat through the whole hot spring and summer of ninth grade for nothing, I was pissed.

It wasn't too hard to figure out what had happened in the aftermath of the Chi-Mos performance. Mr. Teone had jumped to the conclusion that the name "Chi-Mo" was a reference to him and his questionable activities. The content of some of the songs seemed to confirm his suspicions. If he had just ignored it, the matter would certainly have gone away and no one would ever have known. But he had read the band's performance and the zine as a threat to him. In those circumstances, my note about "materials among my deceased father's effects" must have seemed a bit like a blackmail message, implying, perhaps, that my dad had had some information on him that I had had access to. I never did figure out what my dad had been working on when he had been killed, but it was just conceivable that it might have had something to do with his old friend Tit. Even if it didn't, though, Mr. Teone's association with my dad went back quite a long way, and it was likely that CEH had known some potentially damaging information that I theoretically could have uncovered.

Mr. Teone had tried to intimidate me in the boys' bathroom a couple of times, and had maybe even organized the brass instrument attack to drive the message home, but the note had pushed him over the edge and he decided to skip town rather than risk being caught. He was still missing. The speculation was that he had left the country, or that he was being hidden in a secret lair by his fellow porn-Satanists.

At any rate, there went any possibility of Uncle Tony's big surprise party or an illuminating heart-to-heart at Linda's Pancakes on Broadway. Maybe I wasn't descended from kings after all. Rats.

It was all over the papers and the news, of course. There was, however, no mention as yet of the fact that the chain of events that had exposed and toppled Tit's Satanic Empire had begun with the performance of a sucky high school rock band. Nor was it noted that Mr. Teone's flight had been sparked by his narcissistic assumption that a tenth grader's derogatory nickname could only be a veiled reference to him, rather than the result of a faulty aptitude test that equated introversion, social anxiety, and depression with a spiritual vocation. It was quite a story, though. Sam Hellerman was already planning how, once we had a recording of Teone songs available in stores, we would sell our story and make a million dollars.

CHI-MOS ARE REAL ROCK AND ROLL

My mom had come to visit at the hospital briefly during one of my most out-of-it phases. I hardly remember it, but I know I asked her to bring me the CEH library. She had passed the task along to Little Big Tom.

So Mr. Aquino started moaning, then wheezing, and then—well, in a way this was one of the bigger surprises of the whole affair. Little Big Tom and Amanda walked in together, and they seemed to be getting along pretty well. It's not like they came in holding hands and skipping or anything. But Amanda was acting civil toward him, almost friendly, which was quite something. I mean, her eyes were rolling less than usual, and you'd be surprised at what a difference a small thing like that can make. She even pretended to laugh, just a little, when he said "Calling Dr. Howard!" Now, I have no idea why that was supposed to be funny, but you could tell by the look on his face that it was supposed to be a riot. I had never seen Amanda humor LBT like that. As for him, he was clearly in fake-dad heaven. Say what you will about Little Big Tom: it doesn't take much. And a hospital visit can really help pull a fake family together.

One thing about being in the hospital: people always feel they should bring you something when they visit. Amanda brought in this impressive series of drawings illustrating the Chi-Mos story, kind of like the Bayeux Tapestry, except instead of William the Conqueror and the Pope and so forth, the main characters were me, Sam Hellerman, and Mr.

Teone, whom she had drawn as a kind of effeminate Satan. The last one depicted a wailing Mr. Teone being crushed under huge granite letters that spelled "Chi-Mos Are Real Rock and Roll!"

The drawings were childlike and brilliant, almost like real art. I totally wanted to use them for the first Chi-Mos album. Actually we had already tentatively changed the name to the Elephants of Style, me on guitar, Sam Enchanted Evening on bass and animal husbandry, first album *Devil Warship*. Well, there was plenty of time to talk about it. I kissed Amanda on the forehead when she leaned over. She said: "You're the most famous person I know," which was sweet. She was being all Phoebe-esque and nicer-than-usual to *me*, too. Weird.

Little Big Tom had put two and two together and had realized I had been doing research into my dad's youth reading list. So he decided, helpfully, to provide me with a complementary LBT library. He had been impressed that I had swiped his Che Guevara T-shirt, so the LBT books were tilted toward impenetrable and/or goofy books on radical politics that no one would ever read voluntarily anymore. Among them was a beat-up copy of *The Little Red Book,* which is a collection of retarded sayings by this chubby mass murderer from China. (He made an appearance earlier in this story on Sam Hellerman's hand-lettered T-shirt—guy by the name of Mao.) People in the sixties liked to be seen carrying this book around, hoping it would make them appear more radical and cutting-edge and sexy and intellectual. I guess you started out carrying around *The Catcher in the Rye,* and then, when you got a little older and the thrill was gone, you "turned political" and switched to *The Little Red Book* instead. The funny thing is, by all accounts, doing this really *could* get you dates. With the hairy women of the time, perhaps, but still.

There was of course no need to investigate Little Big Tom: he was already an open book, and there wasn't even one little thing about him that wasn't painfully obvious. That was part of his charm, maybe, but it made the LBT library a bit less compelling than he probably imagined. I nodded politely, though, and went along with it.

"Kill the bourgeois pigs," I said. "And the running dogs of the imperial yo-yo or whatever. Except for you and Mom. We need you to hang in there long enough to pay for our college." Amanda nodded solemnly and put her arm around me, and we both flashed him sardonic peace signs.

You've got to hand it to Little Big Tom, though: he was either too clueless or too "centered" to let anything like that bother him. He just smiled back and rumpled our hair.

"Kids today," he said, and we all laughed. I mean, he did.

Just before they left, as I was saying good-bye to Amanda, I made a sudden decision and handed her the bloodstained *Brighton Rock*.

"It was Dad's book," I said. "It's the best book ever written."

As she walked out, she had the book open and was staring at the inside front cover, at the bloody CEH 1965, and I had a pretty good idea what she was thinking. Maybe I'd even tell her the whole story one day if she played her cards right. And if I ever figured it out.

Whatever they were giving me in the hospital was pretty outstanding. They should put it in the water supply or something: the world would be a more peaceful and rewarding place. Life flies by in a nice breeze, and you remember stuff as if none of the boring or unpleasant parts even happened. So I'm not sure if it was before or after the LBT/Amanda visit, and in fact I may be mixing up or joining a couple of different episodes, but there was at least one other significant hospital event, and here's how I remember it.

Mr. Aquino started moaning, then wheezing, and then I saw Shinefield, Syndie Duffy's floppy boyfriend, coming past the curtain. He was followed by Celeste Fletcher and Syndie Duffy. Yasmynne Schmick and Sam Hellerman came in a couple of minutes later. Sam Hellerman discreetly handed me two sealed envelopes as he walked by.

So was Sam Hellerman hanging out with the drama people again? Or had he been all along? Or maybe they had just given him a lift. At any rate, the scene was very much as it had been during his hippie lunch phase. They weren't paying too much attention to Sam Hellerman, though they didn't seem to mind that he was hanging around. And the whole time, even when he was talking to me, he just stared at Celeste Fletcher's ass, even going so far as to reposition himself so as to get a better view whenever she happened to move it out of his line of sight.

The other weird thing was that Celeste Fletcher seemed pretty friendly with Shinefield, though he was still Syndie Duffy's boyfriend as far as I knew. When Syndie Duffy left to go to the bathroom or smoke, Shinefield would move even closer to Celeste Fletcher and touch her butt, acting like it was accidental. I couldn't tell whether she was in on it. Maybe Syndie Duffy and Celeste Fletcher had switched boyfriends or something. I'm not sure how dating politics works in the subnormal/drama world, so I could be misreading it. Clearly, though, on some level what we were seeing was the emergence of a new girl trio, out of the ashes of the Sisterhood. The question was, would Celeste Fletcher or Syndie Duffy end up as the dominant girl? My money was on Celeste Fletcher, because her open flirtation with Shinefield really did seem to give her the upper hand. Yasmynne

Schmick, of course, would be a #3 till the end of her days, but I was glad she was there. She was always nice and usually funny and generally seemed so happy to see me.

Much of the raw information about Mr. Teone's activities and the Chi-Mos' continuing influence at Hillmont came from the conversation between me and this weird-ass group. I was kind of woozy and fuzzy, and the drama people were, no doubt, totally high. Sam Hellerman was ass addled. Yet somehow we figured out a way to exchange information, though I didn't manage to tease out all the implications till I'd had a chance to think it all over during the next few days. It was a pretty interesting topic. The whole time, though, I was holding Sam Hellerman's envelopes, dying to know what was inside them, but realizing that he had sealed them for a reason, and that I couldn't open them till everybody had left.

I'll say one thing: Shinefield was a true fan. He couldn't stop talking about the Chi-Mos and the Festival of Lights and the zine. He had started to call me Chi-Bro. I kid you not. The girls didn't pay too much attention to the band talk, but even they said some nice things, too. I mean, it was ridiculous. We had sucked, probably worse than any band that had ever played at any high school ever. But I guess running the associate principal out of town, even accidentally, counts for a lot.

Just being in a band counts, too. I'm convinced of that. By my calculations, girls find you around fifteen percent more attractive and worth their attention if you're in a band than they do if you're not. It works with subnormal/drama girls, anyway. And apparently, in a different way, of course, it can even work with your own ordinarily ill-tempered sister; it doesn't appear to have much effect on your mom, though. Fifteen percent may not sound like much, but it feels quite substantial when you start the game at close to zero.

Eventually they left, and Sam Hellerman gave me a "we'll talk later" look as he followed Celeste Fletcher's ass past the curtain and out the door. I tore open the first envelope.

It contained $240, my share of the proceeds from the song zine. On the twenty-dollar bill on top of the stack, he had written "Keep making me money, kid." Which was from some movie, I'm pretty sure. Anyhow, it was kind of funny. More money than I had ever had at one time. Liquid assets. Which is not a bad band name if you think about it. Hey, we're the Liquid Assets, and this one's called "Pheromone City...."

I would have been happy if the other envelope had contained more money, but it was a lot thinner, and I could tell by feeling it that inside were a few sheets of folded paper. Documents, information of some kind. I slid my thumb through the flap.

STILL NOT DONE LOVING YOU, MAMA

Before I got a chance to see what was in Sam Hellerman's second envelope, I heard Mr. Aquino begin to moan, and then to wheeze. I hurriedly shoved both envelopes back under my pillow. To my surprise, Celeste Fletcher came back in.

"They're getting the car," she said. "I was hoping I could get your autograph."

I was surprised, to say the least. Or maybe it was here, rather than before, like I said, that I made the calculation that girls like you fifteen percent more when you're in a band. Or no, it was right after that, when she handed me a Sharpie, and then, instead of offering the zine or a piece of paper for me to sign like I had expected, leaned over and pulled her shirt down. She wanted me to sign her tits. I had heard of this before, but come on: how many ordinary guys in lousy high school rock bands ever land in this situation, let alone King Dork? It's not supposed to happen. You know, thinking about it, it's really more like at least twenty-five percent. What was I thinking? Maybe more like forty-four percent, actually. Give or take.

She was pretty demure and tasteful about it, but she also did it smoothly, as though she'd done it many times before. I mean, she pulled the neck of her scoopy T-shirt down and to the left but not low enough to expose the nipple, and simultaneously pushed the breast up from below with her palm, so that the top of it bulged out and up. My guess is that that's not the sort of thing you do well the first time you try it. I don't know if you can picture it, but trust me: it looked fucking amazing.

"Certainly," I said, trying to act as though I had done this many times as well, though my shaking hands probably gave me away. I hadn't touched too many breasts, you know. This was only number four, by my calculations.

So I leaned forward and wrote in a spidery hand: "Best wishes, Thomas Charles Henderson."

She said thanks. But as she was turning to leave, she pulled her top out and glanced down and said, haltingly, "Trombone Chablis Ampersand?" I guess my handwriting was even shakier than I thought. They didn't cover breast autographs in third-grade penmanship, you see, though maybe they should have.

I explained that that was my real name, well, pretty close, anyway. Clearly, though, she knew me as Chi-Mo, and wanted my autograph because I was one of the Chi-Mos, and hey, I might as well face it, I was as much Chi-Mo as I was anything else. She wanted a Chi-Mo autograph, and who was I to deny her? So she came back around with the unsheathed Sharpie and pulled her shirt down and pushed the other breast so that most of its northern hemisphere bulged out and up. This time I wrote, much more carefully: "Nice breast. CM." Which made her laugh and seemed to please her well enough.

"Thanks," she said.

"No problem," I said. "But I'm not sure how long we'll keep that name. What do you think of Sentient Beard?" (Me on guitar, Samerica the Beautiful on bass and upholstery, first album *Off the Charts–Way Off.*)

"Well, it's better than the Stoned Mamalukes."

I was on drugs, so I was a little slow, but not so slow that it didn't click. I could think of only one way she would have known about the Stoned Marmadukes. I realize now that there may have in fact been other ways, especially if she had spent time hanging around with Sam Hellerman. But her re-action gave it away: she realized she had slipped up, and even made a kind of half-motion to cover her mouth, almost as though to stuff the words back in. It looked kind of melo-dramatic and theatrical, and only halfway unintentionally so, which was familiar, too. And that's what clinched it, pretty much. Fiona. Celeste Fletcher was fake Fiona. Note the nice, Schtuppified deformation of Marmadukes, which actually was a vast improvement, and which was another clincher: that's exactly the kind of joke the Fiona of my dim memory would have made while leaving you guessing as to whether it had been intentional or not. Or wait, it was me, not her, who would make that kind of joke; but those were jokes she could get, so presumably she could make them as well. So it wasn't breast number four after all. We were back to breast number one, with whose nipple I had spent so many happy moments in my innocent youth.

Wait. Really? She totally didn't look like Fiona, even

adjusting for the lack of the Fiona costume. Fantasy and reality sure can get in the way of each other, can't they?

When people disguise themselves as other people in movies and no one in the movie is supposed to realize it, you usually don't believe it for a minute. In real life, though, it's not so easy to figure stuff out. I had only seen the original fake Fiona once, in the dark and while a little buzzed, and I hadn't even known Celeste Fletcher or seen her up close at the time. Plus, I had seen the Fiona'd-out Celeste Fletcher mostly from the front, whereas up till now, I'd only examined Celeste Fletcher playing herself from Sam Hellerman's vantage point–that is, from behind. Even without the costume, and as a general rule, that's a totally different look for a lady. Celeste Fletcher's breasts even felt different from how I had remembered Fiona's breasts feeling–but I had had a different focus at that time. I mean, I hadn't had to worry about keeping my handwriting neat and steady. Not to get too philosophical on you here, but in different contexts, and depending on what you're doing, the same rack can be totally different worlds. Anyway, God help 'em if they ever try to make a movie out of this, with the same sexy teenaged actress playing both fake Fiona and Celeste Fletcher in different costumes and makeup. It'll be hard to pull off in movie form. But it worked in real life. I swear to God.

Anyway, there I was at Mercy Hospital in Santa Carla, on the other side of the curtain from the moaning Mr. Aquino, around ninety percent convinced that I was staring at the girl of my dreams, who just happened to have my name scribbled all over her breasts in black Sharpie. What would you have done?

It all went back to Dud Chart. Sam Hellerman hadn't tried to exempt me from the contest, as he had said. Quite the contrary: he had set me up, as he had done with all the Hillmont High School Untouchables, organizing my presence at the party, and advising Celeste Fletcher on how to dress and behave to "push my buttons" effectively when I got there. My point value had been high, and she had wanted to win. Why such a complicated plan? Well, an ordinary Make-out/Fake-out would have been unlikely to succeed because I was well aware of the technique and was always on guard against it, almost maybe to the level of paranoia. There had been Make-out/Fake-out attempts the week before the party, in fact, which I had wiggled out of–maybe those had been part of Dud Chart, too. I don't think you got any points for a failed attempt, so they had to figure out a trickier, more elaborate way. Plus, from what I knew of the Sisterhood, Celeste Fletcher is one of those people who just prefers things to be elaborate. Sam Hellerman is certainly like that. In fact, the Fiona project had Sam Hellerman written all over it, even down to the name, which probably had had a subtle influence on me because it sounded kind of English and rock and roll had made me a devil-head Anglophile.

This had been at an early stage in the Dud Chart game, where the object had just been making out rather than something really serious and extreme like walking around Center Court. Her plan had only been to get to second base in a publicly observable setting. That, and not ladies' week, was why she hadn't wanted me to go down her pants, why she had directed my attention to her tits instead, and also presumably explains her stalling, constantly glancing around the room, and eventual sudden instigation of the making-out part. She had been waiting for the witnesses to show up. Witnesses. How embarrassing.

As for Sam Hellerman, he clearly had his own little obsession going for Celeste Fletcher qua Celeste Fletcher, and her true fake identity made some of his behavior just a bit easier to understand. He had been pissed off and jealous when, according to my slightly exaggerated account, he heard it had gone beyond second base, which hadn't been the "deal." On top of that, he hadn't wanted me to find out the real story, not to mention his role in it. So he attempted to dampen my interest in the imaginary mystery girl and to draw my attention away from the real girl who stood behind her. He wanted Celeste Fletcher to be his imaginary fake girlfriend rather than mine. Pointing to Deanna Schumacher, who had been selected for her glasses and her distant location, had been a diversionary tactic that totally would have worked if I hadn't called her up and if she hadn't been the kind of girl who would say "you'd better come over, then" in that situation. That was just a crazy stroke of luck.

The basic scheme was clear almost as soon as I heard Celeste Fletcher say "mamalukes." I filled in more details later. In the meantime, we were just staring at each other, trying to guess what the other was going to do.

I don't know what normal people would have done. The girl would flounce out of the room in tears. Or the boy would say something along the lines of "leave me, I would be alone." Or they would have a big, soul-baring conversation that would drag on deep into the night, until somebody eventually ended up hitting somebody else with a heavy object.

But we weren't normal people. And this situation (a pretty hot girl standing in front of you with your name scrawled all over her in black Sharpie) doesn't come up all that often. Believe it or not. So what I did was, I reached out to touch the Trombone Chablis Ampersand breast and dipped two fingers under the T-shirt and bra from above. And what she did was to lean into me and to start sticking her tongue into my mouth and saying "mmmm." Soon we were fully making out, and it was just like at the party, except she wasn't in Fiona costume, and I was in pajamas instead of my army coat, and instead of a sound track of distant mod-related music, there was only the sound of Mr. Aquino's moaning.

Soon I had my other hand on the Chi-Mo breast and was moving the TCA hand down to the back waistband of her jeans so it was jeans-underwear-fingers-skin, and instead of resisting like before, she scrunched up so I could reach farther down, though it was a pretty tight squeeze. This was more like it. The autographs were getting smudged, so she said, "You'll have to redo these sometime." Sounds good to me. If you insist.

Then, and you can believe it or not, I don't really care, she reached her hand under the covers, said "Let me see if I can help you with that," and started to give me what I believe is technically referred to as a hand job. Mind-blowing.

I was thinking that there was a fairly good chance of this developing into full-blown ramoning. At this point in the proceedings, however, Mr. Aquino's moans got louder and he started to wheeze. "Someone's coming!" I said. We shared an extremely brief slan look about that hilarious choice of words—yeah, because we slans love our sophisticated jokes—but she quickly disengaged, straightened herself up, reached into her back pocket, handed me a folded note, mimed a little kiss, and left the room.

The new visitor, I kid you not, was Deanna Schumacher, wearing her IHA uniform. She and Celeste Fletcher glared at each other as their paths crossed at the curtain. I shoved the note down behind my pillow with Sam Hellerman's envelopes.

"Who was that?" said Deanna Schumacher.

"Sam Hellerman's illicit lover," I said.

"She seems like a bitch." She sat on the edge of the bed.

"You have no idea," I said. Which was true.

Deanna Schumacher launched into her usual alternating hot/cold, mean/nice, hostile/polite routine. I'll tell you one thing: navigating the twists and turns of a Schumacher conversation is way easier when you're on prescription medication. It's the only way to go. I just bided my time, till, as expected, she finally finished being schizophrenic and we started to make out.

"Let me see if I can help you with that," she said, sticking to the script. But Deanna Schumacher had had a lot of practice with that sort of discreet, sheet-covered help and she knew what to do. It was just like in her room, with a similar sense of urgency and looming time limit, but also with perhaps a bit more confidence on my part. Everything went well, and there were no interruptions. And I was glad all over all over again. Then she left, calling me a jerk, reminding me that Mondays and Thursdays are best, and asking that I say hello to my mother for her.

READING MATTER

When I was sure Deanna Schumacher had left the room for good, I retrieved Celeste Fletcher's note. I had to laugh a little, because I hadn't known what to expect, but I probably should have. It said my band rocked, blah blah blah, and there was a phone number; if I ever felt like killing some time I could call her. "Wednesdays are best, till around ten." Hey, but what about the other day when her boyfriend works late? Maybe that's Sam Hellerman's day. Or Shinefield's. Well, at least the work schedule proved Celeste Fletcher and Deanna Schumacher didn't have the same boyfriend. That sure would have complicated things.

She had written the note before she knew that I would have learned the Fiona secret by the time I read it. But it didn't make much difference. Maybe I should have been more irritated by the deception, but without it, and without her having slipped up and my having realized it, the hospital make-out session wouldn't have occurred, so I was mostly glad it worked out the way it did. Whatever. Celeste Fletcher was hot and I was more or less totally into her, details be damned. Though I had to admit, I preferred her in Fiona drag.

What about Sam Hellerman? Well, he had sold me out, it's true, and the whole thing was a bit embarrassing. But if it hadn't been for his devil-head machinations, none of the making out in my life would have happened at all. None of it. I couldn't be too mad at him. In fact, I thought I really should try to give him some kind of thank-you gift. Plus, we had to keep the band together, at least till we sold our first million records. Only then could we move on to competing solo careers and sniping at each other about our shared women and sleazy escapades in the music press, till we eventually reconcile around the time I record the third in a celebrated series of albums about having writer's block.

The maddening part was that I probably would never end up knowing how many of the results of his plans had been intended and how many had been because things went awry. Or how much he knew, or what he was planning for the future. I could talk to him about it, but I'd never know for sure if he was being completely honest. Plus, he clearly still had the hots for Celeste Fletcher, and I didn't really want the subject to come up. I didn't want him to know about Deanna Schumacher, either, just in case he might tell Celeste Fletcher about her. I certainly didn't want those two knowing about each other. God, no.

‹ ❋ ❋ ❋ ›

I almost forgot Sam Hellerman's other envelope in all the excitement. Eventually, though, I retrieved it from under the pillow and took a look.

In the envelope were two neatly folded pieces of paper. The first was a reverse-exposure printout from the library's microfilm machine. Clearly, Sam Hellerman had resumed the Tit investigation while I had been out. The article reported that in early March 1963, a student had been discovered hanging by the neck from a rope in the gymnasium of Most Precious Blood College Preparatory in San Francisco. An apparent suicide. The student was not named in the article, but it seemed a good bet that his name had been Timothy J. Anderson. In the margin, Sam Hellerman had written, "Killed by Tit?" It was an intriguing notion, though I couldn't see where he got that.

Most Precious Blood College Preparatory. Man, I prided myself on coming up with good names for bands and titles and such, but compared to the Catholic church, I was a rank amateur. Most Precious Blood—probably the best name ever, for a school or a band.

The other page was a computer printout of another, more recent article from the *San Francisco Chronicle,* dated nearly a year before my dad's death. It was about a scandal and shake-up in the Santa Carla city and county governments. The details were cursory, but it appeared to be some kind of corruption scandal. The entire board of supervisors, the chief of police, and several other unnamed officials had had to resign; a few had been indicted, and, interestingly, there had even been a couple of suicides, including a Santa Carla policeman. I didn't see how it could be linked to Timothy J. Anderson, but I guessed Sam Hellerman saw some kind of connection between this story and my dad's death. Perhaps my dad had been involved in the scandal in some way and his suicide was delayed but similar to that of the cop mentioned in the article? If so, it was weird that this was the first time I'd heard of the Santa Carla corruption scandal, as I'd read dozens of articles concerning his death from the time and none of them had mentioned it. But of course, in those articles it had been reported as an accident rather than a suicide. Since my mom was the only person who thought it had been a suicide, as far as I could tell, I couldn't quite put my finger on precisely how they might be connected outside my mom's weird mind.

The most interesting bit to me, though, was the fact that the article quoted a county official named Melvin Schumacher. The quote itself was bland and contentless, something about "respecting the process and seeing it through," but the speaker was Deanna Schumacher's father, clearly.

Now, I'd known that her dad had worked with the county coroner's office, so it wasn't a big surprise to me. The question was, how much did Sam Hellerman know about that situation? Supposedly, he knew nothing about it. Deanna Schumacher had been chosen strictly for her appearance, for the superficial resemblance of her yearbook photo to the Celeste Fletcher "Fiona," and presented to me as Fiona to throw me off Celeste Fletcher's scent. As far as I knew, that was as far as it went. Sam Hellerman had no idea that I had struck up an illicit, blow-job-oriented relationship with her; he still believed that I believed that Deanna Schumacher was Fiona and that she was living in Florida with her suddenly transferred, non-CEH-associated father. But, as so often where Sam Hellerman is concerned, I had a few doubts. Was Deanna Schumacher more deeply involved in Sam Hellerman's schemes than I knew? I had assumed that she had been chosen after the fact, on the basis of her resemblance to "Fiona." But looking at the name "Melvin

Schumacher" in the article printout, another thought occurred to me: perhaps Celeste Fletcher's Fiona outfit had been deliberately designed to make her look like Deanna Schumacher, rather than the other way around. And Sam Hellerman had had a plan, going all the way back to the Baby Batter Weeks at the beginning of the year, before Dud Chart, before the party, that involved bringing Deanna Schumacher into my world.

It sounded crazy in my head when I thought about it. Before the *Catcher* code, before my mom's "Thinking of Suicide?" freak-out, there had been no reason for Sam Hellerman to be particularly concerned about CEH-related issues. The problem went beyond CEH, though. Now that circumstances had arranged themselves so that my life involved making out secretly with both Deanna Schumacher *and* Celeste Fletcher, with Sam Hellerman's role ambiguous, the question took on some urgency. How I proceeded with D. S. and C. F. would in some ways depend on what Sam Hellerman knew and when he knew it. And what he planned to do about it.

So the real question concerning that second article was what Sam Hellerman was trying to tell me with it. Was he trying to tell me something about CEH and Tit and Timothy J. Anderson, or was he trying to tell me something about Deanna Schumacher? I started to rack my brains for a way to find out without his realizing that I knew there was anything to find out.

FIRECRACKER

There was a pay phone down the hall in the hospital, and I used it to call Sam Hellerman shortly after I had opened the second envelope. He seemed pretty pleased with himself.

"You mean you haven't been able to figure it out?" he

said, when I'd as much as told him I hadn't been able to figure it out. "It all makes sense if you look at it a certain way," he added. Well, I doubted that very much. But he said we could get together to discuss it when I got out of the hospital. I tried to come up with a way to get him to talk about Deanna Schumacher without actually mentioning her myself, but I couldn't manage it. The best I could do was:

"So, when you say it all adds up, you mean Timothy J. Anderson and Tit and my dad and the *Catcher* code and Matthew chapter Three verse nine?"

"Uh, yeah," he said, with that "no duh" inflection where you make "yeah" into two syllables, kind of swooping down on the last one.

"Hey, how about that Celeste Fletcher," I said, after a pause, because I couldn't think of anything else to say.

"She's a firecracker," said Sam Hellerman.

There was an uncomfortable silence.

"Really?" I said. I guess there are guys who can sound cool saying that a girl is a firecracker, but Sam Hellerman isn't one of them. Anyway, that exhausted my material, so I said "Later" and hung up.

Life feels a little easier when you don't have to make your own schedule. I didn't have to worry about calling Deanna Schumacher till Thursday, which was a relief. Wednesday, Celeste Fletcher's "safe" day, was right around the corner, though. I was due to be released Thursday, so that meant I'd have to call from the pay phone in the hall. Even though I didn't find calling Celeste Fletcher quite as scary as calling Deanna Schumacher, I was still pretty nervous about it. Maybe you never get used to calling girls on the phone.

I stalled and avoided it for a while, but eventually I got up the nerve to go out to the hall and call from the pay phone.

"Oh, thank God!" she said, when she realized it was me. I kid you not. "Oh, thank God." Could anyone be so happy to hear from me that they would spontaneously burst into a prayer of thanks? Sounds dubious, I know. She said she hadn't been sure I would call her, showing just how little she really understood me and what I was all about. That was okay—I wasn't sure I liked the idea of her being able to understand me that easily anyway.

Our phone conversation was quite long, considering that my half of it was on a pay phone in the hallway of a hospital floor surrounded by angry fellow convalescents who thought I was taking too long and didn't much like what they were hearing me say. It resembled the phone-side scene at the Henderson-Tucci household a bit, in other words, and it was not the first time I'd noted similarities between my house and a sanitarium, I can tell you that.

I knew there was one thing we would have to cover eventually, so I got it out of the way near the beginning. I assured her I wasn't going to tell anyone about us or our activities, past, present, or (and here I knew I was taking an optimistic leap) future. We'd just pretend we hardly knew each other. Okay? She sounded relieved that she didn't have to figure out a way to bring it up, as I'd known she would.

"Because it would be really bad if my boyfriend found out," she said.

I took a stab. "Shinefield?"

"Him too." She laughed, a little nervously maybe. I wasn't sure who her actual real official boyfriend was, but it seemed safest just to adopt a blanket policy of nondisclosure that would cover him along with everyone else. Make things simpler. How had she explained the smudged breastographs, I wondered? Well, I was sure she had it all figured out. She had that air. "And, um, you might not want to mention anything to Sam, either."

Way ahead of you, babe. Not that I thought she was still messing around with Sam Hellerman, too. Did I? Was she? She was a busy girl, but I sincerely hoped not.

"Or Yasmynne."

Okay, this was getting weird. But I didn't want to kill the "Oh, thank God" vibe, so I let it slide. "Don't worry, Fiona. No one will find out."

"Stop calling me Fiona," she said.

"Okay, if you stop calling me Trombone." Because she had started to call me Trombone somewhere during the conversation. But that was a deal she couldn't or wouldn't make, so I guess Fiona was back on the menu in at least a limited way. Plus, for obvious reasons the word "trombone" would now forever bring to mind her breasts, or one of them, anyway. So I suddenly found I kind of liked hearing the word "trombone."

With the nondisclosure agreement out of the way, the rest went pretty well.

"For the record," she said, "I never thought you belonged on the dude chart."

Dude chart? Now, that was hard to interpret. In a variety of ways, that statement went against everything I had understood about Dud Chart, the Sisterhood, and Celeste Fletcher's role in the whole thing. Or at least, it seemed to give the game slightly different implications. Had Sam Hellerman gotten it a bit wrong, or contrived that I should get it a bit wrong? But wait: why didn't I belong on it, if it was a "dude chart" rather than a "dud chart"? What was she trying to say? Who fucking knows? Nevertheless, even though I didn't quite understand it, it was just about the nicest thing anyone had ever said to me. I think. So I said thanks and left it at that. I couldn't think of anything else to do.

On the other hand, "dude chart" may just have been a playful mispronunciation. See, one thing I learned from the conversation really blew me away—and this is so typical of me it's not even funny: Celeste Fletcher was actually in Mr. Schtuppe's English class, and was something of a champion mispronouncer in her own right. I had been too devil-head oblivious even to notice. So while I was obsessing over the mystery girl, the mystery girl had been right under my nose, and we had been reading about Jane Gallagher and mispronouncing the same words from *Catcher in the Rye* all along without my realizing it. Hell God damn. So that's why, when it was finally time to wrap it up, I asked her how things were in Old Nocturnal Emission Hills.

"Libidinous," she said, but she pronounced it so it rhymed with "shyness." She was the real deal. A slan chick with a great rack, a devious nature, and a powerful vocabulary. Not bad at all. I think I'm in love, I thought, whatever I might have meant by that.

ALWAYS THE QUIET ONES

In movies and books there's this thing called a character arc, where the main guy is supposed to change and grow and become a better person and learn something about himself. Essentially, there's supposed to be this part right at the end where he says: "And as for me, well, I learned the most valuable lesson of all." Now, if I were the main guy in a movie, I'd have the most retarded character arc anyone ever heard of. I didn't learn anything. What's the opposite of learning something? I mean, I knew stuff at the beginning that I don't know anymore. Bits of my life simply disappeared. I'm more con-fused than I ever was before, and that's really saying some-thing.

But if you're expecting that touchy-feely "you have touched me, I have grown" character arc stuff, here it is. Because, well, as for me, I have learned the most valuable les-son of all.

As I originally described the King Dork card game, a player automatically loses if he gets a king in his hand. Now I see that it's a little more complicated. You can bluff and fake your way out of getting kicked out of the game. In other words, if you play in such a way that no one knows you have any kings, you stay in. I still need to work out the details, be-cause somehow there also has to be a way that two or more players, like, say, Deanna Schumacher and Celeste Fletcher, can hold the same king card at the same time without realiz-ing it. And maybe some way for the queens to masquerade as each other or something. Anyway, I don't know how you win. Maybe no one ever wins, and you just keep accumulat-ing cards and bluffing about them till everyone dies and is for-gotten.

I don't know how it is if you're a normal guy with one special girl who is your official girlfriend in the approving sight of God and country. Nice work if you can get it, but it's just not available to everyone. So this only applies if you're the schlumpy King Dork type whom girls don't tend to want to associate with in public if they can help it. But here it is, the lesson:

If you're in a band, even an extremely sucky band, girls, even semihot ones like Celeste Fletcher and Deanna Schumacher, will totally mess around with you and give you blow jobs and so forth, provided you can assure them that no one will ever find out about it. Start a band. Or go around saying you're in a band, which is, let's face it, pretty much the same thing. The quality of your life can only improve.

I admit, it doesn't quite rise to the level of an actual Sex Alliance Against Society. Maybe a Sex Alliance Against Society is in the end too much to hope for for some of us. But even though there is a small part of me that reacts with fury and indignation over that fact, another part of me would argue that considering where I was at the beginning of the school year and throughout my entire life previous to it, the current lack of a Sex Alliance Against Society is quite an improvement over the previous lack of a S. A. A. S. This second small part understands where the first small part is coming from, but still, all things considered, it can't really see the flaw in it. Of course, the huge, hunkin' part that's left over has no idea what to think and is still totally confused and melancholy and bitter. So it's not like we're looking at a tremendous change here. My poor, adorable, flimsy character arc: you blink, you miss it, bless its little cotton socks.

Still. I've got two slightly less-than-imaginary secret quasi girlfriends whom I can call on Mondays and Thursdays, and on Wednesdays, respectively, when their official boyfriends are temporarily out of the picture because they're on the late shift at the convenience store.

What you got?

epilogue

SHERLOCK HELLERMAN

We were in my room at the beginning of Christmas vacation, listening to *Ace of Spades*. Sam Hellerman was seated on the floor, leaning against the dresser, with a glass of bourbon between his feet and a couple of my deluxe hospital-issued painkillers, one balanced on each knee. He had promised to delay actually taking them till he had finished explaining his Timothy J. Anderson theory—I didn't want him to pass out in the middle of a sentence—but I could see it was going to be a struggle for him. Sam Hellerman had very little self-control when it came to tranquilizers.

"Once you realize that Timothy J. Anderson was a kid, or a teenager," he said, tapping on the microfilm printout about the hanged student in the Most Precious Blood gym, "the whole thing starts to make a little more sense."

He paused to headbang slightly, and to sing "the ace of spades" a couple times under his breath, but stopped when he saw me giving him a rather desperate "mercy, please, I beg of you" look.

"Okay," he said, after taking a little sip of bourbon. "Starting with that Bible quote you're so hung up on. Why did the mountain monk have the same quotation in his book that Timothy J. Anderson had on his funeral card? You had guessed that the connection might be that they were both monks or clergymen. But they had something else in common, too—they were kids. I mean the mountain story guy was writing about his childhood; Timothy J. Anderson died while still a kid. And that quotation really suits a kid's funeral as much as an I-was-a-teenaged-monk book."

Clearly, Sam Hellerman hadn't actually read *The Seven Storey Mountain,* but I could see his point. "God is able of these stones to raise up children to Abraham." Matthew 3:9–11 did sound like something you might want to quote at a kid's funeral.

The Catholic Church, he added, had had a pretty strict antisuicide policy, especially at that time. Adults who killed themselves weren't allowed to have Catholic burials. Kids sometimes were, depending on their age, according to his research, though, of course, we didn't know the hanged kid's exact age.

"They were changing all the rules around at that time," he said, pointing to the date, 1963, "including the rules about who got to have funerals and all that." I hadn't realized you had to earn the right to have a funeral by dying in the proper manner—it never ends, does it? But of course, a taboo like that doesn't disappear just because they change the wording of something in Rome. Sam Hellerman thought that might be a reason why, even if there had been a funeral, as there appeared to have been, they might not have been eager to draw attention to it by publishing an obituary. "That's assuming everyone believed it was a suicide, whether or not it really was."

"But couldn't you just as easily conclude," I said, "that if suicides didn't get to have funerals, the fact that TJA *did* have a funeral kind of suggests that he didn't kill himself, that he wasn't the one who hanged himself in the gym? How do we know for sure that TJA *was* that kid, and not some other guy?" And then, thinking of Dr. Hexstrom, I added: "And how do we know that the TJA card was even from a funeral? It could have been from just about anything."

"It could have been," said Sam Hellerman. "But it wasn't. It was a funeral, or at least a memorial service. Even if not, though, it doesn't really matter: a kid, a classmate of Tit's and your dad's at Most Precious Blood College Prep, was found hanging in the gym. And there *was* a funeral, which Tit, according to his own note, refused to go to." He conceded that it was possible that this kid was someone other than Timothy J. Anderson, but that it "worked out better" if they were the same person. How well it "worked out" seemed like a funny way to decide whether something really happened or not. But we both knew that this was the sort of game we were playing.

"So it's just a coincidence that my dad happened to be reading a book with the same quotation as the one used at the funeral of a classmate?" I asked, still a little dubious.

"Well," said Sam Hellerman, "it was a popular book."

"*The Seven Storey Mountain?*"

"No," he said. "The Bible."

It was hard to argue with that.

I got up to turn the record over, and when I came back I noticed that Sam Hellerman had only one painkiller left on his knee.

"For crying out loud, Hellerman."

He pointed to the remaining pill knee. "This stuff isn't at all bad," he said. Lemmy was singing "Jailbait."

I coughed. "So you were talking about TJA being a kid. . . ."

"Oh. Right," he said, breathing a little more heavily. "Think about all the stuff that happened this year. Our songs freaked people out because they reminded them of real stuff that happened in the past, even though we didn't mean it that way. So your mom freaked out about 'Thinking of Suicide?' Mr. Teone thought the Chi-Mos' songs were about him and his Satanic Empire. And the same kind of thing happened with Kyrsten Blakeney." He took another gulp of bourbon.

"It was unintentional," he continued. "The connections happened in their heads. But in another way, Mr. Teone's reaction to the Chi-Mos wasn't at all an accident."

I went: "?"

"I mean, there's a nonrandom reason you have the nickname Chi-Mo. The kids in seventh grade gave you the name because they associated 'clergy' with 'child molester.' And the reason for that is that there really were situations, especially in schools like the one Tit attended with CEH, where kids were molested. It's in the news all the time. That's why I think there may have been a pattern. . . ." His voice trailed off.

A pattern. "Really?" I said.

"A pattern from the past re-created in the present," he said, after staring into space for a while. That sounded like a poorly translated fortune cookie. He was losing me. We were halfway through the final guitar solo in "The Chase Is Better Than the Catch."

He looked a little zoned. I punched him in the arm, which seemed to wake him up a bit.

It took some prodding and a bit of patience, but I was eventually able to get it out of him. Sam Hellerman's idea was that Mr. Teone's teen porn operation had been based on a similarly structured system at Most Precious Blood, which he had encountered as a young Tit. When he finally became a shop teacher, and later a principal, he had set up his own organization at Hillmont along the same lines.

"So there was a retro-porn thing going on at Most Precious Blood, too?" I asked, finding it kind of hard to picture, given what I knew about the technology of 1963: home-made secret photography would have been more difficult back then.

"It could have been anything illicit," replied Sam Hellerman. "But I'd guess it would have been sex-related in some way." Check, I thought. It always comes back to ramoning, doesn't it? And it squared, in a general way, with the contents of Tit's note. If Tit had been involved, as a participant or even as a student organizer, in some kind of perverted ramoning situation at Most Precious Blood, what had my dad's role been? I couldn't get my mind around that question, so I shook it out of my head.

Anyhow, I could see the logic, sort of, assuming Timothy J. Anderson *was* Tit's dead bastard. It could account for why Tit had hated "the bastard," and rejoiced in his death. Say Tit had been a Matt Lynch figure, and TJA one of his minions. Tit was infuriated when TJA killed himself in shame and remorse, because it endangered the operation and risked sparking some kind of investigation. Or TJA was going to expose the operation and had to be eliminated, and, as Sam Hellerman had suggested, Tit had killed him and, somehow, made it look like suicide. Or TJA had been the Matt Lynch figure, and Tit a recruit who had turned on him. Or he could have been "talent" like Kyrsten Blakeney. Mr. Teone was clearly deranged, and he'd had to get there somehow. So, long ago, in the depraved halls of Most Precious Blood College Preparatory, a sociopath was born? I guess that was the idea.

But even if that was true in a general way, it seemed like there were a lot of possible variations. I gave Sam Hellerman another "?" look, and said: "So why are you so sure TJA was killed by Tit?"

"It's the patterns again," he said, staring intently and with what seemed like loving devotion at the pill on his knee.

"Patterns. I think Tit probably murdered TJA and disguised it as suicide. Because I'm pretty sure that's basically how he killed your dad, and also kind of how he tried to kill you."

He was talking about the old "knock me on the head with a tuba and blame it on the boxing" plan–I guess the connection there was the elaborate fake explanation for a murder attempt. That was a stretch, and in fact, I didn't believe that the brass instrument scheme had been a true murder attempt. It was just ordinary revenge, and maybe intimidation, as well. But as for Mr. Teone's being involved in my dad's murder– well, it wasn't like I hadn't considered this possibility. One of Amanda's Chi-Mos panels had even depicted a devilish Mr. Teone driving the car that had hit my dad–it was kind of obvious, in a way, if hard to fathom. But somehow, hearing Sam Hellerman say it really creeped me out. And I still couldn't quite see how a fake suicide would fit in to the whole hit-and-run scenario, though I was sure Sam Hellerman was going to tell me, provided he could stay conscious long enough. It was a race against time.

"Could you turn that Funkadelic off?" he said irritably. "It's giving me a headache." I had put on *One Nation Under a Groove* after the Motorhead was finished.

I wanted to use our time wisely, so I refrained from mentioning his lack of good taste and took the Funkadelic record off. I was reaching for the Isley Brothers, but Sam Hellerman made a little cross with his index fingers, so I put on *Young Loud and Snotty* instead. He looked up at me with this TV-commercial "headache gone!" expression. Which I thought was kind of funny.

"See," he finally said, slurring a little after I had shaken his shoulder to wake him up, "the problem with your dad's death was never a lack of information. It was that there were too many explanations. It was a murder, it was an accident, it was a suicide. It can't have been all of those. And the one consistent element, the car crash, is the least likely part."

"But the car crash definitely happened," I said. "It was in the paper."

"Yeah, but if you really wanted to kill someone, crashing into their parked car would be just about the worst plan possible."

Okay, that was actually a good point. People get killed in car crashes when both cars are moving at high speed, and even then there can be survivors. You certainly couldn't be *sure* that a hit-and-run on a parked car would lead to sudden death, though it happens. Plus the damage to your own car would be hard to disguise or explain. I don't know why it hadn't occurred to me before.

Sam Hellerman then began to deliver a rambling, semi-drugged analysis of the inadequacies of the car crash as a murder method, which once again I found kind of creepy at those moments when it hit me that it was my dad's death he was retroactively strategizing about.

"So are you saying it was an accident, then," I said, "as per the official story? I thought your idea was that Mr. Teone *did* murder him."

"See, it's not a believable way to die in an accident, either," said Sam Hellerman with a deep, semitranquilized sigh as Stiv Bators sang "Caught with the Meat in Your Mouth." "There would still be all the same problems. And suicide by hit-and-run makes even less sense. And haven't you ever wondered why your dad happened to be parked in the middle of nowhere at three a.m.?" In perfect hit-and-run position. Yeah, I'd wondered about that.

"None of it seems like it could possibly be accidental," he said. "That's why I figure your dad was already dead when his car was rammed, and that the person who rammed him had set it up that way."

I'll spare you the details of the retarded slurred Q&A whereby I finally arrived at a basic understanding of it, but Sam Hellerman's hit-and-run scenario went more or less like this: Mr. Teone had started up the Satanic Empire operation almost as soon as he started teaching at Hillmont. For some reason, he had seen my dad as a threat and decided he had to get him out of the way. It may have been because of an official investigation my dad had been working on. Or it may have been a private matter between them. There was certainly no one better situated to cause trouble for Tit's fledgling teen porn operation than a cop who had known him all his life and who had at least some knowledge of the shady activities of the past at Most Precious Blood. So he arranged to meet my dad on the Sky Vista frontage road at three a.m. under some pretense. Sam Hellerman wasn't sure how he had actually killed him, but he "liked" the idea that he had rendered him unconscious somehow and rigged up a tailpipe/hose/window apparatus—which is how people do commit suicide in cars on occasion. Then he had rammed the car and driven away. Sam Hellerman also speculated that perhaps Mr. Teone had written the suicide note my mom claimed to have or to have seen, leaving it in the car, or possibly arranging for it to get to my mom directly.

"But why would he go to such trouble to make it look like suicide and then confuse the issue with a faked accident? And wouldn't the cops have been suspicious, and wouldn't they have been able to tell what had really happened?"

To my slight dismay, Sam Hellerman quickly popped the other pill in his mouth, gulped some bourbon, and smiled at me impishly. I knew we didn't have long. He still seemed lucid enough but very tired and uninterested in focusing—I knew the feeling pretty well by now. He picked up the computer printout about the Santa Carla corruption scandal.

"Didn't you read this?" he said.

SHERLOCK HENDERSON

Now, I've got to interrupt Sam Hellerman's explanation with my own explanation. There was something I had to know, and under the circumstances it just wasn't possible to ask it directly. So I had a plan. Fortunately, he was on drugs, which would help. That's one of the reasons I had agreed to let him have some painkillers, in fact.

I reached over, tapped the printout, and said: "so Fiona is back in the picture."

His facial expression and body language were easy to read. He sighed and slumped, looking exasperated and dismayed, like he always did whenever the name Fiona was mentioned. He liked to think he'd taken care of that situation, thrown me off the track, and he was bummed when the subject would still pop up now and again. But it was also obvious that my bringing up Fiona in the context of the newspaper article was puzzling to him. That told me something, but there was still a piece missing.

He looked over the article with a furrowed brow and a little growl of frustration. He couldn't see what I was getting at. Then, eventually, his face cleared: he had figured it out. He mouthed the word "Schumacher" and nodded. Which was frustrating. Come on, Hellerman, I thought, trying to summon as much psychic power as I had in me: don't mouth it, don't mouth it. . . .

"I see," he finally said. "Yeah. No. Those situations have nothing to do with each other. It's a coincidence."

Now it was my turn to sigh. Well, it would have been too easy, I thought. Then, however, he added:

"It must be a different Schumacher. It's a common name."

Which was what I had been angling for. Saying "it's a common [blank]" is always Sam Hellerman's response to an inconvenient coincidence, I was starting to realize. But he had said "Shoe-mocker" rather than "Skoo-macker." That told me that he had never actually spoken to Deanna Schumacher, and was almost certainly not in contact with her. Which was a big relief. Unless he was wilier than even I thought, and had realized what I was up to and had deliberately mispronounced the name. I didn't think so, though. He was too mind fogged to put on much of an act.

Mispronunciation had come through once again.

I put on *All American Boy* and looked at Sam Hellerman, who was staring off into space and speaking kind of quietly but still seemed mostly in control of his faculties.

"The Santa Carla police department had just gone through an embarrassing controversy that involved at least one suicide. They would have wanted to avoid bad publicity from yet another one."

According to Sam Hellerman, the cops would have wanted to cover up the suicide angle and treat the death publicly as an accident or possible vehicular homicide. They may or may not have actually believed the suicide story, though the fact that there was a suicide note that had convinced the widow would have made it more plausible. But whether they believed it or not, they had judged it to be in their interests to keep it quiet and had taken advantage of Mr. Teone's setup.

"So let me get this straight," I said. "You're saying that Mr. Teone arranged the fake suicide, knowing that the cops would want to cover it up; *and*, on top of that, he added a phony car crash, knowing that the cops would prefer that scenario and run with it, instead of investigating it as a murder?"

"Or the cops did the hit-and-run themselves," said Sam Hellerman. "But it works out better–"

"–if it was Teone," I said, finishing his sentence.

"Right."

Of course, I knew something that Sam Hellerman didn't: Mr. Teone may have had some help from an accomplice in the county coroner's office. Melvin Schumacher had known my dad, and his daughter's going to Catholic school probably indicated that he had a Catholic background. Maybe he had even been a student at MPB himself.

In view of this, it seemed to me that the suicide angle needlessly complicated things–if Mr. Teone had wanted to murder my dad, and Melvin Schumacher was willing to help him cover it up, there would have been no need for another layer of subterfuge. I was more than ready to believe that my dad's suicide was all in my mom's head. But Sam Hellerman was trying to fit everything into a single storyline without leaving anything out, so he had to fit the suicide theme in somewhere. And, I had to admit, his story had a kind of symmetry, with a faked suicide at either end.

At any rate, it was possible, though not certain, that Melvin Schumacher had been involved in my dad's murder. And now, circumstances had arranged themselves in such a way that I was getting weekly blow jobs from his daughter. Life is weird.

Let me put it this way: some of it seemed like a bit of a stretch. Sam Hellerman seemed utterly confident in his theory, but then, he always seemed u. c. As Sam Hellerman would say, it "worked out" better if Mr. Teone was behind it all, but that didn't mean it really happened that way. My dad could have been murdered by anybody, not necessarily the guy who wrote the *Catcher* code and whose illicit activities were exposed by our retarded rock band. And despite all this energetic and ingenious reasoning, it was still possible that the whole thing had been a fluke accident after all. There was no evidence for any of what Sam Hellerman was proposing.

When I mentioned this, Sam Hellerman rolled his half-closed eyes.

"Oh no," he said. "That's the way it happened." Then, realizing that I was still skeptical, he groaned and summoned what was left of his strength.

"Look at it this way: what year did your dad die?"

"O-nine, o-six, nine-three," I said automatically.

"And what can you tell me about Mr. Teone's car?"

I saw what he was getting at: he was saying Mr. Teone had had to buy his celebrated Geo Prizm in 1993 to replace the one he had smashed up by ramming into my dad. That seemed like reaching, even for Sam Hellerman. He could have bought the car used anytime after 1993. I regarded him dubiously but went along with it.

"What did he do with the smashed-up car?" I asked.

"Well," said Sam Hellerman, "if you were a metal-shop teacher, and you needed to get rid of an incriminating car, what would *you* do?"

"The Hillmont Knight?" I said, catching on, but still doubtful.

" 'Presentated to HHS by the Class of '94,' " he quoted, as smug as it's possible to be when you're about to slip into a coma. "He turned the evidence into a class project. Much better than pushing it in the reservoir." He was right: Hillmont High Center Court was the last place anyone would look.

I shuddered a little at the image of Hillmont's drama hippies leaning casually against what might have been my dad's murder weapon. Hell, I'd even climbed on it, and swung from its crankshaft lance once or twice. I suddenly realized that, if Sam Hellerman was right, Mr. Teone's constant references to his '93 Geo Prizm might have been more sinister than goofy.

There was one bit of evidence Sam Hellerman hadn't covered, and I was pretty sure he did have a little theory about it that he had just forgotten to mention: the card for the Happy Day Dry Cleaners that had been stuck between the pages of *The Seven Storey Mountain* along with the TJA card. Maybe something to do with the bloodstains in *Catcher,* CEH 1960? That was just a guess. I started to ask Sam Hellerman about this but I noticed that he had finally slipped off. I stared at the wall for a while.

"Hellerman," I finally said, in the direction of his comatose little form. "That is so..." I searched for the word. "...retarded." But then I said, "I don't know, Hellerman," because I really didn't.

I put on *The Kinks Are the Village Green Preservation Society* and lay back on the bed, more or less alone with my thoughts, which under the circumstances didn't have a lot to do with the English countryside of yesteryear.

DUNGEONS IN THE AIR

Any way you sliced it, I was going to have a lot to think about over the Christmas break.

Despite Sam Hellerman's confidence, I knew there were other ways to work it out. Presumably there is an actual story, one that really happened, behind the Tit-CEH-TJA nexus revealed by Tit's note and Matthew 3:9–11, though I'd be willing to bet that if so, it would end up seeming to make even less sense. Life is stupid that way.

It occurred to me that we had worked it out in much the same way we would have worked out the details of a particularly elaborate band. And the whole story, especially the complicated, multiply deceptive murder scheme, was Hellerman through and through. I mean, if Sam Hellerman were a loopy associate principal–pornographer who wanted to get rid of a cop he had known since childhood, that was exactly the sort of plan *he* would have come up with. That didn't necessarily mean that Mr. Teone would have come up with the same plan.

Of course, if Mr. Teone really had murdered my dad, I wanted to know. But I was just starting to realize why I was so unsatisfied with Hellermanian theories on this matter: in the end, I didn't want my relationship with my dad to be about Mr. Teone, or substitution ciphers, or broods of vipers, or pornography, or police corruption, or any of that stuff. And in reality, it wasn't about any of those things, though it's easy to forget that when you're trying to solve codes and piece together an explanation out of scraps of paper and notes in the margins of books. I'm not a good detective, and I don't even really want to be one. The only part of it that matters is that I miss my dad and wish he weren't dead. And that I love making out with Celeste Fletcher and hope to be able to do it again one day. Family values and ramoning. That's reality.

Now, Sam Hellerman had said I was "hung up on" Matthew 3:9–11, and he wasn't wrong, though it took a lot of thinking before I figured out why. It wasn't only because the passage kind of creeped me out and kept popping up. And it wasn't only because the brood of vipers kept reminding me of Rye Hell and the *Catcher* cult. I think it was also because it was something real, a piece of a book people had been reading for thousands of years, a part of the world that existed independently from any of our conjectures. It was because my dad had probably read that quote, probably thought about it, probably wondered, as I had done, what it meant and how it applied to his life and the world. And he had read *The Seven Storey Mountain* and may have wondered why the *SSM* guy had chosen it for his epigraph. In a way, it put my dad in a picture made up of things that weren't entirely imaginary or theoretical. It allowed me to imagine myself in his place in the past. And those opportunities were pretty rare.

Even if every other element of Sam Hellerman's theory turned out to be right, Timothy J. Anderson's relationship to my dad and Tit and the *Seven Storey Mountain* guy could still have been random, unconnected to the rest of the story. And for some reason I found the randomness more satisfying. I imagined my dad, engrossed in *The Seven Storey Mountain,* perhaps attending church with his family. He notices the memorial card, if that's what it was, for someone he has never heard of, on a table, in a pew, or in a missal or hymnal. He stops dead, struck by the coincidence that it uses the same quote as his book's epigraph. He sits there thinking, "Wow, this is spooky and weird," clips the quote off the rest of the card, and keeps it to use as a bookmark. Or he's intrigued by it and starts his own little investigation into Timothy J. Anderson, trying to learn who he was and why his card and his book share the same quotation. That's what I would have done. That's what I *had* done. The thought came closer to bringing my dad "back to life" than anything else I had ever thought of.

And that road of reasoning leads to an entirely different way of looking at it, which is that all of these elements are random and not really connected to each other in any particular way, except to the degree that Sam Hellerman and I tried to make them make sense by coming up with a storyline to tie them together.

Like this: there were two kids in the sixties who were into *The Catcher in the Rye* and who used to write notes to each other in code, often about weird or off-the-wall things, and boast about how they messed around with girls. And one of their classmates had hanged himself in the gymnasium. And one of them used to read a lot of books, and at some point acquired a memorial card, if that's what it was, for a totally unrelated guy named Timothy J. Anderson and used it as a bookmark. And when they grew up, one of them became a cop, while the other became a loopy associate principal with a kind of perverted and illegal way of getting his jollies and earning extra cash on the side. These things happen.

Honestly, I can't decide. One day I look at it one way, and the next I'll think that's nuts and start looking at it another way. Maybe I just haven't hit on the right explanation yet. Or maybe there is no explanation. Around and around, it can drive a person crazy.

There certainly are a lot of avenues for further investigation. I should probably go through my mom's stuff and try to find the supposed suicide note, despite Amanda's plausible conclusion that it doesn't actually exist. Learning a little more about my mom and her relationship with my dad would probably go a long way toward clearing up some of the confusion. I'm not totally sold on that, however. My mom is sad, distant, goofy, mysterious, and beautiful, and part of me feels like I'd prefer to leave her that way. I'm pretty sure we will always fail to understand each other completely. And I know I wouldn't like it if investigating her caused her to fade even more from view, which is what basically happened when I tried to investigate my dad. Anyway, you can't spend *all* your time digging through other people's stuff to try to shed light on your own concerns. Sometimes you just want to switch to obsessing about semihot girls and working on your band for a while.

As I mentioned, Sam Hellerman had written "killed by Tit?" in the margin of the reverse-exposure printout about the hanged kid who may or may not have been Timothy J. Anderson. Thinking it over, it occurred to me that if, decades from now, some kids were to discover this sheet of paper stuck in a book somewhere, it could lead to a whole new wheel-spinning investigation with God only knows how many twists and turns and coincidences and mistaken assumptions and imposed meanings and ingenious errors and peripheral connections to various episodes involving messing around with a variety of hot and semihot girls. Randomly generated dungeons in the air, passed from generation to generation. In the spirit of continuing this grand tradition, I located Little Big Tom's most retarded-looking counterculture book, *Revolution for the Hell of It* (by Free–that's supposed to be the guy's name, I kid you not. Jacket photo by Richard Avedon). Supposedly the author of this book got five years in prison for writing it. Which seems a bit lenient if you ask me. The guy who wrote *The Doors of Perception* got off way easier, though, especially since the worst band in the history of the world, the Doors, named themselves after it. He has a lot to answer for.

I picked up a pen, intending to underline a suitably bizarre section, and maybe compose an off-the-wall message in code based upon it. I found, however, that the book was all marked up already. There was one underlined passage, near the beginning, that said that five-sided objects were evil and proposed measuring the Pentagon to figure out how many hippies it would take to make it less evil by forming a big, smelly circle around it. And in the margin someone, presumably a young, idealistic, right-on Little Big Tom, had pathetically written "Yes!" I kid you not. Well, there was nothing I could add–you can't improve on perfection. I put my pen down, folded up the "killed by Tit?" printout, and placed it in the book between the pages containing this Deep Thought. That oughta confuse the hell out of them, I thought with incalculable satisfaction. All we had to do now was wait.

I glanced over at Sam Hellerman, sleeping peacefully in the corner. Then I got up and went down to the basement and put the book near the bottom of one of the book boxes, feeling as though I were burying the sixties. Even though I guess I really wasn't.

GREAT BOOK, CHANGED MY LIFE, YOU KNOW

It's rather ironic, wouldn't you say, that things ended up arranging themselves so that I spent a considerable chunk of my sophomore year carrying around a copy of *The Catcher in the Rye* everywhere I went? In a sense, I suppose you could even say that *The Catcher in the Rye* changed my life, though I'm not about to commemorate that fact by joining a cult or anything. It set in motion a process by which I learned so much about some stuff that I ended up not knowing anything at all about it. And it indirectly influenced the fact that my rock band accidentally brought down a perverted high school sexploitation empire and freed the little children from the devil-head predations of an evil associate principal. And it happened to coincide with my clumsy venture from pure fantasy to impure reality in the girl arena. Not bad for a sucky book you read only to suck up to teachers holding a gun to your head.

Look, it's not even that bad of a book. I admit it. I can feel sorry for myself while pretending to be Holden Caulfield. I can. And I can see why the powers that be have decided to adopt it as their semiofficial alterna-bible. Things were really, really bad in the sixties. You were always getting kicked out of your prep school, or getting into fights at your prep school, or getting marooned on deserted islands on the way to your fancy English boarding school. And when you finally got off the island, your "old man" was always on your "case," and Vietnam just drove you crazy, plus you were constantly high on drugs and out of touch with reality and it was sometimes a little more difficult than it should have been to get everyone to admit how much better you were than everybody else. It was rough. I get it. I really get it. Up with Holden. I'd have probably been the same way.

In the end, though, the attempt to save the world by forcing people to read *The Catcher in the Rye* and dressing casually and supporting public television and putting bumper stickers on Volvos and eating only weird expensive food and separating your cans and bottles and doing tai chi and going to the farmer's market and pronouncing Spanish words with a cartoon-character accent and calling actresses actors and making up your own religion and so forth–well, the world refused to be saved that way. Big surprise. On the other hand, no one could ever mistake Hillmont High School for a prep school, so at least you accomplished that. I mean, calling it a school involves the kind of generosity of spirit that in other circumstances might get you the Nobel Peace Prize nomination or something. You stuck it to the old man, killed half of your brain cells, *and* dumbed down the educational system: you *are* the greatest generation.

Before all that character arc stuff happened, I might have been able to sing "all we are saying is make high school a little less sadistic" with a little more enthusiasm. Compared to Hillmont High School, Holden Caulfield's prep school troubles seem like a sort of heaven on earth. But honestly, I've got my mind on other things. Girls and rock and roll, I mean. Everything else is trivia.

OUTRO

How we live now:

Christmas break. Band practice. We Have Eaten All the Cake, me on guitar/vox, Spam L. Ermine on bass and domestic hygiene, Shinefield on drums, first album *Slut Heaven*. Working on: "You Look Good on Drugs."

Little Big Tom enters, tilts his head to one side, raises one eyebrow, does a quick, shallow knee bend, tilts his head to the other side, raises the phone he is carrying above his head, and brings it down, straightening his arm in one fluid motion, as though it's a remote and he's changing the channel. Or a phaser on stun.

"There a rock star in the house?"

I take the phone. "Oh, thank God," I say, when I realize it is Celeste "Fiona" Fletcher. Because we've started saying that whenever we call each other.

Fake Fiona: "Trombone!"

Amanda: "Get off the phone. Get off the phone. Get off the phone."

Mom: just about halfway visible from a certain angle, seated at the dining room table at the end of the hall in a cloud of cigarette smoke, staring into her drink. Looking sad and beautiful.

Little Big Tom, sighing: "Rock and roll . . ."

Sam Hellerman: staring ahead inscrutably, fingering bass strings. Saying nothing.

bandography

(AUGUST-DECEMBER)

1. Easter Monday

2. Baby Batter
GUITAR: Guitar Guy
BASE AND SCIENTOLOGY: Sam Hellerman
THIRD ALBUM: *Odd and Even Number*

3. The Plasma Nukes
GUITAR: Lithium Dan
BASS AND CALLIGRAPHY: Little Pink Sambo
VOX: The Worm
MACHINE-GUN DRUMS: TBA
FIRST ALBUM: *Feelin' Free with the Plasma Nukes*

4. Tennis with Guitars
LEAD AXE: Love Love
BASS AND RAT-CATCHING: The Prophet Samuel
VOCALS, KEYS, BUMPING, GRINDING: Li'l Miss Debbie
DRUMMER: Beat-Beat
FIRST ALBUM: *Amphetamine Low*
COVER: white with the album title in tiny black type on
    the back. The band name does not appear anywhere
    on the outside packaging.
SECOND ALBUM: *Phantasmagoria, Gloria*
PHOTO: a police dog licks a broken doll's face.

5. Helmet Boy
GUITAR: Moe
BASS AND PROCRASTINATION: Sambiguity
FIRST ALBUM: *Helmet Boy II*

6. Liquid Malice

7. The Underpants Machine
GUITAR: Super-Moe
BASS AND BOTTLE ROCKETS: Sam Sam the Piper's Son
FIRST ALBUM: *We Will Bury You*

8. The Stoned Marmadukes
GUITAR: Moe "Fingers" Henderson
BASS AND PALEONTOLOGY: Mr. Sam Hellerman
FIRST ALBUM: *Right Lane Must Exit*

9. Ray Bradbury's Love-Camel
GUITAR: Moe-Moe
BASS AND CALISTHENICS: Scammy Sammy
FIRST ALBUM: *Prepare to Die*

10. Silent Nightmare
GUITAR: The Lord of Electricity
BASS AND GYNECOLOGY: Samson
FIRST ALBUM: *Feel Me Fall*

11. The Medieval Ages
GUITAR: St. Moe
BASS AND BODYWORK: Samber Waves of Grain
FIRST ALBUM: *That Stupid Pope*

12. The Sadly Mistaken

GUITAR: Moe Vittles

BASS AND LANDSCAPING: Sam "Noxious" Fumes

FIRST ALBUM: *Kill the Boy Wonder*

13. Oxford English

GUITAR: Moe Bilalabama

BASS AND LOLLYGAGGING: Sam "the Cat" Hellerman

FIRST ALBUM: *What Part of Suck Don't You Understand?*

14. Some Delicious Sky, aka SDS

TREBLE AND VOCALS: Squealie

THICK BOTTOM AND INDUSTRIAL ARTS:
  Sambidextrous

FIRST ALBUM: *Taste My Juice*

15. Arab Charger

GUITAR: me

BASS AND PREVENTIVE DENTISTRY: The Fiend in
  Human Shape

FIRST ALBUM: *Blank Me*

16. Occult Blood

GUITAR AND VOX: Mopey Mo

BASS AND TELEOLOGY: Hell-man

PERCUSSION INSTRUMENTS: Todd Panchowski

FIRST ALBUM: *Pentagrampa*

17. The Mordor Apes

GUITAR: Mithril-hound

BASS AND NECROLOGY: L'il Sauron

PERCUSSION AND STUPEFACTION: Dim Todd

FIRST ALBUM: *Elven Tail*

18. The Nancy Wheelers
GUITAR: Pseudo-Moe
BASS AND OUIJA BOARD: Sam Hellerman
FIRST ALBUM: *Margaret? It's God. Please Shut Up.*

19. Green Sabbath
GUITAR: Monsignor Eco-druid
BASS AND INDUSTRIAL SABOTAGE: The Grim Recycler
DRUMS, PERCUSSION, ACOUSTIC AND SEMI-ACOUSTIC DRUMS, CYMBALS, TAMBOURINES, COWBELLS, CHIMES, GONGS, TOMS, SHAKER EGGS, BONGOS, STICK CLICKS, WOOD BLOCKS, PERCUSSION, PERCUSSION AND MORE PERCUSSION: Todd "Percussion" Panchowski
FIRST ALBUM: *Our Drummer is Kind of Full of Himself*

20. Balls Deep
GUITAR: Comrade Gal-hammer
BASS AND EMBROIDERY: Our Dear Leader
REAL FANCY AND IMPORTANT PERCUSSION: the Lonely Dissident
FIRST ALBUM: *We Control the Horizontal*

21. Super Mega Plus
GUITAR/VOX: Moelle
BASS, PREVARICATION, AND PROCURING YOUNG GIRLS UNDER FALSE PRETENSES: Sam Hell
IRREGULAR TIMEKEEPING: Brain-dead Panchowski
FIRST ALBUM: *A Woman Knows*

22. The Chi-Mos!

GUITAR: the Reverend Chi-Mo

BASS AND BEING AWARE OF HIS OWN MORTALITY:
Assistant Principal Chi-Mo

PERCUSSION AND COUNTING TO FOUR:
Chi-Mo Panchowski

FIRST ALBUM: *Balls Deep*

23. The Elephants of Style

GUITAR: Mot Juste

BASS AND ANIMAL HUSBANDRY: Sam Enchanted
Evening

FIRST ALBUM: *Devil Warship*

24. Sentient Beard

GUITAR/VOX: Mot Nosredneh

BASS AND UPHOLSTERY: Samerica the Beautiful

FIRST ALBUM: *Off the Charts–Way Off*

25. We Have Eaten All the Cake

GUITAR/VOX: Tomcat

BASS AND DOMESTIC HYGIENE: Spam L. Ermine

DRUMS: Shinefield

FIRST ALBUM: *Slut Heaven*

glossary

AC/DC (ACK-dack): the fourth-greatest rock and roll band of all time.

Advanced French (a-VALST flalsh): a form of the French language in which only the present tense is used. Primarily employed for telling time and for describing the activities of this one guy named Jean and this other guy named Claude.

Advanced Placement (ud-VANT-udgd po-LEES-munt): classes that are far easier than regular classes and for which students receive inflated grades. Rumor has it that "work" done in some AP classes can even count as college credit, though it is doubtful that the sort of college that would accept such credit is the sort of college you'd ever want to put on a resume.

anglophile (an-GLOF-eh-lay): someone who is under the mistaken impression that there is something cool or impressive about trying to speak in a fake English accent.

ankh (ANK-ul): the ancient Egyptian symbol of life, often worn as a pendant or tattoo, or emblazoned on drug paraphernalia.

atheism (ATH-iz-im): a religion for people who figure they probably already know everything there is to know about everything.

The Bad Seed (dee BUD sayd): the charming story of a typical American childhood. The second-greatest movie ever made.

Bayeux Tapestry (bay-OOKS tap-ESS-tree): a long strip of material embroidered in the Middle Ages that illustrates the events leading up to the Norman Conquest of England. Starring the Pope, William the Conqueror, a guy named King Cnut [sic], and a lot of guys with swords dressed up as chess pieces.

The Beatles (the RUTT-ulz): four mop-topped lads from Liverpool who set the toes of the world a-tapping. Then they turned into hippies.

be-in (BE-ing): back in the sixties, hippies used to have these, where everybody took drugs and tried to feel important. I think it's pretty much the same as a "happening."

bête noire (bait nwah-RAY): "black beast" in nonadvanced French. It's slightly worse than a pet peeve, though not as bad as a bane, as far as I can tell.

The Bible (the bibble): a big creepy book, the contents of which have influenced and formed the basis for much of the history and culture of Western civilization for thousands and thousands of years. Mention of this book is forbidden in public schools and in progressive right-thinking households, thus ensuring that substantial chunks of history and literature and the culture at large will be virtually incomprehensible to a sizeable minority of the country's population. Highly prized by religious and other wrong-thinking people for these and other reasons.

The Big Chill (tha BEEG cheel): a nauseating movie about everybody's parents. If anyone has ever tried to make you dance around to oldies while doing the dishes, you have this movie to thank for it.

bitch (beetch): an uncooperative female. Also, a cooperative female. Additionally, among girls, a rival. Or ally.

Black Sabbath (BLAY-ack suh-BAWTH): pentagrams, inverted crosses, capes, tights, drugs, de-tuned guitars, unlimited recording budgets—what could go wrong? The eighteenth-greatest rock and roll band of all time.

Blue Oyster Cult (blue iced occult): maybe rock and roll music wasn't meant to be this intellectual and sophisticated, but they're still the twelfth-greatest rock and roll band of all time.

Boomers (boh-OM-ers): the Most Annoying Generation.

bourgeois pigs (bore-GOYCE pegs): what people in the sixties used to call their parents.

Brighton Rock (BRIG-a-thon rawk): the best book ever written.

bubblegum (BOOB leh-GYOOM): this is, in the end, more or less the Lord's music.

Jimmy Buffett (JUM-ee boo-FAY): a weird old hippie dude featuring Hawaiian shirts and terrible music. On special occasions, a **boomer** dad will sometimes put on a little Jimmy Buffett costume, fix drinks with umbrellas in them, and bring them over to his "old lady," biting his lower lip and doing this weird, slow-motion dance-walk. If there is a more gruesome scenario on this earth, I cannot think what it might be and do not want to know in any case.

callipygian (CALL-ippy-DJEE-ahn), also **callipygous**: Describes a woman with large, shapely, or otherwise lovely, remarkable, or impressive buttocks. By way of the Greeks, those ancient, horny, clever bastards. The day I learned there was a word for this was the day I regained my interest in living and faith in humanity.

Carrie (CARE-ree-AY): normal students stage an elaborate **Make-Out/Fake-Out** on a shy, freaky girl, joke-electing her prom queen and then dumping a bucket of pig blood on her head. She turns out to have special powers and destroys them all. All proms should turn out like that. The fourth-greatest movie of all time.

The Catcher in the Rye (KAT-sha-rin R'lyeh): don't fight it. Relax. Clear your mind and let the magic take hold of you.

You're floating, floating on air. Take the book. Go on, take it. You know you want to. That's it. Nice and slow. Isn't it so much easier this way? One of us, one of us, one of us ...

Cocksparrer (HOT-spur): working-class English punk band who could have been the Sex Pistols if they had played their cards right. But they didn't.

cock tease (kok TAYCE): an attractive female whose behavior is erratic, unpredictable, or otherwise unsatisfactory.

collage (koe-LODGE-ay): a piece of paper with things cut out from magazines glued on it in an attractive or arresting pattern. Has replaced the expository essay as the preferred means for assessing a student's academic progress in American public schools.

concupiscent (con-koo-PISK-unt): wide open and up for anything.

D and D (DAN-dee): a role-playing game played only by very cool guys.

dilettante (dial-TAN-tay): one who can never stick with anything for more than a couple of minutes. An unjustly maligned lifestyle.

The Doors (duh DERZ): there is an extremely well-organized conspiracy among **boomers** to cultivate the fiction that this band doesn't totally suck. The worst thing in the history of the universe.

Dr. Dee (der DAY): Queen Elizabeth I's astrologer. He put a hex on the Spanish Armada, saving England and ensuring that, four hundred years later, **the Beatles** would end up singing in English rather than Spanish. He was also given a weird code by angelic beings he saw in a crystal, and probably needed medication that hadn't been invented yet.

Dr. Who (dra-WOO): a more sophisticated, English version of *Star Trek*.

Bob Dylan (BAY-bee ZIM-er-mn): there was a time in my

life when I fervently wanted to be Bob Dylan. Then I realized that practically everybody else in the world wanted to be Bob Dylan, too, and that if we all got our wish, being Bob Dylan would be so common that it would be completely meaningless to be Bob Dylan, even for the actual, original Bob Dylan, and the world would essentially end up exactly the same as it was before. The alpha Bob Dylans would beat up the less alpha Bob Dylans, the female Bob Dylans would confuse the hell out of the male Bob Dylans, the teacher Bob Dylans would make the student Bob Dylans read *The Catcher in the Rye,* the parent Bob Dylans would call continual inane family discussions with the kid Bob Dylans, and the sadistic, psychotic structure of the universe would be more or less preserved. Nature is a **bitch.**

epigraph (a-PIG-rape): an obscure quotation at the beginning of a book designed to make the author of the book seem smarter and more well-read than its readers. An epigraph that doesn't make the reader feel confused, small, worthless, and stupid is an epigraph that has failed. Therefore, the best epigraphs have no discernible relationship to the contents of the books they adorn.

epilogue (EPP-ul-oh-gay): just when you think the book is over, there are suddenly like twenty more pages to go, because some writers just don't know when to stop. Don't read epilogues: it will only encourage them.

epitaph (epp-EE-toff): an obscure quotation on a tombstone, designed to make the dead guy's life seem less pointless.

Europe (YOUR-ip): we beat these guys in World War II.

Foghat (foe-GAT): the fifth-greatest rock and roll band of all time.

Funkadelic (FUN-kee-assgroove-a-TELL-ick-ness): the funkiest band in the world, unless you count the Isley Brothers.

337

genuflect (g-NU-fuh-lect): sometimes, the church only requires one half of a person's body to be kneeling.

gifted and talented (gif-TED and tal-on-TED): gifted and talented students are those who have figured out that if you make a little effort to leave the right impression, very little will be expected of you in the end.

Gilligan's Island (GILL-gan SIS-land): a television show, certain episodes of which contain the secret to the meaning of existence, concealed by means of coded messages and obscure symbolism.

Che Guevara (chee goo-ey-VAH-ra): a Latin American revolutionary famous for his sexiness and hip T-shirts. A cross between Elvis and **Charles Manson.** An inexplicably adored Holden Caulfield for the political-minded.

George Harrison (GORE-jer-us ISS-un): guitar player and Siddhartha-type. The hairiest of all **the Beatles.**

hemisemidemiquaver (HEE-mee-SUM-thin-ore-UDD-er): a sixteenth note. Many guitar players believe the object of the game is to play as many of these as possible, leaving as few spaces as they can for the entire song. It's a test of endurance.

Hitler (HIL-ter): a thoroughly evil totalitarian mass murderer from Germany. Seriously, you can't get more evil than him. Admirers of other totalitarian mass murderers take comfort in the notion that at least their guy's evilness doesn't meet this standard; plus they point out that in their guy's dictatorship everyone who is not murdered gets free health care and education.

Humanities (hum-in-AN-uh-teez): the study of random things, characterized by self-admiration and extremely easy assignments.

homoeroticism (home-AY-oh-RAW-tick-iz-um): dudes being turned on by dudes, or dudes ridiculing other dudes by behaving as they believe dudes who really are turned on by dudes behave with respect to those dudes they are turned on by, under the impression that this is hilarious or otherwise worthwhile. As irritating as this is for dudes who in fact are not turned on by dudes, it must be even worse for those who are.

horological (whore-a-lodge-ICK-el): related to clocks or time.

Invasion of the Body Snatchers (in-WAY-shun off THE BUD-ee SNITCH-ehz): no one has yet come up with a better hypothesis for why our society is the way it is. The third-greatest movie ever made.

The Jam (the JIM): fake-mod dolphins from around the eleventh century. Breaks the ice at parties. The twenty-third-greatest rock and roll band of all time.

Joan Jett (John JET-ah): guitar player for the Runaways, the fourteenth-greatest rock and roll band of all time.

Johnny Thunders (joe NEETH-un-derz): the name of a **Kinks** song, and the guitar player for the **New York Dolls.**

The Kinks (thee KEEN-uck-ess): the third-greatest rock and roll band of all time.

KISS (nites in SERV-iss uv SAY-tan): considering the fact that KISS is four middle-aged guys in mime makeup, it's extremely impressive that they somehow managed to swing becoming the eleventh-greatest rock and roll band of all time.

Timothy Leary (tee-MOTH-ee lee-AHR-ay): famous college professor turned drug fiend from the sixties.

Led Zeppelin (leads a-PEEL-in): hey, gang! Let's all get stoned and head down to the Mississippi Delta and watch four goofy-ass English guys in wizards' hats and girls' blouses play "the blues" and teach us everything there is to know about elfin princesses; gossamer wings; the tooth fairy; the land of Winken, Blinken, and Nod; the wise and dark and mystic pilgrim brooding in the mist; and Puff the Magic Dragon. Come on, it'll be magical.

Lemmy (let-me): "singer" of **Motorhead.**

libidinous (LI-bid-IGH-ness): one of the many fancy-pants ways to say "horny."

magnanimous (MAG-na-MIN-ee-us): if you are generous and kind of full of yourself, this word is for you.

Make-out/Fake-out (MACK-it FACK-it): a public humiliation technique that owes its power to the reliably universal desire to possess what one is not allowed to touch. Analogous to the game called keep-away, the object of which is to take possession of a ball that is held just beyond one's grasp, or tantalizingly offered only to be tossed to another player at the last moment.

Mamelukes (maym-LUCK-ayce): mounted warriors recruited from slaves, who dominated Egypt for several centuries till they were destroyed by Mehemet Ali Pasha in 1811. And a great fucking band name.

Charles Manson (CHAR-less mon-SOON): the world's most famous **Beatles** fan, the ultimate **boomer,** and the Voice of his Generation.

Mao Tse-tung (Meow TAY-zee-tongue): a Chinese communist revolutionary who managed to thin out the Chinese population considerably, earning him the admiration and gratitude of a small but irritating segment of **The Most Annoying Generation.** Author of *The Little Red Book,* about which the best that can be said is: well, at least it's not a big red book.

George Michael (YORE-gay Mich-elle): there's lots to say about this guy, perhaps, but the shorts alone are bad enough.

Monty Python (MIN-tee PITH-ee): short for Monty Python's

Flying Circus. A documentary series on everyday life in Great Britain.

Most Annoying Generation, The: see **Boomers**

Motorhead (MELT-er red): the seventh-greatest rock and roll band of all time.

multiple personality disorder (em-py-DEE): a feminine courtship strategy.

The New York Dolls (the NEW-ark DOY-leez): a New York transvestite version of the **Rolling Stones**. The fifteenth-greatest rock and roll band of all time.

normal (nor-MAL): lacking in taste, compassion, understanding, kindness, and ordinary human decency.

obsequious (ob-see-CUE-ee-us): a fancy-pants way to describe a suck-up.

orgasmic (or-JAZZ-um-ick): of, like, or pertaining to being glad all over.

partner (pard-NAIR): a euphemism for spouse or significant other. When a woman reaches the age where everyone starts to giggle whenever she refers to her "boyfriend," and if the dude won't marry her or if she doesn't think "husband" sounds special enough, and possibly if she wants to preserve ambiguity as to whether or not she is a lesbian, she will usually settle on "partner." I have no idea why guys use this word, unless it's because their girlfriends or wives are a little touchy and they'd rather not get into it. This situation could be worse, however, as there are misguided parents out there who, I kid you not, like to introduce each other by saying things like "this is my lover, Don," which can be quite a bit more nauseating.

PE (pay: as in, you will): "physical education." I believe the Nazis used to make people dress in gay outfits and play tennis and do exercises in school, too.

Suzy Quatro (SOO-zee cue): hot rock and roll chick developed by the same guys who masterminded **the Sweet**. She was also in this TV show called *Happy Days* about people in the fifties who had seventies clothes and hairstyles.

The Ramones (duh rah-MOAN-ayz): if you can pull off the juvenile delinquent style when you are in your thirties and beyond, you are doing all right. The eighth-greatest rock and roll band of all time.

ramoning (ra-MAWN-in): a form of the verb "to ramone" (derived from the French *ramoner,* to scrub out a chimney). The point of human existence, i.e., **sexual intercourse**.

roach (rootch): the stubby end of a marijuana cigarette, held in a clip and smoked till it can be smoked no more, after which it is swallowed. This is believed to confer upon the stoner what are thought to be the magical properties of the plant itself, such as leafyness, harmlessness, listlessness, lack of short-term memory and motivation, and a slightly greenish coloring.

The Rolling Stones (the KID-nee stains): the Star Trek of rock and roll. The thirteenth-greatest rock and roll band of all time.

Rosemary's Baby (ROH-zmer-eeze BABB-ee): scary evil devil people trick a skinny foxy chick into being ramoned by Satan so they can raise the resulting half-human/half-devil baby themselves and take over the world. The best movie ever made.

Samhain (sam-HANE): a Celtic festival marking the summer's end, which was supposedly the origin of our Halloween. Funny people with capes, medallions, and large rings sometimes go to the park on whatever day they imagine Samhain to have been to do fake ancient rituals, drink wine from a box, and listen to heavy metal music. It's a fun adventure.

sex (six): an abbreviation for **sexual intercourse**.

sexual intercourse (secks-YOU-all IN-ter-co-URS): a pathetic attempt to make ramoning sound less sexy.

Slade (slah-DAY): four English guys who couldn't spell to save their lives. The sixth-greatest rock and roll band of all time.

slans (slawns): aliens who can communicate telepathically; also, earthlings whose superior intuitive powers allow them to dispense with verbal communication at least some of the time. Both face continual extermination attempts by enraged normal people.

The Small Faces (theez MALL FASH-ists): the poor man's **Who**. The nineteenth-greatest rock and roll band of all time.

The Smiths (da smurfs): music for when you are sad.

Stalin (sta-LEEN): Russian communist dictator who managed to thin out the Russian and Eastern European population considerably, earning him the admiration and gratitude of a small but irritatingly vocal segment of **The Most Annoying Generation**. A lot of them are a little embarrassed by this now that he has fallen from favor, an embarrassment they will often celebrate by avoiding the subject, buying a sports car, smoking a joint, or taking out the recycling.

Paul Stanley (pole STAIN-lee): the singer-guitarist of **KISS**, described, with a straight face, as The Lover in all promotional materials. Has set the industry standard for announcing songs in a high-pitched squeal at live shows.

The Sweet (the Sweat): maybe they were only the second-greatest rock and roll band of all time, but they made the first-greatest album of all time (*Desolation Boulevard*) and the all-time greatest song in the history of music ("Fox on the Run").

Thin Lizzy (TEEN LEZ-ie): Ireland's greatest contribution to Western civilization. The ninth-greatest rock and roll band of all time.

veganism (WEE-gun-izz-im): a religion for people who never feel particularly hungry.

The Velvet Underground (thee VULV-uh TUN-dra): you can tell how badly someone wants to come off as a hipster by how fervently he or she pretends to have been into this group since early childhood. They were my favorite band as a zygote. The tenth-greatest rock and roll band of all time.

Vicodin (vick-OH-dun): medicine to help mothers forget they are mothers.

The Vietnam War (tha VITE-nam wair): for **The Most Annoying Generation,** the most fascinating and important topic in the world. For everybody else, not. When people from The MAG begin to reminisce about it, it's a good time to balance your checkbook, catch up on your homework, learn a foreign language, or do the *New York Times* crossword puzzle. Don't worry—they'll still be talking when you're done.

wanton (wahn-tahn): sexy, horny, game, chewy, delicious.

weltschmerz (well-cha-MERZ): German for "world-weariness." This is a reasonable reaction to life on this earth, and it's great that there's a word for it, but if you can figure out a way to slip it into ordinary conversation, you're a better man than I.

The Who (the hoe): the greatest rock and roll band of all time.

Wishbone Ash (vish-BONE-ay ASS): the, let's see, 65,893rd-greatest rock and roll band of all time. Just kidding, guys. But I guess you really had to be there. . . .

The Yardbirds (they ARD-varks): the sixteenth-greatest rock and roll band of all time.

Frank Zappa (flank zeh-PAH): if all hippie music had been this weird and good, maybe that subculture wouldn't have been such a total waste of brain cells.

THANKS TO:

My editor, Krista Marino, and everyone at Delacorte Press;

my agent, Steven Malk;

plus Belle, Matil, Chris Appelgren, Paul Caringella,
Shauna Cross, Joanna Hatzopoulos, Marion Henderson,
Amanda Jenkins, Bobby Jordan, Tristin Laughter,
Rebekah Leslie, Beth Lisick, Paige O'Donoghue,
Christine Portman, and Ethan Stoller.

Bobby Jordan

FRANK PORTMAN (aka Dr. Frank) is the singer/songwriter/guitarist of the influential East Bay punk band the Mr. T Experience (MTX). MTX has released around a dozen albums since forming in the mid-eighties and continues to record and tour. *King Dork* is his first novel.

www.frankportman.com